S0-BKR-091

"A DAZZLER! A FAST-PACED NOVEL
OF PASSION AND INTRIGUE...DON'T
MISS THIS ONE!"
—Susan Elizabeth Phillips, *New York Times*
bestselling author of *Fancy Pants*

SOLITAIRE

"A CLASSY NOVEL...GLAMOUR, GREED,
AND GLORY-SEEKERS—AN EXPLOSIVE
COMBINATION...I LOVED IT!"
—Sandra Brown, *New York Times*
bestselling author of *Mirror Image*

Berkley Books by Norma Beishir

A TIME FOR LEGENDS
ANGELS AT MIDNIGHT
DANCE OF THE GODS
SOLITAIRE

SOLITAIRE

NORMA BEISHIR

BERKLEY BOOKS, NEW YORK

SOLITAIRE

A Berkley Book / published by arrangement with
Moonstone-Solitaire, Inc.

PRINTING HISTORY
Berkley edition / April 1991

ISBN: 0-425-12646-3

A BERKLEY BOOK® TM 757,375
Berkley Books are published by The Berkley Publishing Group,
200 Madison Avenue, New York, New York 10016.
The name ''Berkley'' and the ''B'' logo
are trademarks belonging to Berkley Publishing Corporation.

PRINTED IN THE UNITED STATES OF AMERICA

10 9 8 7 6 5 4 3 2 1

For Maria, who made
it possible . . .

And for Tony and Collin,
who made it worthwhile.

It is when you give
of yourself that you
truly give.

—Kahlil Gibran,
The Prophet

sol·i·taire (sol·i·tair) **n.** 1. a diamond or other gem set by itself. 2. a card game for one person in which cards have to be brought into a particular arrangement.

—*Oxford American Dictionary*

SOLITAIRE

⇄ The International Polo Federation World Championships Berlin, August 1989

The ball took a wild bounce and skittered into an open area of the polo field. The momentum of the eight galloping horses carried the players well past it. Jordan Phillips, playing the number three position for the North American team, blocked the Argentine player's attempt at reaching the ball. He checked his mount, urging it into an abrupt turn as he raised his mallet and took aim.

"Leave it, Jordy!" One of his teammates, Lance Whitney, was in a better position for a shot at the ball. Though Jordan had good reason to doubt his old friend's judgment these days, he backed off, lowering his mallet as he moved into position to block the closest opposition between Lance and the goal. The big Argentine, the only rider in that position, was racing for an interception of the ball's anticipated flight toward the goal, moving to defend against a score.

The moment the necessary pivot hoof of Jordan's black pony touched the ground, he signaled the horse with legs and reins into a swift, fluid turn with almost no break in speed. He could hear the familiar clunk of the mallet making contact with the ball from behind him, and out of the corner of his eye he saw the ball streaking past him. He bore down on the horse and rider angling toward the ball, approaching on the Argentine's mallet side. At the speed at which the horses were traveling, anything wider would have been dangerous. It would also be a foul. Jordan ignored the danger of the impending collision as he drove his horse's shoulder into that of his opponent's mount. He felt the bone-jarring hit as the other horse stumbled but quickly recovered its balance and stride. He kept the weight

1

of his own horse leaning into his opponent's, riding him off the line of the ball as it raced toward the goal.

Then he saw Lance—approaching the Argentine from the other side—riding straight into his opponent. He opened his mouth to call out to his teammate, but it was too late. In the next instant, Lance's mount crashed forcefully into the Argentine's, which sent the animal tumbling toward Jordan, and then all three horses went down. Reacting instinctively, Jordan launched himself from his saddle, rolling free of the thrashing animals. He was momentarily dazed; he could vaguely hear shouts from the stands and was only dimly aware that people were rushing across the field toward them, that the play had been brought to an abrupt halt. Nothing was clear as two men helped him to his feet.

"Are you all right?" one of them asked.

He nodded, dusting grass and dirt from his pants and jersey. "I think so."

The first thing he did was look for his horse. She was standing with the other two, several yards away, and appeared to be all right. He started forward, then stopped abruptly as he saw that another player was sprawled on the turf several yards away, surrounded by people. He couldn't tell who it was. Pushing his way through the human barrier, he discovered it was the Argentine. The man wasn't moving and didn't appear to be breathing.

Jordan turned to the man on his right. "Is he dead?" he asked cautiously.

The man shook his head. "Unconscious. They've sent for medical assistance," he said gravely.

Jordan, still slightly disoriented, tried to recall those last critical seconds before the collision. Lance. Lance had been responsible for this. The man's personal problems were now becoming everyone's problem. Jordan realized he had let it go too far. By keeping quiet about it, he was placing other players' lives—and his own—in jeopardy. *End of the line, friend,* he thought, his anger mounting as he pushed his way back through the crowd, in search of Lance Whitney. His teammate was nowhere to be seen.

Jordan caught up with one of the grooms. "Where's Whitney?" he demanded, wiping perspiration from his face with the back of his hand.

The boy stepped back. "He left the field—I don't know—" he stammered, very much aware of Jordan's rage.

"Never mind," Jordan said tightly. "I'll find him."

Up in the stands, Sloane Driscoll was on her feet, straining to look over the heads of the anxious spectators. With one hand she held on to her wide-brimmed blue hat in the brisk autumn breeze that caught her long auburn hair. Wide, gray-blue eyes reflected the fear she was experiencing as she scanned the field in search of Jordan. The announcer's voice rattled on excitedly over the loudspeakers, but Sloane understood so little German she had no idea what he was saying. She turned to the woman on her left, the slim dark woman in black. "What's he saying, Gaby?" she asked.

The other woman craned her neck, trying to get a better look. "Three players are down—one seriously injured." She never took her eyes off the field.

Sloane's hand flew to her mouth. "Jordan!" she gasped. She had to go to him. She started for the exit before her friend could stop her.

"He's on the Argentine team, Sloane!" Gaby called after her. "It's not Jordan! Jordan's not hurt!"

As Sloane picked her way through the crowd, she could hear the blaring siren of the ambulance making its way across the polo field. Her heart was beating wildly in her throat. He had to be all right. If anything happened to Jordan, she wasn't at all sure she could deal with it. Especially now, after so much had gone wrong between them. She'd almost lost him once— but without Jordan, nothing else mattered. . . .

"You goddamned son of a bitch—we could have both been killed!"

Jordan stood at the stable entrance, his dark eyes blazing with anger as he pulled off his polo helmet. Throwing it down in a forceful movement, he advanced on his teammate menacingly. In the shadows, Lance was crouched over his malletier, a rectangular leather travel case used for polo equipment, which lay open on the floor. He stood up as Jordan approached, brushing bits of straw from his white pants. "It was an *accident*—" he began in a faltering voice. Lance tried to drop the small transparent bag of white powder he held behind him into the malletier, but the action did not go unnoticed.

Jordan raised his right hand as if to strike the other man, then raked it through his dark hair, a gesture of frustration mingled with barely controlled rage. "Accident?" His laugh was hollow. "It was an error in judgment—on your part, friend!" he snapped. "You're so damned strung out on coke you couldn't find your way to the john without a road map!"

"I haven't been doing any drugs!" Lance protested, taking a step backward.

"Cut the crap, pal!" Jordan growled. Poised in an angry stance, legs spread apart, his whole body rigid, he unconsciously tapped the whip he held in his right hand against the palm of his left. "Save it for someone who doesn't know you like I do."

"Jordy, you've got it all wrong." The other man was clearly intimidated. "I swear it!"

"You fucking bastard!" Jordan lunged at him, shoving him back against one of the stall doors with such force that, had he been paying attention, he would have heard the boards crack. Lance put up a struggle, but it only served to further infuriate Jordan. He slammed his fist into the other man's abdomen, forcing a wail of pain that came out as a gasp. Finally, galvanized by fear, Lance managed to raise his knee sharply into Jordan's groin, pushing him away.

Jordan fell to the ground but quickly got to his feet again. His fist smashed into Lance's jaw, and Lance crumpled to the ground in agony. Jordan dragged him up again by the collar of his polo jersey. By this time, the other man was too weak to put up a fight, and attempted once again to talk to his assailant. "Jordy, you've gotta listen—" he moaned.

"Shut your goddamned mouth!" Jordan snapped, slamming him against the wall again. "You just listen, you bastard, and listen good." His face was dangerously close to the other man's. "You want to put your own life on the line, that's your business. Go blow your brains out, if you have any left—I don't give a damn about that! But do it somewhere other than the polo field, got it?" Jordan released him abruptly, and Lance slid down the wall into a crouching position. "One more time, Whitney, and I go to Gavin Hillyer. I don't think I have to tell you how easy it's going to be to replace you on the team.''

As he turned to walk away, Lance lunged at him from behind. In the next instant, both men were on the floor, rolling around in the dirt, arms flailing as they clawed at each other. Jordan pinned Lance down on the ground, straddling him as he struck him again and again. His hands found the other man's throat, and he began throttling him, unable to control his rage. . . .

BOOK ONE
CLUBS

♊ New York City, July 1986

The Grill Room at the Four Seasons has often been referred to as a kind of "publishing central"—a gathering spot for high-level publishing executives, influential editors, high-powered agents, and their best-selling authors. Countless megabuck deals—and celebrations of the results of those deals—have taken place at any one of the Grill Room's booths or tables, all of which are well spaced in the large rectangular dining room with its towering, metallic-curtained windows, French walnut paneling, and floral displays that change with the seasons.

One such celebration took place on a hot summer afternoon, possibly the hottest of the year. That day Sloane Driscoll's fifth novel, *Fallen Idols,* officially hit the number one spot on the *New York Times* best seller list. The book was her fifth consecutive best seller and by far the most commercially successful to date. It was a major triumph, not only for the author, but for the two women with whom she celebrated that day: her agent, Cate Winslow, one of the most influential literary agents in the business, and Adrienne Adamson, who was not only Sloane's editor but also the driving force behind at least half a dozen names regularly making best seller lists around the country. Together, they had launched those five internationally successful novels, and Sloane knew that Cate and Adrienne, each in her own way, had had as much to do with the books' successes as she had herself. She paused now, her eyes moving from one to the other: Cate—petite, stylish, a fashionable woman, her dark coloring an indication of her Greek heritage, who'd been called a shark by some and a genius by others;

Adrienne, confident and attractive, with a warm, congenial manner that concealed the fierce determination that often showed itself when she was fighting for a book she believed in during weekly editorial meetings. Sloane was close to both women, and yet there was a part of her that envied each of them, envied their self-assurance, their perfect balance of career and marriage—something she'd never been able to accomplish herself.

She raised her glass in a toast and smiled. "To both of you," she began, raising her head in a way that revealed heavily mascaraed eyes, previously hidden in the shadows of her wide-brimmed red hat. Carelessly, she flicked a strand of auburn hair over her shoulder. "Without you—both of you—I'd probably still be hustling back in Chicago!"

Cate and Adrienne raised their glasses to hers. "And to the next five best sellers," Adrienne added.

Cate only smiled, remembering that first meeting she'd had with Sloane in Chicago eight years earlier. How very like Sloane the comment had been. "I think you've come a long way since you left Chicago," she pointed out.

Sloane's grin was wicked. "Eight hundred and nine miles, to be exact," she said lightly.

Cate's gaze was level. "You know perfectly well what I mean," she said carefully. It was going to be one of those days. Sloane was, quite simply, a hell-raiser, and Cate suspected that nothing short of death was ever going to change her. Not that anyone at the Holland Publishing Group really wanted to change her. In the beginning, Sloane's natural brassiness had been a constant source of irritation to the publicity department. They'd tried to create an image for her but discovered that she was far too much her own person to be successfully molded into what they'd had in mind. She was not a woman who was easily restrained. In the end, they found that her bold approach to giving interviews—and ultimately to promoting her novels—had gained her a notoriety that sold books far more effectively than the methods used by their more conservative authors.

"Word has it you're going on tour again soon," Adrienne said as the waiter placed their dessert—the specialty of the house, chocolate velvet cake—in front of them. "Another twenty-two cities in twenty-five days, I believe."

Sloane gave an exaggerated groan. "I really don't mind going on tour—in fact, I enjoy it. Gives me a chance to catch up on all the latest gossip with the bookstore managers," she insisted. She loved nothing more than good gossip and had achieved a rapport with personnel in bookstores across the country that enabled her to hear all the latest about "the competition," her term for other best-selling authors. "But until last week, I thought it was fifteen cities. Even people in the path of a hurricane get more advance notice than this!"

Adrienne laughed. "I'd think you'd be accustomed to it by now." Then she added, "Do you have any idea how many writers would sell their souls to trade places with you?"

"Only too well," Sloane assured her. "Just eight years ago I was one of them—remember?" She finished her Brandy Alexander. "I suppose I'm still finding it hard to believe that anyone could actually envy me."

Cate smiled. "You have a great deal going for you, Sloane," she reminded her client. "What more do you want?"

She shrugged. "I wouldn't mind looking like Christie Brinkley," she confessed.

Their conversation was interrupted at that point by the manager of the restaurant, who asked Sloane to sign the leather-bound guest register, an honor extended to only their most frequent and celebrated guests. She obliged, and he left them alone to finish dessert. "Talk about timing," Adrienne commented with a sly smile as he walked away.

"I've got a hell of an idea for a new book," Sloane announced then, changing the subject abruptly. "As a matter of fact, I can't wait to get started on it." Then, with a slight shrug of her shoulders, she added casually, "But it will have to wait—until after the book tour."

"You could probably turn out a synopsis before you leave," Adrienne suggested. Sloane was one of that rare species of writer who could actually write fast without sacrificing quality.

Sloane shook her head emphatically. "I don't think so. I'm leaving for France in two days—and I'll be gone almost three weeks. That doesn't leave much time for writing." She scooped up the last morsel of cake and popped it into her mouth.

"France?" Adrienne turned to Cate, slightly confused. "Did you know about this?"

"No," Cate admitted, "not until just now." She looked across the table at Sloane. In the eight years they'd worked together, a strong bond of friendship had developed between herself and her client, but Cate had discovered early on that Sloane could be difficult when she wanted to be and at times had been impulsive, unpredictable, and infuriatingly stubborn. There were times when Cate could have cheerfully strangled her, and she suspected that this was going to be one of those times. "What on earth are you going to France for *now,* of all times—" she started.

"I *could* say I really need a vacation," Sloane said casually, pausing to finish her drink.

"But that's not the real reason, is it?"

Sloane shook her head. "It's the start of the polo season in Deauville."

Adrienne shot her a quizzical look. "When did you become interested in polo?" she asked. "I thought indoor sports were your cup of tea." It was an old joke between them, stemming from the question Sloane had been asked most often about her books: had the sex scenes come from her own experiences?

"When I decided to write about it," Sloane answered with a smile.

"Well, Mom, what've you got in mind this time?" Ten-year-old Travis Driscoll sat on one corner of Sloane's big brass bed in the blue and white bedroom overlooking Central Park, watching his mother pack. "Gambling, dancing till dawn, or skinny-dipping in the nearest fountain?"

She looked up at him suspiciously. "None of the above," she said emphatically. "And while we're on the subject, where do you get such ideas?"

He cocked his head to one side and gave her a puzzled look, as if he were surprised she didn't already know the answer. He was a handsome boy, with dark hair and dark brown eyes, and his looks still left his mother baffled. He didn't look like her—and he sure as hell didn't look like his father. *Maybe he's a throwback,* she thought, amused.

"You know, Mom—those newspapers they sell at the supermarket. The ones on the racks next to the checkout," he said. "The ones with the stuff about babies from other planets and junk like that."

"When did you start reading that trash?" Sloane asked disapprovingly.

"Right after I started reading *Playboy*," he answered with a mischievous grin.

Sloane stopped what she was doing. "You are *definitely* too young for *Playboy*," she told him firmly.

He laughed. "Don't worry, Mom—I don't read it—"

"I know—you just look at the pictures," she said at the exact moment he spoke the same words.

"Nothing gets by you, does it?" he asked cheerfully. He got up off the bed and headed for the door.

"I really wish you'd go with me," she told him then.

"I'd like to, Mom, but you know how it is—previous engagements and all," he said with feigned sophistication. He was ten going on forty, Sloane decided. Too smart for his own good. But he had made plans with his friends, and Emma, their housekeeper of six years, would be there to look after him as always. School would be starting before she returned, so she decided not to push it.

He scurried out of the room. A moment later, he poked his head in the doorway. "Hey, Mom—can we order a pizza tonight? One of those monster-sized deals with everything on it—except the little fishes?"

"Anchovies," Sloane supplied.

He shrugged. "Whatever. Can we get one?"

She turned to look at him, hands on her hips in a firm stance. "Travis, my love, has anyone ever bothered to tell you that man—or boy—does not live by pizza alone?"

"Only you," he answered. "Anyway, I was only thinking of you."

She shot him a dubious look. "Of *me*? Since when?"

"Since now," he said promptly. "I know you gave Emma the night off, and I know you hate to cook—"

"You know I *can't* cook," she corrected.

"I was just being nice."

"I'll just bet you were."

"Well—what's it gonna be, Mom?" he asked impatiently. "Can I call 'em now?"

She looked at him for a moment, then gave a deep sigh. "Go ahead," she surrendered. "But don't you dare try to con

Emma into ordering pizza every night while I'm away!'' she
called after him as he hurried away to call in the order before
she changed her mind. "She'll be forewarned!"

She shook her head, smiling. He was spoiled, no doubt about
that . . . but she had no one to blame but herself. *I created the
monster,* she thought with mild amusement. She'd never denied
him anything. But bringing up a child alone—especially an
only child—was never easy, whether one was a Rockefeller
or a bank teller. The temptation to indulge was overwhelming.
She'd always felt that somehow she had to compensate for not
having been able to give him a father. Still, no father had to
be better than growing up with the man who'd fathered Travis,
she told herself again and again. Over the years she hadn't
exactly shown good judgment in her relationships with men.
It reminded her of her high school chemistry class—when she'd
had a bad habit of mixing the wrong chemicals. With disastrous
results. Taking her past track record with the opposite sex into
consideration, she'd decided long ago that true love was definitely not in the cards for her. She'd devoted all her time and
energies to her son and her career and had been quite pleased
with the results. She didn't need a man in her life to complicate
things now.

By the time she'd finished packing the last of her three
suitcases, Sloane was exhausted. Now she had a good excuse
to call it an early night, and she was glad Travis had conned
her into ordering pizza.

Catching sight of herself in the full-length mirror on the
closet door, she paused. *We usually avoid mirrors, Bela Lugosi
and me,* she thought wryly. The face looking back at her was
a face that might be described as interesting or even striking,
depending upon the visual acuity of the beholder, but not clas-
sically beautiful. *Beautiful only if he's got a cane and a dog,*
she told herself. She'd always thought her face was a little too
round: when she smiled broadly, she mused, she looked as if
she might be storing nuts for the winter. She would have liked
a perfect oval face. *Not Christie Brinkley,* she decided. Still,
she did have high cheekbones, and her complexion was flawless. Her hair was good. One couldn't have everything, she
told herself. The body was not bad. She had curves in all the
right places and was not overweight. Her breasts were full and

still firm. She was, however, a little broad in the beam. Thank
God for shoulder pads and hats. They gave the illusion of
balance. But her best asset was the one she couldn't see when
she looked in the mirror: her imagination. She'd written five
best sellers. She was a bona fide celebrity. *Maybe some people
really do envy me,* she thought with a degree of satisfaction.
But I'd still like to look like Christie Brinkley.

"It's a well-known fact that your publisher paid you a two-
million-dollar advance for *Fallen Idols.*" The interviewer was
an attractive but conservatively dressed woman in her early
forties, pleasant but unmistakably professional. "It's been rumored that you've just signed a new contract for a record-
breaking advance. Is this true?"

Sloane smiled, completely relaxed before the television cameras in spite of the question put to her. From past experience,
she knew where it was leading. "That's right," she affirmed.

"None of the reports specified exactly how much," the interviewer went on. "Care to enlighten us?"

Sloane's gaze was level. "Let's just say it made me—and the
IRS—very happy," she said easily. Personally, she didn't care
who knew what she'd been paid for her books. Though most authors did, Sloane regarded her advances much in the way a child
did a new toy. A born show-off, Cate had called her.

Cate had been the one who decided on that aura of mystery.
Sloane thought it was silly, but she usually let Cate call the
shots when it came to business. And Linc had agreed with Cate
one hundred percent.

Linc. Glancing past the interviewer momentarily, Sloane
could see Linc Marsden standing in the shadows just off cam-
era. He was a tall, handsome man in his early forties, with
thick, coffee-brown hair that teased the collar of his shirt and
fell in a deep wave across his forehead, and a mustache that
was always immaculately trimmed. His face looked as if it
could have been the model for a Roman coin, and his eyes
were a deep, vivid blue. As always, he was dressed impeccably
in one of the expensive suits paid for from the exorbitant sums
he charged her annually to serve as her personal publicist. *The
picture of British reserve,* Sloane thought wryly. Without the
expensive suit and the carefully cultivated image he was quite
a different man—and having gotten to know that man inti-

mately, Sloane wasn't at all sure she liked him.

The rest of the interview went smoothly, but Sloane was still relieved when it was over. In less than four hours she was leaving for France, and she still had what seemed like a million things to do before her departure.

"We have to talk," Linc told her as they left the television center together.

"You'll have to make it fast." Sloane's eyes scanned the busy street in search of a taxi. "I'm in a hurry."

"Don't be absurd," he said crossly. "Stop by the office tomorrow around ten—"

She shook her head. "No can do," she told him, still looking for a cab. "At ten tomorrow morning, I'll be in France."

"France?" He grabbed her arm. "Whatever are you going to France for?"

"You're the fifth person to ask me that," she said with a wintry smile. "Not that it's any of your business, but I'm meeting friends in Deauville."

"You can't just take off like this!" he argued. People around them turned to look, but neither of them noticed. "You have a tour coming up—in case you've forgotten!"

She shook herself free. "I haven't forgotten anything."

"I have interviews lined up—*Time,* another *People,* a spot on the *Today* show—" He was quite clearly flustered.

She looked at him. "These are already scheduled?" she asked. She waved to a passing cab, but it went on by.

He hesitated for a moment. "No, but—"

"Then there's no problem," she said promptly. "Just don't schedule anything until after October first. I should be back from the book tour by then."

"Why do you have to go to France *now*?" he pursued. "Is someone dying?"

She turned on him angrily. "*You* might be if you don't back off," she warned, resenting his interference. "If you absolutely have to know, I'm going to Deauville on a research trip—and if I'm lucky, I just might squeeze in a little R and R while I'm there. God knows it's been ages since I've had a real vacation!" She hailed another taxi.

"You could have at least consulted me before you made your plans," he reprimanded her as the taxi came to a stop at the curb.

She opened the door to get in, then turned on Linc again, her eyes blazing with anger. "Let's get something straight right here and now—*you* work for *me*!" she snapped. People were staring, but Sloane didn't care. "*You* consult *me* before you schedule anything, got it?"

Now he was angry, too. "Just where do you think you'd be now without me?" he demanded.

"Probably a hell of a lot better off!" she shot back at him. "You know, for the past six years you've been pushing me in directions I don't want to go—and, quite frankly, I've had it! You've tried to tell me how to smile, how to talk to the press, how to dress, how to wear my hair! I let you drag me to that idiotic makeup artist—and ended up looking like a Picasso! I'm beginning to feel like a puppet! The Sloane Driscoll doll—wind her up and she'll smile for the cameras, talk like a nice, boring lady who doesn't answer half the questions put to her and who is so bland that the answers she does give aren't worth hearing! You could use that stupid image you created for me as part of a military training film—how to put an entire nation to sleep at one time!"

"Hey, lady!" the cabbie interjected impatiently. "Are you going or not?"

"I am!" Sloane drew in a deep breath, then let it out again. "I'll come by the office, Linc—when I get back!" She got into the cab and slammed the door, making it clear she did not intend to share the car with him.

As the driver negotiated the heavy crosstown traffic, Sloane thought about it. She wasn't sure whom she was angrier with—Linc for being so pushy or herself for letting him get to her. How much of her hostility toward him was personal? she wondered now. She told herself she didn't need him. She'd never agreed to the image he'd proposed for her. It was like a dress bought two sizes too small: it didn't fit. Dani Havilland, Holland's promotions manager, and Caroline Forrest, the publicity manager, saw to it that she got all the publicity she needed. She was a star—and she no longer needed Linc Marsden.

But it hadn't always been that way. Holland had given her first novel an impressive promotion, but Sloane was convinced it wasn't enough. Her ego refused to take a back seat to anyone, and she'd convinced herself that she needed a personal publicist. After *Revelations* became a best seller, she began looking for one. No firm had come more highly recommended than Lincoln Marsden Associates. Linc had worked with several big-name authors and achieved spectacular results. The fact that he was also extremely attractive had not been a factor in her decision to hire him; she hadn't been interested in him as a man. Indeed, the two locked horns right from the beginning. But somewhere along the line, that highly charged business relationship had turned personal—and physical. The affair hadn't lasted. She'd quickly discovered that Linc the man was even more demanding and unreasonable than Linc the publicist.

Men, she thought now. *Who needs 'em?*

At Kennedy Airport, Sloane checked her bags and made her way through the bustling East Wing terminal, where departing international flights boarded, to the gate where she would board an Air France flight to Paris. From there, she would fly on to Deauville. Traffic had been heavier than usual all the way from Manhattan, and a drive that normally took only thirty minutes had taken almost an hour.

Boarding the plane, she found her seat by the window, as she'd requested, and put her carry-on bag in the overhead compartment. *It's going to be a long night,* she thought as she settled in and fastened her seat belt. She took out one of the books she'd brought along—books on polo to help her learn the rules of the game so she wouldn't feel totally stupid in Deauville—and started to read. It promised to be an interesting trip. She'd been invited to Deauville by Gabrielle Millano, her college roommate. Gaby, as she was called by her friends, had married an Italian businessman nine years ago and spent most of her time in Europe. Her husband, Carlo, was a polo enthusiast and onetime player who followed the important matches religiously. He'd transferred his love of the sport to his wife, who in the past few years had sent Sloane letters bearing postmarks from all over the world, describing in detail—sometimes graphic detail, Sloane recalled with amusement—the life-styles of the polo players and other "horse people." Her letters had inspired the novel Sloane wanted to write—and led to the invitation to Sloane to join them in Deauville. Gaby had told her on the phone a week earlier that a good friend of theirs, who at age thirty was already a nine-goal player riding with the American team, was willing to talk with her and "show her the ropes." "Knowing Jordan, he'll teach you about more than just polo," Gaby had said cryptically.

Nine-goal rating, Sloane thought. *Polo players have a handicap, just like golfers—only in reverse. The higher the rating, the better the player. This Jordan Phillips must really be good.*

She didn't put the book aside until a flight attendant brought her dinner. Even then, she continued to mentally drill herself on polo terminology and trivia. She hadn't been on a horse in years, and she had never been to Deauville, though she'd heard a great deal about it. All in all, it promised to be an interesting three weeks.

⇄ Deauville, August 1986

C-r-r-rack! The small white ball skimmed the ground, streaking toward the goal like a heat-seeking missile zeroing in on its target. The eight mounted players, four in red and white jerseys and the other four in blue, charged after it, the sound of their horses' hoofbeats like a distant rumble of thunder to the spectators up in the stands. Another powerful hit sent the ball rocketing well past the goalposts. There was a loud burst of applause from the stands as the players, wielding their mallets like lethal weapons, turned their mounts and headed back across the field. The announcer's voice boomed over the loudspeakers, describing the action in rapid French.

"He's the number three in the blue jersey." Gabrielle Millano was a tall, reed-thin woman in a sea-green linen suit and matching picture hat that offset her sharp, angular features and straight, shoulder-length black hair. She sat with Sloane at a table in that section of the stands known as the Village, pointing out one of the players as Sloane trained her binoculars on the polo field. Gaby's husband, Carlo, who normally would not have permitted anyone to disrupt his enjoyment of the game, discussed an important business deal with a French financier. Around them, the spectators were all elegantly turned out, the women in their summer linens from the top designers in Paris. "Linens and cottons for day, all the important jewels for night," Gaby had told Sloane when she invited her to join them. Sloane had felt her white linen suit with its blue camisole and seed pearl epaulets, and the wide-brimmed white hat, were too formal for polo, but now that she was there, she realized it was entirely right for polo in Deauville.

"I see him," Sloane said finally, fixing her binoculars on the blue number three.

"What do you think?" Gaby wanted to know.

Sloane shrugged. "He's either a madman or one hell of a bluffer," she observed.

"No, I mean about *him*," Gaby specified. "Isn't he gorgeous?"

"It's hard to tell from this distance," Sloane answered without diverting her attention from the field. "Especially since he *is* wearing a helmet and face guard." The blue number three scored another goal for his team.

He really is good, Sloane thought. Even though she was hardly an expert on polo, she could see that he was a force to be reckoned with. She followed him with the binoculars. Idly, she wondered what he looked like up close—without the helmet and face guard. Gaby said he was gorgeous. *Probably conceited as hell, too.*

The American team was leading—four goals to their opponents' two—when the bell sounded to indicate that only thirty seconds remained of the second chukker. The players rode off the field, many of them to change mounts. Sloane followed the blue number three with her binoculars. He swung out of his saddle with an easy gracefulness that spoke of confidence, of years of perfecting his equestrian skills. He pulled off his helmet, but she still couldn't get a close look at his face. He was dark, she noted, as he ran one hand through his hair. He handed his pony over to a groom who'd brought him another.

By the end of the third chukker, the American team had set a swift pace. Sloane missed the shot that sent the ball bouncing free of the tangle of horses and riders. It came to rest midfield. She did see number three's dapple-gray pony break from the pack, moving like quicksilver as he executed yet another long, cracking hit. The ball skittered across the field but was intercepted by the opposing team. Another goal for the opponents. Then the American team took possession of the ball. Their all-out attack was clearly an upset to the other team, which committed two fouls by the time the horn sounded to indicate the end of the chukker.

"Come on—I'll introduce you to Jordy," Gaby told Sloane

as the players rode off the field for a half-time break. As they made their way through the crowd, Sloane noticed a number of the spectators migrating to the field itself. "It's an old tradition," Gaby explained. "Mashing down the divots."

Approaching the picket line, Sloane observed a group of players from both teams laughing together, some seated in lawn chairs, the others sprawled out on the grass. "Apparently, the rivalry ends when the horn blows," she commented.

"Most of the time, but not always," Gaby said with a knowing smile. "Ah—here he comes. Jordan!" she called out, waving to him.

Sloane turned. The man walking toward them was pulling off his helmet. He was tall and well built, a fact that was easily discernible from the way his perspiration-soaked polo jersey clung to every muscle of his broad, well-developed chest. Open at the neckline, the shirt gave an inviting glimpse of thick chest hair. Her gaze returned to his face as he came closer. His features were strong but regular. His eyes were dark but seemed to crackle in a way that suggested some hidden fire concealed within their depths. His damp, dark hair curled around his ears, and Sloane found herself thinking indecent thoughts—and wondering if her own face was as flushed as his.

"Jordy, this is Sloane Driscoll," Gaby was saying. "Sloane, Jordan Phillips."

Sloane extended her hand. "I'm pleased to meet you," she said formally. She knew she was staring at him, and she felt like an idiot.

Jordan took her hand, gave it a little squeeze but did not release it. "So it's not a pen name," he guessed.

"No," she lied, shaking her head. "I confess to everything." *Except my real name,* she thought.

He grinned. "Do you, now?"

Sloane knew she was blushing, but she was unable to do anything about it. *This man has a bad effect on you,* she was thinking. *Like drinking too much champagne.*

Jordan's smile was disarming. "Gaby's told me a lot about you," he said.

Sloane laughed. "Don't believe a word this woman says!" she warned.

"I seldom do," he assured her. "After all, they don't call her Gaby for nothing."

"Stop talking about me as if I weren't here, you two," Gaby interjected, stepping out of the way as a young groom leading two horses passed too close for comfort.

Jordan ignored her. "However," he continued, still holding Sloane's hand, "I think I have to trust her this time. This old harpy's said some very flattering things about you. I think you must be one of the three people in the world she actually likes."

Gaby took a step toward him menacingly. "If I didn't like *you*, Jordy Phillips, I'd never let you get away with the things you've said to and about me!"

"You'd never be able to stop me, love," he told her. "I'm bigger than you—and a damned sight stronger." With that, he released Sloane's hand and swept Gaby up in his arms, lifting her a good ten inches off the ground.

"Put me down, you idiot!" Gaby scolded, pummeling his left shoulder with her fist. "People are staring!"

"Since when does that bother you?" he asked as he lowered her to the ground.

"One of these days—" Gaby warned, feigning anger. "Look what you've done! Now I smell like horse!"

"It's better than that perfume you were wearing," Jordan said easily, taking a large glass of ice water offered to him by a young blonde in pants and a T-shirt that looked to be two sizes too small, who looked at him with open adulation. The girl was so starry-eyed she didn't even seem to notice that he hadn't so much as acknowledged her presence. Sloane, however, was painfully aware of her. *Why should it bother me?* she wondered as the girl finally disappeared into the crowd.

Jordan drank half the water from the glass, then doused himself with the rest. "It's hotter than blazes out there," he commented, gesturing toward the polo field. Then he handed the glass to Gaby. "Do something with this, will you?"

"I know what I'd like to do with it," she told him.

He ignored her threat and turned to Sloane again. "Where are you staying?" he asked.

She looked at him for a moment. "The Normandy."

He nodded, raking his fingers through his hair. "I'm at the Royal. We'll have dinner at the Normandy—tonight, eight?"

She was stunned for a moment. He was making plans for them to have dinner—and he hadn't even asked her!

He saw the look on her face and laughed. "You *do* want to talk polo with me, don't you?" he asked, amused.

"That's why I'm here," she managed, still stunned by his presumptuousness.

"I'm more cooperative on a full stomach." He took the reins of the fresh mount his groom brought him. "Tonight, then?"

She nodded.

"You may end up getting more than you bargained for," Gaby confided as he mounted and rode away.

Sloane only smiled. She was thinking of her high school chemistry class.

"Watch carefully, now," Jordan instructed. He took the salt and pepper shakers and placed them side by side on the table in front of her. "This is how we practice passing strategy. This player," he said, pointing to the salt, "sends his teammate on in front of him." He moved the pepper several inches. "When he's about thirty yards ahead, he'll drive the ball past him as hard as he can."

"If he doesn't get spilled first," Sloane commented.

"Let's have a little respect here, woman. This is serious business," he scolded, grinning. "After this guy makes his hit, he's going to pull up and wait for the other guy to hit back to him. That one goes after the ball, looks back to see how his buddy's positioned, then picks up speed before he makes his hit."

Sloane's voice dropped to a conspiratorial whisper. "The waiter's staring at us," she told him.

"If he doesn't like what he sees, he doesn't have to look," Jordan said with mock indignation.

It had been a pleasant—and informative—evening. Jordan was not only attractive, he was the most appealing man she had ever met. He answered her questions and entertained her with anecdotes about his travels as a professional polo player. "Polo is basically pretty simple: high goals and low morals," he said with a sly wink.

"Do you always play with the same team?" she asked over dessert.

He shook his head. "I'm a free-lancer," he answered. "It's a lot like prostitution: I play for the highest bidder—whoever happens to make me the best offer. After this, I'm off to

Argentina to play on another team." He paused. "Not everyone operates that way. A good many players play for only one sponsor. Playing with the same guys all the time does have some definite advantages, especially for a newcomer to the pro ranks."

He talked about his days as a club player at Myopia near Boston. "We'd all go out the night before a match—both teams," he recalled. "Each team would do their best to get the other team skunked so they wouldn't play worth a damn the next day. Trouble was, we'd all end up drunk. When we got together for breakfast the next morning, we'd all be too hung over to eat, but no one would admit it. Everyone forced himself to eat, then we'd all go off somewhere and barf our guts up."

Sloane made a face. "Sounds like fun."

"It was. It just proved an old theory that all polo players are egomaniacs," he said, reaching for his wineglass. "No one would admit to being weak. They'd torture themselves first."

"You sound as if you miss those days," she observed.

His eyes met hers. "I do," he said quietly. "Don't get me wrong—professional polo is my life—but there are times I miss playing just for the fun of it."

She frowned. She knew the feeling only too well.

There are five capitals of world-class polo: Palm Beach, Buenos Aires, England's Windsor Great Park and Cowdray, and Deauville. Of the five, any genuine polo patron will attest to the fact that Deauville is the most fun. Polo enthusiasts, most of them high-gear types whose calendars are filled with meetings and business trips and countless social engagements, will invariably strive to pencil in Deauville on their agendas for the last three weeks of August each year.

Eight teams and their entourages converge on the chic French resort each summer to compete for some fifteen cups, the most coveted being the Coupe d'Or. To compete, each team must have an overall rating of at least twenty goals and be able to pay the two-thousand-dollar entry fee. Generally this is not a problem for the typical high-goal team, which customarily consists of a rich, top-rated team captain, a rich friend, and two ''money'' players. When this is not the case, there is a team sponsor who is a patron of the game and who assembles a group of top-level money players to compete under his colors. Sponsors have become increasingly important to the game in recent years as paying the pros, maintaining a string that averages six ponies for each player, and covering their travel expenses can run into a million dollars or more each year.

During their three weeks in Deauville, the teams play every day except Monday. They're on the field by nine each morning, either practicing or competing. Because of their rigorous schedules, they usually lead a rather staid night life, usually nothing more than dinner at one of the restaurants favored by the ''horse people,'' such as Café le Drakkar. Occasionally, they visit the casinos or nightclubs like Regine's in Deauville or Jimmy's, across the river in Trouville. On one Monday each season, the gauchos serve up an *asado*, a traditional Argentine beef barbecue, on the field near the stables.

Sloane enjoyed the barbecue. Mingling with the other players, many of whom had wives and children who accompanied them on the road, she was able to see a side of Jordan he never presented when they were alone. He spent all of his free time with her and had been most cooperative, sharing personal experiences with her and even inviting her to the early-morning practice sessions, but she'd always had the feeling that he held back a vital part of himself. Not so with his fellow players. They were, for the most part, like one big, happy, extended family. At the barbecue everyone, from the players and patrons to the grooms and other members of the teams' staffs, joined in the revelry. There was a camaraderie among the players, many of whom had known each other and played together for years.

Jordan was especially close to Lance Whitney, who played main offensive for the American team. Lance was slightly older than Jordan, tall and as fair as Jordan was dark. Over the delicious meal, they reminisced about their years in professional polo for Sloane's microcassette recorder. ''Half the time,'' Lance recalled, ''we'd end up in a country where we didn't speak the language and a city where we didn't know our way around. When we weren't too exhausted to go out at night, we'd always manage to get ourselves lost. We couldn't stop to ask directions—they couldn't understand us, and we couldn't understand them—so it was all quite hopeless.''

"We *did* manage to break down the language barriers on the polo fields,'' Jordan put in as he reached for a beer. "After you've played as long as we have, you just know somehow when you're being called a no-good S.O.B. in any one of a dozen languages!'' He opened the bottle easily and took a long swallow.

"And we heard *that* a lot,'' Lance said with a laugh. "In the good old days, when Jordy and Max and I teamed up, we were real hell-raisers—weren't we, Jordy?''

Jordan's expression changed quite suddenly. "Yeah,'' he said darkly. "Yeah, we were.''

"Max?'' Sloane was looking at Jordan, and his reaction to Lance's comment aroused her curiosity.

Lance noticed it too. "Max Kenyon,'' he said uneasily. "We were teammates—and buddies—way back when.''

Were, Sloane thought, puzzled by the abrupt change in Jordan's mood. *That, apparently, is the key word*. She made a mental note to ask him about it later.

Gaby accused Sloane of being more interested in the man than in the polo player, but Sloane categorically denied any attraction. "I'm not looking for a man, and you know it,'' she insisted. "Just because I'm on a diet doesn't mean I can't look at the menu.'' In fact, it was all business between them. They always talked about polo. She asked the questions and he provided the answers, and it was all quite simple.

On the surface.

"There are times when I feel like a nomad,'' Jordan confessed as they walked together across the polo field, his pony trailing behind them. It was still quite early, just after dawn, and his team was gathering for a practice session. The stands were empty now and the grass moist with dew. A soft, salty breeze blew in from the English Channel, and the morning air smelled incredibly fresh. "A week here, two weeks there, maybe a month somewhere else.'' One of the horses clustered on the other side of the field whinnied. Ears perked, Jordan's mare lifted her head and nickered in response. He patted her neck affectionately. "I haven't been stateside since February.''

"Where's home?" Sloane asked, brushing a strand of hair off her face with one hand. It was unusually cool for Deauville in August, and she was beginning to wish she'd chosen something warmer than the royal blue linen slacks and red shirt she was wearing.

"Massachusetts," he answered. "Martha's Vineyard, to be exact. I grew up there. My parents live in Boston now, but to me Moonstone is still home. I keep my ponies there and breed and train horses for polo—when I have the time."

"I take it you have no other family. No brothers or sisters—" She wanted to say, "No wife, no fiancée," but resisted the impulse. *Why should it matter to me?* she asked herself.

He shook his head. "I'm an only child. What about you?"

Sloane frowned. "I'm the one asking the questions, remember?"

He looked at her oddly. "Touchy subject?"

"No, just personal."

He nodded slowly. "I see. It's all right for you to *ask* personal questions—you just won't answer any, right?" he concluded.

She folded her arms across her chest in a defensive gesture, looking down at the ground as she walked. "Something like that," she said quietly.

"Jordan!" One of his teammates rode toward them on a big chestnut gelding. "Are you going to stick and ball with us or not?"

He turned to Sloane for a moment as if he wanted to say something, then changed his mind. "Be right there," he responded. He mounted his pony, then looked at Sloane one more time. "Planning to stick around?" he asked sharply.

She nodded.

"Good. I think you'll find it educational." As he rode away, she felt a small shiver course down her spine. She was thinking of what she'd said to Gaby: *Just because I'm on a diet doesn't mean I can't look at the menu.*

Looking at Jordan Phillips made her want to forget that "diet"—and the promise she'd made to herself a long time ago.

"I see I've been replaced. And all this time I've thought I was irreplaceable!"

Jordan tightened the cinch on his saddle, pulled down the flap with a sharp jerk, then adjusted the stirrup. He didn't turn around. The soft, seductive feminine voice addressing him was only too familiar. "I think you're in the wrong camp, Jilly," he said tightly.

"Am I?" Her tone was one of amusement.

"I doubt your husband would approve."

"Whether or not my husband approves is of no interest to me," she said simply. "I do as I please."

"No one knows that better than I do," he said, taking a deep breath.

"Are you afraid to look at me, Jordan?" She was taunting him.

"Dammit, Jilly, go bother someone else!" he snapped angrily as he swung around to face her. People around them had begun to stare, but he was too annoyed with her to notice— or to care. "I've been bitten, remember? I'm immune to your venom now."

"Are you really?" Jilly Fleming Kenyon was still one of the most beautiful women Jordan had ever seen—and he'd seen plenty. She was tall and full-figured, with black-lashed green eyes and dark red hair that cascaded in heavy waves past her shoulders. Her soft, delicate features were made to look sharp, almost feline, by the dramatic makeup she always wore. She was wearing a low-cut blue silk dress, and even now Jordan found it impossible to look at her without remembering what she'd been like in bed: a tigress with a magnificent and willing body that seemed to have been designed to give pleasure. She'd always been daring, willing to experiment sexually. But beyond that, he could not recall what he had seen in her, what had made him come so close to making her his wife. She was spoiled, self-centered, manipulative—all the things he hadn't been able to see until the sexual spell she'd cast on him years ago had been broken.

"You loved me once," she said softly, almost as if she'd read his mind.

He frowned. "At least we had one thing in common."

She took a step closer. "I did love you, whether you believe me or not," she said softly, placing her hands on his shoulders. Jordan felt his body begin to respond against his will. "I still do."

She started to kiss him, but he grabbed her wrists and pushed her away. "Come off it, Jilly," he said harshly. "We both know you've always been too much in love with yourself to have any genuine feelings for anyone else . . . including Max."

She smiled. "I've never loved Max. You know that."

"Of course not," Jordan said coldly. "You married Max to get back at me—just like you made sure I caught the two of you in bed at Chukka Cove to get back at me. What's the matter, Jilly? Isn't revenge sweet enough for you?"

"You still want me, Jordan—I know it and you know it." She tried to kiss him again, but he turned away. "Remember how it was with us? No one could satisfy me like you did."

"Well, *I* wasn't satisfied!" he exploded to the surprise of everyone milling around the grounds. "Go on back to Max, Jilly—you're wasting your time here."

"Am I?" She laughed. "You're a fool, Jordan. The woman you've been spending all your time with is just using you!"

"Coming from an expert like yourself, I'm sure that's a qualified opinion," he said, turning away from her abruptly.

"She'll dump you as soon as she has what she really wants," Jilly predicted. "And when she does, you know where to find me."

"Don't hold your breath." He turned back to his horse as Jilly spun on her heel and walked away.

Neither of them saw Sloane, standing only a few yards away, watching them.

"How much do you know about Jordan, Gaby?" Sloane asked.

They were walking along the bleached-out *planches*, the long boardwalk along the beach that had been built back in the 1920s. Out on the beach, sun-bronzed bodies and large umbrellas resembling tents in bright shades of red and blue dotted the white sand. Beyond that, men and women on horseback rode at the edge of the surf, talking and laughing loudly.

If Gaby was surprised by the question, she gave no indication of it. "About as much as anyone could, I suppose," she answered. "He comes from a good New England family— grandfather made a killing in the stock market, mother's from a well-known Social Register family. Jordan, I'm afraid, has always had a bit of the devil in him. He was kicked out of all the best schools on the East Coast. Carlo and I met him at Palm Beach seven years ago. He was just making a name for himself in polo then, and a number of sponsors were interested in him. So were the women, for that matter. More females flocked around him at the picket lines than flies around the horses.''

''What about Jilly Kenyon?'' The strong, salty sea breeze blew Sloane's long hair around her face.

''Jordy met Jilly in Sydney years ago, when he was just getting started in international polo.'' Gaby paused. ''Her father was one of the top-rated Australian players. His nickname was 'the Tasmanian Devil,' and he sure as hell lived up to it. He was a real monster on the polo field. For Jordan and Jilly, it was like spontaneous combustion, according to the tales I've heard. Apparently everyone—including Jilly—expected to hear wedding bells, but it never happened.''

''Why?'' Sloane asked carefully.

Gaby shrugged. ''Nobody knows. Jordy just ended it one day and refused to talk about it,'' she recalled. ''I don't think Jilly ever forgave him. Six months later she married his best friend, Max Kenyon, who's one of the top players in England right now. If you choose to believe the rumors, she did it to spite Jordy.''

''Sounds like a real charmer,'' Sloane remarked. They both stopped walking as a brightly colored beach ball bounced across the boardwalk in front of them, followed by a small child.

''Charmer?'' Gaby gave a little laugh. ''Not Jilly. Serpent, maybe. Or shark or piranha. But definitely not a charmer.''

Sloane leaned on the railing, staring out at the water absently. ''Then what did he see in her?'' she asked.

''That's easy. Sex—the same thing every man sees in Jilly,'' Gaby replied. ''Except poor Max—he's so smitten with her it's sickening. They say love's blind, but in Max's case, it's brain dead.''

''I suppose he still sees her—Jordan, I mean.''

Gaby nodded. ''More frequently than he'd like, I suspect,'' she said. ''They're barely civil to each other, which is more than I can say for Jordy and Max. When they're on opposing teams, the polo field turns into a war zone.'' She turned to look at Sloane, smiling slyly. "You *are* interested in him, aren't you?"

Sloane made a face. "You know me better than that, Gaby."

"Exactly—I do know you." Gaby made it clear she was not about to let go easily. "Listen—the two of you have been making mating calls at each other all week, and it's frustrating as hell watching you because neither of you is doing anything about it!"

"If I *were* going to 'do anything about it,' as you put it, I certainly wouldn't let you watch," Sloane told her.

"You know what I mean," Gaby said accusingly. Reaching into her clutch bag, she took out a key and pressed it into Sloane's hand. "This is the key to that cottage Carlo and I bought at Honfleur. We just completed the decorating, but we're not going to be able to make use of it this time around— business meetings and all here in town."

"What am I supposed to do with it?" Sloane asked.

Gaby smiled. "If you have half the brain I give you credit for, you'll use it," she said. "Let's go on down to Ciro's for lunch. I'll give you the directions . . ."

"Would you believe I've played Deauville every year for the past six years, and this is the first time I've even been inside the door?" Jordan asked as he and Sloane entered the elegant Casino d'Été.

She looked up at him with a sly smile. "No gambling spirit?" she asked in a teasing voice.

"Plenty of gambling spirit. No energy," he admitted solemnly. "After playing most of the day, I'm usually dead by ten o'clock."

She smiled. "You don't know what you're missing."

"I do now." She was, he decided, the most maddeningly complicated woman he'd ever met. Why did she continually send out mixed signals, coming on to him one minute and cool and distant the next? What did she expect of him? After Jilly, celibacy had taken on a whole new appeal, but looking at Sloane now, in that midnight-blue silk with its plunging neckline, he felt as if he were being teased. He wanted her. It had been a long time since he'd wanted one particular woman and not just someone to take care of his physical needs. Not since Jilly, damn her. Jilly had ruined him, made him incapable of trusting or loving any woman. Even now, as much as he wanted Sloane, wanted to make love to her, he still didn't trust her. In her own way, she was as much a user as Jilly had ever been. A celebrity. A successful author who was interested in him only as a polo player. But, dammit, he still wanted her!

"Shall we try our hand at roulette?" Sloane was asking.

He grinned. "Why not?" The damned tux was driving him crazy. Why did the casino have those stupid rules about formal attire? he thought, shifting his neck in the uncomfortably stiff collar. "Let's go take their money," he said with a forced cheerfulness as he steered her toward the cashier.

They bought a stack of big black chips, each worth five hundred francs, then found empty chairs at one of the roulette tables. Sloane put ten chips on the twenty-four black. "We're probably going to lose our shirts," Jordan commented skeptically.

"You look perfectly fine to me without a shirt," she said with a grin, recalling all the mornings she'd watched him practice without the benefit of a helmet—or a shirt.

He seized the opportunity immediately. "Maybe I should find out if you do as well," he said with a suggestive smile.

She changed the subject abruptly. "What happened to all that confidence and optimism?" she asked stiffly.

"I checked it at the door." *Damn!* he was thinking.

"*Rien ne va plus,*" the croupier barked, indicating that no more bets could be placed.

Sloane held her breath momentarily as the wheel was spun and the ball began its rollicking dance of luck. As the wheel began to slow down, the ball hopped and skipped a few times before coming to rest on the twenty-four black. Squealing, Sloane clapped loudly with delight.

The croupier took care of the other players' bets then turned to Sloane again. "Will you stay on the twenty-four, mademoiselle?" he wanted to know.

She looked at Jordan, who nodded. "Leave it," she instructed.

Again, their number came up. Before she realized it, Sloane was on her feet, screeching with delight and hugging Jordan, who was taken completely by surprise at her unexpected show of emotion but not about to point it out to her. *Maybe*, he thought, *this wasn't such a bad idea after all*.

By the time they left the casino, sometime around midnight, their winnings and losses left them with a profit of close to thirty-five thousand American dollars. "We should spend this on something frivolous—like a vacation in Tahiti," Jordan suggested, intimating that since they'd won it together, they should enjoy it together. Sloane pretended to ignore his suggestion.

But soon, he promised himself, she would want him.

As the sun rose over the eastern horizon into the cloudless summer sky, the players began to gather on the field. Jordan didn't see them. He was concentrating on the shot he was about to make. Galloping his horse at an angle that would place the ball at his right, he kept his eye on it, now no more than a tiny white speck on the dark green polo field. He rose in the stirrups, placing his full weight on the irons as he braced himself for the shot. His body reacted instinctively, gripping with his thighs and his knees to enable him to keep his position on the horse. He twisted around, cocking his wrist so that the mallet was high above his head and would gain momentum on the downward swing. Timing the move carefully, he brought the mallet down in a wide arc when he was no more than a few feet from the ball, the impact so forceful that it sent vibrations all the way up his arm to his shoulder. His follow-through was smooth, and the ball went sailing down the field.

Checking his mount, he turned and rode back to the picket line where Sloane was waiting. Leaning against the bumper of her dark green rented Peugeot, she was dressed more casually than he'd ever seen her: lavender cotton slacks and a pale gray cotton shirt, a lavender-and-blue print scarf tied loosely around her neck. And no hat. That was the first thing he noticed. She was almost never without a hat. Her long hair blew around her like a shimmering banner in the soft wind. *If only she'd go a little lighter on the makeup*, he thought, *she'd look ten years younger*.

It didn't bother him that she was five years older than he was. It wasn't that much of a difference. But he had a feeling that it did bother her. Why? He pushed the thought from his mind as he dismounted and walked over to her. "Let's see how much you've learned," he said cheerfully. "What was the shot I just made?"

She responded quickly. "Offside forehand."

He raised an eyebrow in mock surprise, but the tone of his voice indicated he was impressed. "You *are* a quick study," he commended her. "Maybe I should teach you to play."

"Think I couldn't learn?" she asked.

"It's not easy," he said.

She rose to the challenge. "Okay—you're on."

"When do you want your first lesson?" he asked, grinning broadly.

"No time like the present."

"Whatever you say," he agreed. He led her over to the horse. "This is the front of the horse—and this, of course, is the back," he explained with great seriousness.

"I know a horse's ass when I see one," she snorted. "That's the part that reminds me of you."

"Touché," he said with a laugh as she mounted. "I take it you've ridden before?"

"A long time ago." She adjusted her position in the saddle. "Now what?"

He pulled off his helmet and gave it to her. "Put this on," he instructed.

She slipped the helmet on and fastened the chin strap. "You know," she confided, "the hardest part of doing this book is going to be trying to write about how the player thinks, what he feels during the action. No matter how much research I do, I'm never going to be able to capture that because I've never done it myself."

"Is that all that concerns you?" he asked, grinning up at her. "Easily remedied, my dear." Before she could respond, he leaped behind her onto the horse and urged it into a full gallop, heading across the field where the other players were engaged in a scrimmage.

"Jordan!" Sloane screamed, still reeling from the shock of his unexpected action. She gripped the front of the saddle as best she could as he wrapped his left arm around her waist and gathered the reins in that hand. "Do you know what you're doing?"

He laughed again. "I always know what I'm doing, love," he assured her.

"I can't look!" she wailed as they approached the tangle of horses and riders.

"If you don't look, you'll miss the whole point," he told her. Bending forward, around his passenger, he executed a flawless shot. The force of the mallet's impact sent the ball flying toward the goal.

"Hey, Phillips—stop showing off!" one of the other players called out to him as the action came to an abrupt halt.

"Just showing the lady how it's done," Jordan responded. He leaned against her shoulder. She was trembling. "You okay?" he whispered.

"About as well as can be expected," she said breathlessly.

"I wouldn't let you fall," he assured her. "Just lean back against me."

She did as he told her. He liked the feel of her, so close to him, not protesting, just allowing him to hold her as the horse cantered back toward the picket line. He slowed his mount to a walk. His lips brushed against her cheek lightly. He wanted her. He had, right from the beginning . . . and he believed now that she wanted him, too. And time was running out for them. In a week she'd be returning to New York, and he'd be off to Argentina. Unconsciously he held her a little tighter.

Catching her breath, her hand found its way to her neck. "My scarf!" she gasped, suddenly realizing it was gone. "I must have lost it out there somewhere."

"We'll find it." He turned the horse and headed back across the field, still at a walk. He was in no hurry to let go of her.

"There it is," she said, pointing to the long strip of material in a heap on the ground. He rode over to it and scooped it up with his mallet, offering it to her. She plucked it from the mallet head, then twisted around as best she could to look up at him. "So—chivalry isn't dead!" she declared as she pulled the mallet off. "I—"

She didn't have the opportunity to finish before his lips found hers, kissing her briefly, with a tenderness he didn't know he was capable of until that moment.

Sloane returned to her suite at the Normandy as soon as he took her back to her car. Even now, just thinking about what it had been like, being in his arms, feeling his lips on hers, made her tremble. She was certain that what she felt was more than mere physical desire, but she was unable to identify it because she'd never experienced it before. Gaby was right all along. She *did* want him—even if it was only for one weekend, even if she never saw him again. A man like this, she was absolutely certain, came along once in a lifetime, and, no matter what, she wanted one perfect, idyllic weekend with him.

She opened her bag and took out the key Gaby had given her. The cottage at Honfleur. It sounded like just what she had in mind, the perfect place for a perfect weekend. But how should she approach him? She had the feeling he wasn't the kind of man who was attracted to overly aggressive women. He'd want to be the one to initiate a physical relationship between them. But hadn't he done that this morning, out on the polo field? Surely she hadn't misinterpreted the way he held her, the huskiness in his voice, the way he kissed her. Still, she couldn't just go back to La Touques and say, "Hey, want to spend the weekend with me?" Not even in this liberated age. Not with an old-fashioned man like Jordan.

Finally, she came up with an idea. She scribbled a note to him, telling him where she would be and inviting him to join her if he liked. She put it in an envelope with his name on it. It took her less than ten minutes to pack a bag. She stopped by the Royal and left the note at the front desk, knowing he would get it as soon as he returned from practice.

Thirty minutes later, she was on her way to Honfleur.

ॐ Honfleur, August 1986

The cottage was situated on a hill high over the little fishing port. From the narrow gravel road leading up to it, Honfleur, with its armada of fishing and pleasure boats in the harbor, could be seen to the north. Beyond that, cargo ships and ocean liners were visible out in the Channel. To the west, the city of Le Havre was in full view beyond the estuary of the Seine. As the car began its steady climb up the hill, Sloane recalled that Gaby had told her the view was best at night, but she hoped she would have better things to do with her evenings than take in the view.

Would he show? she wondered as she brought the car to a stop in the circular driveway. She believed he would. She believed he had made his intentions clear that morning on the polo field. She had made hers clear when she left him that note at the Royal. *He'll be here*, she reassured herself as she entered the house and put down her suitcase.

On the outside, the cottage looked like a very old Norman farmhouse, built from plaster and wood beams and partially covered by a lush growth of ivy. The roof was covered with thatch—from which, she'd been told, wildflowers would sprout in the spring. The grounds surrounding the house were thickly shaded and abundant with flowers: roses, asters, delphinium, dahlias, and heather. The inside, however, was quite another story: a perfect blend of the old and the new. The walls were covered with finely pleated damask in rich shades of rose, blue, and green. There were tall windows and four-poster beds and antiques everywhere, yet the bathrooms and kitchen were newly renovated and ultramodern. Sloane smiled to herself. Of course it had been renovated; she couldn't imagine Gaby living anywhere, even for a few weeks out of the year, without all the modern conveniences.

She took the bottle of Dom Perignon she'd picked up in Deauville to the kitchen and filled the ice bucket she found there. Tonight, if Jordan showed, would be a celebration. Only the best, she'd promised herself. Then she took her bag upstairs to the master bedroom and unpacked. She hadn't brought much, figuring she wouldn't be needing a lot of clothes this weekend. She took out one special item—a daringly low-cut nightgown of rose-colored silk trimmed in ivory lace—and draped it over a chair in one corner of the room. *Yes,* she told herself, *this weekend is going to be one he'll never forget. And neither will I.*

Standing at the window for a moment to enjoy the view, she saw the car coming up the drive. Jordan's rental car. She hurried downstairs to greet him, opening the front door just as he raised his hand to knock. He grinned, pointing to the wicker basket he carried under his left arm. "Gourmet to Go," he greeted her. "There's a lady in Deauville who says you'd die up here without a can opener."

"Gaby has a big mouth," she muttered, stepping aside to let him pass.

He put his suitcase on the floor and gave her the basket. "Nice place," he commented, looking around. "Came up here to work, did you?"

She smiled, placing the basket on a nearby table. "Actually, I came up here for a little peace and quiet."

He frowned. "You should have told me," he said, his expression properly apologetic. "I invited the whole team. They're on their way."

She laughed. "Like hell you did!"

He broke into a grin. "Okay, so I'm stretching it a bit."

"You're stretching it a lot," she disagreed.

He nodded. "I'm surprised you asked me," he said then, coming a little closer. "Aren't you afraid to be alone with me? I might try to seduce you."

She threw back her head and laughed heartily. "Phillips, I've come to the conclusion that you're basically harmless," she teased him. "All talk and no action."

His eyebrows arched as a wicked gleam came into his dark eyes. "It's action you want now, is it?" Before she could open her mouth to respond, he grabbed her hand and pulled her up the staircase.

"Jordan Phillips, you're insane!" she laughed, stumbling along after him. "It's three o'clock in the afternoon!"

"So?" He didn't stop until he reached the top of the stairs. "Which way?"

It took her a second to realize what he was talking about. "Second door on the right," she gasped breathlessly, still gig-gling.

He pulled her into the bedroom, then dragged her against him roughly. "Stop laughing at me, woman," he growled. "It's hard to be romantic when the lady's got an attack of the giggles."

"You're a Neanderthal," she told him. "And I'm not laugh-ing at you. I'm laughing because all of my plans for a romantic evening just went down the tubes. All my good intentions—"

"Good, if not honorable," he said softly. "And we both know all about good intentions . . ." His mouth came down on hers in a slow, lingering kiss.

She pulled away long enough to catch her breath. "The road to hell is paved with good intentions," she whispered, lowering her head to kiss the hollow of his neck.

"Heaven, hell, I'm not sure which this is. Maybe both." His hands moving down her back, he cupped her buttocks and pressed himself against her as he started kissing her neck. "Don't know how long I can wait," he breathed.

She threaded her fingers through his hair as he lifted one hand to unbutton her gray cotton shirt. He lost his patience after the third button and ripped the thin fabric all the way to the waistband of her slacks. He cupped one breast in his hand, making small circles around the nipple with his thumb until it became a small, hard knot of desire. He backed up and sat on the edge of the bed, drawing her close. With one arm around her waist, he started kissing her breasts, teasing the nipples with the tip of his tongue, then taking one between his lips, sucking at it lazily. She stroked his handsome head, offering herself to him, wanting to give herself completely to him, to the need and desire that engulfed both of them like a fire out of control. "Don't stop," she breathed as he withdrew.

"Only for a moment, love," he promised, unzipping her slacks. He pushed them down over her hips, followed by her sheer panties. Everything fell in a heap on the carpet around her ankles. She stepped out of her sandals and reached for him again. Tugging impatiently at his polo shirt, she managed to pull it up over his head. She dropped it on the floor and sank to her knees, unbuckling his belt. As she unzipped his pants, she realized he wasn't wearing anything underneath. His erection sprang forward as she reached out to touch him. "Careful," he chuckled. "Don't want the party to end too soon now, do you?"

She shook her head. "No more than you do," she said simply. He raised himself slightly so she could pull his pants off. She worked them down over his muscular legs, her fingers trembling.

"Damn!" she muttered under her breath.

"The boots?" he asked, amused.

She looked up at him, frustrated. "Do you *always* wear them?"

He grinned devilishly. "Almost always, love."

"I'll bet you don't see too much action, then," she commented as she unbuckled the straps across the tops of the scuffed brown leather boots, unzipped them, and struggled to pull them off. "At last!" she gasped, rocking back on her heels.

Impatiently, Jordan reached down and grabbed her shoulders, pulling her to her feet again. "Now, where was I?" he asked with a wicked grin as he started nuzzling her breasts. She shivered pleasurably when he began to suck at them again.

Abruptly, he pulled her down onto the bed beside him and hovered over her. His lips met hers again and ignited a fire deep within her core. She caressed him, each well-defined muscle of his chest and shoulders burned permanently into her memory as she did so. She ran her fingers through the thick mat of dark hair covering his chest as he nibbled at that sensitive hollow just behind her left ear. She felt his hand slide easily between her legs, testing the dampness there as he explored her gently. She reached for him again, taking his hard, quivering organ into her hand, stroking it with her fingertips. She started to tremble as he brought her to a fever pitch of ecstasy.

He let out a low groan, and she knew he was trying to hold back. "Now," she whispered. *Relieve the agony for both of us,* she was thinking. "Now, Jordan—please, now—"

"Now . . ." he muttered. With one quick, sharp movement, he was inside her. She let out a muffled cry, and he silenced her with his lips. He stroked her hair gently, as if he were soothing a skittish colt. "That's it, love," he said huskily. He drew her long legs up over his slim hips as he started to thrust, moving faster as he began to lose control of himself. She clutched at him, moving with him, urging him on. She could feel his entire body shudder violently as he came. As if afraid he might somehow slip away from her, she pulled him down to her again, holding him close. She stroked his hair, feeling his breath hot against her breast.

How long had it been since she'd known anyone who made her feel like this?

"Are you all right?" Jordan asked.

The room was in total darkness, but he had no idea how late it was. Not that it mattered. From the minute they came into the bedroom, nothing else had been important. Now he lay on his back, holding her in his arms as she nestled against his chest, silent, unmoving. "Couldn't be better," she said softly, kissing his moist flesh. She loved the musky, definitely male scent of him, the lean hardness of his body so close to her own.

He fingered a strand of her hair. "You really surprised the hell out of me," he told her then.

She raised her head slightly. "How did I surprise you?" she wanted to know.

"The message you left at the hotel, coming here . . ." He smiled, letting his fingers roam over her shoulder blades. "For the past two weeks, you've been keeping me at arm's length. I was beginning to think you really weren't interested."

She was silent for a moment. "I wondered the same thing about you," she said finally.

He laughed at the thought. "Me? What was I supposed to do?" he asked. "You wouldn't even let me close enough to kiss you good night! The closest I got to physical contact was the other night at the casino—and even then, I wasn't sure it wasn't just the high of winning at the roulette table.''

"That was an excuse," she said, stroking his chest, making small circles with her fingertips as she kissed his chin fleetingly.

"Was it, now?" he asked, pleased. "And this? Coming all the way to Honfleur? What's this all about?"

"A way we could be completely alone. No phones ringing, no one knocking at the door."

He thought about it. "In that case, let's stay here," he suggested. "The whole week."

She looked up at him, her heart skipping a beat. "You're serious, aren't you."

"Damned right I am," he told her. "Gaby and Carlo won't be using it. They're tied up in town. It's not that far to Deauville—I can still make practice early every morning. And here we can be alone, as you said. In other words, no interruptions. No one would know we're here."

"I'd have to let my housekeeper know where to reach me," she told him. "My son—"

"Of course," he agreed.

"And Gaby."

"Telling Gaby is like telling the wire services," he grumbled, rumpling her hair. "But under the circumstances, I guess we really don't have a choice there."

"Whatever you want," she purred, kissing his chest again.

"Whatever *I* want?" he asked, his tone suggestive. "In that case . . .''

When Sloane awakened the next morning, Jordan was sleeping soundly beside her. She lay there for a long time, looking at him, wanting to touch him yet not wanting to disturb him. He was, she decided, the most beautiful man she'd ever seen. Beautiful. She smiled to herself. He'd probably laugh if she were to tell him that—but to her, he *was* beautiful.

Eventually she sat up, slowly so she wouldn't wake him. The first thing she saw was the nightgown, still draped across the chair. The nightgown she'd bought three days after she'd arrived in Deauville—for the express purpose of seducing him. Seducing him! She almost laughed aloud at the thought. She still wasn't sure who had been the seducer and who the seduced last night. She thought about the unopened champagne in the ice bucket and the picnic basket downstairs. So much for that romantic evening she'd planned.

But it *had* been romantic—if a little more intense than she'd anticipated. Jordan had been like a racehorse eager to break from the starting gate, but he was a wonderful lover. He seemed to know just how and where to touch her, as if they'd been lovers forever instead of two people making love for the first time. They'd made love again and again throughout the afternoon and night, unable to get enough of each other. Even now she wanted him, wanted his touches and kisses, wanted to feel him inside her again. She wanted him to hold her, to hear him say he wanted her. Last night, Jordan had made her feel as no other man ever had, and she couldn't get enough of that.

She put on her robe, a deep rose silk that matched the night-gown, and went into the bathroom. She was mortified by the face in the mirror that greeted her. Everything had ignited between them so quickly yesterday that she hadn't realized—until now—that she'd forgotten to take off her makeup. Now she looked like a raccoon, her heavy black mascara and liner smudged around her eyes in lopsided dark rings. *Thank God Jordan's still asleep,* she thought as she opened the large jar of cleansing cream on the counter and began smoothing it over her entire face. She plucked several tissues from a box on the shelf. *I certainly wouldn't want him to see me like this.*

"I wondered where you'd gotten to."

Startled, she swung around. Jordan stood in the doorway, smiling at her. He hadn't bothered to dress, and the sight of him, even at a moment like this, aroused her. "I thought you were still asleep," she said, turning back to the mirror before she forgot what she was doing.

He made a face. "I always heard after making love like we did, the woman was supposed to wake up all rosy-cheeked and dewy-eyed," he commented with a grin. "Where did I go wrong?"

"I forgot to take my makeup off," she said, wishing he hadn't seen her this way.

He smiled and took the tissues from her. With his left hand, he cupped her chin and lifted her head, tilting her face to the light. Gently, he wiped away the cream, and with it all traces of makeup. "Too much war paint," he said, softly but meaning it, his dark eyes twinkling with amusement. He then paused to inspect his work. "By God, there *is* a woman under all that fancy artwork!" he declared triumphantly, dropping the last of the soiled tissues into the wastebasket.

"Stop examining me as if I'm one of your polo ponies being prepped for sale!" she protested indignantly.

"I don't consider you one of my ponies, and I certainly wouldn't sell you at any price," he assured her, planting a kiss on her forehead.

Her eyes narrowed suspiciously. "I'm not sure, but I have a feeling I'm supposed to be flattered by that comment."

"It's as close to a compliment as I ever get," he told her, kissing her again. Then he slapped her bottom lightly. "Get dressed, woman—we're due in Deauville in an hour."

On Sunday, Jordan wasn't scheduled to play, so they stayed in Honfleur. They went down into the old village and explored the *vieux bassin*, the old harbor with its assorted fishing boats and old houses facing the docks, tall, narrow, slate-roofed houses that looked as if they'd been pushed together by the inevitable process of growth and expansion over the centuries. They went to see the sailors' church, St. Catherine's, on the north side of the harbor, built entirely of raw timber by ship-builders in the fifteenth century and whose roof resembled an upturned ship's hull, and ended up at Ferme St.-Siméon, an old Norman-style restaurant on a slope of a hill overlooking the English Channel.

"The last time I asked you a personal question, you told me in not so many words that it was none of my business," Jordan recalled over lunch. "So before I ask again, tell me—is your personal life still off limits?"

"I never said it was none of your business," she said, avoiding his eyes. "I said I was supposed to be the one asking the questions."

"Same thing."

"Same question?" she asked, putting down her fork.

He took a bite. "For starters."

She shook her head, looking down at her plate. "There's really not much to tell," she said quietly. "Before *Revelations* was published, I led a very unglamorous life. I grew up in

Chicago. My roots are very Middle American, nothing spectacular. Two nice parents, a nice kid brother, a nice dog—''

''A nice husband?'' he wanted to know.

She shook her head again. ''No nice husband. No nice anybody in that department,'' she said stiffly.

''You have a son. Did you buy him at Sears?'' he asked, attempting to break the tension the question had raised between them.

She raised her eyes to his and smiled weakly. ''I wish I had.''

''Meaning what?'' he pursued, not about to let her off easy.

''Meaning that Travis is one of the few good things that's happened to me,'' she said simply. ''I've never considered having him a mistake—but his father was.''

He was silent for a moment. ''So—the story of your life is not exactly a Cinderella tale, as you implied,'' he said finally.

''More like *Jaws*.''

He reached across the table and covered her hand with his own. ''Don't you believe in happy endings?'' he asked.

Sloane frowned at the thought. ''Only in books and movies,'' she answered regretfully.

''Are you excited?''

They were in bed. The sun was rising on the eastern horizon, heralding the start of a new day. *The* day. The Coupe d'Or. *Our last day together*, Sloane thought, looking up at him as he hovered over her. *Possibly the last day I'll ever have with you, Jordy*.

Pressing himself against her gently, he gave her a lascivious grin. ''What do you think?''

''Nut!'' She slapped his shoulder playfully. ''I was referring to the match!''

''I know what you were referring to.'' His lips brushed hers fleetingly. ''This is what *I'm* talking about.'' He nibbled lightly at her earlobe. Under the sheets, one hand roamed the length of her body.

She giggled. ''I always thought athletes didn't do this sort of thing just before an important game,'' she said as his lips trailed down her neck to her collarbone and down over her breasts. Under the sheets, their legs entwined, and the hair on his legs felt mildly abrasive against her smooth skin. ''Something about stamina, I believe—''

"My stamina is just fine, thank you," he said with a husky laugh. He raised his free hand to her breasts, and with the tip of his index finger he traced a line down the deep cleft between them. "I've played almost every day since we came here. Have you ever known me to abstain?"

She buried her fingers in his hair. "Can't say that I have," she conceded. Next to the deep bronze of his skin, she decided that she looked almost too white.

His hand moved to the side of her left breast, plumping up the mound of soft white flesh. Bending his head, he took the erect nipple into his mouth and began to suck deeply. She arched her back and moaned, giving herself up to the wave of intense pleasure that swept through her, stroking his hair, holding him so he wouldn't pull away too soon.

Where had she gone wrong? she asked herself now. She'd thought only a weekend—one perfect, sensual weekend with a man she'd wanted from the minute she laid eyes on him. But what she felt right now was more than just sexual desire. It was different, but she couldn't identify it because she'd never felt it before. Like the chemicals she'd mismatched in that chemistry class many years ago, something had gone wrong.

It had blown up in her face.

Jordan and Max Kenyon, who was playing for the British team in that final match, jostled for position on the ball while Lance Whitney made a neck shot that sent the ball flying off toward the goal. At a table in the Village with Gaby, Sloane watched the heart-stopping action through high-powered binoculars. A near collision between two players brought her to her feet abruptly. They looked as though they were engaged in actual combat! "I think they're trying to kill each other," she worried aloud, lowering her binoculars slowly.

"I told you—when Jordy and Max compete, it's a bloody war zone." Gaby sipped her white wine. The sleeveless white dress she wore seemed to enhance her summer tan and dark coloring. "Over the years, they've had more than a few near disasters."

Sloane looked at her. "Over Jilly," she concluded.

Gaby shook her head. "I think it has more to do with pride

than with Jilly," she said as she put her glass down. "Max has it in his head that Jilly wants Jordan again, but Jordan was the one who dropped her, so I really don't think he's made any overtures."

Max may be right, Sloane thought, recalling what she'd seen that day at the picket line.

"Max is just dotty for his wife, but the crazy man thinks every guy in the world wants to get Jilly in the sack." She smiled wickedly. "Trouble is, most of them already have."

"Has she ever made a play for Carlo?" Sloane asked, settling into her seat again.

"Is she on crutches?"

"Not the last time I saw her."

"Then she hasn't made a play for Carlo," Gaby said promptly.

Sloane turned her attention back to the polo field. The play was fast and furious now. The British team appeared rattled. Two fouls were committed, which gave Jordan's team two penalty shots, one from the forty-yard line and one from the sixty. Still, by the time the bell sounded, indicating that only thirty seconds remained of the third chukker, the British team led by two goals.

Sloane put down the binoculars and got to her feet. "Where are you going?" Gaby asked.

"To wait for Jordy at the picket line. I have a feeling he's going to need cheering up."

Gaby smiled wryly. "I suggest verbal comfort," she said, eyeing Sloane's sapphire-blue linen dress. "The smell of horse is a dead giveaway."

"That bastard was out for blood," Jordan declared angrily as he dismounted at the picket line. Turning his mount over to one of the grooms, he walked toward Sloane with the athletic ease that came from years of riding every day, of playing year-round. He pulled off his helmet and raked one hand through his damp, tousled hair, his careless fingers leaving furrows in its thickness. His face was flushed and moist with perspiration. Sloane met him with a cool, damp cloth, wiping his face thoroughly before she handed him a large glass of iced tea.

"It *was* close, wasn't it?" She swatted at a large horsefly that circled her head like a vulture watching a carcass.

"Too close. We damn near collided." He finished the tea and put his glass on top of the cooler they'd brought along, now sitting on the hood of the car. "The son of a bitch should be suspended."

Sloane didn't respond. She was busy swatting the air in a vain attempt to bring down her insect assailant.

Jordan laughed for the first time. "Are you having a problem with flies today?" he asked, clearly amused by her plight.

"Bugs," she said crossly. She rolled up the program from the day's match and took one last shot, finally smashing the fly against the fender of her car. "Bugs in general. Flies, gnats, bees—you name it. Haven't they been bothering you?"

Jordan grinned. "Tell me, love—would *you* want to bite someone who'd just spent the hottest day of the year out there?" he asked, gesturing toward the polo field.

Sloane grimaced at the thought. "Point well taken," she said agreeably. She poured him another glass of tea and one for herself.

He took the glass she offered him, his eyes still fixed on the polo field. "I should have been ready for him," he said finally. "Maybe I need more practice."

"Don't be so hard on yourself."

"I have to be," he said tightly. "I want to be the best, Sloane. One doesn't get to be *numero uno* by making excuses for a lousy performance."

"Maybe your four-star performance this morning took too much out of you," she teased, trying to cajole him out of his low spirits. Putting her glass aside, she reached for his damp jersey, pulling it up over his head—much to his surprise.

He laughed as she tossed it aside. "Just what do you think you're doing, woman?" he asked. "There are people around—"

"Relax," she said, running the wet cloth up his arms and over his chest. "I don't intend to remove anything below the belt." She came closer as she attempted to wash his back.

"That's too bad." He trapped her in his arms. "It could have been interesting."

"To say the very least," she agreed. "But we're getting plenty of attention right now."

"If they don't like what they see, they don't have to look." He kissed her forehead.

She embraced him gently. "You're like a naughty little boy who thinks he's gotten away with something," she told him.

"I have," he said with a grin.

"Not here, you haven't!"

He refused to let her go. "Come to Argentina with me, Sloane," he said then. "We're good together. Why settle for just a couple of weeks when there could be so much more?"

"I can't," she said quietly, frowning.

He looked unconvinced. "You can't—or you won't?"

"I can't," she insisted. "I told you about the book tour."

"And after that?" he wanted to know.

"After that I don't know," she admitted.

"I'll be playing in California," he told her. "Eldorado. Meet me there."

"I'll try."

He shook his head. "Not good enough."

"It's all I can promise right now."

"If you don't show, I'll come looking for you," he warned.

She raised her head to kiss his lips gently. "Fair enough," she said simply, pulling free of his embrace. "I've got to get you another jersey."

He watched her, puzzled. Was he asking more of her than she was willing to give?

The score was 6–4 at the throw-in signaling the start of the fourth chukker. The American team scored two goals in rapid succession. Jordan rode off Max Kenyon in a dangerous show-down that kept just within the designated limits, thwarting Kenyon's attempts to block the goal.

At their table, Gaby divided her attention between the match and watching for Carlo, who, having been detained by yet another business meeting, was missing the entire final game. "He gets me hooked on polo, then runs off and leaves me at the matches to fend for myself," she lamented. Sloane found it hard to keep her mind on the polo field with Jilly Kenyon sitting two tables away. Jilly, she had to admit reluctantly, was a beautiful woman, the kind of woman who made men fall all over themselves like lovesick schoolboys, the kind of woman *she* had never been. It was obvious why Jordan had been attracted to her, she thought miserably.

Watching Jilly made Sloane miss the shot that gave the American team their twelfth goal—and the Coupe d'Or. Her thoughts were interrupted by the sound of the horn ending the chukker—and the game. She looked up as the players rode up to the stands and dismounted, and Deauville mayor Anne d'Ornano stepped forward to present the cup. The players were surrounded now by their girlfriends or wives, joining in the moment of triumph. Sloane got up and headed toward the jubilant crowd, eager to congratulate Jordan. When he saw her, he motioned to her to join him. "Smile, love," he whispered, slipping his free arm around her waist as he and Lance Whitney hoisted the magnificent cup high in the air. "The cameras are everywhere." The crowd cheered as flashbulbs popped around them.

"We're probably going to make the cover of *Paris-Match*," she told him.

He grinned. "Among others."

"Jordy!" Lance interrupted then. "We're all going to Jimmy's over in Trouville to celebrate tonight. You coming?"

Jordan looked at Sloane and smiled. "Not if I get a better offer, friend," he answered.

The bedroom was in darkness. Jordan, alone in bed, lay on his side, sleeping soundly. Sloane stood at the side of the bed, fully dressed, watching him for a long moment. She wanted to touch him one last time but knew she couldn't risk waking him. He wouldn't understand why she was leaving like this— and she couldn't explain it to him. She wasn't sure she understood it herself. She knew only that she couldn't bear the idea of having to look into those incredible dark eyes of his, eyes that had always made her feel as if she were on fire, and tell him good-bye. She didn't want to leave him with memories of a hasty good-bye at the airport. She wanted him to remember her as they'd been tonight, making love more fiercely than they had before. *She* wanted to remember *him* that way—the triumphant polo champion who'd claimed the coveted Coupe d'Or, then passed on the team's jubilant celebration in Trouville to spend his last night here with her.

Come with me to Argentina. We're good together. His own words. Just like that, putting all of his cards on the table. No empty promises. Live only for the moment and don't think about tomorrow: that had been the basis of their brief relationship. He'd never promised anything, and she hadn't asked him to. He wanted her with him—but for how long? If she had agreed to go, how much time would they have together? How long would it last? Why did it matter?

I have to leave him before he leaves me, she thought. She resisted the urge to kiss him good-bye. She walked purposefully to the bedroom door and gathered up her luggage, then looked over at Jordan one last time. He was exhausted; he hadn't moved a muscle since she got out of bed.

She turned to the door again and walked out—without looking back.

↻ Buenos Aires, September 1986

On the polo field at Palermo Park, the play was fast and furious. Shouts between teammates and heated curses hurled at opponents mingled with the groan of leather, the crack of locking mallets, and the snorts and grunts of the straining horses.

"Whitney's not up to par today, but Phillips gets better every time he plays. He's going to be a ten in no time." Gavin Hillyer, watching the match with his wife, scrutinized each player on the field as carefully as a jeweler would examine a diamond. At fifty-three, Hillyer was a tall, slightly overweight man with a hawklike face and thinning hair the color of gunmetal. He had at one time been a world-class polo player himself and, though he seldom played these days, was still actively involved with the game. His White Timbers team sponsored some of the best players in the world, and he bred only the best polo ponies and racehorses on his farm in Texas. Hillyer, a steel magnate rumored to be one of the richest men in the world, had only one objective when it came to polo: to put together an invincible forty-goal team. He'd come here scouting for players and had already recruited Lance Whitney.

"You talk as if you can buy players the same way you buy your horses, Gavin," his wife observed wryly. Nadine Hillyer looked, as she always did, as if she'd just stepped from the pages of *Town and Country*, impeccably dressed in her black-and-white print Oscar de la Renta and the rope of baroque pearls her husband had given her for her birthday. At forty-nine, she could easily pass for thirty-nine, thanks to the skill of the best plastic surgeon in Beverly Hills. She maintained her trim figure with regular sabbaticals to the Golden Door Spa, and her perfectly styled silver-blond hair was courtesy of her favorite colorist at Kenneth in New York. She spent a fortune each season on her wardrobe and made the pages of *Women's Wear Daily* with great regularity. She justified the expense by maintaining she had to look good for her husband at business dinners, on the polo circuit, in the newspapers and magazines. She was the perfect hostess and traveling companion, an unlisted asset of her husband's corporation.

"In a sense, I do," he said mildly, returning his attention to the polo field as the throw-in got the fifth chukker off to a rousing start. "Every man has a price. Some are worth it, some not. Most aren't."

"You obviously believe this Jordan Phillips is," Nadine concluded.

"I think he might be." Hillyer frowned. "Unfortunately, I don't know what kind of monies he's looking for. Phillips has always been a free agent—never showed the slightest interest in playing for one sponsor." ·

Nadine smiled. "I'm sure you'll find a way to persuade him, darling," she said confidently, reaching across the table to pat his hand. "You always do."

Jordan pulled off his helmet as he led his sweating mount to the picket line. His groom was tending another horse, so he tied the exhausted animal to the side of the trailer and, putting his helmet and mallet aside, proceeded to remove the pony's tack. It had been a long day, and he was glad it was over. He was so physically drained he could barely stand. He could feel the beads of perspiration on his face and upper lip, could feel it trickling down the back of his neck into his already damp shirt. "Easy, *amigo*," he soothed the tired horse. "Easy."

"If I didn't know better, Jordy Phillips, I'd think you were avoiding me."

He immediately recognized the female voice addressing him from behind. "Gaby," he said. It was almost a groan. "Where's Carlo?"

"He's coming. He ran into an old friend." She gave a little laugh. "It still amazes me how many old friends my husband has—wherever we go."

"He's that kind of guy. People like him," Jordan said absently. He pulled off the horse's saddle and started working on the bridle.

"I wanted to talk to you alone," Gaby said then.

"That's what I was afraid of."

"Have you talked to Sloane?"

"No," he said curtly. "Is there any reason why I should have?"

She hesitated for a moment. "I thought the two of you really had something going in France," she said, slightly confused by his attitude.

"We did—business." His voice was tight, controlled. "Research for her book, remember?"

"She wasn't doing research at Honfleur," Gaby pursued, not about to show him any mercy.

Jordan removed the bridle, jerking it from the horse's mouth in a manner that made the animal pull away abruptly. "Are you sure about that?" he asked coldly.

"Oh, come on, Jordan!" Gaby scolded. "Surely you don't think—"

He turned to face her. His face was flushed and moist with perspiration, his hair tousled and damp. His eyes reflected his irritation with her interrogation. "How would I know *what* to think?" he asked, annoyed, running his fingers through his hair. "Maybe she needed to know how a polo player rates in bed. How should I know what she wanted from me—other than research?"

"That's ridiculous!" Gaby insisted.

"I agree. It *is* ridiculous."

"Phillips—I'd like a word with you if you have a moment." As he approached, both of them recognized Gavin Hillyer.

Jordan looked at Gaby, grateful for the interruption. He didn't want to talk about Sloane or what had happened between them. The truth was, he didn't know himself. All he knew was that he woke that morning at Honfleur and she was gone. "Will you excuse us?" he asked in a low voice.

She nodded. "We'll continue our talk later," she said.

"There's nothing to continue. It was over in Honfleur."

She looked unconvinced but departed without protest.

Jordan turned to Hillyer. "What is it you want to talk to me about?'' he asked politely. As if he didn't already know.

Hillyer grinned. ''I'm about to make you an offer you won't be able to refuse.''

''You know, of course, that I've always been a free-lancer.'' Jordan sat down in a nearby lawn chair. Picking up the wet towel draped over the back, he mopped it over his face and neck, then ran it over his damp hair.

Hillyer sat down too. ''I'm aware of that,'' he acknowledged with a solemn nod. ''I realize that it does have advantages—''

''Financial advantages,'' Jordan specified, unsmiling. ''As a free agent, I'm able to play for the highest bidder. The way I see it, by committing myself to one team, I stand to lose money.''

''Possibly.'' Hillyer lit a cigar. ''But then, I'd be willing to wager that no sponsor's ever offered you a guarantee of two hundred fifty thousand a year.'' He put away his gold lighter.

Jordan raised an eyebrow in surprise. ''Is that what you're offering me, Mr. Hillyer?'' he asked carefully. How many players—outside of a handful of Argentine ten-goalers—were worth that much to any sponsor, even one as rich as Gavin Hillyer?

''All you have to do is say the word,'' Hillyer told him, taking a long drag off his fat cigar.

''You flatter me.'' Jordan wiped his face again and stared thoughtfully at the vacant polo field for a moment. The mid-afternoon sun beating down on him was unbearably hot. He ignored the physical discomfort. He was not impressed by the money Hillyer offered; he came from a moneyed family and had grown up with all the advantages that money could buy. Everything he'd ever wanted had always been handed to him. Still, he'd never been content just to be a rich man's son. He wanted more than anything to prove himself, to make it on his own. He wanted to be a success in his own right, on his own terms. Hillyer's offer—the fact that a man like Gavin Hillyer wanted him for the White Timbers team and was willing to pay such an exorbitant price to get him—was proof that he had done just what he'd set out to do.

He looked at Hillyer. ''I'll have to think it over,'' he said evenly, even though the decision had already been reached.

• • •

"My wife is worried about you, Jordan." Carlo Millano, a man of average height and build whose Italian heritage was readily apparent in his dark good looks and heavily accented English, sat across from Jordan at a small table in a crowded, dimly lit bar in Buenos Aires.

Jordan forced a smile. "She has no reason to worry about me—especially if you're referring to Sloane." He finished his beer and signaled the bartender for another.

Carlo raised an eyebrow questioningly. "You are sure?"

"Yes I *am* sure!" he snapped. "She was in Deauville to research a book. We had a few laughs together. She got what she wanted, and she split. End of story."

"Is that all it was to you?"

"What else would it be? You know me, Carlo—I swore off the opposite sex a long time ago."

"So you would like everyone to think."

Jordan raised a hand to silence him. "Please—don't play shrink, okay?" he asked. "I get enough of that from Gaby."

A waitress brought his beer. He smiled up at her. She was a knockout, and the way she looked at him told him she was attracted to him. For a moment, he entertained the idea of making plans to see her later but quickly dismissed the idea.

I'd be better off in a monastery, he thought ruefully.

Why couldn't they just leave it alone? Jordan wondered as he showered that night. First Gaby, then Carlo. Couldn't they see that he didn't want to discuss it? It was over. Sloane had walked out of his life as unexpectedly as she'd entered it, and that was that. It *had* been good between them, apparently better for him than for her. She was the first woman with whom he'd let down his guard since that morning he found Jilly in bed with Max at Chukka Cove. It had been a stupid move on his part, he realized now, but he'd learned his lesson. Never again would a woman use him. From now on, he was going to be the user.

Stepping out of the shower, he grabbed a towel and rubbed his hair vigorously, then dried himself. Hearing a knock at the door, he wrapped the towel securely around his middle and went into the next room to answer it. "Who is it?" he called out as he approached.

"Room service," responded a muffled voice from the other side.

"There must be some mistake," he said as he opened the door. "I didn't order any—" He stopped short when he saw Jilly, dressed provocatively as always in slim black silk pants, a white silk shirt buttoned low to show cleavage, and a red scarf tied around her long neck. "What the hell do you want?"

She smiled appreciatively at the sight of him wearing only a towel. "It would appear I'm just in time," she said in a low, suggestive voice.

Jordan was perturbed and didn't bother to hide his feelings. "What do you want?" he asked again, losing patience.

"Do you even have to ask?" She pushed past him and entered the room, then swung around to face him, still smiling. "Don't you think you should close the door, darling?"

He shook his head. "This won't take long, I'm sure."

She laughed. "Suit yourself. I happen to think you look very appealing—but I doubt the hotel staff will approve."

Jordan looked down at himself, suddenly aware of his own state of undress, then closed the door. "What is it with you, Jilly?" he asked, turning to face her again. "It's been over three years. We've spoken ten words to each other since the day you—since you married Max. Why now?"

"Maybe I've finally realized what a mistake I made in letting you get away from me." She took a step closer.

"You didn't let me get away, as you put it. I left," he reminded her. "You used Max to make me jealous. Are you using me now to make him jealous?"

She laughed again. "I don't have to make Max jealous," she said, putting her arms around his neck. "He's insanely jealous. He'd kill you if he knew I was here."

"Is that what you want, Jilly?" Jordan asked coldly. "Does it turn you on to have men fighting over you?"

"*You* turn me on, Jordan." With a movement as swift as that of a snake striking its target, she reached down and pulled his towel away.

Jordan made no move to cover himself. "You came here to get laid, is that it?" he concluded.

She kissed him deeply, pressing herself against his naked body. "You never used to be so crude," she whispered, stroking him. "But if that's what turns you on, it's perfectly all right with me."

His first impulse was to throw her out, send her back to Max, who undoubtedly deserved her. Then he remembered the promise he'd made to himself in the shower. From now on, he would be the user. If Jilly was going to throw herself at him, he'd sure as hell take her to bed. He reached down and unbuttoned her shirt, then released the front closure of her lacy bra, exposing her full breasts. "That's it, darling," Jilly whispered as he squeezed them, rubbing his thumbs back and forth across her nipples. She unzipped her own pants and pushed them down over her hips. Underneath, she wore nothing but a lacy black garter belt and black stockings.

Obviously she came prepared, Jordan thought as he pushed the shirt off her shoulders and slid the straps of the bra down her arms. Jilly shed the garments quickly and backed across the room to the bed, pulling him with her. She lay on the bed, smiling up at him seductively. "Make love to me, Jordan," she said softly. "Just like we used to."

He looked at her, unsmiling. Make love? Love had nothing to do with it. She'd come to him for stud service, and that was all she was going to get. He looked down at himself, puzzled. He was still not erect. Before, just the sight of Jilly nude made him hard. Had the circumstances been different, he might have thought it funny. He'd always said Jilly could give a dead man a hard-on, and here he was, having trouble getting it up for her.

She lay on the bed, her legs spread invitingly. Her hair fanned out on the sheets like a wide red halo, and even lying down, her breasts stood high and firm. Just below the lacy garter belt was that familiar delta of curly red hair. She was still beautiful, he thought as he lay down beside her. Propping himself up on one elbow, he started fondling her breasts. Her rosy nipples hardened at his touch. He pinched them lightly, but as he bent his head to suck them, she stopped him. "Aren't you even going to kiss me?" she asked, openly confused.

"No," he said simply. "If it's candlelight and romance you want, go home to your husband." His mouth closed over one nipple, and he sucked fiercely as he continued to fondle the other breast. She arched her back and moaned as he continued to suck.

"Take it easy," she gasped. "You're getting too rough, darling."

He finally released her aching nipple and turned his attention to the other breast. Jilly started touching herself, hoping he would follow suit, but he seemed more interested in her breasts at the moment. She was frustrated and confused. He was hurting her. She tried to push him away, but he was not about to stop until he was ready.

"Jordan—please!" she moaned.

He raised his head and looked at her, then at himself. Nothing was happening for him. He knew he should feel desire, but all he felt for her was anger. He wanted to hurt her as she had once hurt him. Silently, he slid one hand between her legs. Parting the moist lips with his fingers, he stroked her. She was already wet, but that didn't surprise him. Jilly was always ready for sex. He slid two fingers up inside her, moving in and out, faster and faster, rubbing her clitoris with his thumb until she started to writhe and moan beneath him. He brought her to a sharp orgasm with his hand. She begged him to take her, but by then he'd realized nothing was going to happen with him. He was not going to be able to finish what he'd started, and the realization was devastating for him. He released her abruptly and got to his feet. Jilly, bewildered, looked on as he hastily collected her discarded clothes and threw them at her.

"Out!" he roared. "Get dressed and get out!"

The look in his eyes frightened Jilly. She dressed quickly and fled without protest. After she was gone, Jordan sat down on the edge of the bed, slumped over, his face in his hands. Why had he ever let it go that far? Why had he even let her in? Jilly was out of his life—and he wanted to keep it that way. He looked down at his limp organ, and he was baffled. This had never happened to him before. Never. Why had it happened now? he asked himself.

Jilly thought he was punishing her by refusing her. He could see it in her eyes. She thought he just didn't want to have sex with her. Thank God she didn't suspect the truth.

That he *couldn't* perform sexually with her.

"What's his problem?" Carlo wondered aloud.

"Your guess is as good as mine," Jordan responded with a

shrug. The two men watched from the sidelines as Lance missed what should have been an easy shot. "He hasn't been himself since he got here."

"He's always been a good player."

"He's sure as hell no good today." Jordan thought about it as the chukker ended abruptly at the sound of the bell and the players headed back to the picket lines to change mounts. Lance's game was off. Way off.

"I guess everyone has their off days."

"I guess," Jordan agreed with a nod, only half listening.

As the players rode back onto the field, Jordan noticed that Lance's new mount was more than a little skittish. In fact, Lance was having a hard time controlling the animal. The pony bucked, trying to unseat his rider. Lance was fighting to maintain control, but from where Jordan stood it looked as if he were fighting a losing battle.

"Looks like he has another problem," Carlo observed.

Jordan frowned. "As if he needs more problems."

"He should have the good sense to switch mounts."

"I wonder if he's got any sense at all."

Even as Jordan spoke, Lance's mount lurched forward wildly, tossing him off like an old rag doll. He hit the ground with what appeared to be a fair amount of force. Jordan watched for a moment, waiting for Lance to get up. He didn't—at least not right away.

"Got the wind knocked out of him," Carlo speculated as the two men started across the field.

"Yeah." Jordan wasn't really listening.

While Carlo pushed his way through the crowd gathering around Lance, who had finally pulled himself up to a sitting position, Jordan caught up with the groom who had grabbed the pony and was leading it back to the lines. The animal had calmed down the moment Lance was off his back. A quick check of the tack immediately revealed the reason to Jordan. Someone had put a piece of tin—it looked as if it might have been the top of a can, but it had been cut in a way that made the edges jagged and very sharp—under the saddle. With Lance's weight in the saddle, it would have been pressing into the pony's back, causing a great deal of pain.

Why? Jordan wondered. *Why would anyone deliberately do this?*

• • •

Over the next few days, Jordan played even more fiercely than he had before, but even polo could not relieve him of the anger and tension he now felt. He came off the field as filled with pent-up frustration as he had before the first throw-in. He rode as if he were being pursued by the devil himself and played like a man possessed. Nothing gave him any degree of respite.

At night, he eschewed any kind of social life and spent his time at the stables with the horses. He missed his own polo ponies back in the States—quarantine laws in many foreign countries often made it impossible for him to use his own horses in international tournaments—and gave his affection freely to the animals made available to him here in Argentina. Horses, he decided, were fortunate. They mated, but that's all it was, just mating. No feelings, no emotional investment on either side. No broken hearts in the equine world. *Maybe it's better that way,* he thought.

"You're a lucky son of a bitch," he said aloud, peering through the darkness at a splendid bay stallion belonging to one of the Argentine players, a horse used for breeding purposes but never for polo. "They even hold the mare for you."

"Taken to comparing notes with the studs now?"

Startled, Jordan swung around. Lance was entering the stables, and from his unsteady gait Jordan could tell he was quite drunk.

"Is this a private war, or can anyone enlist?" Jordan asked, sensing his friend's dark mood. Lance's spirits had been low since their arrival in Buenos Aires, but he'd never been willing to talk about it, and Jordan had been too preoccupied with his own troubles to question him.

"Private." Lance sat down on a bale of hay, unable to stand on his own. He slumped over, his face buried in his hands.

"Paula isn't going to be too happy to see you like this," Jordan pointed out, still stroking his horse's head as it nickered softly.

"Paula won't be seeing me at all," Lance said simply.

"You've heard from her?"

Lance shook his head, looking up again. "From her lawyer. She's filing for divorce."

"Why?" Jordan knew they'd been having problems, but he'd had no idea divorce had even been discussed.

"That should be obvious, pal. She doesn't want to be married to me anymore." He pulled out a flask and took a swig.

"Don't you think you've had enough?"

"Hell, I'm just getting started," Lance retorted, finishing off the flask.

"You don't want the divorce."

"No, I don't want the divorce," Lance said bitterly. "We're a fine pair, you and I. We both let our women get away from us. I thought you were a fool to let Sloane go. After Jilly, you finally got a good—"

"I didn't let Sloane go," Jordan snapped. "She left entirely on her own." He turned away, staring thoughtfully into the darkness. "And, for the record, she wasn't mine to lose."

"Wasn't she?" Lance smiled drunkenly in the shadows. "Didn't look that way from where I sat."

"Looks can be deceiving," Jordan said crossly, turning back to the horse again.

"Listen—take some advice from a guy who's been there, buddy boy," Lance drawled, slurring his words. "That ten-goal rating's a great high, I know. This whole game's a high. But the number ten's not going to keep you warm at night. It won't make love to you and make you feel like the best thing to come along since the wheel when the rest of the world's giving you a shitty way to go. I know, I've been there. I lost my woman. If you're smart, you'll go after yours."

"Thanks for the advice, Doctor," Jordan growled. "I'll call you when I need your couch again." Unwilling to listen to Lance's preaching, Jordan turned and stalked out of the stables, leaving his friend alone to sober up.

Lance took another drink, then reached into his pocket and took out a small bottle containing several red capsules. He took one from the bottle and popped it into his mouth, then washed it down with the bourbon in the flask. "And you won't do it for me either," he declared. "But you sure as hell dull the pain, don't you?"

⇄ New York City, September 1986

"This scene doesn't really do anything for the story," Adrienne told Sloane, reviewing the notes she'd made on a yellow legal pad. "I think it should be cut—" She looked up, hesitating for just a moment as she realized that Sloane had not heard a word she'd said. "Would you like to talk about it?" she asked.

Sloane didn't reply, didn't even acknowledge the question, but continued to stare absently at the bookshelves across the room.

Adrienne shook her head, amused but a little concerned, too. Sloane had been like this ever since she'd returned from France. Time for drastic measures. She put down her pen and took a deep breath. "I think this manuscript's hopeless, and we should just forget about it," she stated with a totally straight face. "What do you think?"

"What?" Sloane said distractedly, waving her hand in a dismissive gesture. "Oh . . . do whatever you think is best."

"Sloane, for God's sake!" Adrienne said, laughing. "You haven't heard a word I've said!"

Sloane's head jerked up suddenly, bringing her back to the present with a rude start. "I'm sorry," she apologized. "I've had a lot on my mind—"

"Obviously." The editor smiled knowingly as she placed her elbows on the desk and propped up her chin with both hands. "You just gave me the nod to run your manuscript through the shredder." Pushing her chair back from the desk abruptly, she rose to her feet and walked around to perch on one corner of the large desk. "It's the polo player, isn't it?"

she asked, smoothing the front of her dark blue silk jacquard dress.

"What polo player?" Sloane asked in a mildly irritated tone.

"The polo player with whom you were joined at the hip in Deauville." Noting the look of surprise on Sloane's face, she smiled. "I *do* read *Paris-Match*."

"You can't believe everything you read," Sloane responded sullenly, looking away.

"I didn't have to read anything. The pictures said it all." Adrienne picked up the current issue of the French magazine and passed it to Sloane. It was open to a photo layout taken at Deauville. She and Jordan were in a number of the photos, and with the exception of the action shots taken on the field, they were always together.

"He's gorgeous," Adrienne voiced her approval.

Sloane nodded slowly, thoughtfully. "Even more so in the flesh," she agreed.

"Who is he?"

"His name is Jordan Phillips. We met through mutual friends," Sloane told her, still staring at the photographs and remembering what it had been like, being with him at Honfleur. "He taught me the basics of polo."

"And that's all?" Adrienne looked unconvinced.

"Why would you think there might be anything else?"

"You don't exactly look as if you're interviewing him in those pictures," Adrienne pointed out, nodding toward the magazine in Sloane's hand.

Sloane was silent for a long moment. "All right—it wasn't all business," she admitted with a frown. "Is that what you wanted to hear?"

"That depends," Adrienne said slowly, folding her arms across her chest. "How bad is it?"

Sloane looked at her. "How bad is what?"

Her laugh was skeptical. "Come on, Sloane—at the risk of sounding trite, you're obviously carrying one huge torch for this man," she stated. "As your friend, I'm worried about you. As your editor, I have to worry about how this is going to affect your work."

Sloane shook her head. "Don't worry—I'll make my deadline," she promised.

"Right now, that's the least of my worries."

Handing the magazine back to Adrienne, Sloane got to her feet slowly. "I had the most wonderful week of my life with Jordan Phillips at the most romantic hideaway I've ever seen," she said carefully. "He was gorgeous and sexy and fun to be with, and he made me feel more alive than I've ever felt—"

"And you let him get away?" Adrienne cut in, her tone disbelieving.

Sloane shook her head. "I'm a realist, Adrienne," she said. "I knew when I met him it wasn't going to last."

"When did you become clairvoyant?"

"For God's sake, Adrienne—he's too young!" Sloane exclaimed, her tone a mixture of indignation and frustration.

Adrienne looked at her suspiciously. "Just what do you have in mind that he's too young for?" she asked slowly.

Sloane scowled at her. "You know damned well what I'm talking about."

"How much younger is he?"

"Five years."

"Five years!" Adrienne looked more relieved than surprised. "You're worried about *five years?*"

"In some cases, five years can be a hell of a difference," Sloane maintained, clearly unhappy about it.

"Not for you," Adrienne disagreed. "You've always been young for your age."

Sloane looked at her. "Thanks. That's just what I needed to hear."

"You know what I'm talking about," Adrienne insisted.

"This is all pointless," Sloane stated in a low, controlled voice, her eyes scanning the room. "It's over. It didn't last. It wasn't meant to last. He knew it and I knew it."

"You didn't want it to last?"

"No—yes—oh, shit, I don't know, Adrienne," Sloane said crossly. "It's hard to know what I want or don't want from a man I've known for only a few weeks."

Adrienne looked dubious but didn't comment. "What about him?" she asked finally. "What did he want?"

Sloane turned to face her again. "He wanted me to go to Argentina with him."

"So—*he* wasn't ready to end it," Adrienne concluded.

"I'd hardly call asking me to go to Argentina making a commitment," Sloane said with a wintry smile.

"Is that what you want from him? A commitment?"

"Stop twisting my words," Sloane growled.

"That's what editors are for," Adrienne pointed out. "Especially when the author can't seem to get the words right herself."

Sloane gave her a tired smile—but not a word in response.

"When will you be back, Mom?"

"Two weeks." Sloane was packing her bags. She stopped what she was doing and looked at her son suspiciously. "Why am I getting the feeling you may actually miss me this time?"

He gave her a sheepish grin. "Maybe just a little," he confessed reluctantly.

"You sound as if you hate to admit it."

"I don't want it to go to your head."

She smiled faintly. "I see."

"Cate called," he said then.

Her head jerked up again. "When?"

"About an hour before you got home." He peeled the banana he'd brought with him into the bedroom and took a bite.

"Why didn't you tell me then?" she asked.

"Wouldn't have done any good. She said she'd be out, that she'd probably be back around four," he remembered. "She said she has to talk to you before you leave, that it's important. Must have to do with money."

She smiled. "To you, anything that's important has to mean money," she chided him. "The only things in life that matter to you have dollar signs in front of them."

"You bet!" he responded enthusiastically. "That's why I've decided to become a writer."

She shook her head. "Wrong profession for a little capitalist like you."

"Why? It pays good."

"Only when you can get the publisher to let go of it," she pointed out, shooing him off the bed. "Go ask Emma for two plastic bags."

"Are we about to commit family suicide?"

"No, silly. I need them for my suitcases. She must have

thrown away the ones I had.''

"Sure thing." He ran out of the room, dropping the banana peel on the carpet in the doorway.

She looked at the clock radio on the nightstand. Three forty-five. On the chance that Cate might have returned to her office early, she picked up the phone and dialed Cate's number. The answering machine came on at the third ring. "Damn!" Sloane muttered under her breath. She left a brief message and hung up, hoping she'd hear from her agent before she left.

In a way, she told herself, this tour was going to be a blessing. Tours were always frantic and left her exhausted. Maybe she'd be so busy she wouldn't have time to think about Jordan.

Aboard an Aerolineas Argentinas flight bound for New York, Jordan Phillips leaned back in his seat and drew in a deep breath. In another hour, they'd be landing at Kennedy. He considered his options. He could get a local flight on to Massachusetts, but he decided against it. He was exhausted. What he needed right now, and needed desperately, was a good night's sleep. He decided to crash at his father's regular suite at the Plaza—the one he kept year-round for all the times he popped into Manhattan on business—and take a PBA shuttle from La Guardia to Martha's Vineyard first thing in the morning.

He rubbed his eyes and stifled a yawn. It had been a long flight, and he was beginning to feel a little stiff. Even first class didn't allow enough space for him to stretch his long legs. He was tired of sitting and too tired to do anything else. Except think. He'd done a lot of thinking in the past five hours. He stretched his legs as best he could and rolled his shoulders in an exaggerated shrug in an attempt to work out the kinks in his muscles. If only it were so easy to work out all of his problems.

Not so long ago, he'd thought he had all the answers. After Jilly, after that morning at Chukka Cove, he'd sworn off emotional involvements. He'd resolved never to let himself care again, never to let any woman make a fool of him as Jilly had. Of course there had been women in his life since then, but there hadn't been any degree of emotional involvement. He thought he'd managed to successfully separate sex from love.

And then he met Sloane Driscoll.

With Sloane, at the cottage at Honfleur, he'd experienced something he'd never known before, not even with Jilly. The feelings she aroused in him, so strong and yet so impossible to identify, had taken him completely by surprise. He had asked her to go with him to Argentina because he'd believed she'd felt them too. Apparently, he thought dismally, he'd been wrong. Their time together couldn't have meant much to her at all. She'd walked out on him that night without so much as a good-bye. Not even a note. Nothing. He recalled now how angry he'd been that morning when he woke and discovered she was gone. What he still didn't understand was why he had been angry. How many women had he bedded over the past few years—and abandoned in much the same manner in which she'd left him?

He waved off the solicitous flight attendant who offered him a drink. Anything alcoholic right now, exhausted as he was, would certainly knock him out. The past few weeks had been sheer hell. His frustration at Sloane had been compounded by the sting of defeat at the hands—and the mallets—of the Argentines his team had faced in the finals. He felt he'd played his best, but the Argentines had been that much better. Three goals better, to be precise. And Lance. Lance Whitney had been useless on the polo field. His impending divorce was having a devastating effect on his performance. He didn't give anywhere near one hundred percent of himself in Buenos Aires; it was obvious to anyone who watched his game.

And then there was Jilly, damn her. His inability to perform sexually with her still bugged the hell out of him. That sort of thing had never happened to him before.

Jordan frowned. Gaby was so goddamned positive that he'd been reading Sloane wrong, that she hadn't been using him. Even Carlo had pleaded her case. Why? What difference did it make now? Whatever they'd had in France was over now, and she was the one who'd ended it. And even while he told himself he didn't care one way or the other, he realized that it did matter. It mattered more than he would have liked. A part of him still wanted her, wanted to find her and find out where he really stood with her. *Why do I give a damn?* he asked himself again.

The point was that he did give a damn. He wanted her, and she'd walked before he was willing to let her go. And by the time his flight landed in New York, he realized he had to know why she did what she did, why he felt the way he did.

And only Sloane herself could provide the answers.

Jordan disembarked from the plane at one of the gates of the International Arrivals terminal and made his way to the closest immigration booth. Taking out his passport, he handed it to the inspector, who looked at it momentarily, punched up some keys on his computer, then stamped and returned it to Jordan. "Welcome home, Mr. Phillips," he said pleasantly.

Jordan nodded, hoisting his flight bag up over his left shoulder easily. "Thank you. It's good to be home."

By the time Jordan got through the long lines at customs it was ten-thirty. He'd hoped to get into Manhattan and make contact with Sloane's agent before she left for lunch. He smiled to himself, remembering that Sloane had told him once that Cate Winslow often took three-hour lunches to meet with her clients or editors with whom she was currently negotiating. *Must be nice,* Jordan thought with mild amusement.

He made his way to the nearest pay phone, got the number of the Winslow Literary Agency, and dialed it. On the operator's instructions, he started feeding coins into the slot.

A woman's voice answered on the second ring. "Good morning, Winslow Agency."

"Cate Winslow, please."

"Who's calling, please?"

"Jordan Phillips—I'm a friend of Sloane Driscoll's," he said, not knowing how else to identify himself to the agent.

"One moment, please."

He was put on hold before he could open his mouth to object. Moments later, a soft yet authoritative feminine voice came on the line. "Cate Winslow," she identified herself. "What can I do for you, Mr. Phillips?"

"I need to find Sloane Driscoll."

Cate laughed. "At least you're direct about it," she commented. "She told me about you, Mr. Phillips."

This last statement took Jordan by surprise. He wondered what Sloane had told her but didn't dare ask. "I need to reach her, and I thought you might give me her phone number—''

"I'd be happy to, since I know she'd want to see you,"
Cate began, "but it wouldn't do any good. Sloane left this
morning on a promotional tour."

He paused momentarily. "When will she be back?"

"October first."

He shook his head, forgetting that the woman on the telephone couldn't see him. He couldn't wait that long. Wouldn't
wait. "Where was she going?" he asked aloud.

"Miami," Cate answered. "Of course, she'll be somewhere
else by tomorrow. I don't have her itinerary, but when she
calls in, I'll tell her you called."

"No—don't do that," he said quickly. "I mean, I'd rather
surprise her. Why don't you just give me her address . . .''

Sloane looked at her watch as the taxi inched its way through
the heavy traffic on the Van Wyck Expressway approaching
the airport. Eleven-fifteen. She hoped she didn't miss her flight.
It was scheduled to depart in half an hour. *Why today of all
days?* she asked herself. Why hadn't she left earlier? Why did
that truck have to end up overturned on the expressway today
and not tomorrow or yesterday? What else could go wrong?
She didn't even want to think about it. The airline would probably lose her luggage somewhere between New York and
Miami. That could go wrong—for starters.

She leaned back in the seat and drew in a deep breath. This
tour was getting off to a great start. *An omen?* she wondered
as the taxi passed through the main entrance at Kennedy Airport. *I probably won't make it to Miami. The plane will be
hijacked, and I'll end up in Cuba. But then, look at the bright
side: no planes have been hijacked to Cuba in years.*

The cab slowed to a stop at the TWA domestic flights terminal. Standing on the curb as a porter collected her luggage,
she didn't notice the man in the back seat of the taxi passing
by as it headed for the exit.

And Jordan didn't see her.

↻ St. Louis, September 1986

Alone in her suite at the Adam's Mark Hotel, Sloane contemplated the view of the Gateway Arch illuminated by floodlights. She was looking at it without too much interest, without really seeing it, because her mind was on other things. She was thinking about the long, tiring day just now winding down—a seemingly endless round of television and radio interviews—and the long day facing her tomorrow, signing books at a bookstore in the St. Louis Centre, a mall within walking distance of the hotel. The following day, she'd give an interview to a local magazine, then on to Dallas, the next whistle stop on her tour. Thank God it had been changed back to fifteen cities. It meant she didn't have to make a mad dash from bookstore to airport at each stop. It meant she had the luxury of time, however limited, to relax. To catch her breath. And on the negative side, it meant she had time to think.

Sloane frowned, still staring into the darkness that gave the window a mirrorlike quality. She was thinking about Jordan again, wondering where he was, what he was doing . . . whom he was with. Arms crossed, her hands agitatedly rubbed the tautness of her upper arms. She didn't want to think about Jordan. She didn't want to care about whom he was with. She didn't want her memories of Deauville—and more specifically, of Honfleur—to intrude on her otherwise orderly life. It had been wonderful, and she'd never regret her brief time with him, but it was over now, and she had to get on with her life, as she was sure he had. Staring at her reflection in the mirrored panes, she found herself looking for the ravages of time in her face, the tiny lines that would inevitably appear around her

72

eyes, the grooves along either side of her mouth that would invariably deepen—as she did whenever she looked in a mirror these days. She hadn't given such things a thought until Jordan entered her life. But now . . .

Suddenly she felt terribly alone. She hadn't talked to Cate since she left on the tour, almost a week ago. Cate and her husband, Sean McCarron, a Manhattan psychiatrist, were presently vacationing in England. They'd left two days ago, as far as Sloane knew. Adrienne was off speaking at a writers' conference in Denver. Sloane hadn't heard from Gaby since Deauville, although Emma had mentioned that there were two letters from her waiting at home. Sloane realized how few close friends she actually had. How many people were there in whom she could really confide? She could count them on the fingers of one hand. God, even her own son seemed to be avoiding her these days, cutting their telephone conversations short but insisting that everything was "fine." He was growing up. He had a life of his own now. *And he's just like his mother,* Sloane thought, not sure if she was happy about it or not. *Everything's "fine" even when it's not.*

Like now. . . .

Seated at a table at the front of the bookstore, Sloane, dressed stylishly in a black silk skirt, burgundy blouse, and a wide-brimmed burgundy hat, observed the bustling activity within the mall. It had been an exceptionally good day for her. The bookstore was crowded from the minute it opened that morning and had continued to do a thriving business throughout the day. She'd signed so many books that she ended up with a bad case of writer's cramp, but it gave her tremendous satisfaction to know that so many people were reading her book.

"We've sold sixty copies so far," the store manager told her as he opened another carton of books and stacked them neatly on the table beside her. "Keep this up, and we'll have sold every copy we've got in stock by the time you leave."

Sloane gave him a tired smile. "We have less than an hour," she reminded him. "Think we'll make it?"

He grinned. "So far, so good."

As he headed toward the stockroom, his arms full of empty cartons, two women approached Sloane, books in hand. She looked up at them and smiled pleasantly as she took the books, chatting briefly with them while she autographed each copy. By the time she was finished, there were four more people waiting. And two more after that.

She stole a quick glance at her watch as she paused in the middle of signing one book to flex her aching right hand. Fifteen minutes to go. *Thank God,* she thought. *If I have to sign one more book, my hand will fall off.*

Almost as if on cue, another book was thrust in front of her. Exhausted, she forced a smile. As she lifted her head, she caught sight of a boot—a riding boot—hiked up on the metal folding chair on the other side of the table. Her head jerked up abruptly, her pulse racing. Jordan was smiling down at her. "Hi, love," he greeted her.

"Jordan!" she gasped. "I-I thought you were in Argentina—"

"I was," he said with a nod. "My team lost."

"I'm sorry." She didn't know what else to say.

He shrugged. "There's always next time," he said, as if it didn't really matter.

Sloane knew it *did* matter. They all mattered to Jordan. Obviously, he didn't want to talk about it. "How did you find me?" she asked.

"It wasn't easy," he admitted, pursing his lips thoughtfully. "You cover your tracks very well."

"I didn't cover anything," she assured him, so happy to see him that she forgot her vow to put those three weeks in France behind her. "I didn't exactly expect you to be looking for me." She stood up. Time to call it a day. The timing couldn't have been better. "Did you call my publisher, or—"

"Yeah, I did. After I called your agent," he said. "Cate Winslow gave me your address. Your publisher gave me a bad time."

Sloane laughed, even though she knew to him that probably wasn't funny. "And?"

"I went to your apartment. Fortunately for me, your son has a big mouth."

"You talked to Travis?"

He grinned. "You'd better keep that boy away from the press."

Sloane stuffed some loose items—bookmarks, promotional

brochures, and other advertising matter—into her shoulder bag. "What, exactly, did he tell you?"

"Everything I wanted to know and more."

She looked mortified. "I'll kill him!"

Jordan laughed. "Ah, he's a good kid—if only his mother were as straightforward," he remarked.

She eyed him warily. "Meaning what?"

"I'll never tell." He looked around momentarily. "How much longer do you have to hang around here?"

"I don't," she said, pulling the bag up on her left shoulder. "I'm finished."

"Good," he said promptly. "We can walk back to the hotel together."

She gave him a quizzical look.

"You *are* staying at the Adam's Mark, aren't you?"

"Yes, but—"

"So am I."

She hesitated for a moment, wondering how he knew. Then it hit her. Of course. Her all-knowing, all-telling son had squealed. She made a mental note to have a talk with him as soon as she got home.

"Sloane?"

Jordan's voice interrupted her thoughts. Her head jerked up abruptly. "What?"

He reached out and took her hand. "I've missed you."

She swallowed hard. "I've missed you, too."

He smiled. "It would seem we've got a lot of catching up to do."

She nodded again. "Give me five minutes, okay?"

"Five minutes. A second longer and I'm coming after you."

"Deal."

She thought about it as she headed toward the back of the store to find the manager. She wasn't sure why he'd come. She wasn't sure it even mattered. But she was curious. Why had he gone to so much trouble to find her? What did he want from her—aside from the obvious?

And even more important, what did she want from him?

It was raining hard when they left the bookstore. "Damn!" Jordan muttered under his breath as he held the door for Sloane.

"It was clear as the proverbial bell when I walked over from the hotel."

She laughed. "There's a saying here," she began as she unfurled her umbrella and held it over both of them, "if you don't like the weather in St. Louis, stick around—it'll change."

He put one arm around her as they crossed the busy intersection outside the center and walked a block east to Broadway. He talked about Argentina, about his team's defeat, about Gaby and Carlo, and about Lance's unexpected divorce. The only thing he didn't talk about was his reason for being here.

The umbrella offered little cover from the driving rain. The sky was so dark it looked almost like night as they walked, skirting puddles in their path. "Argentina must have been a disappointment," Sloane commented as they turned the corner at Broadway and Locust. "Were all the *señoritas* flat-chested and knock-kneed?"

He stopped suddenly in his tracks and stared at her as if she'd slapped him. "Is that all I am to you, Sloane?" he asked, barely able to control his anger. "A stud? Some kind of goddamned sex machine?"

She stared at him, bewildered by his unexpected reaction to what she'd intended as a joke. "No—of course not!" she said. "I only meant it as a—"

He glared at her. "What did you really want when you invited me to Honfleur?" His handsome face was dark with rage. "Did you need to know how a polo player would perform in the sack? Did you need to check out a physical specimen? Or was I just any old port in a storm?"

"Now, wait a goddamned minute—"

"I guess I wasted my time coming here—unless you'd like a quick roll in the hay," he said coldly.

Reacting without thinking, her hand lashed out across his face. He recoiled, his dark eyes flashing. Sloane drew back, as astonished as he was. "I'm sorry—" She reached for his arm, but he pushed her away.

"So am I," he said sharply. Without another word, he turned on his heel and walked away, his anger such that he was oblivious of the pouring rain.

Sloane stared after him for a long moment, too stunned to think clearly. Still not certain why her offhand remark had so offended him, she snapped out of her daze and caught only a glimpse of him as he disappeared into the crowd.

"Jordan—wait!" she called out as she ran after him, seeking him out in a sea of assorted umbrellas as he stalked down the busy street, unable to keep up with his long, athletic stride. "Jordan!"

If he heard her calling to him, he gave no indication of it. He kept walking, crossing Fourth Street against the light. Sloane ran after him and was nearly hit by a taxi. The driver hit his brakes, causing a loud squeal on the wet pavement. "Hey, lady!" he shouted angrily. "Watch where the hell you're goin', will ya?"

Sloane didn't respond. She didn't even hear him. She ran after Jordan, finally catching up with him at the Fourth Street entrance of the Adam's Mark. "Jordan—listen to me, dammit!" She grabbed him, pulling him around to face her. Her tone was urgent, pleading. "What I said back there—I didn't mean anything by it! It was a joke! I had no idea you'd take it that way!"

He looked at her, droplets of water streaming down his face from his rain-soaked hair, its damp thickness showing the furrows made by his raking fingers. There was still anger in his dark eyes, and raindrops glittered from his thick, dark lashes. "I don't deny sex was good between us," he said tightly, "but dammit, Sloane, sex is available anywhere, anytime, for the asking! I didn't have to come this far for it! I came because I wanted *you*—even if you did walk out on me in France!"

She stared at him momentarily, reluctant to make any confessions herself just yet. "I—I wanted you, too," she said finally. "I wanted more than anything to go with you to Argentina, but I couldn't—"

"You didn't have to just sneak off in the middle of the night like that."

"I had my reasons," she said, deliberately avoiding his eyes as she moved under the brightly lit port extending across the sidewalk from the glass and chrome doors to the street.

His jaw tightened visibly. "Not good enough."

She lifted her head slowly, her eyes finally meeting his. "Okay—I didn't want to get hurt," she confessed, drawing a deep breath.

"What made you think I'd hurt you?" he pursued, his eyes narrowing suspiciously.

She shook her head. "You wouldn't understand," she said quietly, closing her umbrella.

He wasn't about to let go. "Try me," he pressed.

"History has a way of repeating itself," she said evasively.

"Meaning?"

"You know the saying, 'Lucky at cards, unlucky in love'? Well, I've always been great at cards," she said.

He lifted his hand to wipe away a single droplet that rolled down her cheek—or was it a tear? He studied her for a few seconds, as if not knowing just what to say. "There are no guarantees," he said finally. "There are never any guarantees. I don't know what the future holds any more than you do, love. All I know is that we had something pretty damned good in Deauville—and I think it's worth taking a chance on. I don't know about you, but I don't want to give up on it without at least trying. I want us to be together. I want to risk it."

She looked up at him. "You came a long way to tell me that."

He gave her a tired smile. "Doesn't that tell you something?"

"It tells me you need to have your head examined," she said, keeping her voice light.

"Maybe you're right," he said, realizing her joke was a defense mechanism of sorts. He pulled her close. "Maybe I don't have both oars in the water, I don't know. All I know is what I feel right now, at this moment." He paused. "What's it going to be, Sloane?"

She put her arms around his neck and kissed him longingly. "Let the games begin," she whispered as he embraced her tightly.

"Do you make a habit of this, woman? Luring unsuspecting men up to your room and disrobing them?" Jordan chuckled as Sloane unbuttoned his shirt.

"You're soaked through to the skin," she said seriously as she slipped the damp shirt off his shoulders and pulled it down his arms. "You're going to have to get out of those wet clothes. All of them." She tossed the shirt aside carelessly.

He grinned. "I will if you will."

She made a wry face. "My clothes aren't wet," she reminded him.

"They will be—after I dump that ice bucket over there on you." He nodded toward the bar across the room.

Sloane laughed. "I thought you didn't want me to see you as a stud."

He kissed her forehead. "Correction—I said I didn't want you to see me *only* as a stud." He started to unbutton her blouse.

"Jordan!"

His mouth came down on hers as his fingers fumbled with the tiny buttons down the back of the blouse. "I *have* missed you, love," he whispered in her ear. He peeled the burgundy silk down her arms easily. With one hand, he unhooked the front of her lacy bra and bared her breasts. Her nipples grew hard as his hand caressed her. In the back of his mind, he wondered if he would have the problem with Sloane that he'd had with Jilly in Argentina. If he did, what would he do?

As if she'd read his mind, Sloane unzipped his pants, exposing him. As her fingers stroked him, he could feel the heat growing within his groin. He didn't have to look; he knew what was happening. There wasn't anything wrong with him after all! He wanted her now as much as he had before she'd left him in France—physically and emotionally—and there wasn't the slightest doubt in his mind that he was going to have her. All the way. And she wanted him just as much. He unbuttoned the front of her skirt and let it fall to the floor. He freed her of the rest of her clothing while she pushed his pants down his muscular legs. All the while they kept kissing each other, quick, darting, eager kisses. Teasing, flirting kisses exchanged in a lighthearted mating ritual.

"We've got to have a talk about these damned boots, Phillips," she lamented as she dropped to her knees on the carpet in front of him. He settled into a large chair while she pulled the boots off and followed them with his pants. She was on her knees between his legs, looking up at him. He took her face in his hands and bent his head to kiss her hungrily. She withdrew slowly and lowered her head between his thighs. He shuddered involuntarily when he felt her lips on him, kissing

him, nuzzling him. He stroked her hair as she started licking
and sucking at him.

"My God!" he gasped, feeling as though he might actually
explode. "Oh . . . sweet Jesus!" Unable to stand it any longer,
he pushed her back on the carpet and came down on top of
her. "We almost got rained out there," he muttered in her ear
as he kissed her neck and shoulder. "Wouldn't want the games
to be over before they even begin, would you?"

"No," she breathed as he lowered his head to nuzzle her
breasts. He sucked at her nipples, first lazily, then with a
demanding impatience. She arched her back, offering herself
up to him, digging her nails into his back as he sucked fiercely,
pinning her to the floor with the weight of his body. Her legs
parted willingly as he entered her, sliding in as easily as if they
were two parts of the same puzzle that fit together perfectly.
His hips started to move, slowly at first, and she moved with
him, urging him on, trapping him inside her.

"That's it, love," he growled as she shuddered against his
thrusts, her orgasms increasing in intensity. "Yeah, that's
it . . ." It *was* as good as before, he told himself. Better. She
wanted him as much as he wanted her, and the weeks they'd
been apart had only intensified their hunger for each other.
Whatever her reasons for leaving had been, it didn't matter
now. It wouldn't happen again. He'd make sure of that.

As he came, and his whole body tensed and shuddered, she
reached up and wrapped her arms around his neck, drawing
him down to her. He buried his face in her shoulder, kissing
her again and again while she stroked his hair.

"Welcome back," she whispered.

Sloane lay captive in Jordan's arms in the darkness, a willing
prisoner resting against him, threading her fingers through the
thick mat of hair covering his hard-muscled chest. His deep,
even breathing indicated he was fast asleep. She pressed her
lips to his flesh. She'd been so heady with passion, so spent
from the urgency of their lovemaking, that she barely recalled
being carried to bed in the cradle of his strong arms. She wasn't
sure how long they'd held each other in silence, not needing
words because their bodies had said all there was to be said—
for the moment. It felt now as if they'd never been apart at

all, as if they'd always been together. She still had some reservations about the future, but here in his arms none of it seemed to matter.

Trying not to wake him, she slowly, carefully extricated herself from his embrace. She sat up on the side of the bed and lowered her feet to the floor. But just as she started to get up, Jordan's arm shot out, encircling her waist, pulling her down to him again. "Where do you think you're going?" he growled.

She twisted around, rumpling his hair playfully. "Now, what do people usually do when they get up in the middle of the night?"

"I know what most people do—but what do *you* have in mind?" He refused to let go of her.

She poked him in the ribs. "I was planning to go to the bathroom—if you don't mind."

"And if I do mind?"

"Then we have a serious problem."

He lifted his head off the pillow to kiss the underside of her breast. "I'm not letting you sneak out on me again," he told her.

She laughed. "The bathroom is right over there," she pointed out. "I can't get out without you seeing me, so there's really not much chance of my escaping."

"There's always the window."

"We're eight floors up. Even I'm not that foolish."

"Maybe I'll handcuff us together," he mused.

"And just how would I finish the tour?"

"Simple. I'll go with you."

"That would be interesting."

"To say the least," he agreed.

"And what about your other obligations?" she asked. "When's your next match?"

"December. In Los Angeles. And I'm taking you with me," he informed her.

Her eyebrows arched in surprise. "Are you, now?"

He nodded. "Damned right I am."

"Don't I have anything to say about it?"

He shook his head. "Not really."

"It's nice to know where I stand in this relationship," she

commented, amused. "Don't tell me—you're one of those men who likes your women barefoot and pregnant."

"Not at all!" he responded with mock indignation. "Shoes are necessary—especially in good restaurants!"

She roared with laughter. "You're terrible!" She pried herself free and moved away quickly, beyond his grasp. "I'll be right back."

"You have one minute," he called after her as she closed the door. "Any longer than that and I'm coming in after you!"

"You've got carpet burns on your back, love."

Sloane was sitting up in the bed, the sheet pulled up around her waist. Jordan, lying next to her, traced the red marks on her bare back with his fingertips. "Now, whose fault is that?" she wanted to know.

"You started it," he chuckled. "Want me to kiss them and make them better?"

She giggled. "Think it'll help?"

He grinned. "I guarantee I can make you forget they're there." Raising himself up on one elbow, he pressed his lips to her back. "How's that?"

"Mmmmm . . . better."

He kissed another spot. "And here?"

"Much better."

"Here?"

"Ohhh . . ."

His lips moved up to her shoulder. "Got any on the flip side?" he muttered in a low, suggestive tone.

She smiled, rolling her head back as he sat up and folded his arms around her. "Sorry," she droned. "I was on my back the whole time, remember?"

His hands cupped her breasts, his thumbs making slow, lazy circles around her nipples, making them harden at his touch. "Do you believe in preventive medicine?" he asked in a low, husky voice.

"Definitely," she purred. "But since when do you need an excuse to do exactly as you please?"

His fingers pulled gently at her taut nipples. "You're absolutely right," he said, pulling her around until she was lying across his lap, cradling her easily with one arm. He kissed her hard while his hands continued to work at her breasts. Finally, when she was breathless, he lowered his head to her breast and started to suck at her aching nipples, claiming her with an intensity that left her dizzy with longing.

But Jordan wanted to claim more than just her body.

BOOK TWO
HEARTS

⮀ New York City, October 1986

"Are you in love with Jordan, Mom?"

Sloane looked at her son out of the corner of her eye. "What, may I ask, brings this on?" Jordan had gone to the Plaza to collect the last of his things from his father's suite, and Sloane realized now that Travis had been waiting for just this opportunity to grill her about the state of their relationship.

He perched on a stool at the bar, looking at her expectantly as she filled an ice bucket and put a bottle of Bollinger Brut to chill. "Are you?" he pursued.

"I don't know," she said carefully, reluctant to discuss her feelings for Jordan with Travis or anyone else.

"Doesn't look that way from where I sit," he commented, unconvinced.

She turned to look at him, her eyebrows arched in surprise. She was trying hard not to smile and failing miserably. "And when did you become an authority?"

He propped his elbows up on the bar, resting his chin in his hands. "C'mon, Mom—I wasn't born yesterday."

She gave a short laugh. "I know when you were born. I was there, remember?"

"Don't change the subject," he said stubbornly. "I've seen the way you two look at each other, the way you're always touching and holding hands. Geez—you even let him move in!"

She could hardly keep from laughing. "I see—and that's a dead giveaway, is it?"

He invaded the bowl of mixed nuts on the bar. "You never let anybody else move in with us," he pointed out in a casual tone.

She checked the liquor cabinet to see if she needed to have Emma order anything. "For your information, Dr. Freud—" she started.

"Dr. Freud?" Travis made a face. "Who's he?"

"A famous psychiatrist," Sloane clarified. "And Jordan hasn't moved in with us, as you put it. He's only staying with us for a little while. He lives in Massachusetts."

"I see." Travis was thoughtful for a moment. "Then it's just sex."

Sloane was momentarily stunned by his directness. "W-What—" she stammered, almost speechless.

"He does sleep with you," Travis reminded her.

She felt the color coming to her cheeks and busied herself in the lower part of the liquor cabinet so he wouldn't see she was blushing. She'd never once given a thought to how her very observant son would perceive her relationship with Jordan. The day they returned to New York, two weeks ago, Jordan had moved in with her. They had never discussed it; it was simply something that was mutually understood. They knew they would be together. *Had* to be together.

"Mom?" Travis's voice cut through her thoughts.

She finally turned around, as composed as she could manage. "What?"

"Just for the record," he said as he hopped down off the stool, "you have my blessing."

"What do you think of this one?"

Sloane shook her head disapprovingly. "It's too big. I'd think it would be terribly uncomfortable."

They were standing at one of the jewelry counters at Saks Fifth Avenue, admiring a selection of rings and bracelets. A large crowd of Saturday shoppers milled around them, many of them laden with bulky packages and shopping bags, checking out the counter displays. "What about that one?" Jordan asked, pointing out a large diamond solitaire.

"It's lovely, but I'm not really into diamonds," she told him, adjusting the brim of her blue felt fedora.

His eyebrows shot upward in surprise. "Now tell me—what kind of woman isn't 'into' diamonds?" he demanded, his tone teasing.

"*This* kind of woman," she replied, her stance firm as she shoved her hands down into the deep pockets of her unconstructed dove-gray jacket.

He laughed. "And what stones, pray tell, *are* you into?"

"Sapphires," she said promptly. "The bluer the better."

"Anything to be different!" he declared, rolling his eyes upward as he made a gesture to the heavens.

"While we're on the subject, what are *you* into?" she questioned him. "You're obviously here looking for something."

"A watch," he answered too quickly. "My father's birthday's coming up."

Sloane smiled wickedly. "Then you'd better stop wasting your time on the rings and go on over to the watch counter," she advised, nodding in that direction.

He hesitated for a fraction of a second. "I have a better idea," he said. "Let's take a walk up to Cartier's."

As they walked up Fifth Avenue, they paused from time to time to check out some of the elegant displays in the shop windows. Sloane was particularly taken with a beautiful blue fox coat. "I take it you're not a conservationist," Jordan observed with a wry smile as he watched her gush effusively over the coat.

The light in her eyes dimmed abruptly. "You don't approve, do you?" she guessed.

"My mother has at least half a dozen furs," he told her. "And I approve wholeheartedly of *you*—even if you are a material girl."

She smiled, relieved. "A material girl in a material world," she quoted the song.

"Definitely." He came to a stop at one of Cartier's display windows facing Fifth Avenue. "What do you think of that one?" he asked casually.

Her gaze followed the direction of his hand. In the window, surrounded by a matching bracelet, choker, and earrings, was a simple but stunning sapphire solitaire ring. "Is that one also too big?" he asked.

She pursed her lips thoughtfully. "I think I could live with that one."

He looked surprised. "Live with it?"

She laughed. "I think it's the most beautiful ring I've ever seen," she admitted, "but this is all a colossal waste of time—unless, of course, you're planning to buy it for me." She hooked her arm in his and kissed his cheek affectionately. "Come on—let's go buy a watch."

"Media coverage—that's the answer."

Sloane laughed. "Heaven help you if you ever become dependent on the media to aid your career," she told him as they walked hand in hand along Central Park South a few days later. "It's great when they love you, but when they don't, developing a thick hide is your only chance of survival."

Jordan shook his head. "If polo's going to gain the mass appeal other sports already enjoy, we *do* need them. Most people have an image of polo as a rich man's game—fast, expensive, and glamorous," he pointed out. "What they don't realize is that it's generally *not* expensive for spectators."

Sloane shoved her hands down into the large pockets of her trench coat. "So what's the game plan?" she asked.

"For starters, the USPA's working with the International Management Group, the same sports marketing outfit that worked magic for golf and tennis." Jordan stopped to buy two hot dogs and two cans of soda from a vendor on the outskirts of the park. "What do you want on yours?" he asked, pulling his wallet from his back pocket.

"Mustard and sauerkraut." She turned up the collar of her coat to further block out the brisk October wind. "Try the pretzels," she recommended. "They're like the Empire State Building—it's just not New York without them."

He laughed. "You know, it's downright amazing how many times I've been to New York yet never really been here." He handed her one of the hot dogs and a soda, then turned back to the vendor. "Two pretzels, please." Noting the amusement on the other man's face, he winked. "I've got to pamper her. She's pregnant—craves stuff like this all the time."

"Jordan!" She punched his arm.

"Keep this up and you won't have room for dinner tonight," he warned.

"Fat chance." She took a bite. "Getting back to your problem, I think you should be warned in advance. Wait until you're interviewed by a hostile reporter."

"I've already had my first unpleasant experience," he said, biting into the pretzel. "You're right. These are good." He washed it down. "I was interviewed by a woman in Texas last year. She approached me right after the match, and we talked for a long time. I did my damnedest to get it all across to her—the dedication, the sacrifices, the hard work, the whole bit. But when we were finished, all she really seemed interested in was finding out if I used Polo cologne. Made me feel like I'd wasted my breath."

Sloane finished her hot dog and licked dabs of mustard from her fingertips. "I hate to break this to you, angel, but that's tame," she said. "I can tell you some *real* horror stories."

He grimaced. "Thanks for the warning."

As they approached Grand Army Plaza, Jordan noticed half a dozen horse-drawn hansom cabs lined up at the curb. "Another of those you-haven't-really-been-to-New-York-till-you've-tried-it experiences?" he asked.

She nodded. "They were the limos of yesteryear. In the thirties' movies, scores of lovers ventured into Central Park by night in hansom cabs," she told him. "Just check out the late movies on TV—any night of the week."

He winked. "I have better things to do with my nights—and so do you." Finishing his soda, he tossed the can into a nearby trash can. "Taking a ride in the park sounds like a good idea, though." He took her hand. "Shall we?"

She looked up at him and smiled. "Why not?"

Jordan and Sloane held hands and enjoyed the sights in the park as their driver, a personable young woman in top hat and tails, indicated various points of interest along the way.

As they approached the Plaza Hotel, Jordan pulled Sloane close and kissed her. "How do you feel about having dinner at the Plaza?" he asked.

Sloane nodded and smiled approvingly. "Sounds wonderful to me. Trader Vic's? The Edwardian Room?"

"Actually," he said with a wicked gleam in his eye, "I was thinking of room service."

When Sloane woke the next morning, it took her a few seconds to remember where she was. Then it came to her. Jason Phillips's suite at the Plaza. They'd spent the night there—and what a night it had been! She rolled over on her side, expecting to put her arms around Jordan, and was surprised to find herself alone in the big bed. She paused for a moment, listening for the shower. Nothing.

"Good morning, sleepyhead." Jordan appeared in the doorway, wearing his pants but no shirt or boots. He was carrying a tray laden with food.

She sat up, pulling the sheet up to her chest to cover her nakedness. "What's this?" she asked, still not quite awake.

"Room service—as promised."

"You promised me room service for dinner," she reminded him, pushing her tousled hair back off her face with one hand.

"Last night there were more important things on my mind than food," he defended himself. "I take it you're hungry."

"Famished," she admitted. "Let me get dressed—"

"No need to dress," he said quickly, balancing the tray on one hand as he waved her off with the other. "We're having breakfast in bed."

"Nothing doing," she protested. "That's how I got cheated out of dinner, remember?"

"This time I'll let you eat. Scout's honor."

"I'll take that as a promise," she said. "What are we having?"

"You're having eggs, ham, and juice." He placed the tray in front of her.

She looked up at him questioningly. "And what are you having?"

"Depends on how cooperative you are," he replied with a leer. His dark eyes roved over the curves of her body, outlined by the clinging sheet.

She looked at him accusingly. "How do you ever play polo?" she asked. "Your mind's always in the gutter."

"Eat your breakfast," he ordered, settling down on the bed next to her. "You're going to need your strength."

"I'll bet." She reached for the juice. "Aren't you eating?"

"I already did," he said. "Some of us *do* get out of bed before noon, you know. Now, eat your breakfast," he repeated firmly, tapping the edge of the tray.

"Gladly." She lifted the cover on one of the plates. Scrambled eggs and ham had never smelled so good. She reached for the cover of the smaller plate. "What's this—" She stopped short as she raised the lid to reveal not food but the choker she'd seen in Cartier's window, a wide band of filigreed white gold set with one spectacular sapphire. She looked up at him. "Jordan, why—" She couldn't find the words.

He smiled. "Does there always have to be a reason?"

"No, of course not." It was a stupid thing to have said. She picked up the necklace and fingered it as if making sure it was real. He was so unbelievably impulsive . . . and she was so completely in love with him it was scary.

"Can I safely assume you like it?" he asked, taking it from her. As she lifted her hair off her shoulders, he put it around her neck and fastened the clasp.

"I love it," she said in a low, faltering voice. *And I love you,* she wanted to say. She leaned on him, her hands on his strong shoulders, and kissed him deeply, lingeringly.

By the time her thoughts returned to her breakfast again, it was cold.

"I think I'm in love with him, Cate," Sloane confided. She put down her wineglass in an emphatic gesture that indicated a mixture of hopelessness and frustration.

Cate smiled patiently. "You've just now figured it out?" she asked, trying to conceal her amusement because she sensed Sloane's ambivalence.

They were having lunch at Ernie's, a lively, noisy Italian restaurant on the Upper West Side. With its Corinthian columns demarcating the freestanding bar, snakelike patterns of ceiling ducts and conduits in au courant colors, and the wall of pay telephones integrated into a bare wall, its decor could actually be described as "nondecor." It was well on its way to becoming *the* Upper West Side singles' watering hole.

"I don't *want* to be in love with him." Sloane took a forkful of her angel hair pasta. "I don't want to be hurt when I lose him."

Cate gave her a puzzled look. "What makes you think you're going to lose him?" she asked, not sure she understood.

"Come on, Cate—you've seen Jordy," Sloane said seriously. "He's young, gorgeous, rich, successful—and if that's not enough, consider his personality. I've seen the way women look at him—young, nubile, beautiful women. He could have any of them. All he'd have to do is say the word.''

Cate eyed the beautiful sapphire necklace Sloane wore. "I think you can be fairly certain he's not handing those out by the gross," she commented, tasting her salmon.

"All right—we have a wonderful relationship," Sloane conceded. "I'm the last one to even try to deny that. I'm not denying he's as happy as I am—now. But how long can it last?"

"You might be surprised." Cate reached for her glass.

"Jordan needs a women who's free to travel with him whenever and wherever he goes. He needs someone who's got the time and ability to organize things for him." She put down her fork. "He needs someone young enough to give him the big family he wants."

"What he needs and what he wants may be two entirely different things," Cate said quietly, sipping her kir. "When have you ever been so happy with what you needed?"

"Cate—"

"It's like telling a child he needs spinach when what he really wants is ice cream," Cate continued.

"I'm thirty-six years old. A little late to be starting a family—again," Sloane said sullenly.

"That doesn't make you ready for the retirement home," Cate maintained. "I've got six years on you—and I don't consider myself a fossil yet."

"I have a son. A ten-year-old son. To have a baby now—"

"You can," Cate insisted. "The question is, do you want to have a baby now?"

Sloane paused momentarily. "That's just it. I don't know," she confessed. "I thought I didn't, and yet I look at Jordan and . . ." She shrugged helplessly.

"Maybe you should think about it. Seriously."

Sloane smiled wearily. "This is all premature," she insisted. "He hasn't exactly asked me to stop taking the pill . . . but he has asked me how I'd feel about it."

"Then he's obviously considered it," Cate concluded. "I doubt a man who's not sure of a relationship would question the woman about having his children."

"Yeah. I guess." Sloane looked unconvinced.

"You know, Sloane, you never cease to amaze me," Cate said then. "For someone who's always been so sure of herself professionally, you're incredibly unsure of yourself as a woman."

"Maybe it's my lousy track record in that department that does it," Sloane offered. "I've always been a better writer than I have been a woman."

Cate frowned. "And maybe your own view of yourself has a lot to do with that."

"Maybe." Sloane looked at her watch. "Look . . . I'm going to have to run."

"Without dessert?" Cate was genuinely surprised. "You who can't resist Ernie's special Death by Chocolate?"

"Today I'll have to," Sloane insisted. "I have a fitting I can't put off. Jordan has special plans tonight he's been very mysterious about—and he's insisted I have a drop-dead dress."

Auntie Yuan's, on First Avenue at Sixty-fourth Street, is a dazzlingly chic Chinese restaurant, its ultradramatic black interior highlighted by strategically placed spotlights and beautiful pink orchids, with Mozart playing on the sophisticated stereo system. Its chefs, who have lent an international flavor to the cuisine by adding unusual ingredients such as quail and salmon to their dishes, have given Auntie Yuan's the reputation of being a Chinese restaurant for those who don't like Chinese restaurants.

"Try the lobster," Jordan recommended as they looked at the menu. "It's the best they've got."

Sloane smiled, drawing a conclusion. "You speak from experience?"

He nodded, putting the menu aside. "I discovered this place right after it opened. I love Chinese food," he told her. "I think I've tried every dish they offer—including the seven-course tasting platter." Tonight, he was finding it hard to concentrate on dinner—or on anything else other than Sloane. She looked smashing in her long-sleeved black crepe dress that fit like a glove, hugging every curve of her body. Cut diagonally between her breasts, it exposed the upper left half of her body under a very sheer black net. Her breast was covered—barely— by a black crepe flower edged with glittering black sequins.

She wore the choker he'd given her—the only jewelry she needed with that dress—and her long hair was anchored in a loose knot on top of her head.

"Have I told you how beautiful you look tonight?" he asked with an appreciative smile.

She smiled back. "No, but you can tell me now—and as often as you like."

"I intend to." He paused. "At the risk of sounding crude, I'd love to pluck your petals."

"Maybe later," she told him.

"Definitely later," he corrected.

The meal was most enjoyable, but Sloane was puzzled by Jordan's uncharacteristic silence. He seemed to be watching her throughout dinner, as if he wanted to say something to her but was waiting for the right moment. Twice she asked him what was on his mind, but he only shook his head and insisted it was nothing.

After dinner Sloane excused herself. "Travis went out with friends tonight," she explained. "I think I'd better make sure he came in before curfew."

"My mother tried to impose a curfew once," Jordan remembered. "It didn't work."

"I can believe that." More than once she'd tried to imagine what he'd been like as a child—a rich, spoiled, only child. He was probably an unholy terror. "I'll be right back."

"Yeah."

She went back to the ladies' room and added a touch of lip gloss and a spray of Magie Noir over her collarbone, then made her call. Relieved to learn from Emma that Travis was not only home but in bed and sound asleep, she returned to their table.

The plates had been cleared away. In their place were two glasses of champagne and a small silver tray holding two fortune cookies. As she approached, Jordan snatched up one of the cookies. The other, she discovered upon closer inspection, was cracked.

"Why do I get the cracked one?" she asked as she seated herself across from him. "You checked the fortune and didn't like it, so you took the other one—right?"

"Eat your cookie," he ordered.

She wrinkled her nose. "Nobody ever eats them," she insisted. "You just read the fortunes."

"I eat them."

"That figures."

"Dammit, Sloane, will you quit bellyaching and eat the goddamned cookie or do whatever you're going to do with it?" he asked impatiently, taking her by surprise.

She looked at him, baffled by his strange mood. "Anything to make you happy," she said, forcing a smile. *Humor him*, she thought. As she picked up the cookie, it fell apart in her hand. She took the tiny slip of paper and read it slowly: YOUR FUTURE IS AS LOFTY AS THE BOUNDLESS HEAVENS. "Now they tell me," she commented lightly. As she started to put it down, she noticed something had been written on the back. Turning it over, she read it three times before the message, written in Jordan's familiar scrawl, sunk in: *Let's get hitched!*

"You have a warped sense of humor, Phillips," she said, looking up. But one look at his face told her it was no joke.

He wasn't laughing. He wasn't even smiling. Shadows played across his handsome face as he watched her intently, waiting for her answer. "This isn't a joke, is it?" she asked feebly.

His gaze held. "Do I look like I'm joking?"

She shook her head. "No. No, you don't."

He reached across the table and covered her hand with his own. "Well, love, give me the bottom line," he said gently. "What's it going to be?"

"Yes," she whispered, even though instinct told her to run, to get as far away from him as fast as she could. "Yes."

♻ Martha's Vineyard,
   November 1986

To Bostonians and denizens of the Cape Cod area, it's known simply as "the Vineyard"; sometimes, its name is given as Martha's Vineyard Island, presumably to let tourists know that this is a separate place out to sea. According to island folklore, it was given its unusual name by seventeenth-century explorer Bartholomew Gosnold, who found wild grapes growing there—and promptly named the vineyard in honor of his daughter. In those days, whaling brought prosperity to an otherwise poor island. Today, it boasts a successful commercial vineyard and winery, a thriving lobster hatchery, and—in the summer months, when the island's year-round population of ten thousand swells to some sixty-five thousand—a booming tourism business. The main draws for tourists—Edgartown, Oak Bluffs, and Vineyard Haven—are all on the northern part of the island. Its southern shores tend to be more secluded, with private beaches and even more private residents. People like Jordan Phillips, who harbored a secret passion for privacy.

Moonstone was the most beautiful part of the Vineyard's southernmost shore. It was thirty acres of prime real estate surrounded by a high gray stone wall with imposing black iron gates at the entrance. The large, beautifully restored Victorian farmhouse, complete with a sturdy porch swing and colorful stained-glass windows, had been built in the mid-1800s. Thanks largely to Jordan's mother, Andrea—an intelligent and cultured woman with a real passion for history and art—it was filled with antiques, many of which dated back to the Civil War. There were enormous stone fireplaces in the living room and master bedroom, four-poster beds adorned with fine quilts, and large, overstuffed chairs that were incredibly comfortable. Only the large, fully equipped kitchen belonged totally to the twentieth century.

The grounds were thickly wooded with pine and oak, and the air smelled strongly of trees and the nearby ocean. A long shell-rock drive led to a two-story stable that looked more like a huge Cape Cod house than a stable; it was painted white with red shutters and trim, and had tack trunks next to each stall door. There was an immaculate hedgerow around the entire structure. Topping the weathervane atop the single vented cupola on the roof was a figure of a polo player. Wood-chip paths connected the stables, the larger brood mare barn, the service building, the bunkhouse, and the feed barn to each of the paddocks.

Sloane hadn't been at all surprised when Jordan wanted to spend Thanksgiving at Moonstone. She'd expected it. After all, he'd grown up there; it was his home—when he wasn't on the road—and it held a special place in his heart. Sloane had never been to Martha's Vineyard before, but she'd heard all about it and had been looking forward to the trip.

"I think Travis has overcome his disappointment at having to miss the Macy's parade," she told Jordan, watching her son from the bay windows in the master bedroom as he explored the grounds near the main house.

"What about you?" he asked as he came up behind her, placing his hands on her shoulders. His lips brushed lightly against her hair as his hands moved down, gently kneading her upper arms.

She shook her head. "I was never all that wild about the parade."

"You know that's not what I meant," he said, kissing her neck. "How do you feel about coming here, about leaving New York, your home—"

"I'm with you and my son," she said simply. "That's exactly where I belong."

"In the beginning, when I first got involved with them, she didn't think much of me." Jordan recalled his early relationship with polo legend Ian Welles, who'd been his coach and mentor, and Ian's daughter, Dusty, as he and Sloane walked on the grounds at twilight. "The more Ian treated me like a son, the more Dusty resented me. She was jealous as hell for a long time. I tell her she has me to thank for the quality of her game today. She pushed herself to the max back then, trying to compete with me. We were on the polo field physically, but in reality she was competing for her father's attention. Or so she thought."

Sloane smiled. "Sounds like sibling rivalry."

"It was, in her eyes. Dusty was an only child. She was accustomed to having her father all to herself—they were very close," he said, picking up a twig. He absently peeled off the few tiny leaves that still clung to it, then cast it aside. "Then I came along and took part of that away from her."

"When did it change?" Sloane asked.

"When Dusty was mature enough to understand that I hadn't replaced her in Ian's affections." Jordan smiled at the memory. "About that same time, she developed a huge crush on me. She was sixteen at the time. I think Ian always hoped it would end up more than that, but the chemistry wasn't there for us."

Sloane looked at him. "Not at all?"

He shook his head. "At least not on my part. I thought of her as a kid sister, the sister I never had."

She was silent for a moment, surprised by his statement. "Do you miss not having brothers and sisters?" she asked.

He shrugged. "Sometimes. Growing up an only child has its advantages, sure, but it's damned lonely for a kid growing up like I did, with no families living close by and no one my own age within walking distance. I always swore I'd never have just one child—I'd want a whole houseful."

Sloane forced a smile. "That's asking for it."

"Doesn't Travis ever miss not having a little brother or sister?"

"If he does, he's never said anything," Sloane replied. "Of course, Travis grew up in Manhattan, and some of his cohorts are right there in the same building, and those who aren't are within walking distance or close enough to reach by bus or subway."

"You let your son go out alone on the subway?" It was Jordan's turn to be surprised.

"Of course. Travis can take care of himself." She smiled.

"He's every bit as tough as he sounds sometimes."

They stopped at the feed barn on their way back to the house so that Jordan could check on the biweekly grain delivery. Sloane was surprised to discover that an entire building was required for the feed at Moonstone, and that so many different types and brands were used. "We get the dehydrated alfalfa cubes at the racetrack," Jordan told her. "The rest we buy from a dealer on the mainland. We mix it ourselves here to get just the right balance—pelleted grain, sweet feed, beet pulp."

"I know people who aren't as picky about their baby food," Sloane commented wryly.

Jordan laughed. "These horses are thoroughbreds," he offered in explanation. "They're high-strung, and they need a lot of grain in order to maintain their condition. In the morning they get a little hay—a timothy-clover mix—and a blend of pellets, sweet feed, whole oats, and the alfalfa cubes. Every evening we give them beet pulp pellets in a full bucket of water. It gives them extra roughage and encourages the fussy ones to eat. Annie Hall's our fussiest eater—nothing much appeals to her." He nodded to two of the stable hands as they passed.

"It all sounds so complicated," Sloane said, amazed at the meticulous care given to every aspect of the horses' feeding and grooming. But horses were Jordan's bread and butter. He was as particular about his horses as she was about her books.

"Complicated—but entirely necessary," he maintained. "The young horses get vitamin and mineral supplements, and some of them are getting biotin for their hooves. One of our mares is on antihistamines."

She forced a smile. "Looks like I've got a lot to learn."

What she wanted to learn at that moment, however, had nothing to do with horses. It had to do with Dusty Welles.

"He's been a real bastard these past few days—more so than usual." Jordan's stable manager, Cappy McCullough, was a short, chunky man in his mid-fifties with graying hair in desperate need of a barber's touch, a weatherbeaten face, and startling blue eyes. He stood near the white rail fence, watching a magnificent black stallion prance impatiently in the paddock, snorting and tossing his head. "It's like he knows his days as a stud are over."

Jordan, in jeans and a red polo shirt, hoisted one boot up on the bottom rail while leaning against the top. "I can't say I blame him for being indignant," he remarked as he studied the animal thoughtfully. "I wouldn't want to be fixed either."

Cappy grinned, pulling his tattered old slouch hat low over his forehead to block out the sun. "There were times your folks considered it, you know." Cappy had been running things at Moonstone for almost twenty years and had known Jordan since he was a boy. Watching him grow up, seeing the boy become a man, Cappy had witnessed the sowing of almost all of Jordan's wild oats and had doubted he would ever really settle down. Jordan, the mischievous boy with a knack for talking himself out of any scrape, had become a handsome man with a lethal amount of charm. Women of all ages were drawn to him, and it was apparent early on that Jordan loved women. Cappy recalled now how Andrea Phillips had worried about his freewheeling life-style. There had been so many women in his life, and she was afraid he would never be willing to settle for just one.

Cappy said nothing of this to Jordan, just looked at him and smiled. He looked on Jordan as one of his own, and he had three boys of his own, all grown and married now. None of his own sons had ever loved horses the way he did. The way Jordan did. None of them had ever shared that bond with him as Jordan had. Cappy had taught Jordan to ride. He'd taught Jordan everything he knew about breeding and training thoroughbreds, and Jordan had learned a great deal more. Horses in general and polo in particular were the great love of Jordan's life. Until now. He was willing to bet that Andrea Phillips was not only pleased but greatly relieved.

"My parents were beginning to think the only daughter-in-law they'd get would have four legs and a tail," Jordan was saying, grinning like the cat who'd swallowed the proverbial canary. "Sloane was a real surprise for them."

"They liked her, did they?"

"Of course. I knew they would."

"I hear Gavin Hillyer's been on your trail again," Cappy said then.

Jordan nodded, his eyes on the stallion. "He's made me a very impressive offer to play for White Timbers."

Cappy studied him for a moment. "What answer did you give him?" He was almost afraid to ask.

Jordan pursed his lips as he considered his next statement. "I told him I'd have to think about it."

"But you've already made up your mind," Cappy guessed.

"He offered me a quarter of a million annually," Jordan said then.

"You don't need the money," Cappy reminded him. "Your father would sponsor a team for you—"

"It's not the money," Jordan insisted. He looked at Cappy, studying him for a long moment. "You don't think much of Hillyer, do you?"

"I don't know the man," Cappy said honestly. "I only know what I've heard."

"Which is?"

"That he has no respect for horseflesh and even less for the men on the horses' backs," Cappy answered. He wasn't pulling any punches. "He plays his men and his ponies till they drop."

"Every player worth his handicap plays every chukker with all he's got," Jordan pointed out.

"Not to the point of putting lives on the line," Cappy disagreed. "The way I hear it, Gavin Hillyer's a cold, unfeeling bastard with ice water for blood." Spotting something that clearly bothered him several yards away, he ended the conversation abruptly. "That goddamned idiot. I've told him at least a dozen times I'll not tolerate smoking near the stables." He promptly went off to reprimand the groom he'd seen lighting up.

Jordan stared after him, still bothered by what he'd said about Hillyer and not quite sure why it bothered him.

"Accident, my ass," Ian snorted angrily.

The telephone connection was poor, but even so Jordan was able to detect the skepticism in Welles's voice. "How else can you explain it?"

"I don't know," Ian answered, frustrated, "but there have been too damned many so-called 'accidents' lately for me to buy those lame excuses I've been hearing."

Jordan's laugh was hollow. "We haven't exactly got the competition running scared these days," he pointed out.

"You can thank your friend Whitney for that."

"He's had a lot of problems lately." In spite of his own feelings on the subject, Jordan felt the need to defend Lance. "Paula filing for divorce hit him pretty hard."

"Stop making excuses for him," Ian growled.

Jordan paused. "You don't think *Lance* is behind this?" he asked, surprised.

"Hardly. He's just making it easy for whoever is," Ian concluded.

Jordan thought about it. There *had* been too many so-called accidents recently, and all of them, now that he stopped to think about it seriously, had involved members of the White Timbers team. In Argentina, it had been Lance. Two weeks later, a White Timbers player had taken a bad fall during a scrimmage—his girth had broken, though rumor had it that it had actually been cut—and ended up in the hospital with a concussion and two broken ribs. In Chicago, one of the players had been killed in a fall. The man's helmet had been damaged, and rumors still circulated that it had somehow been tampered with. Jordan wasn't sure he bought that. He'd always thought everyone had overreacted to the incident.

Now he wasn't so sure. Ian Welles was not a man given to overstatement. If he were so concerned, maybe there was something to all of this after all.

"Any idea what the motive might be?" Jordan asked.

"Revenge looks like a good bet from where I sit."

"Come on, woman—it's time to get up!"

Jordan whipped the quilt off the bed and threw it to the floor. Grabbing Sloane's ankles, he dragged her across the bed and she screamed, swinging her arms furiously in protest. "Let go of me, dammit!" she shrieked. "Have you gone completely mad?"

"It's time to get up," he repeated insistently.

"Make up your mind, will you?" she grumbled, pulling herself upright. "Last night you couldn't wait to get me into bed and now you can't wait to get me out! Which is it going to be?"

"Depends on the moment," he said with a grin. "Right now I need you up and about, because if you stay in that bed—like that—much longer, I'm going to end up there with you, and I don't want to do that." He unbuckled his belt as if to illustrate his point.

She smiled suggestively. "What a wonderful idea." She reached for him, but he backed away. "Now, *there's* a first," she teased. "Jordan Phillips saying no to sex!"

He leaned back against the wall, arms folded across his chest, bending one leg as he braced his foot against the wall. "I'd love to accommodate you, sweetheart, but it'll have to wait until tonight."

"The world must be coming to an end," she declared with a wave of her hand. "The day you turn down—"

"Never mind the sarcasm." He tossed her the robe lying on the chair next to him. "Just get up and get dressed before I weaken. We have a busy day ahead of us."

"A man who doesn't truly love horses has no business in polo," Jordan told Sloane as they walked along the long row of red-shuttered box stalls. Horses poked their heads over the half doors, ears pricked, many of them whinnying softly in recognition when they saw him. "A real polo player, the one who truly has it in his blood, must love horses. He might be a callous ass to his wife or lover. He may even neglect his kids if he has any. He may be guilty of ignoring his elderly, bed-ridden mother—but to his horses, he's got to be a prince."

Sloane smiled, pushing her hands down into the deep pockets of her oversize royal blue sweater. "Are you that bad?"

He grinned. "Worse. You, of all people, should know that," he pointed out.

"I'm biased," she reminded him.

"You'd better be."

As they walked, he paused at intervals to give each horse an affectionate pat on the neck or stroke a muzzle. Sloane was touched by his gentleness, the obviously strong feelings he had for each animal. He treated them with more kindness and affection than some people gave their children. He'd make such a wonderful father, she realized now.

She was intrigued by the names on the aluminum plates on

each door. "Key Largo . . . Maltese Falcon . . . Casablanca."
She looked at Jordan suspiciously. "Unless I miss my guess,
someone around here is a big Bogart fan."

"Guilty," Jordan confessed with a grin. "Bogey was my
idea of a man's man. Loved his movies."

She read another nameplate, then looked at Jordan again.
"Annie Hall?"

He shrugged. "She's always been a little flaky."

She went to the next one. "Solitaire—what a beautiful
name," she commented. "Where did that come from?"

He shook his head. "She's the best there is on the polo
field—one of a kind," he said, stroking the mare's neck.
"When I was learning to play polo, my father bought her for
me—the only experienced polo pony I owned at the time. I
called her my solitary advantage, but 'Solitary Advantage'
didn't seem an appropriate name for a beautiful lady, so she
became 'Avantage Solitaire'—'Solitaire' for the sake of sim-
plicity." He paused. "Ian always said the name didn't really
matter—out on the polo field they're all 'You sorry S.O.B.'—
but for her, I just felt I had to come up with something as
special as she is."

"She's beautiful," Sloane agreed, stroking the horse's velvety muzzle. "Were all of these horses bred for polo?"

"None of them were really bred for it," Jordan answered.
"They all started life as racehorses. Unfortunately, most of
them couldn't cut it at the track. We saved their lives by buying
them."

"Saved their lives? How?"

"When racehorses don't live up to expectations, they're
often sold to butchers," he explained. "For dog food."

"Dog food!" Sloane looked horrified.

He nodded, frowning. "It's a sad fact," he said grimly.
"Most of the horses you see on the polo fields, particularly at
the club level, were saved from slaughter by the players riding
them." He patted Solitaire's neck again. "This old girl's about
ready for retirement. She's too old to play pro anymore. I'm
going to make sure her twilight years are good ones. She'll
never leave Moonstone again, as long as she lives."

"Looks like it was love at first sight for you two," she
commented, observing the affection between the man and the
mare.

He smiled. "You sound as if you don't believe in it," he said.

"I never have," she admitted, "until now."

"Hillyer seems to have noticed the unusual number of accidents occurring within the ranks of his own team," Ian told Jordan when he called from Dallas. "He's taken precautions—to protect himself. He's increased his insurance coverage on everyone on the team—and probably on all of his horses as well."

"Sounds completely within character—for Hillyer," Jordan said without reservation, cradling the telephone receiver on one shoulder as he sat on the edge of the bed, pulling his boots on.

"Guess he figures if one of you meets with an untimely end, at least he won't have lost anything," Ian suggested only half-jokingly.

"Like I said, it sounds just like him. Anything else been happening?"

"No. It's been quiet—so far. Unless you count the truck breaking down. Something to do with the brakes, I think. Nothing major."

"I take it there were no horses in the trailer at the time." *But if there had been . . . God, I must be getting paranoid!*

"Are you really going to marry my mother, Jordy?" Travis asked, perched on the top rail of the fence, watching Jordan saddle one of his horses.

Jordan glanced over his shoulder at the boy. "I wouldn't have asked her if I didn't intend to go through with it, sport," he said, checking the saddle's girth.

"Think she'll go through with it?"

"Why wouldn't she?" Jordan's tone was casual as he turned his attentions back to the horse.

"Mom's specialty is beating the hasty retreat," Travis told him. "She never keeps anybody around for long."

"There's a first time for everything," Jordan said, wondering how many she'd "kept around" in the past.

Travis shook his head solemnly. "Not with Mom. She's one of those people who's afraid of being committed."

Jordan couldn't help laughing. "I think you mean afraid of commitment, don't you?"

Travis shrugged. "Whatever."

"Why do you think she's afraid of commitments?" Jordan asked, adjusting the stirrups.

"Like I said. Nobody ever stuck around for long." Travis climbed down off the fence. "Not even my father."

"Maybe she just never cared enough about anyone," Jordan offered.

"Maybe." Travis approached him. "I think she loves you, for what it's worth."

"Thanks for the vote of confidence, sport." Jordan rumpled his hair. "Come on—your first riding lesson's about to begin."

"Your son thinks you'll back out before the wedding bells get a chance to ring." Jordan put his arm around Sloane's shoulders as they walked barefoot in the wet sand, the legs of their pants rolled up to midcalf. The cold surf lapped at their feet, washing away their footprints in the sand almost as soon as they were made. The morning sun seemed to rise out of the Atlantic Ocean like an angry red fireball, heralding the start of a new day.

Sloane avoided his eyes. "Why would he tell you that?" she asked carefully.

"I don't know, other than he says you're afraid of being committed," he said, quoting Travis with a deceptively straight face.

"What?" Sloane looked up at him and started to laugh.

"I think what he was trying to say was that you're afraid of commitments," Jordan said, kicking some seaweed from his left foot. He told her what Travis had told him. "He didn't realize I knew about your penchant for retreating firsthand."

Sloane's face colored visibly. The cool morning breeze blew her long hair in all directions as she attempted to push it out of her face with one hand. "My son has a big mouth," she said tightly.

"He worries about you," Jordan told her. "He also worries about himself. I think he'd like to have a father."

"I know."

"He's got it in his head that you'll pull a disappearing act before the last 'I do' is said,'' Jordan said then. He bent to pick up a piece of driftwood, absently drawing an abstract design in the wet sand.

"Travis has a vivid imagination," Sloane maintained.

He looked up at her. "Is that all it is, Sloane, a child's active imagination?" he asked dubiously. "Or is that why you keep stalling?"

"You shouldn't put too much stock in some of the things Travis says," she responded. "He's a born bullshitter. Comes by it naturally."

"And you haven't answered my question."

"I'm not going anywhere."

He straightened up and threw the driftwood several yards ahead of them on the beach. "That's good, because I love you and I don't intend to let you get away from me again," he said seriously.

She stared at him for a moment, her eyes wide and her mouth slightly open, but she said nothing.

"You never really say the words, Sloane," he said then, his stare mildly accusing. "Oh, you've said it when we're making love, in the heat of passion—but never any other time."

She looked down at the sand, where he'd drawn their initials in a huge, lopsided heart. "You know how I feel."

He nodded. "I think I know, but I want you to tell me. I want to hear the words. Not in bed, not when we're making love. Right here. Right now."

Her eyes met his. She hesitated for a moment, then nodded. "I do love you, Jordan," she said softly. "It's hard to say the words because it makes me feel so damned vulnerable. I don't want to be vulnerable ever again."

"Even with me?"

"Even with you," she admitted reluctantly. "It's never worked for me. I figured I just didn't have it in me to sustain a relationship. When I met you . . . there was something there, I felt it right away. But I was afraid to care. I didn't want to get hurt."

He touched her face gently. "Who hurt you? Before, I mean."

"No one," she said quickly. Too quickly. "What makes you think—"

"Anyone who's afraid of being hurt has been burned before," he reasoned. "I know. I've been there. Now—who hurt you?"

"No one," she repeated firmly.

"Love has a lot to do with trust," he reminded her. "Do you trust me, Sloane?"

"With my life," she said simply.

He caressed her cheek tenderly. "I'm giving you one hundred percent, love," he told her. "I expect no less in return."

"I love you," she insisted. "But you have the advantage, Jordy. You had a wonderful childhood with two parents who adored you—and each other. You grew up knowing love. I didn't. I don't have any role models in that department to draw from. I've got a lot to learn."

"Meaning?"

"It's a long story."

"We have all the time in the world."

She shook her head. "Not yet, Jordy. I can't. Not yet," she said quietly. "Be patient with me, okay?"

He placed his hands on her shoulders and pulled her around to face him. "I had a great childhood, true, but it didn't make me a smashing success in the romance department," he said wearily, his hair ruffled by the soft, salty breeze blowing in off the ocean. "I've had a pretty lousy track record myself."

"At least you know what a good relationship is."

"Yeah." He took her in his arms. "And I'm going to show you what it is, too, love," he promised.

On Saturday, Travis went into West Tisbury with Cappy and two of the stableboys. Jordan and Sloane took the opportunity to go riding alone on the grounds, and Sloane was surprised at how easily the riding lessons she'd taken as a teen-ager came back to her. Having ridden hard all morning, they dismounted in a thickly wooded area and allowed their horses to walk along slowly behind them, cooling down.

"What was it like, growing up here?" Sloane asked, wondering what it must have been like to live at Moonstone as a child, to have every advantage. "What was it like to feel happy and secure? To feel as if you belonged somewhere?"

"I never really gave it much thought," Jordan confessed, pulling leaves from a low-hanging branch as they walked. Autumn had definitely come to Martha's Vineyard, and except for the pines the trees had turned all the shades of the season, from yellow to orange to gold to brilliant red. "I guess when you've always had it, you just take it all for granted."

She nodded. "I suppose."

He looked at her, her face dappled by the sunlight streaming through the trees, and he wondered what kind of world she had come from. She obviously didn't like to talk about it. Even in France she'd put up a good front, but he'd had the feeling it wasn't the typical middle-class American family she'd described. "What was your childhood like?" he asked hesitantly.

"Like a 'Movie of the Week.'"

"Meaning?"

"Bad marriage, troubled kids, that sort of thing," she answered vaguely. "Sort of like growing up in a prison camp—I spent all my time trying to escape."

"Why?" he pursued.

She brushed it off with a shrug. "A lot of reasons."

"Is that why you became a writer?" he asked. "To fulfill some kind of emotional need?"

"In a way." She frowned. "Mostly, though, I did it for the money. I figured it was my ticket to a better life."

"And was it?"

"Sure. I'm not complaining. I like making a lot of money. I like seeing my name on my published books and on the best seller lists. I still get a kick when I see my name on the cover, when I see someone in a bookstore buying one of my books . . ."

"But?"

She looked at him. "What makes you think there's a flip side?"

"Chalk it up to instinct."

She nodded slowly. "Yeah, well . . . I love what I'm doing, for the record. I love being a star, if that's what it's called," she said. "In the beginning, it wasn't easy. I don't think I've ever worked harder for anything in my life. Even after that first sale, Travis and I still lived hand-to-mouth for a long time. I owed a lot of people a lot of money, and most of my first advance went to pay back debts. Even Cate. She loaned me money to get me through the weeks of waiting for that first check.''

"But you made it.''

"I made it, yes. I learned to be a survivor at an early age,'' she recalled. "I lost what illusions I had left during my first year as a professional. I discovered very early that there's more to publishing a book like mine than sitting down at the type-writer and writing.''

"Like what?''

"Like selling myself.'' She gave a tired little laugh at the look of surprise on his face. "I think Molière said it best: First you do it for love, then you do it for a few friends, and finally you do it for the money. When I started doing it for money, my life was no longer my own. I've been told what to say, how to dress, how to talk—there are times I'm not sure who I really am or what I want anymore.''

Jordan studied her for a moment, touched by her confession. Dropping the reins, he reached out and took her in his arms. "I think I know,'' he said softly. "Let me help you know, too.''

She clung to him. She needed him as she'd never needed anyone. She needed to know he loved her, that her beautiful bubble was not going to burst.

Hillyer called two days later. "I need you in Chicago right away,'' he announced without preamble. "How soon can you get a flight?''

"I can't—that is, I'm not,'' Jordan responded without hes-itation. "We had an agreement, remember? I'm supposed to be off—''

"As they say in the military, all leaves are canceled until further notice.'' It sounded like a joke, but there was no humor in Hillyer's voice. "Whitney's been injured. He'll be out of commission two weeks minimum.''

Jordan was silent for a moment. "What happened?'' he asked finally.

"Loose girth. He went down headfirst during a scrimmage. The horses' hooves clipped him in the ribs and right shoulder.'' There was a pause on the other end. "Now—how soon can you get here?''

Jordan frowned. "Tonight," he agreed reluctantly. He would have to call the airlines. "Tomorrow morning at the latest."

"No later."

The receiver clicked in Jordan's ear. He drew back and stared at it for a moment, then hung up slowly. As soon as Hillyer got what he wanted, that was it. End of discussion. But the man's abruptness wasn't what bothered Jordan now.

He was thinking about Lance, about the accident. Hillyer hadn't said much about it, but what he had said hadn't made any sense. There had been so many "accidents" lately, they could have renamed the team the Four Horsemen of the Apocalypse. It was unheard of. *A loose girth,* Jordan thought, disturbed. *No player worth his salt would ever mount without checking out his tack first.*

Not even Lance.

"But you said—" Sloane began.

"I know what I said," Jordan responded, annoyed, as he threw his clothes into a suitcase. "Hillyer wouldn't take no for an answer."

"I hope this isn't going to become a habit."

"Something's not right," he said, troubled. He hadn't even heard what she'd just said. "I just can't put my finger on it."

She looked mildly confused. "What are you talking about?"

"He would have never mounted without first checking his tack."

Sloane looked dubious. "You said yourself Lance has had a lot of problems lately."

Jordan slammed the suitcase shut. "He's not that far gone. Not yet."

Something definitely was not right.

↺ New York City, December 1986

"I've always loved Christmas in New York," Sloane confessed as she and Jordan walked down Fifth Avenue. They were both loaded down with brightly wrapped packages in assorted sizes. The stores were unbelievably crowded, even for Manhattan at Christmastime, and it was a cold, blustery day, but neither of them complained. They were enjoying themselves too much to be thwarted by the crowds or the unpleasant weather. "I love the decorations, the department store Santas— I even love the crowds, such as they are."

"I haven't spent a Christmas at home in three years," Jordan said, looking at her over the mound of packages in his arms. "I was in Palm Beach the past two years, and in '83 I was playing in Argentina and Chile. I missed being home. It's just not the same, especially in another country. Christmas at Moonstone's nothing at all like New York, but it was always a big deal to me . . . one of those rare times I could catch up with my folks and really unwind. For a week either side of Christmas, friends were in and out, and we always ended up in Boston on New Year's Eve."

"I spent my first New Year's Eve in New York in the middle of an unruly mob at Times Square," Sloane recalled as they crossed the busy intersection at Fifth Avenue and Fifty-first. "It was just something I had to do."

Jordan grinned. "Like the Empire State Building and the pretzels and the hansom cabs, right?"

"Exactly. After that, it was always the Plaza or the Waldorf or someplace like that, but the first time, it had to be Times

Square." She paused thoughtfully. "I've always wanted to do Times Square again."

"If that's a hint, forget it," Jordan told her. "I've heard all about Times Square on New Year's Eve, and there's no way on earth I'll go anywhere near it. Not even for you."

"Travis wants to go. I can't let him go alone," she maintained, struggling to prevent the smallest packages from falling from the top of the stack she was carrying.

Jordan came to a halt at the skating rink in Rockefeller Center. "For the record, I don't plan to try to tell you what to do—unless what you plan to do is dangerous, like what you're suggesting right now. There's no way you're going out among the riffraff, even if I have to lock you in the closet. If Travis wants to see New Year's Eve at Times Square, he can watch it on TV like sane people do."

Sloane put her packages down and paused to catch her breath. "Do you plan to be a wicked stepfather?" she asked in a mildly teasing tone. Her cheeks were flushed from the cold, and her hair was blowing in the wind from beneath her black fur hat.

"Nope. Just a sensible one." He watched the skaters below them for a long moment, his breath vaporizing in front of his face and his hair ruffled by the brisk wind. "Tell me, love, once we're married, how would you feel about spending Christmas at Moonstone and New Year's Eve here?" he wanted to know. He was still looking at the ice skaters, but his mind was on other things.

She took his packages from him, put them down beside hers, and kissed him. "I'll be happy anywhere—as long as we're together," she assured him.

He returned her kiss. "You sure?"

"Absitively posolutely."

"Just remember—you said it." He glanced at his watch. "Hungry?"

"Famished. When are you going to feed me?" she demanded.

"Right now—" He stopped short as he slid his hand into his back pocket, then looked up at Sloane, clearly embarrassed. "Maybe *you'd* better take *me* out to lunch," he suggested with a sheepish grin.

"Why? What's wrong?" she asked, concerned.

"It would appear someone's picked my pocket."

"At Moonstone, we always have a real tree," Jordan told Travis as they hung ornaments on the twelve-foot artificial Scotch pine in Sloane's living room. "We go out on the grounds and find one that looks good—always a nice big one—then we chop it down and take it home. We deck it out with every light, ornament, and garland we can put our hands on." The memories brought a smile to his lips.

"And end up with pine needles all over the floor." Across the room, Sloane, dressed in an emerald-green, crystal-pleated, two-piece lounger, removed an assortment of elaborate ornaments from a large box.

"That's half the fun—the pine needles and the smell of the real thing," Jordan insisted, shifting on the ladder to look at her. "You've got to loosen up, city slicker."

"You can have all the real trees you want, Phillips, as long as you're willing to clean up the mess," she told him, trying to make him believe she was serious but failing miserably.

He shot her a grin over his shoulder. "We'll see." He picked some silver tinsel off his heavy cranberry sweater.

"Just what do you mean by that?"

"You'll see," he promised.

"That's what I'm afraid of."

"What were your Christmases like in Chicago?" he asked casually as he climbed higher on the ladder.

She frowned, her mood changing abruptly. "Bleak," she said quietly. "No money, no job, and a newborn baby to worry about." *Among other things,* she was thinking.

"And before that? When you were a child?"

"Uneventful."

He paused on the ladder to untangle a string of multicolored lights. "How did you make ends meet?" he asked, genuinely interested.

"I was a Jackie-of-all-trades," she answered. "Mostly, I lived by my wits." Sloane took a broken ornament from the box, looked at it for a moment, then put it aside. For Sammy Douglas, living by her wits had been second nature. But that, she reminded herself, had been another lifetime.

A smile teased the corners of Jordan's mouth. "Sounds intriguing."

She shot him a look. "I didn't do *that*," she said, opening another box. "Get your mind out of the gutter, Phillips."

"Whatever you say, love." He winked at her. "That reminds me. Where's the mistletoe . . . ?"

Amid a sea of ribbon and torn wrapping paper, Travis enthusiastically examined each of his gifts. Sloane sat with Jordan on the couch, her head on his shoulder. "Just make sure you don't open anything that doesn't have your name on it," she warned the boy.

"When are you going to open yours?" Travis wanted to know, eyeing them both suspiciously.

"Right now," Jordan announced. He got up from the couch and took a huge package wrapped in silver foil paper and royal blue ribbon from under the tree and deposited it on Sloane's lap.

She looked up at him. "What is it?" she asked stupidly.

"There's only one way you're going to find out, sweetheart," he said in his best Bogart imitation.

"Sure. Why didn't I think of that?" She pulled at the paper furiously, leaving it in a heap at her feet in a matter of seconds. Lifting the lid of the huge box, she gasped with delight. Inside was the blue fox coat she'd admired that October afternoon on Fifth Avenue. She thought she was going to cry. "I don't know what to say—" she began, her voice cracking.

"Don't say anything. Just try it on."

"I don't think it would look too good over this outfit," she said, wrinkling her nose.

"No," he said with a sly grin, "but it would look great with just a teddy."

She shook her head. "Not here. Later." She looked at Travis, who hadn't appeared to have heard a word they'd said, then back at Jordan. "Now, open yours. The big one wrapped in red foil."

He found the package in question and dropped onto the couch beside her to open it. It was enormous. "What on earth is in here—a polo pony?" he asked as he picked at the carefully taped edges of the package.

"Not quite."

He pulled the paper loose and discarded it, then opened the box. Inside was another, smaller box, this time wrapped in green foil. "What the hell—" he began, baffled.

"Open it," she urged.

He did—and discovered yet another package, this one even smaller and wrapped in gold foil. By the time he'd opened five boxes, each one just slightly smaller than the one before it, he was completely perplexed and could have cheerfully strangled her. "Would you mind telling me just where all of this is leading?" he asked, frustrated.

"You'll see," she promised.

"After I open how many boxes?"

"Two more. Scout's honor."

The last box was extremely small and wrapped in royal blue paper. He held it up and shook it gently. "There's nothing in here, right?" He grinned. "This is the oldest gag in the book, you know."

She tapped the box with her index finger. "Open it and find out," she pressed him.

"Sure. I'll humor you." He opened it slowly, certain she was more excited than he was. The contents of that box took him completely by surprise. Nestled in a bed of dark blue velvet was a gold medallion on a heavy chain. Engraved on the medallion was the Moonstone logo, a Pegasus in flight with crossed polo mallets behind it.

"I gave the jeweler photos of the logo on the door of your Jeep," Sloane explained.

"It's perfect," he said, staring at it thoughtfully. He couldn't remember when anyone had ever given him such a personal gift.

"Let me put it on you." She took it from him and slipped her hands up around his neck to fasten the clasp. Their eyes met momentarily, then their lips met in a slow, lingering kiss.

"There's no mistletoe," she whispered between kisses.

"That's okay," he told her. "I can fake it if you can."

"How do you want it done?"

Two men sat in the shadows of a small, dingy tavern outside Fort Lauderdale, a place chosen for their clandestine meeting because they knew it was a place where neither of them would be recognized. Two beers sat in front of them on the small, scratched wooden table, warm and untouched. Neither of them was interested in drinking. They both had more important business on their minds.

"I don't give a damn how it's done. I just want it done. The end justifies the means."

"Yeah. Right."

"The method will be your choice."

"Whatever works, right?"

The other man nodded. "Whatever works. That's the bottom line."

♻ Los Angeles, December 1986

The Beverly Hills Hotel, a pink stucco fortress with satellite bungalows, sprawls over twelve acres of some of the world's highest-priced real estate in the heart of Beverly Hills, and beckons to those whose dreams have yet to be fulfilled. Though by no means the largest luxury hotel in town—nor the poshest—it is a legend in its own time with a loyal following who swear it's the only place to stay. Everyone knows who's been there, who will be there, and who's doing what with whom while there. More deals, of all types, have been concluded there than anywhere else on earth, and more celebrities and would-be celebrities have chosen it as the place to be seen.

Travis would have enjoyed it, Sloane thought sadly. She made a mental note to bring him sometime when he wasn't in school, recalling how resentful he'd been at being left with Emma.

"I made the reservation for a bungalow," Jordan told Sloane as they drove past the tacky neon sign bearing the hotel's name and headed up the long, sweeping driveway lined with thousand-foot palm trees on either side. "I figured we'd have more privacy."

Sloane, admiring the beautiful sapphire solitaire engagement ring on her left hand, only smiled. She knew exactly what he had in mind because she was thinking the same thing.

As Jordan brought the rental car to a stop near the main entrance, the doors were opened immediately for them by a hotel employee, who turned the car over to one of the valet parking attendants, and then escorted them across the red carpet extending from the driveway to the lobby entrance.

"They do tend to go overboard," Jordan muttered under his breath, mildly annoyed at all the fuss.

Sloane smiled patiently, giving his hand a little squeeze. "I believe they call it pampering the guests."

He made a wry face, tugging irritably at his tie. "I can only hope they don't have someone stationed in the johns to hand out the paper."

Once checked in, they were escorted to Bungalow Five by smiling, joking bellhops, two of a staff of sixteen. Sloane tried to hide her amusement as Jordan tipped each of them and rushed them on their way. "Not anxious to get rid of them, are you?" she asked as he locked the door.

"A little pampering goes a long way as far as I'm concerned," he said, heading for the bar. He pulled off his tie and slipped out of his gray tweed jacket, dropping both on a nearby chair.

"The people who usually stay here expect such treatment," she reminded him. "They not only expect it, they demand it." She took off her wide-brimmed gray hat and placed it on a table near the door. "This bungalow, for example—it's seen royalty come and go. Queen Juliana, the Shah of Iran, Princess Grace—the hotel spends as much as $750,000 every year redecorating to suit a particular guest. For Queen Juliana, for example, the gardeners put in a tulip patch. Room service delivered specially prepared filet mignons—rare—to the Duke and Duchess of Windsor for their pugs. Howard Hughes took four bungalows every time he stayed; he had an electronic communications center hidden under one of them. A chef and switchboard operator were on call, just for him. Did you know he actually paid the gardeners to cut the grass in the middle of the night because he slept all day and worked all night?"

"No. I didn't know that." He studied her for a long moment, as if trying to determine what was going on inside her head. He'd been born into wealth, yet this was more her world than his, and she had an almost childlike fascination with it. "You love all of this, don't you."

"What?"

"The perks and privileges granted to powerful people," he said with an expansive gesture. "A tulip bed for a visiting Dutch queen, filet mignon for a duke's dogs, an oddball billionaire's unreasonable demands—that kind of star treatment appeals to you, doesn't it?''

She took off the white jacket she wore over a simple gray dress. ''You picked this hotel,'' she pointed out.

He nodded. ''Yes, I did, but that doesn't answer my question, love,'' he said, swirling a small amount of brandy in a snifter as he crossed the room to her.

Sloane hesitated momentarily. ''Yes,'' she said finally, ''it does fascinate me. Famous, powerful people, royalty, they all appeal to me—they have ever since I was a little girl. They were the far-off, the unattainable. I've spent my entire life wanting to be one of them, to live the way they do . . . I suppose that's why I write about people who do. I live the fantasy through them.''

''You've accomplished a great deal for yourself,'' he said, putting down his glass. He placed his hands on her shoulders and met her eyes with his own. ''You are a star in your own right, Sloane. People recognize you even when you aren't signing books in a bookstore. You get star treatment wherever you go.''

''Most of the time,'' she conceded. ''Still, there are times . . . times I feel like I'm still on the outside looking in.'' She ran her hands up his arms slowly as she spoke in a low, somewhat uncertain tone. ''Even now . . . I'm not really one of them. Not yet. Not in my own mind. I wasn't born into it, Jordy. I've had to fight for it, to work myself to death for every bit of recognition I've had. I've had to give up a lot and make more compromises than I care to remember, and, dammit, no matter what I've accomplished, there's a part of me that never stops wanting.''

''I was born into it,'' he began, kissing her forehead, ''and I did have things pretty much handed to me, but it didn't really make things easy. Why do you think I'm here right now, playing for Hillyer? I don't even like the man—and I don't need his money. What I need from him is something money can't buy.''

''And what's that?'' Sloane asked, returning his kiss.

He'd started to say ''my own self-worth,'' but the intimacy of the physical contact between them shot his concentration to hell. ''Right now,'' he said huskily, ''I need you.''

• • •

The four-thousand-seat Equidome of the Los Angeles Equestrian Center in Griffith Park was filled to capacity with enthusiastic polo fans cheering and shouting in response to the action taking place on the indoor field. From her midfield front-row seat, Sloane had what had to be the best view in the place. Out on the field, Jordan's pony broke from a muddle, shooting ahead of everyone but the opposition's number one, who slugged the yellow ball up the field. Jordan urged his mount into a gallop, racing after the ball with the opponent quickly closing in on him from the near side. The decibel level in the Equidome immediately rose to a loud roar. The ball had come to a stop about twenty-five yards from the goal, right of center. It worked to Jordan's advantage. The opposing number three was trying to connect and ride him off the line. Jordan veered to the right just enough to stay clear of the attempted interference and executed a neck shot that banged into the goal like a bullet. The bell sounded the end of the chukker—and the match. As the crowd went wild with applause, Sloane could barely hear the announcer's voice calling the final score over the loudspeakers. Jordan's team had won with a score of 15–11.

"Hard to believe this place almost went under a few years back, isn't it?" Jordan stated more than asked as he and Sloane walked back to the stables afterward.

She looked at him, surprised. "Went under?" It was indeed hard to believe after seeing the turnout for the match.

Jordan nodded. "Back in '83, when it was more equestrian center than polo center, the L.A. Lancers and the National Polo League were the product of a joint venture of Walton's Polo and Equestrian Centers of America. Things were great—for a while. Then the partnership went down the tubes and the center filed for bankruptcy."

"Then how did all of this come about?" Sloane asked with a wave of her hand.

"A Chapter Eleven reorganization," he explained, handing over his mount to a groom as they entered one of the show barns. "A new group of investors put up a million and a half in working capital, and the bank holding the lien made a loan for the same amount. They did a lot of construction—banquet room, tack shop, more stall space—added an instruction program, and went from primarily celebrity polo to serious professional matches.''

''Impressive,'' Sloane commented, running one hand down the railing outside one of the stalls.

''Damned impressive,'' he said, swinging around to face her. He leaned back against the wall and crossed his arms over his chest. ''One of these days, when I'm too old to play myself—when I'm too blind to even see the ball, let alone hit it, and too arthritic to climb into the saddle—I'd like to spend my twilight years running an operation like this.''

Sloane laughed. ''Planning to retire anytime soon?''

''It's something to think about,'' he said, his tone as serious as the expression on his face. ''Something to plan ahead for. It's not something I could do on the spur of the moment.''

She put her arms around his neck. ''Not 'I'— 'we,' '' she corrected. ''Something *we* can do.''

Dinner that evening was at the Center's Polo and Riding Club, and Sloane found it to be an experience unlike any other. The Equidome parking lot had been transformed into an enormous dance floor populated with polo followers dressed to kill and exhausted players with their saddle-strained posteriors. Jordan introduced Sloane to his friends as his fiancée with the explanation that they would be ''tying the knot very soon.'' They were invariably surprised by his announcement, and Sloane wondered if it was because he was getting married— or because she was the woman he had chosen to marry.

''Thanks for consulting me,'' she said with mock anger in her voice when they finally managed a moment alone.

He raised an eyebrow questioningly. ''Are you telling me you don't want to marry me right away?''

''What's the rush? We have plenty of time.''

''Jordy!''

The female voice that interrupted their exchange just short of a declaration of war belonged to a young woman picking her way through the crowd, waving to him as she approached. She was tall and slim, wearing a simple green wraparound dress and little jewelry. As she came closer, Sloane saw that she was quite attractive, with strong but decidedly feminine features framed by thick, coffee-brown hair that hung loosely around her shoulders. She grasped Jordan's arm affectionately as soon as she was close enough to do so. "You're one hard man to track down, Jordy Phillips," she scolded him. It was clear to Sloane that the pair were friends of long standing—or were they more than just friends? she wondered.

"Oh, come on!" Jordan scoffed. "You always know where to find me."

He looked at Sloane, who'd been observing the exchange with disapproval, ready to dislike the other woman on principle. "Dusty, this is Sloane Driscoll—soon to be Mrs. Jordan Phillips," he introduced her. "Sloane, my surrogate sister, Dusty Welles. Her real name is Kirsten, but nobody ever calls her that anymore. We call her Dusty because we spend so much time eating her dust."

Sloane couldn't hide her surprise as she shook Dusty's hand. The younger woman certainly didn't *look* like a polo player. She'd pictured a huge amazon of a woman who could compete with the men on their own level physically. "I've heard a great deal about you," she said.

Dusty glanced at Jordan suspiciously. "If you believe everything he tells you, you probably have a preconceived image of me as a juvenile, spoiled brat," she said with a twinge of amusement in her voice and an obvious deep affection for Jordan in her eyes. Sloane wasn't at all sure she liked that in spite of his introduction of Dusty as his "surrogate sister."

Jordan held up his hands in protest. "I haven't said a word!"

"I'll bet you haven't!" Dusty turned back to Sloane again, her face serious now. "You're actually going to marry this idiot? Do you have any idea what you're getting into?"

Sloane laughed, going along with the joke. "I'm beginning to."

"The stories I could tell you!" Dusty declared with a wink.

Jordan cut her off. "You just forget about those stories. I'm having enough trouble getting this woman to the altar," he complained, downing the remainder of his drink.

"Speaking of trouble," Dusty started, nodding toward the crowd on the makeshift dance floor, "here comes a friend of yours."

Jordan frowned. "Damn!" he muttered. "Just what I don't need."

Sloane's eyes followed his gaze. The man coming toward them looked Latin. He was tall, with a lean yet muscular build. His hair was dark, almost black, and his olive complexion deeply tanned. Dressed casually in a white cotton polo shirt and tan trousers, he moved through the crowd with a seemingly natural self-confidence as if he knew the eyes of half the women there were on him. "Who is he?" she asked, Jordan's reaction to his appearance leaving her more than a little curious.

"Antonio Alvarez," Jordan said grimly. "The Argentine asshole himself."

"A polo player," Sloane concluded, convinced she was the only one present who didn't recognize him immediately.

"He's good—trouble is, he knows it," Dusty commented.

"An ego problem?"

"He went to the Muammar Qaddafi School of Charm," Jordan told her. "He's got the ego that ate Palm Beach."

Sloane finished her drink. "I take it he's not one of your favorite people."

"You take it right," Jordan responded. "He's been a god-damned thorn in my side ever since I went pro. Last year I played against him eight times—and that son of a bitch beat me every time."

Sloane looked at him but said nothing. What she saw in his face was all too familiar: the pain of wanting the unattainable, of wanting something so badly it hurt.

Of wanting something and not being able to do anything about it.

The four thousand seats in the Equidome that had been filled with enthusiastic fans the previous afternoon were, for the most part, empty now. The large, cavernous building was dark except for the huge lights directly over the playing field. The ball shot across the arena with lightning speed, all six horses and riders charging after it. The sound of a mallet striking the ball seemed to echo through the entire building. One of the players shouted angrily at an opponent, his verbal assault peppered with profanity. The ball shot free of the muddle of horses and riders, rocketing toward the opposite end of the indoor field. Jordan, riding a bloodred bay that stood out among the other horses, broke away from the pack. Another player followed close behind, approaching on Jordan's off side, swearing loudly in Spanish. With a powerful nearside foreshot, Jordan sent the ball smashing into the goal.

From the stands, Sloane and Dusty, among the few spectators present during the practice session, watched the action with interest. "It's amazing how intelligent, well-bred men turn into sewer-mouthed barbarians the minute they have a polo mallet in their hands," Sloane observed wryly.

"They can't help themselves," Dusty told her, amused. "It's like an addiction—once you're hooked, there's no way out."

"Is it always like that?" Sloane asked, her eyes still on the field. She flinched inwardly when Jordan nearly collided with Alvarez in what appeared to be a showdown of sorts.

"Almost always," Dusty said with a nod. "My father was bitten by the bug long before I was born. He wanted children— three sons—so he could have his own family team. He got me instead, so he had to make do. I was the son he never had— me and Jordy."

"Then he wanted you to play." It was more a statement than a question.

Dusty nodded. "Eventually. After I proved I could handle a horse as well as any of the boys—including Jordy." Their conversation was interrupted by the loud, angry shouts of the players out on the field as Jordan successfully blocked his opponent's attempt at goal. "All right!" Dusty shouted enthusiastically, turning to Sloane again. "Dad says he should already have been awarded the ten."

"Ten what?" It didn't register in Sloane's mind.

"The ten-goal rating," Dusty clarified. "The best there is."

"Oh," Sloane said stupidly. "I guess I've got a lot to learn to be a player's wife."

A lot, she thought, wondering if she ever could be the kind of wife Jordan needed.

"Your game's a little off these days," Nadine Hillyer told Lance as he dismounted outside the arena. She'd gone to a great deal of trouble to choose just the right attire—a rose silk dress and matching hat—to make her look seductive but stylish. Lance didn't seem to notice at all. "I wonder—is the problem professional or personal?"

"Neither," Lance responded tightly, tempted for a moment to walk away. He wasn't in the mood to be interrogated by the boss's wife—or whatever the hell she'd come there for.

"Funny—I always thought you were a better player than that," she remarked as she came closer. "Lately, though—"

"Did your husband send you here to check up on me?" he demanded angrily. Even as he spoke the words, he silently wished he hadn't.

"Gavin doesn't know I'm here." Her right hand stroked his upper arm gently. He seemed oblivious of the overtures she was making. "It was entirely my own idea, I assure you."

He looked at her suspiciously. "Why?"

"Why not?" She smiled. "Don't you think I'm interested in polo?"

"Not really," he said frankly, turning back to the horse.

"Well, you're wrong." She continued to caress his arm, but if he was aware of it, he gave no indication. "I'm very interested."

"Look, Mrs. Hillyer—" he started, his patience wearing thin.

"Nadine," she corrected.

"Nadine," he repeated, his attention still focused on his pony, "I appreciate your concern, okay? But I'm fine. Really. I just had an off day, that's all."

"If you say so." She withdrew her hand, reluctantly dropping it to her side. "My husband hates to lose, Lance. I would genuinely hate to see him drop you from the team." Her voice was soft and low, but the message it carried was all too clear.

Lance frowned. "Thanks for the vote of confidence," he said sarcastically. He removed the horse's bridle.

"Forewarned is forearmed," she said. "I only want to help—if you'll let me."

He didn't look at her. "Thanks, but I don't need any help."

"Fine," she said, finally giving up. "The offer stands if you change your mind." She turned on her heel and walked away.

Lance still didn't turn around. He listened to the sound of her retreating footsteps, then drew in a deep breath and drove his fist into his saddle, frustrated. "Damn!" he muttered irritably. The last thing he needed right now was to antagonize the man who sponsored him. He didn't need to add to his own problems, especially now. Hillyer had already been on his case about his lousy performance. He'd sworn there would be immediate improvement—but could he deliver? He had tried—dammit, he had really tried—but ever since Paula filed for divorce, nothing had gone right for him. It was as if she'd taken what luck he'd had as part of the divorce settlement. Damn her—didn't she know how much he'd loved her, how much he still loved her? Didn't that count for anything?

This was his father's fault, as everything else that was wrong in his life had been his father's fault. The old man had been dead almost ten years now, but he continued to control Lance's life from beyond the grave. Lance had always enjoyed polo, but he'd never wanted to go pro. His father had wanted that for him. His father had wanted to fulfill his own dreams through his only son. Things might have been different, though, had the old man lived. He would have been able to walk away, to live his own life and let his father do the same. But fate had chosen to intervene and screw things up for both of them.

In his mind, Lance could still see it as clearly as if it had happened yesterday: his father playing that afternoon at Oak Brook, near Chicago . . . the players, eight men part of a long-standing rivalry, all braced for blood . . . the ball racing down his father's side of the field . . . he was in hot pursuit, mallet high, eyes low, charging his target . . . he bent from the saddle to attempt an offside neck shot, missing his mark . . . the mallet caught the pony's forelegs, bringing him down . . . Lance's father fell from the saddle as the horse came down hard on top of him. . . .

The old man had lasted three days after that, with the help of machines and medical science, but he'd been little more than a vegetable. Death had been a blessing. He could never have stood the humiliation of being an invalid, of having to depend upon others for even the simplest tasks like eating or going to the bathroom. But when he died, he left Lance with a burden: that of having to carry on for his father, of having to realize his father's dreams at the expense of his own.

Realizing his father's dream had cost Lance the only woman he'd ever loved. Paula had never been capable of being a polo player's wife. The constant travel, the endless hours fieldside, the nonstop polo talk had never appealed to her. She'd never been willing to sacrifice her own goals, as Lance had. She had a successful career in Paris as editor of a top fashion magazine, and she'd made it clear that she intended to put down roots in Paris whatever Lance decided to do with his life.

He reached into his pocket and pulled out the small vial he was never without these days. Removing the cap, he shook two red capsules into his palm and swallowed them quickly. He'd become so good at it that he didn't need water to wash them down. He was so wrapped up in his own thoughts that he didn't see Jordan, who stood several yards away, watching him.

The play was fast and intense. Since it was only a practice game, there weren't many spectators in the Equidome that afternoon. A few of the players' wives sat together in one section, doing more talking than watching. The other spectators were scattered throughout the stands, a few of them seated alone.

One man sat in the uppermost reaches of the stands, isolated from everyone else entirely by choice. He was wearing jeans and a black leather jacket, and the top half of his face was hidden by sunglasses so dark it would have been impossible to see his eyes, even at close range. He watched the action impassively, waiting for the right moment to make his move. When it came, he acted without hesitation. Taking a specially modified rifle with the best scope available attached to it from a garment bag he'd brought with him, he made sure no one down below could see him, even if someone happened to look his way. When he was convinced he was hidden in the shadows sufficiently to protect himself, he positioned the rifle, took careful aim, and fired only once. That was all that was necessary. He was a crack shot, good enough to hit his target from that range on the first try. No one took notice of the shot that had been fired. The echoes within the cavernous empty space of the Equidome made it sound more like a mallet connecting with the ball than a gunshot. In the next instant, one of the horses on the playing field below went down, its rider just managing to roll clear of it before the animal hit the ground.

The play came to an abrupt halt. The few people sitting in

the stands were on their feet now, moving closer to the rails in an attempt to get a closer look. The players had all dismounted and were clustered around the disabled horse and rider.

The man in the black leather jacket raised his dark glasses just long enough to take in the scene before collecting his equipment for a quick and unobtrusive departure.

Quick and clean, he congratulated himself mentally. *Don't take unnecessary chances and don't let anybody get a good look at your face.*

Those were the most important rules of the game.

Jordan brought the car to a jerky stop in front of the Beverly Hills Hotel. As he pushed the door open and got out, an attendant appeared to take his keys. He said nothing, crossing the red carpet to the entrance in long, quick strides. He nodded absently to the uniformed doorman, Smitty. He did not speak. His mind was on Lance, on what he'd seen at the Equestrian Center. He wasn't sure what disturbed him more—the suspicion that Lance was doing drugs or seeing the way Nadine Hillyer had been coming on to him. Jordan had heard all the stories about Mrs. Hillyer's sexual escapades, but until now that's all they'd been—stories.

Surely Lance wasn't involved with Hillyer's wife, of all people. He had to know he'd be playing with fire. He had to know what Hillyer would do to him if he ever found out. Trouble was, Lance was vulnerable. His wife had just left him, and he'd spent most of his time since licking his wounds. The pain of the divorce, compounded by Lance's growing love-hate affair with polo, would make him susceptible to the attentions of a woman like Nadine Hillyer. In the end, though, it could do irrevocable damage to his career.

Jordan was halfway to Bungalow Five when he remembered that Sloane would be waiting for him in the Polo Lounge.

"There's been an accident at the Equidome," Ian told Jordan over the phone. "Eric's pony had to be put down."

"Why? What happened?"

"Nobody knows for sure. The pony went down during the fourth chukker—for apparently no reason. Wasn't hit in any way," Ian said. "The vet was there right away, but there was nothing he could do. Said it was the damnedest thing he'd ever seen."

"In what way?"

"The bone wasn't just broken, it was shattered," Ian answered grimly. "Reminded me of that filly, Ruffian." Ruffian had been a promising thoroughbred before her fall during a highly publicized race some years back. "The fracture was so bad it broke the flesh—there was blood everywhere."

"And nobody knows why?"

"No apparent cause," Ian confirmed. "No injury, nothing."
He's right, Jordan thought. *It doesn't make sense.*

"It's done."

"Are you sure no one will detect your involvement?"

"Come off it, man. I ain't stupid. Nobody'll ever suspect a thing."

"You just make damned sure no one ever traces any of this back to *me*."

In Bungalow Two, Nadine Hillyer relaxed in a hot, fragrant bath scented with jasmine. Her husband had left over an hour ago for another of his dreary business meetings. Lately it seemed he had more meetings than usual and more of them were taking place at night. Normally, Nadine was unable to face a long evening of making small talk with the wife of one of Gavin's business associates and would beg off with one of her dreadful headaches, but lately Gavin had stopped asking her to accompany him. She didn't question him about it because she was grateful to be left alone with an evening to do as she wished.

Stepping out of the tub, she pulled a thick towel from the rack and dried herself carefully. She paused, catching sight of herself in the full-length mirror. Dropping the towel, she straightened up, checking her naked body from every angle. She was pleased with what she saw: large breasts helped by silicone implants, still high and firm; a small waist made possible by regular trips to the Golden Door and daily exercise; slim hips and a flat stomach, the result of liposuction and a recent tummy tuck. She hadn't had to do anything about her legs: they'd always been long and shapely.

She let her hands glide slowly over her breasts. Her nipples hardened at her touch, and Nadine gave a little gasp of delight. It had been a long time since they'd felt a man's touch, a man's lips. Too long. Gavin hadn't touched her in weeks—he'd had too much on his mind, he claimed—and it had been months since she'd parted company with the handsome young golf pro who'd taken care of her needs during their stay in Florida. He'd been a wonderful lover, and she missed him—missed the pleasure he'd given her—terribly.

Nadine loved Gavin in her own way, but oddly enough she didn't feel guilty about her extramarital affairs. She'd never dream of leaving Gavin for any of them. As far as she was concerned, it was no different than a visit to her hairdresser or her plastic surgeon. It was a service. They serviced her in bed. They took care of her needs her husband didn't have time to be bothered with.

Her thoughts turned to Lance Whitney. His wife had recently left him. There was no other woman in his life at the moment, she was sure of that. He no longer participated in the polo postmatch social scene. He spent his evenings alone in his room—he hadn't even bothered to reserve a bungalow or even a suite this time—and he seldom ventured out of that room when he wasn't practicing or playing. *Such a waste,* Nadine thought. He was a beautiful man—young, strong, and handsome. The kind of man she preferred in her bed. And he needed a woman now as much as she needed a man.

What a perfect arrangement, Nadine reasoned.

Lance was alone in his room, just as Nadine had assumed he would be. He was sprawled out on the bed, shirtless, his heart pounding and his mind racing, unable to even think straight. The amphetamines sure as hell kept him charged up; if it weren't for the barbiturates, he'd probably never sleep.

As he rolled over on one side to retrieve the bottle of Nembutal from the drawer in the nightstand, he was halted by the sight of his wife's—soon to be ex-wife's—beautiful, smiling face. Why did he still keep Paula's photograph by his bedside? he wondered now. *I must be a masochist. I must enjoy torturing myself,* he concluded.

He'd just opened the drawer when he heard someone knocking at the door. He quickly slammed it shut again and scrambled to his feet. Raking a hand through his mussed hair, he crossed the room and opened the door. Nadine Hillyer, impeccably dressed as always in a rose-colored silk blouse and gray wool skirt, stood in the hallway smiling. He looked at her dumbly, wondering why she seemed to be following him. "Oh—hello, Mrs. Hillyer," he finally managed, rubbing his chin thoughtfully. *Her again,* he was thinking. *Just what I need right now.*

"Nadine," she insisted. "Have I come at a bad time?"

There's never going to be a good time, he thought. "No," he lied. "No, it's not a bad time."

"May I come in, then?"

He stared at her for a moment, then nodded. "Sure." He pushed the door back, stepping aside so she could enter.

She came to a halt in the center of the room and looked around. "You really should have taken a suite, you know," she said, her disapproval of his accommodations clear in her voice.

He shook his head. "I don't need that much space," he said as he closed the door. "Let me guess why you're here, Mrs. Hillyer—"

"Nadine," she said again, determined to break through that wall of formality.

Lance nodded. "Nadine," he said quietly as he crossed the room to her. "Let me guess why you're here. You told your husband about our conversation this afternoon—"

She put her small clutch bag on the bureau and turned to face him again. "My husband knows nothing of our conversation."

"Then why are you here?" he asked sharply.

She studied him for a moment. "Has anyone ever told you that you have one huge chip on your shoulder?" she said, mildly annoyed.

"Touché." He dropped down onto the edge of the bed. "It's been one of those years."

She leaned back against the dresser, supporting her weight on her hands, and looked at him speculatively. "I heard about your wife," she said finally. "I'm sorry."

He waved his hand dismissively. "Win a few, lose a few,"

he said with forced indifference in his voice.

"I think you could use a friend," she said softly, letting him know she'd seen through his facade. "I'd like to be that friend—if you'll let me."

He looked at her suspiciously. "Why?" he asked. "Why would you care?"

She smiled. "I could say I'm doing it for my husband," she said carefully. "I could say I'm concerned about your performance—about how it will affect the team."

"You could," Lance said with a nod, "but that's not the real reason, is it."

Nadine shook her head. "I know what you're going through," she said, her eyes meeting his. "I've been lonely too. My husband loves me, about as much as he's capable of loving, but he's a busy man. Over the years the more successful Gavin's become, the less time he's had for me, for our marriage." She knelt down in front of him and unzipped his pants. If he were surprised, he gave no indication of it. He made no move to stop her when she took his limp organ in her hand and stroked it. "You must be very big when you're hard," she said softly.

He said nothing but reached out and unbuttoned her silk blouse. As he unhooked her lacy bra, her breasts spilled out, the large, dark nipples still soft. He cupped them in his hands and squeezed them. "You're pretty big yourself," he said hoarsely.

He knew this was insane. To bed Hillyer's wife was professional suicide . . . but he couldn't have stopped himself now if he'd wanted to. From the minute he let her into his room, he hadn't stood a chance. She'd come to get laid, and he had no intention of disappointing her. Jesus, what she was doing to him with her hands. . . .

"You *are* big," Nadine whispered, lowering her head to kiss it. She fondled his testicles as she nuzzled him, licking the tip as if it were a melting popsicle. When she finally took it into her mouth, he thought he was going to explode. She sensed it and released him abruptly, but he grabbed her and held her there.

"Don't stop!" he groaned, forcing her to her knees again.

"You're ready to come," she whispered, rising to her feet

slowly. "I don't intend to let you—not until we're both ready." She placed one hand on the back of his head and guided him to her breast. He nuzzled the velvety nipple for a moment, then started licking it. Nadine shivered with pleasure as he began to suck at it lustily. She held him there, refusing to let him stop as he tugged at the waistband of her skirt. Finally releasing the zipper, he pushed it down over her slim hips and thrust his hand into her sheer panties, rubbing her roughly as he continued to suck at her breast. She let go of him long enough to push the panties down, certain in his impatience he was going to rip them. "Careful, darling," she said with a throaty laugh. "It might prove embarrassing if I have to explain to my husband how my clothing came to be ripped." Lance turned his attention to her other breast as she stepped out of the panties that slid to her ankles easily once she'd gotten them over her hips.

He pulled her down onto the bed with him, kissing her roughly as he kicked off his pants. He tried to mount her, but she stopped him. "Not yet," she said firmly, rolling him over on his back. She straddled his head, rocking her hips so that his tongue could only lap at her intermittently as she moved over him. Finally, frustrated, he grabbed her buttocks and held her firmly as he attacked her with his lips and tongue, licking her until she began to writhe and moan, trying in vain to pull away. As she reached an explosive orgasm, he pulled her down, plunging himself into her, impaling her on his shaft as he exploded within her. She fell off him, more thoroughly satisfied than she had been in many months.

As they struggled to catch their breath, she snuggled against him, stroking his chest. "I have a feeling," she began in a low, soft voice, "that you and I are going to be *very* good friends."

They met in a noisy, dimly lit cocktail lounge in North Hollywood, a sleazy nightspot frequented by overly made up hookers and young men in long hair and black leather. No one seemed to notice that they looked almost comically out of place in those surroundings, least of all the two of them.

"Can it be done?"

"Sure—it *can*. Ain't too much I can't pull off—but it won't be cheap."

"How much?"

A pause. "I'll have to let you know."

"When? How soon?"

"You'll know as soon as I do."

"And no one will detect your hand—or mine?"

The other man grinned. "That's one of the rules of the game, pal."

♻ Palm Beach, February 1987

"I've been to Florida seven times in the past eight years and never once had a chance to really enjoy it," Sloane commented as a guard waved them through the gates of the Palm Beach Polo and Country Club. "It's always been the same old song and dance—straight from the airport to the hotel, on to a bookstore to sign some books, maybe do an interview or two, then off to the next whistle stop."

"I come to play polo," Jordan said simply, keeping his eyes on the road as he followed a black Mercedes up the drive and brought the car to a stop in the semicircular driveway. "I can't say I've ever seen much of Palm Beach beyond the polo club."

A valet opened the car doors for them. Sloane got out of the car, smoothing the front of her raspberry basketweave linen dress as Jordan came around to join her. She took in her surroundings as he steered her toward the entrance. Everything spelled stylish elegance. This was Jordan's world, the world into which he had been born. The world in which she still sometimes felt like an interloper, she thought as he led her through the entrance foyer. Though Sloane Driscoll, the bestselling novelist, had grown accustomed to such elegance, Sammy Douglas, the streetwise hustler from Chicago, took it all in with the eye of someone on the outside looking in. The part of her that was Sammy still saw this world from the outsider's view, and Sammy had never belonged in this world.

"Phillips." Jordan gave his name to the maître d' who checked all bookings at a lectern near the door. "We're with the Hillyer party."

The man brightened with recognition. "Ah, yes—Mr. and

Mrs. Hillyer are already here," he said. "This way, please."

They were escorted to a large table near the windows where Gavin and Nadine Hillyer sat with Ian and Dusty Welles. Hillyer and Ian got to their feet as Jordan and Sloane approached the table. Sloane acknowledged each of them politely while Jordan held a chair for her, but it was Hillyer's wife who immediately caught Sloane's attention—cool, polished Nadine, in her peacock-blue tiered wool crepe Valentino with a large black hat. The woman was looking at her intently, and it made Sloane slightly uncomfortable. She could almost feel Nadine Hillyer's animosity reaching across the table, clawing at her like a vicious animal. Why? she asked herself. What could this woman possibly have against her? Not that she cared whether Nadine liked her or not, but she was more than a little curious since they didn't even know each other.

"Good to see you again, Sloane." Dusty's words cut through her thoughts. "I called your condo last night, and you hadn't arrived yet. We weren't sure you were going to make it."

"Neither were we," Sloane admitted with a forced smile. "We had to stop over in New York. I had to tape an interview for *Good Morning America*, and it took longer than we expected." Jordan had been cross and impatient during that two-day delay. Sitting in the Green Room while she was being interviewed had definitely not been his idea of fun.

A waiter bringing their drinks—the Spanish Codorníu Jordan preferred—interrupted their conversation momentarily. Sloane, never having tried it before, sampled hers cautiously.

"Get used to it," Dusty advised.

Sloane gave her a quizzical look, not sure what she was talking about.

"Jordan's impatience," Dusty clarified. "That's just his way. He doesn't like to wait for anything."

Sloane smiled wearily. "I'm finding that out the hard way," she admitted. She glanced across the table at Nadine Hillyer, who said nothing as she concentrated on her drink. "Do you come here often, Mrs. Hillyer?" she asked pleasantly, attempting to draw the woman into their conversation.

Nadine didn't smile. "Quite often when we're in town."

"The food must be excellent."

"Passable," Nadine responded with an indifferent shrug.

Sloane struggled to suppress the anger that threatened to surge forth, knowing it would accomplish nothing to tell the woman exactly what she thought of her high-and-mighty attitude. She mentally reminded herself that it was Gavin Hillyer who paid Jordan that quarter of a million annually that was so damned important to him. In her own world, she knew her mind and spoke it, but she was not on her own turf, and she had to consider Jordan's position.

"She's an odd one," Sloane remarked to Dusty as they filled their plates from the sumptuous buffet spread out on the enormous, T-shaped table.

"Who?" Dusty reached for the gazpacho.

"Nadine Hillyer."

"Oh, her." Dusty smiled knowingly. "Pay no attention to her behavior. I suspect she's on the prowl again."

"On the prowl?"

Dusty nodded, lowering her voice to a conspiratorial whisper. "Nadine doesn't know you're alive unless you happen to be young, gorgeous, and male. Especially male."

"I'd heard rumors."

"About her bed-hopping? I think her husband's the only one who hasn't heard those rumors," Dusty said. "The word on the street is that she's snared herself a new young lover—someone almost young enough to be her son."

Sloane glanced over her shoulder toward the table where Nadine still sat with her husband. "She has a preference for younger men?"

"The younger the better, I hear."

"Interesting." It was also disturbing for Sloane.

Dusty quickly changed the subject as her father approached. "Try the cracked crab, Sloane," she recommended brightly. "It's delicious. The gazpacho isn't bad either . . . ."

"Alvarez seems a little flat," Gavin Hillyer observed as he and his wife watched the action from the Hillyers' box at the Palm Beach Polo and Country Club. His White Timbers team was playing Antonio Alvarez's Diablos Rojas powerhouse foursome, and the previously unbeaten Argentines were trailing his team at the half. Hillyer was openly pleased about the score. "He's played four matches in the past seven days. If he keeps that up, he'll burn out in no time.'' Alvarez's overzealousness was going to be White Timbers' gain.

Nadine smiled, a cool, glacial smile. ''You've had your eye on him too?'' She finished the last of her Pimm's Cup and signaled for a refill.

Hillyer never took his eyes off the polo field. ''I always have one eye on the competition,'' he said tightly as one of Alvarez's teammates converted a penalty attempt.

''I'm sure,'' Nadine said with a secret smile that her husband would not have understood had he even noticed it—which, of course, he hadn't. Smoothing her crepe marocain print dress over her knees primly, her gaze swept the field in search of Lance Whitney's blue-and-white number one jersey. She hadn't seen or spoken to him since their arrival in Palm Beach, and she was eager to make contact. As always, she knew she had to be careful. If Gavin ever found out about her extracurricular activities, he'd divorce her without a moment's hesitation. And she had no intention of giving up the prestige of being Mrs. Gavin Hillyer.

''Alvarez's boys were playing at a disadvantage,'' Jordan told Sloane as they crossed the field after the match, arms around each other. ''Their horses were just released from quarantine last week.''

Sloane laughed. ''Since when do you make excuses for winning?'' she asked, having a hard time keeping her hat on in the brisk, cold wind. She'd always thought of polo as a hot-weather sport and had been surprised to learn that matches were played not only on cool days like this one but on snow in places like St. Moritz.

''Who's making excuses?'' With his free hand, Jordan pulled off his helmet and carried it by its chin strap. ''I'm only saying it was an easy win. Had they had the opportunity to practice more, the competition would have been a lot tougher. I've played Alvarez before and lost to him more than I care to remember. He's a mean bastard—on the field and off.''

Sloane hesitated for a moment. ''Worse than Maxwell Kenyon?'' she asked finally.

Jordan's jaw tightened visibly. ''Max Kenyon is a bastard of another kind,'' he answered, an angry undercurrent in his voice.

"Why are you still so angry with him, Jordy?" she asked, not sure even as she spoke that she really wanted to know the answer.

"Why shouldn't I be?" he shot back at her irritably.

"He was your friend once. I remember Lance saying that in Deauville."

"Once," Jordan said flatly. "I don't need friends like Max Kenyon."

"Because of Jilly," Sloane concluded.

"I was involved with Jilly, and Max moved in on her. In my book that's not a friend," he said simply.

Sloane wouldn't let it go, even though she could tell that Jordan didn't want to discuss it. "If you don't still have feelings for Jilly, what difference does it make that she's married to Max?" she pressured him.

Jordan stopped walking. "Don't push it, Sloane." His eyes were cold, and his voice held a warning note. "What there was between Jilly and me was over a long time ago. It's not over with Max because Max won't let go. That's all there is to it, so don't go blowing it out of proportion."

End of discussion, Sloane thought unhappily. At least as far as Jordan was concerned it was. Sloane, however, couldn't shake the feeling that Jordan's anger at Max and his refusal to talk about it was an indication that the past—specifically, his past with Jilly—still mattered to him.

Gavin Hillyer was on the telephone with an associate in Houston when Nadine left their suite at the Breakers, Palm Beach's most luxurious hotel, and went to the Royal Poinciana where Lance was staying. Wearing a wide-brimmed black hat, dark glasses, and a full-length Blackglama mink coat so she would not be easily recognized, she crossed the lobby at a fast clip and ducked into an empty elevator. As the car began its slow ascent, she leaned back against the wall and drew in a deep breath. This, she was certain now, was going to be a very complicated affair. And risky. Certainly not as simple as bedding the Mexican gardener or the boy who came by regularly to clean the pool. It had always been so simple. She'd taken them to bed in her own home when Gavin wasn't around and was not expected to return soon. With Lance, that wasn't going to be possible. She saw him only when she and Gavin attended matches in which the White Timbers team played. She had to sneak around to meet him when her husband was otherwise occupied, always risking discovery, but for Nadine that risk made their affair all the more exciting.

She looked both ways down the long corridor as she disembarked from the elevator on his floor. Good . . . not a soul in sight. She found Lance's suite with no problem; he'd taken a suite only at her insistence and only because she was paying for it. She tapped impatiently on the door. Why didn't he answer? What was taking him so long? When Lance finally let her in, he was in his robe—and, Nadine was certain, wearing nothing underneath. "Where were you?" she demanded irritably.

"On the phone. You got a problem with that?" He closed the door as she crossed the room to the couch and removed her hat and dark glasses. "I wasn't expecting you."

"Obviously." The open pill bottle on the table caught her eye as she took off the mink coat. She knew he'd been doing drugs; fortunately for him, her husband didn't. Nadine idly wondered if he'd been using cocaine as well. She turned to face him. "I've missed you."

He gave her a lazy smile. "Have you, now?"

"Yes, I have." *He's higher than a kite,* she thought. Not that it really mattered to her. He could be in the Twilight Zone for all she cared as long as his body was in good working order. She started to unzip her dress. "Come over here and I'll show you how much . . ."

At a pub in Lantana, the regulars listened to the music of a Scottish pipe and drum band while two men seated alone near the door ignored the live entertainment. They were engaged in a serious conversation, their voices kept as low as possible, oblivious of their surroundings.

"This is the one."

The other man studied the photograph for a moment and smiled coldly. "One of those pretty-boy types, huh?"

He took the photo back and put it away. "That's about it."

"Seems a shame to mess up that pretty face, don't you think?" He waved off the waitress who had come to see if they wanted another drink.

"I couldn't care less. Only the end result matters."

"I guess. Got any special way you want it done?"

"I'll leave that up to you."

"Right. Only the end result matters."

"Just make sure—"

The other man raised a hand to silence him. "I know. Make sure it looks like an accident."

"Exactly." He stood up, tossing a few bills on the table to cover their drinks.

"When do I get my money?"

"I'll call you—after the job is done."

And he left, not once looking back.

So this is Palm Beach, Sloane thought as she entered the all-white, Spanish-style Esplanade complex on Worth Avenue. A town that liked things the way they were back in the 1930s and could afford to keep them that way. A haven for deposed royalty from all over the world. An exclusive, elite community in which the Duchess of Windsor had reigned socially but was refused a credit card at the Palm Beach Saks Fifth Avenue because of a legendary trail of unpaid bills she and her husband had left in the course of their travels. A small town with big bucks, where it takes no more than a phone call to have the police drive by your home hourly when you're out of town or in the middle of a messy divorce and concerned about being harassed.

Sammy Douglas would have loved this place, Sloane decided, amused.

She paused to glance at the slim gold watch on her left wrist, the diamond-studded Piaget Polo Jordan had given her as an engagement present. Sammy would have loved *that,* too, but it wouldn't have remained in her possession for more than forty-eight hours. It would have gone straight to the nearest pawnshop. Whatever else Sammy was, she was a hard-core realist. Back then, she would have needed the money more than she needed a watch. Sloane Driscoll, on the other hand, could easily have both—and more besides. *You've come a long way since the old days in Chicago,* she thought with satisfaction.

She was meeting a reporter for the *Palm Beach Daily News*— nicknamed the "Shiny Sheet" because of the slick paper it had been printed on for many years—at the Café l'Europe, and she was fifteen minutes early. Sloane had long ago made it a hard-and-fast rule never to be early for an interview. It made her appear too eager, and that was an impression she did not want to make. She strolled along at a leisurely pace, checking out some of the shops, something she hadn't had a chance to do until now. She'd prepared carefully for this interview as she always did, from arriving precisely on time to knowing what she would and would not discuss with the interviewer to the white linen suit and hat with striking black accents that projected a professional yet stylish image. It was all a part of the game, she reminded herself now. *The fine print in the contract: author must look the part at all times.*

The heels of her black patent leather pumps clicked on the terra-cotta tiles as she strode along, taking in the offerings in the shop windows. It was when she passed the Krizia shop that something caught her eye—a woman—a tall, redheaded woman dressed in royal purple. Sloane knew who it was without seeing her face. Jilly Kenyon. Sloane watched her intently, mentally bracing herself for battle. *I have to face the enemy sooner or later,* she thought. *It might as well be now.*

Jilly turned as Sloane entered, smiling like a cat who'd just gotten the neighbor's canary in her sights. Sloane found it secretly amusing that Jilly chose to make up her eyes in a way that made her look feline. It suited her perfectly. *That's Jilly,* Sloane thought, facing her now. *A common alley cat.*

"Why, hello, Ms. Driscoll," Jilly greeted her sweetly. "This is an unexpected surprise."

There's so much phony sugar in that voice, she should come with a warning from the surgeon general stamped on her ass, Sloane thought wryly. "Why is it a surprise, Mrs. Kenyon?" she said aloud, putting a special emphasis on the "Mrs. Kenyon."

"I didn't think you got away from Jordan long enough to do such mundane things as shopping." Jilly was still smiling, looking as if she'd devoured someone. "And please—do call me Jilly."

I know what I'd like to call you, but not in public. "Of course," she said, returning Jilly's smile with all the sincerity Jilly had given it. Outwardly, she ignored the remark Jilly had made about Jordan, but she still felt the sting. She did not invite Jilly to use her first name.

"I haven't had the opportunity to congratulate you on your engagement," Jilly was saying. "It came as quite a surprise."

Sloane raised an eyebrow; her smile was forced but convincing. "Why is that?" she asked evenly. She was sure Jilly had every intention of telling her even if she hadn't asked.

Jilly's gaze met hers head-on. "When we saw you together at Deauville, Jordan said you were only there to research a book."

"Things change," Sloane pointed out, determined not to be intimidated.

"Very quickly, I'd say. He certainly didn't act like a man about to be married when we were together in Buenos Aires." Though the words were innocent enough, Jilly made it quite clear what she meant by "together."

Sloane stiffened as if she'd been struck but tried hard not to let it show. "It happened very quickly."

"Obviously." Jilly was still smiling, knowing she'd hit her mark.

Sloane checked her watch, her mind racing for an excuse to leave as quickly as possible. "I really must run," she said, her tone deceptively calm. "I'm meeting a reporter at Café l'Europe—"

"Of course," Jilly agreed with a nod. "Do give my love to Jordan, won't you?"

Sloane stopped halfway to the door and turned to face Jilly again. "I'll be happy to, Jilly—but then I'm sure you'd much rather do it yourself." She walked out, not giving Jilly a chance to respond. It wasn't until she was well away from the Krizia shop that she let go and began to shake violently.

Had Jordan been with Jilly—in bed with her—in Argentina? It was all Sloane could think of as she sat through the interview. . . .

"The goddamned son of a bitch!"

Jordan dismounted at the picket line, handed his mount over to a groom, and stalked to the car angrily. Pulling off his helmet, he threw it aside. "It's the same fucking shit every time he's involved."

"Who?" Sloane had arrived late, having driven around for the past two hours trying to cool off after her confrontation with Jilly. She had missed most of the match in progress.

"Alvarez. He's subbing for Preston Wolcott on the Alamo Express team—as if having been up against that bastard once this week wasn't enough." He threw down his gloves and whip. "Where have you been?"

"I had an interview, remember?" She offered him a glass of water.

He wiped perspiration from his forehead with the back of his hand. "Yeah," he said irritably. "I thought you were going to be back in time for the match."

"I had a couple of things to take care of." Her thoughts were still on her chance meeting with Jilly. "I have to fly back to New York, Jordan. Tonight."

He slammed his glass down on the hood of the car with such force that it smashed. "New York?" He spat it out. "What the hell for this time?"

"I've got a manuscript to finalize—remember?"

"How long?" he asked, not bothering to hide his displeasure.

"What?"

"How long do you have to be up there?"

She shrugged. "I don't know," she said in a quiet, controlled voice. "Look, I'm not crazy about this either, but I do have a deadline—"

"Yeah." The coldness in his voice sent shivers coursing through her. Normally, she would have hated leaving him even for a day, but after what had happened that afternoon, all she could see when she looked at him was Jilly—and the two of them making love. She couldn't deal with that. She needed to get away, to think. "You planning to be here for the finals?" he asked.

"I hope so."

"I guess I can't expect more than that, can I?" he asked in an acid tone as a groom brought him a fresh horse. He mounted, then turned to Sloane again. He opened his mouth as if to say something, then changed his mind abruptly and rode off onto the polo field.

What do I do if Jilly was telling the truth? Sloane asked herself.

⇌ New York City, February 1987

Sloane and Cate were having lunch at the Sea Grill in Rockefeller Center. Normally, it was a restaurant Sloane preferred during the warmer months when the outdoor Summer Garden was open, but the interior decor *was* lovely, and she was quite partial to good seafood, particularly scallops.

Today, they were meeting to discuss an offer Cate had received for the television rights to *Fallen Idols*. The agent was also delivering the contracts on that book from Sloane's French publisher. And Cate was more than a little curious about her decision to fire Linc Marsden, and Sloane knew it.

"I should never have hired him in the first place," Sloane reflected as she reached for her fork. "He's good at his work— at least he's been good for some people. But I didn't need him. I know that now."

Cate only smiled. "It took you long enough to realize that."

Sloane looked at her, realizing for the first time that Cate had never approved of her decision to hire Linc. "Why didn't you ever say anything before?" she asked.

"You made it clear it was what you were going to do, no matter what," Cate reminded her. "There was no point in trying to talk you out of it, and I decided it couldn't hurt to have the man on your side, even if you discontinued the arrangement later on. He does, after all, have quite a stellar reputation."

"He's also an unmitigated ass," Sloane said, taking another drink. "I knew that right from the beginning, but, dammit, I wanted more than anything to be a name author. I wanted my books to sell on the strength of my name alone. I thought Linc

Marsden, for all his arrogance, could give me that.''

"You know how I feel about that,'' Cate said smoothly. "The product has to be there before anything else can happen, and in your case, the product was definitely there.''

"But I had to make the public aware of it. You know I'm a fighter.''

Cate smiled knowingly. "Jordan's not going to have an easy life with you,'' she observed.

"I have a feeling it's not going to be easy for either of us,'' Sloane said darkly.

Cate eyed her warily. She knew Sloane well enough to know that something was bothering her, and that her concerns were not connected to her books or to Linc Marsden. She suspected that it had to do with Jordan. Still, she didn't push. She knew Sloane would tell her if and when she was ready.

But knowing that didn't stop her from being concerned.

Sloane's thoughts were definitely not on television deals or foreign rights or even her confrontation with Linc Marsden when she returned to her apartment late that afternoon. She was thinking about Jordan. She wanted to talk to him. She needed to talk to him. She had to ask him about Jilly, about Argentina—even if she still wasn't sure she really wanted to know the answer.

She stared at the telephone on the table beside the couch for a long time. She picked it up twice but put it down again without dialing. The third time she dialed the number in Palm Beach but hung up before a connection was made. The fourth time she let the call go through, but there was no answer. He was probably out at the polo grounds. He'd be in later in the evening, but she wouldn't be able to call him then. That evening she had to put in an appearance at a party being given at the Rainbow Room by the publishers of *Top Sellers,* a popular book review publication. She wasn't looking forward to it, but felt an obligation to attend. It went with the territory. *Part of my job description,* Sloane thought wryly.

"Hi, Mom.''

The sound of Travis's voice interrupted her dismal specu-lation about the evening ahead. She looked up as he came into the living room and dropped the canvas backpack he carried to school on the first chair he passed. "Hi, sport," she greeted him with a tired smile, extending one hand to him. He crossed the room and sat down next to her.

"What're you doing here?" he asked, kicking off his shoes.

She laughed. "I live here, remember?"

"Not lately," he reminded her with a grin. "Anyway, I thought you'd be heading back to Palm Beach as soon as you finished your business with Adrienne."

She raised an eyebrow. "Are you by any chance trying to tell me you've missed me?" she asked, amused by his macho front.

"Did I say that?"

"No, but—"

He made a face. "Well, I guess it wouldn't hurt to admit that I'm used to havin' you around," he confessed with a sheepish grin.

She rumpled his hair. "That's big of you."

"When's Jordy coming?"

Sloane frowned. "He's not," she said quietly. "He's still in Florida. I'll be going back next week."

"Damn!"

"Travis!"

He frowned, looking down at his feet. "Sorry, Mom," he said, his disappointment obvious.

She smiled understandingly. "That's all right, sport," she assured him. "You like Jordy, don't you?"

Travis nodded. "Jordy's the closest thing I've ever had to a father."

Sloane was silent for a moment. "You've missed that, haven't you—having a father, I mean."

He didn't answer at first. "I love you, Mom—don't get me wrong," he began hesitantly. "But there are things I'm into now that call for a man's help." He looked up at her with a weary smile. "Let's face it—you wouldn't pass the physical."

Sloane smiled. "Well, thank you—I think."

"You know what I mean."

She nodded. "I think I do, yes." She put one arm around him, drawing him close. "Just between you and me, I kinda like having him around too."

Travis grinned. "For the same reasons, right?"

She smiled at the thought. *Yes, son, there are things I need a man around for too.* "Pretty much so, yes," she said aloud.

"You really ought to marry him right away," he told her. "Guys like Jordy don't come along every day, you know."

She held him close. *How well I do know,* she was thinking.

It was past midnight when Sloane let herself into her apartment, having stayed longer than she'd planned at the publishing party. Emma and Travis were no doubt fast asleep by now. As she started to make her way through the darkness to her bedroom, so accustomed to her surroundings that she normally didn't need to turn on the lights to maneuver successfully, her foot hit something on the floor, causing her to stumble. She bent to pick it up. A man's shirt had tangled around her heel. At first she thought it was Travis's, but on closer inspection she decided it was too big. It looked like one of Jordan's, but what was it doing there on the floor?

Taking a few steps further, she encountered a boot . . . then another. Her heart began to beat a little faster. She clutched everything in her arms and went into the master bedroom. There, she found his pants in a heap on the floor by the bed. He was here! He had to be! Spotting the bright line of light under the bathroom door, she went to investigate.

He was in the shower, humming "Rhinestone Cowboy." Sloane closed the door and leaned against it, resisting the impulse to fling the door open and literally throw herself at him. "I thought you had a match," she called out to him above the roar of the shower.

"So did I," he responded. "We lost."

"I'm sorry." She kicked off her shoes.

"Not as sorry as that bastard Alvarez is going to be next time we face off," he assured her. "Did you take care of everything you had to do here?"

"Yes." She put her silver evening bag on the vanity and unzipped her black cocktail dress.

"You work nights now, too?"

"Sometimes. But not tonight—unless you call attending a monster rally work."

He laughed. "Monster rally?"

"You've heard me talk about Guy Raymond before." She

took off the black sequined skull cap she wore over the wild, curly look her hairdresser had given her for the occasion.

"Ah, yes—the *National Enquirer* of the publishing business."

"The one and only," Sloane said with a short laugh. "He held a big party at the Rainbow Room tonight. Everyone showed just to see what he had up his sleeve now."

"Must have been exciting. Do you have any idea what time it is?"

"Not really." She removed her black seamed stockings, then took off her slip and bra. "That's what I like about my work— we don't punch a time clock."

"Is that supposed to be a hint?"

"Take it any way you like." She peeled off her sheer underpants.

"Funny."

"You been here long?"

"Long enough." There was a momentary silence. "You weren't here when I got in, so I thought I'd surprise you. I stripped and got into bed to wait, but the surprise, it seems, was on me."

"The trail of clothes through the living room was intentional . . ."

"Yeah."

She looked at the closed shower door and smiled as an idea came to her. "I suppose I could make it up to you . . ."

"Yeah? What've you got in mind?"

"This." She opened the shower door and stepped inside, wrapping herself around him as the water poured over both of them. "What do you think?"

He grinned. "I think it's a good start," he chuckled.

"Only a start?" she asked, water streaming down her face as she stood directly under the shower head, her body taking the full force of the water pouring from it. Mascara ran down her cheeks in heavy black streaks, and her hair was plastered against her head, neck, and shoulders unflatteringly, but neither of them cared as they embraced, their bodies molding together, their arms and legs entangled.

"A damned good one," he said as his mouth came down on hers. "God, I've missed you."

Thoughts of how foolish she'd been to leave Palm Beach with so much unresolved anger, of how confused she'd been, of how she'd begun to doubt his love, all seemed to disappear down the drain with the water as they kissed. Jordan's hands slid down Sloane's back, gripping her buttocks as she stroked his chest, keeping her balance with one arm still wrapped around his neck. He was already hard, pressing into her, trying to enter her there in the shower. She parted her legs willingly, but as she did so, she slipped on the slick tiled shower floor. Her knees buckled and she went down, pulling Jordan with her. He regained his balance quickly and dragged her to her feet again. "This isn't going to work," he chuckled as he reached past her to turn the water off. "You're not up to this tonight—your balance is always off when you drink."

"For your information, I haven't been drinking!" she spluttered indignantly.

"Of course you haven't," he teased as he opened the shower door and grabbed one of the thick, royal blue bath towels off the rack. "You got tipsy on iced tea, right?"

"I'm not tipsy!"

"Just the same, I don't think it's safe for you to walk to bed alone," he insisted as he wrapped the towel around her and scooped her up in his arms. "You might fall and break something—and then where would I be?"

She giggled. "Depends on what I broke."

"Exactly. I'm not taking any chances."

"Jordan, you're crazy!" she told him, laughing, as he carried her into the bedroom and deposited her on the bed. Lowering himself, he covered her wet, naked body with his own. She wrapped herself around him, holding him close as his mouth sought hers in the darkness. She returned his kisses with an ardor that matched his own, threading her fingers through his thick, damp hair. He pressed himself into her, making his desire known. She screeched loudly when he started nibbling at her neck. "You need a shave!" she scolded him.

"It'll have to wait," he muttered against her neck. "I've got more urgent needs to take care of right now." He attacked her hungrily with little love bites.

She writhed beneath him. "Depends on what you've got in mind, buster!" she laughed, digging her nails into his shoulders.

"Sssh!" he hissed. "You'll wake the kid!"

"Nothing wakes the kid," she assured him, trying in vain to wriggle free of his grasp. She shrieked as he tasted the sensitive flesh behind her ear. "Jordan! That tickles!"

"Quiet, woman!" he commanded as his lips found hers again. As her lips parted willingly, his tongue plunged into her mouth, possessive and demanding. He pinned her to the bed with his body, supporting his weight on his elbows as they continued to kiss hungrily. Her hands moved down his back, tracing each muscle as they continued their journey to his narrow hips, over his buttocks. Her fingers snaked between them, capturing his hardness in her grasp.

"You have been waiting a long time!" she chuckled. He gave a low, pleasurable moan as she stroked him with eager fingers. She guided him into her, wrapping her legs around his hips. "Now, Jordy," she breathed. "Now . . ."

"Yes . . ." Thrusting his hips, he plunged more deeply within her. As he started to gyrate, she moved with him, lifting her hips off the bed to meet his thrusts. He kissed her again as she picked up his rhythm. "I love you, Jordy."

"Then don't . . . ever run out . . . like that . . . again!" He continued that wild, primitive rhythm within her as she contracted herself, pulling him inside her, holding him there.

"I didn't run out on you . . ." Her voice was barely above a whisper.

"The hell you didn't!" His whole body tensed as he exploded within her. His breathing was labored as he lay on top of her, his face buried in her breasts.

Sloane didn't respond. She just stared at him in the darkness, speechless. Until that moment, she hadn't realized he was angry with her.

"Did you sleep with Jilly when you were in Argentina?" Sloane asked.

They were lying in bed the next morning, bodies entwined, physically spent after a long night of intense lovemaking. Jordan looked at her, clearly surprised by her question. There was something else in his expression, too, something that was gone before she could identify it. "Is that why you left?" he wanted to know.

She frowned. "Did you?"

He sat up, running a hand through his tousled hair. "I don't know why they always refer to it as sleeping with someone," he said with a heavy sigh. "Nobody ever does any sleeping."

Sloane propped herself up on one elbow. "You did, didn't you?" she asked again. "You went to bed with that woman."

He looked at her. "Who told you that?"

"I got it straight from the horse's mouth," Sloane answered honestly. "I ran into Jilly at the Esplanade in Palm Beach, and she—"

He shot a finger at her accusingly. "She told you I was in bed with her, and you believed her—just like that!" he said crossly. "That's terrific. That's just terrific."

"Was she telling the truth?" Now Sloane had to know.

He hesitated, tempted for a moment to lie, then shook his head. "Yes—and no."

"It can't be both, Jordan," she said irritably. "Which is it? Yes or no?"

He sucked in his breath and let it out slowly. "After you took flight in France, I'd pretty much had it with women," he admitted. "I was carrying around a lot of anger. I felt used—first by Jilly, then by you. As it happened, Jilly turned up at my door at the worst possible moment."

"Which I'm sure was intentional on her part," Sloane put in.

"I'm sure," Jordan agreed with a nod.

"And you took her to bed," Sloane concluded, angry but trying not to let it show.

"She made it quite clear she'd come there to get laid," he recalled. "I decided to oblige her—but the joke, as it turned out, was on me."

"She changed her mind." It was more a statement than a question.

He shook his head. "No—Jilly was a more than willing participant," he said quietly, looking more than a little embarrassed. "I wasn't."

"You changed *your* mind?" Sloane gave an inward sigh of relief.

"In a manner of speaking." His eyes met hers. "I couldn't get it up for Jilly—and believe me, I tried. I tried damned hard."

She stared at him, puzzled. "You were—"

"Impotent," he confessed, looking down at the sheets. "I couldn't finish what I'd started, so I sent her away. She never knew, of course. She thought I just didn't want her—which, now that I think about it, I really didn't."

"You were never impotent with me," Sloane said then.

"I know." He paused. "When I came to New York to find you, I was confused. I didn't know what I felt or what I wanted. That tryst of ours in Honfleur turned my life inside out. I knew I had to find you to find out why I was so screwed up."

She frowned. "You thought if you could perform normally with me—"

"When I came here, I thought all I wanted was to get you out of my system," he said quietly. "But then when we were together again, everything changed. I realized I was in love with you. I didn't want to be—but, dammit, I was."

Sloane smiled as she sat up behind him and put her arms around his neck, resting her head on his shoulder. "I didn't want to be either," she said softly. "But here we are. What do we do about it?"

He smiled wearily. "We let nature take its course, love."

♫ Sydney, March 1987

The Hotel Inter-Continental Sydney on Macquarie Street is Sydney's newest and most luxurious hotel, opened in 1985. Incorporating the impressive sandstone facade of the hundred-year-old colonial treasury building, it evokes the opulence and Victorian splendor of the 1850s gold rush. From their suite on the twenty-fifth floor, Jordan and Sloane enjoyed a panoramic view of the harbor and the striking architecture of the Opera House complex over their room service breakfast. Sloane was enchanted by the view, but Jordan, who had been there many times before, was more interested in reading the *Sydney Morning Herald* that was delivered with breakfast.

"Planning to hit any of the bookstores while we're here?" he asked casually as he scanned the entertainment pages.

"Of course." Sloane watched his face for a negative reaction, but there was none. "Cate and Dani taught me early on to maximize every opportunity for self-promotion wherever I happen to be." After Palm Beach, she was reluctant to discuss such plans with him but decided she couldn't just sweep it under the rug. He had to accept it, just as she had to accept that part of his life she couldn't change.

"In this case, the timing's perfect."

She put down her fork, surprised by his comment. "How so?" she asked.

He passed the newspaper across the table to her. "The Australians couldn't have given you a better welcome if they'd planned it this way."

She looked at the pages in her hand. The book section seemed to leap out at her: *Fallen Idols* was number one on the best seller list! Sloane let out a delighted shriek. "I can't believe it!"

He raised an eyebrow. "You've never been on a best seller list before?"

"Yes—but *Fallen Idols* was just published here last week," she explained. "It's never happened this quickly before." She kept staring at the page in front of her. "I should call Cate. What time is it in New York right now?"

Jordan looked at his watch, making a few mental calculations. "Seven A.M. here . . . we crossed the International Date Line . . . it's four o'clock yesterday afternoon there."

Sloane laughed. "Yesterday?"

He nodded. "It may be Thursday here, but it's still Wednesday in New York."

"I'd better call her now, then." She got up and started across the room to the phone, but as she passed Jordan, he hooked an arm around her waist and pulled her down onto his lap.

"Not so fast, woman." His voice was a low growl as he held her, wriggling frantically, against him. "If you're going to celebrate with anyone, it's going to be me." He nibbled lightly at her earlobe, and she let out a shriek, laughing at his sudden playfulness.

"I have to call her before she leaves the office," she insisted, putting up a halfhearted struggle as his hand found its way inside her rose silk robe.

"Call her at home. She won't mind." His mouth came down hard on hers as he pushed the top of her robe open and caressed her insistently.

Ten minutes later, she'd completely forgotten about calling anyone.

Jordan slow-cantered the dapple-gray horse toward the ball that had come to rest at midfield. As he approached the small white sphere, he held his ready position until he was almost on it, mallet raised high above his head in anticipation of the shot he was about to make. Swinging the mallet downward in a wide arc, he could hear the familiar clunk as it made contact with the ball; he could feel the vibration of that impact travel up his arm to his shoulder as he completed the follow-through. The ball streaked through the air, bouncing on the rich green turf several yards down the field. Jordan gave chase to it, but Lance, coming from the opposite direction, was closer. Lance raised his mallet in preparation for a head-on shot. Jordan reined in his pony, watching with interest. This was Lance's first practice game since his accident, and it showed.

Lance's arm came down in a less than fluid swing that was definitely off the mark. The mallet head made contact with the ball and pushed it sideways, the abrupt reversal of direction giving it a topspin. He jerked his horse around roughly to go after it. Jordan shook his head in irritation. *What's his problem?*

"Let's take a break," Jordan called out, removing his helmet as Lance rode up to join him. It was more a command than a suggestion.

Lance frowned. "I need the practice," he insisted. "Another hour?"

"I agree you need the practice," Jordan snapped, "but another hour won't do it for you, friend. You're making too many judgmental errors. That last shot was sloppy as hell."

"Thanks a lot, *friend*!" Lance shot back at him bitterly. "Just what I needed to hear!"

"You needed to hear the truth, and that's what you got." Jordan tucked his helmet under one arm. "You need to clean up your act before Hillyer replaces you—which I'm surprised he hasn't done before now."

"Screw you!" Lance reined in his pony and rode off alone in the opposite direction. Jordan didn't try to stop him. Lance was in no mood to listen to reason, and Jordan himself needed time to cool off.

He saw Jilly, perched on the hood of her car, watching him from the sidelines. Just what he didn't need right now. She was wearing a red silk crepe dress that was hiked up to show off her shapely legs, and Jordan was sure the pose was intentional. Jilly had always been a tease. She got her kicks turning men on, even if she had no intention of letting it go further than that initial stage of arousal.

"Hello, Jordan," she purred as he dismounted and led his horse toward her. "I thought I'd find you here."

"Don't you have anything better to do than follow me around?" he asked, not bothering to conceal his annoyance.

She gave him a feline smile. "Perhaps—but nothing I'd

rather do, angel," she told him.

"And where, may I ask, is your husband while you're playing shadow?"

"Max is playing in Mexico. He won't be back for two weeks, just in case you're interested."

"I'm not," he assured her. "Didn't he insist you go with him? I thought he kept you on a pretty tight leash."

Jilly hopped down from her perch and followed him as he walked away from her. "I insisted on staying," she said. "I knew you were coming. I wanted to see you."

"You wasted your time. I don't want to see you," he said coolly.

"I never waste my time, Jordan," she said softly as she came up behind him. "You know that." She tried to put her arms around him, but he pushed her away forcefully.

"I know a lot more about you than I'd like to know," he said contemptuously, handing the reins of his pony to a waiting groom.

"You didn't always feel that way."

"Let's just say I got tired of playing your little games," he said in a tight, controlled voice. "Like that stunt you pulled in Palm Beach."

She looked at him with feigned innocence. "What stunt?"

"You know damned well what stunt!" he snapped, turning on her in anger. "Telling Sloane we were together in Argentina."

"We were together in Argentina," she reminded him, running a scarlet-tipped nail down his hard-muscled arm. "It's certainly not my fault you weren't willing to finish what we started that night."

Jordan frowned. She still didn't realize that he hadn't been physically able to finish what they'd started that night. "You came looking for me," he said aloud. "You should know me well enough by now to know that when I really want a woman, I come after her. I don't wait for her to come to me."

Jilly smiled slyly. "Is that how it is with you and your fiancée?"

"That's none of your business," he said sharply as he pulled off his gloves and got into his car.

Jilly wasn't about to let up on him. "I'd think that might be a little hard to do," she said, pulling the keys from the ignition before he could start the engine.

"Dammit, Jilly, give me the fucking keys!" he said angrily as she tried to pull them away. He grabbed her wrist and squeezed it hard as he pried the keys from her fist. "I'm tired of your silly word games," he said as he slipped the key back in the ignition and started the engine. "Whatever you've got to say to me, why don't you just say it and get it over with?"

She leaned against the car door, smiling down at him. "I'm not playing games, Jordan," she said, reaching through the window to stroke the side of his face. He pushed her hand away. "I just thought you might find it hard to find the time to be alone with her since she spends so much time making all those public appearances. Why, just this morning I heard she's going to be interviewed on channel nine this week. I admire her, I really do," she insisted. "I was never very good at having a career of my own."

"Really? I thought you were a superstar in the world's oldest profession," Jordan said coldly.

Jilly ignored his sarcasm. "She's really quite good at promoting herself."

He frowned. "She's an ambitious woman."

"So I've noticed," Jilly acknowledged with a nod. "Think you'll be able to live with that?"

"Get to the point, Jilly," he said impatiently.

"You always did prefer a woman who was willing to stay by your side, make you the center of her universe," Jilly recalled. "Think you can handle being married to a celebrity, a woman who's more successful than you are?"

"What I think," he began in a barely controlled voice, "is that you've gone to a lot of trouble to start trouble. Take some friendly advice, Jilly. Save it—you're getting nowhere fast." He threw the car in reverse, unbalancing Jilly as he backed off.

But as he drove away, catching a glimpse of Jilly in the rearview mirror as she scrambled to her feet, he realized she'd hit her mark. He did wonder if he was going to be able to deal with Sloane's incredible success on a long-term basis.

Alone in his suite at the Inter-Continental, Gavin Hillyer stared at the papers spread out on the table in front of him. He couldn't believe that what he was seeing was real. It was like a bad dream—his worst nightmare come to life. Southwest Steel, the company founded by his great-grandfather and run by three generations of Hillyer men since, was in deep financial trouble, and Gavin Hillyer had no idea how it had happened.

He'd been on the phone with his people in Houston since three o'clock that morning. No one had been able to give him any acceptable answers. Profits were down. Way down. He was only too aware of that. They were heavily in debt. He knew that, too. It wasn't the first time on either count, and things had always been business as usual. Why was it different now? Why couldn't his people give him any concrete answers to the problems he was facing?

He looked at his watch. He was supposed to have called Nadine in Los Angeles at four in the afternoon California time. It was now six-thirty there. He thought about it for a moment, picked up the phone, then changed his mind and put it down again. Nadine would simply have to understand. He had more urgent problems to deal with at the moment than his wife's latest tummy tuck or whatever the hell she'd gone to that overpriced doctor of hers for this time. He'd never understand her obsession with trying to look eighteen forever. Sure, she'd had a lot of young lovers, men young enough to be her son; she'd never known he'd even suspected it, let alone had been certain of it. He'd known all along. He didn't really care, as long as she was discreet about it. He pretended not to know because it would never do to let her think he approved. This way, he'd always have something to hold over her head, to keep her in line if that became necessary.

Sex had never been high on his list of priorities: polo and horse racing and business were all better than an orgasm as far as he was concerned. For him, sex had always been quick. He'd mount her, satisfy himself, and be done with it. He'd always had more important things on his mind. Like now. . . .

They always met in bars, and always in bars that were not their normal turf. Sleazy bars in lower-class neighborhoods. Places where they would not run into anyone either of them knew. This time, it was a small pub on Sydney's waterfront, a place where stevedores hung out after work. They sat alone in a corner of the crowded room, drinks in front of them that had not been touched.

"You blew it."

"Couldn't be helped."

"The hell it couldn't."

"I know what I'm doing, dammit! Next time, it'll come off without a hitch."

"See that it does."

"That's one of the rules of the game, pal."

At the Royal Horse Show Grounds, a horse and rider broke from the player they'd been guarding and attempted to intercept the oncoming ball. He'd had the inside position on the opposing number one, perfectly placed to turn back any attempted pass by the other team. By turning to meet the ball, he left the player free and the goal exposed.

Jordan swore under his breath, knowing he wasn't in a position to move himself and keenly aware that his teammate's decision left him with only one chance. He had one shot at the ball. If he missed. . . . One powerful neck shot sent the ball flying down the field—and right in front of the opposition's number four, who hit it easily toward the goal. It was expertly intercepted by the opposing forward, who had an easy knock-in for the goal.

"Son of a bitch!" Jordan swore angrily, watching the play but powerless to do anything about it. The bell sounded to end the third chukker, and he turned his pony and headed back toward the picket line. He dismounted and turned the sweating horse over to a groom, then yanked off his helmet in a manner that indicated his anger and frustration. He looked at Sloane, who'd been watching the match from the hood of their rental car, but said nothing as he peeled off his gloves. He accepted the glass of ice water she offered and downed it quickly.

"It was a bad move, wasn't it," she said finally, breaking the silence.

"It was a goddamned stupid move," he responded crankily, pouring himself another glass of water from the cooler in the car. "He was in the right place at the right time, and he blew it."

"Everyone makes mistakes," Sloane offered in a weak defense of Jordan's teammate.

"That wasn't a mistake. It was stupidity, pure and simple," Jordan growled, mopping his face and neck with a damp towel. "He's not green, Sloane. He's been playing close to fifteen years now. He's got a nine-goal rating. He knows better."

"Don't you ever make mistakes?" she asked, attempting to calm him down but in fact having the opposite effect.

"Not deliberately," he snapped, throwing down the towel. He grabbed his helmet and went off to find the groom looking after his mounts. Sloane didn't go after him. She sat on the hood of the car, watching him disappear into the crowd of players, grooms, and hangers-on. He'd been edgy since he returned to the hotel after practice yesterday, and Sloane had the feeling his mood now had to do with more than just a bad move by a fellow player.

What was really bugging him?

"You certainly turned things around in the fourth chukker," Sloane told Jordan over dinner at Primo's Lafayette that evening. The restaurant, located two miles east of Sydney in Elizabeth Bay, is considered one of the area's finest establishments. It caters to a wealthy clientele amid plush surroundings, as it has since the 1930s. Its menu offers an international cuisine, with predominantly French and Italian dishes.

"Barely, love. Just barely." Jordan looked over the menu. "What looks good to you?"

"*Everything* looks good to me," she said. "I'm so hungry I could eat a horse!"

He laughed, the first time in days. "Fortunately, that's the one thing that's not on the menu."

"It's good to hear you laugh again," she said then, putting down her menu. It had been frustrating, not knowing what was bothering him, not being able to talk to him about it, since he wouldn't confide in her. He'd been so moody the past couple of days. Thank God he was finally in better spirits. Maybe now they could talk about it.

"Why shouldn't I? We won, didn't we?"

She raised her glass to him. "I never doubted you would."

"And to celebrate that hard-won victory," he went on, taking a small, gift-wrapped box from his pocket, "I picked this up for you this afternoon." He passed it across the table to her.

It came as a complete surprise. She took it from him and peeled the paper away slowly, as if it were a fruit she were preparing to eat, rather than attacking it in her usual manner. What she found beneath the paper was totally unexpected: a box of Cracker Jack.

Sloane looked up at him and smiled. How like Jordan this was. "I assume there's a special meaning behind this," she stated in a questioning tone.

"Most people check out the toy surprise first," he hinted, gesturing toward the box in her hand.

"Except you." Cracker Jack was his favorite junk food; he was almost never without at least one box.

He was visibly impatient. "Just open the damned box, woman," he ordered.

"All right, all right—just keep your pants on, Phillips," she told him as she opened it with some difficulty. Inside, in a small plastic bag, was a stunning black opal ring set in an antique gold band. She looked up at Jordan. "Is it real?" With Jordan, one never knew.

"Of course it's real," he stated indignantly. "I didn't get it out of a gum machine."

"No," she conceded, "you got it out of a box of Cracker Jack."

He took it from her and slipped it on the ring finger of her right hand. She moved her hand in the light, admiring the streaks of red, yellow, and dark green running through the oval-shaped black stone. "It's beautiful," she told him. "I've never seen a black opal before."

"They're mined only in Australia."

"What's the occasion?"

"I have a proposition for you."

She looked at him suspiciously. "What kind of proposition?"

He raised his wineglass. "That we not allow our professional obligations to take over our private lives," he said, his face suddenly serious. "That we make time to be alone together—and not just in bed. That our marriage be our top priority."

Sloane smiled, raising her glass to his. "I couldn't agree with you more."

• • •

"I can't believe this!" Jordan raged, throwing his shirt down on the bed. "What happened to that promise we made to each other not to let our professional responsibilities take priority over us?"

"You're acting as if I'm taking off for New York for a month!" Sloane, still in her robe, followed him across the room, unable to understand his anger.

"We had an agreement!" he snapped.

"You don't have to remind me!" She threw up her hands in exasperation. "It's only lunch, Jordan—a lousy lunch date with a reporter who can guarantee my name will turn up prominently in the Australian press—"

Jordan turned on her abruptly, his dark eyes blazing with fury. "I thought you'd been doing a damned good job of that all by yourself since the day we got here!" he exploded.

"It's part of the job!" she shot back at him.

"It's *always* part of the job!" he responded bitterly. "A TV interview here, a newspaper story there, an appearance in a bookstore somewhere else—what's it going to be tomorrow, Sloane?"

"I have no idea!" Her anger rose to match his. "Maybe nothing—but if there is something, I'm going to do it! I don't stop you from playing polo, and I don't expect you to stop me from promoting my books!"

"Stop you!" His laugh was mirthless. "I seriously doubt that anyone or anything could stop you!" He yanked the closet door open and pulled a shirt off its hanger with such force that the hanger came off the rod and fell to the floor. He stormed out of the room, slamming the door in his wake.

Sloane knew the interview wasn't going to be any good. Her heart wasn't in it. She was preoccupied with thoughts of Jordan, of their argument. Her answers to the reporter's questions came across flat and lifeless, without much enthusiasm. She just couldn't make herself care, one way or the other.

I should have canceled, she thought, pondering the view of Sydney Harbor from one of the open-air tables on the flagstone pavement of the Waterfront restaurant, a beautifully reconditioned old building on Circular Quay West. From under the awning, she glimpsed the masts and sails of an old schooner.

Normally, she would have enjoyed the interview and the cold seafood platter she'd only been picking at for the last hour. But today, she had other, more important things on her mind.

She was thinking of Jordan.

He'd been an unreasonable, selfish bastard.

As Jordan handed the groom the mallet he'd broken while making an unnecessarily vicious nearside foreshot, Jordan's opinion of himself echoed Sloane's. With another, undamaged mallet, he rode back onto the polo field at a slow canter, his mind not on practice but on Sloane. He'd behaved badly this morning. He'd let his temper get out of hand. He'd said a lot of things he didn't really mean.

He hadn't planned to blow up at her like that. Under normal circumstances he wouldn't have. Damn Jilly! The woman had successfully planted the seeds of doubt in his mind. Did he really resent Sloane's success? He told himself he didn't. He'd admired her for who and what she was, right from the beginning. He was proud of her accomplishments. But a part of him harbored the secret fear that eventually her career would take her away from him. Her hunger for fame would eventually become stronger than their love. And then there was the question Jilly had raised, the one he couldn't yet answer.

Could he deal with having a wife who was more famous, more successful than he was?

It was the first time they'd met in a public place other than a bar.

The park was small and crowded, lots of noise. The two men walked, not stopping, not even pausing for a moment. They were engaged in a serious conversation.

"You bring the money?"

"I said I would, didn't I?" the other man asked irritably. He took a thick brown envelope from his pocket and handed it over. "Count it if you like, it's all there."

He grinned. "I'll take your word for it." He stuck it inside his black leather jacket. "Can't count it here. You never know what kind of unsavory element might be hanging around."

"Suit yourself. I'll be in touch."

"Yeah." He watched the other man walk away, and once

again he was puzzled. What was his game, anyway? It didn't make any sense. Normally, he wasn't one to question his clients' motives, but this one really piqued his curiosity.

What was he *really* after?

BOOK THREE
DIAMONDS

♻ New York City, May 1987

Sloane lay in bed, the blue and green silk comforter pulled up to fully cover her nakedness. Beyond the closed bathroom door, she could hear Jordan singing "Rhinestone Cowboy" in the shower. She smiled to herself. *Turn on a faucet and Jordy will sing "Rhinestone Cowboy,"* she thought with mild amusement. The man she'd fallen in love with was one delicious mass of contradictions. So unpredictable in so many respects, he was actually quite a creature of habit in others. Singing "Rhinestone Cowboy" in the shower. The Cracker Jack he was almost never without. His passion for Chinese food. His love of old movies.

What wasn't predictable was his response to the demands of her work. He'd never been thrilled when her professional obligations separated them, even for a day. She understood that because she wasn't thrilled about those separations herself. What she didn't understand was why the problem had suddenly grown to such incredible proportions while they were in Australia. Sloane suspected that someone, maybe even a reporter, had said something to set him off. She knew Jordan had a lot of pride—and she was only too aware of his terrible temper. She knew the fact that she was so successful wasn't easy for him to deal with. He didn't relish being constantly reminded that the woman he was going to marry was an internationally successful author whose name was practically a household word. A woman who made more money than he did as a polo pro.

Sloane thought about it. They both had a great deal to come to terms with if they expected to make their marriage work;

she with Jilly and that part of Jordan's past that couldn't be changed, and he with those aspects of her work that would always make impossible demands on her time. She frowned. They were getting off to a great start. Just great. If only they could just ignore all the problems and go off to Moonstone, get married and shut out the rest of the world forever. If only it were that easy.

Realistically, she knew it wasn't. Jordan had taken the first step after their argument in Sydney. She recalled now what he'd said to her that night when he finally returned to their hotel. . . .

"I've been a fool, Sloane."

"Yes, you have."

"I let my goddamned ego get out of hand. I wanted you there with me for my big moment—or to soothe my injured pride had we lost the match—"

"I wanted to be there for you, Jordy. I thought you knew that."

"Let me finish before I lose my nerve. I love you. I don't like the idea of being separated by our professional responsibilities—yours or mine. I probably never will. But I'll get used to it. I'll have to because I'm sure as hell not going to let it come between us . . ."

"I love you, Jordy," she said aloud.

"Now, that's the way I like to start the day."

The sound of Jordan's voice brought her abruptly back to the present. She looked up. Jordan was standing at the foot of the bed, a thick towel wrapped around his waist.

Sloane stretched, a slow, sensuous, feline stretch. "You act as if I've never told you before," she said with a lazy, satisfied smile that came from a long, delicious night of lovemaking.

"Oh, you have," he conceded, "but I never get tired of hearing it."

"You have an ego as big as five polo fields!" she said with a laugh, snatching his pillow from beside her on the bed. She threw it at him, but he caught it easily and tossed it back to her. She grabbed it to throw it again, but before she could make her move, he lunged onto the bed, landing beside her. She started to get up, but he grabbed her wrists, pinning her down. She tried to pull herself free, and they engaged in a playful struggle. She started to giggle uncontrollably as he straddled her, pulling the comforter off her easily with one hand. She reached up and yanked the towel away, slinging it across the room in one quick movement. He looked down at her with a menacing grin. "You really shouldn't have done that," he scolded playfully.

She looked at him with a devilish gleam in her eye. "From the looks of you, I'd say I was just in time," she disagreed as she pulled him down to her for a kiss.

"Hmm . . . you may be right," he muttered. Then he pulled back the sheet and made love to her.

Jordan replaced the telephone receiver and leaned back on the couch, his arms folded behind his head. It was done. Getting Hillyer to put someone else in his place for a few weeks had been easier than he'd expected. Hillyer, as it turned out, was high on a player he'd just recruited, a French nine-goaler White Timbers had played against at Palm Beach. He saw Jordan's request for time off as the perfect opportunity to see what the Frenchman could do. At least that was what he'd told Jordan. Jordan suspected he was actually scouting for a replacement for Lance, who hadn't been playing well since his accident.

Lance. Jordan frowned. Lance had a lot of emotional baggage to get rid of before he could play again as well as Jordan knew he could. The divorce action had hit him hard. He'd been in love with Paula since they were kids just entering college in Virginia. He'd believed in long-term relationships and thought they would always be together.

Thinking about Lance and Paula made Jordan realize just how easily a relationship could be destroyed by career conflicts. They'd been pulled apart by a world neither of them really wanted. It was going to be even harder for Sloane and him. Polo was his life. There was nothing else that could make him feel so fulfilled, emotionally and physically. He loved the physical and mental challenge, the feeling of living on the edge, the sense of power—and danger. Sloane loved her work just as much. She loved being in the spotlight. She loved being recognized wherever she went, of being a celebrity. In her own words, she loved playing God—creating worlds and lives and controlling them with a stroke of her pen. How had she put it?

I love being in control. With my books, I control my characters and their destinies as I can never control the real world I live in. He understood that. He respected it. He even admired her for it. But could they each continue to live in those worlds, so vastly different from each other, yet manage to create a middle ground for the two of them together?

The bar was in lower Manhattan, near Battery Park. It was fairly deserted that night; perhaps four or five people had come in all evening. The bartender watched boxing on the portable TV set at one end of the bar.

The two men, the only customers in the place at the time, sat at the table farthest from the bar, keeping their voices low as they talked.

"Do you foresee any problems?"

The other man shook his head. "Should be easier than the others," he predicted. Then, after a brief pause, he added, "I want half the money up front."

"That wasn't our original agreement."

"I don't give a fuck what our original agreement was or wasn't," the other man snapped irritably. "You're into me for a lot of money, man. A *lot* of money. I need a little insurance."

"You'll get your money. When the job is done, as always."

He shook his head. "No good, man. You been keepin' me damned busy. I don't know what your game is here, but I know if you get put out of business, I'm not comin' up on the short end of the stick."

"Nobody's going to put anyone out of business."

"Not me, anyway. Half up front, or I don't work."

He studied the other man thoughtfully for a moment. "All right, dammit!" he snapped finally. "Half up front. I'll have it for you tomorrow."

"Cash."

"Cash."

The other man grinned. "I knew you'd see it my way."

"Is this really necessary?"

Travis stood on a low stool, arm extended like a scarecrow's and looking just about as comfortable, as a tailor made adjustments in the dark blue suit he wore. He made a face, clearly unhappy with his predicament.

"Yes, it is," Sloane insisted with an emphatic nod. "You need a new suit anyway—and since you *are* going to England with us, this is as good a time as any for a fitting."

"It's a pain in the ass," he grumbled.

"Travis!"

"Well, it is," he insisted stubbornly, letting out a loud yelp when the tailor accidentally stuck him in the left ankle with a straight pin.

"I'm sorry," the man muttered apologetically, patting his shoulder.

"Anyway, why can't I buy one off the rack like we get everything else?" he asked.

"Because you can't. A good suit will look like hell without a proper fit," she maintained.

"I'm not a suit person anyway," he argued.

"You are when the occasion calls for it," she told him as the tailor finished what he was doing and got to his feet. "You can go change back into your jeans now," Sloane told Travis.

Walking up Fifth Avenue, they passed a window display featuring a magnificent wedding gown covered in antique lace and thousands of tiny seed pearls. "You gonna have a dress like that?" Travis wanted to know.

She shook her head. "Nothing that elaborate," she said, openly admiring the dress even as she dismissed it.

"When are you going to do it?"

She looked at him. "Do what?"

"Marry Jordy."

"I don't know yet," she answered truthfully. "We haven't set a date yet."

Travis looked perplexed. "What are you waiting for?"

She rumpled his hair. "Christmas," she joked. "Come on— we've got to get going."

The truth was, she'd been asking herself the same question. And she still didn't know the answer.

"Are you sure you feel up to doing a live interview?"

Jordan sat down on the edge of the bed. Sloane lay back against the pillows, raising herself slightly to take the two aspirin he'd brought her. Once she'd put them in her mouth, he offered her a glass of water he'd brought from the bathroom, holding it to her lips as she sipped slowly.

"I'll be all right," she insisted. "I'm just a little dizzy, that's all. I have a headache. It'll pass."

"This interview is that important?"

She drew in her breath as she lay back again. "They're all important, Jordy," she told him.

He forced a smile. "You're the most driven woman I've ever known," he said in a tone that made her doubt he meant it as a compliment.

"I've had to be." She was silent for a long moment. "When I got started in this business, my only ace in the hole was Cate. She stood behind me, fought for me. Aside from that"—she shrugged—"I had nothing. No money, no connections, no track record to convince a publisher I was worth a gamble, nothing. Just Cate—and a lot of nerve and maybe just a little luck."

"And talent," he put in, brushing an errant lock of hair off her face.

She smiled wearily. "Talent's a lot like beauty," she said, giving his hand a little squeeze. "It's all in the eye of the beholder."

"Even I can tell a good book from a bad one," he insisted.

"Who can't?" She intertwined her fingers with his. "Trouble is, we all have our own ideas of good books and bad books. Anyway, I've worked too damned hard to get into the publishing game to let the harsh realities get the best of me." She frowned. "I had to be aggressive, to be willing to dig in and fight like hell sometimes. I've worked my ass off since day one to make a name for myself. I guess it's become so deeply ingrained in me that the habit's hard to kick, even now that I've achieved my goal and don't have to be nearly as aggressive."

Jordan looked at her for a moment but said nothing. Finally, he took her in his arms and held her close. For the first time, he felt as if he understood.

↻ London, June 1987

The polo fields at Windsor Great Park have an almost too perfect appearance. Precisely manicured and uniformly green without so much as the slightest variation in color and shade, it appeared as if each blade of grass on the smooth, even surface had been trimmed to exactly the same height. Beyond the fields, the Round Tower of Windsor Castle created an impressive backdrop, and a soft breeze wafted through the trees in the park. The sky that had been gray and overcast that morning had cleared by noon, and the only evidence that remained of the downpour of the night before was the dampness on the grass that made the playing surface slick and treacherous.

Despite the conditions on the field, the match in progress was hard and fast. Sloane, dressed in a royal blue two-piece dress, sat in a lawn chair on the sidelines, watching the play through high-powered binoculars. She almost wished she hadn't come. She was always nervous when Jordan played under these conditions. His pony had slipped twice during the second chukker, and two other players had taken spills. Now, the opposing teams were facing off at midfield. As the umpire bowled the small white ball into the cluster of horses and riders, the play resumed abruptly with the groan of leather and the clatter of locking mallets. Chaos ensued as the ball was knocked clear of the throw-in. Sent flying off in different directions with each shot, opposing players in blue and yellow jerseys fought for control of it. Horses made sudden stops and starts, spinning and lunging in pursuit of the ball. One horse went down, its rider rolling clear of it as it tumbled to the ground awkwardly, then quickly scrambled to its feet again. The action was brought to a halt until the player had remounted. Within minutes, a pair of riders were jostling for position on the ball. Jordan was one of them. He executed a flawless offside neck shot, swinging his mallet low in front of his dun pony. The impact of that shot sent the ball streaking off at an angle toward the goal. Seconds later, the white-coated judge, positioned beyond the goalposts, waved a white flag over his head to indicate a score.

The bell sounded to end the third chukker, and the players pulled in their horses and headed for the picket lines to change mounts. Sloane breathed a sigh of relief and allowed her binoculars to sweep over the crowd of spectators briefly, lingering for a moment on the box where members of the royal family watched the match. The Queen, seated with Prince Phillip, was in periwinkle blue with a matching hat; the Princess of Wales, to the Queen's right, wore a lovely white dress with large red polka dots and a wide-brimmed red hat; and on Diana's right was the Duchess of York—easily recognizable even from a distance with her luxuriant red hair—in buttercup yellow.

Their presence here today didn't come as a surprise to Sloane; they were often in attendance at the polo matches, particularly when Prince Charles was playing. Today, both the heir to the throne—who was considered well worth his four-goal status because he was a great crowd draw—and the duchess's father, Major Ferguson, were playing for Jordan's opponents, the Guards Polo Club. Sloane smiled to herself. No wonder the press was out in full force today. And no wonder none of them had been bothering her.

She wasn't sure if she liked that or not.

"Argentine players have been banned from playing here since the Falklands conflict," Jordan was saying as he dressed for dinner that night, in response to a comment Sloane had made about the conspicuous absence of any Argentines from the rosters at Windsor. "I guess I can count my blessings that Alvarez won't be showing his face here."

"I can't say I blame Queen Elizabeth for holding a grudge." Sloane, in a simple, one-shoulder green silk dress, was seated in front of the large mirror over the dressing table, applying a dab of lip gloss to her lips with the tip of her little finger. "I remember reading somewhere that when Prince Andrew served there with the Royal Navy, the Argentines would fire their missiles with the cry, 'This one's for you, Prince Andrew!' ''

Jordan moved behind her, looking over her head into the mirror as he knotted his tie. "I doubt the Hurlingham Polo Association will lift the ban anytime soon," he speculated, tugging his collar with a grimace. "They're not crazy about the future king possibly 'consorting with the enemy' even in sport. In a way it's a shame, because most of the best players are Argentine. They bring a lot of excitement to the game."

"Except for Alvarez, of course," Sloane added.

"Alvarez is a good player—but he's also a first-class prick," Jordan said.

"They're not overly fond of foreign players at all, are they?" Sloane guessed, remembering how few players at Windsor weren't British.

"They're just concerned about sidelining their own players," Jordan offered in explanation. "That's why only two foreign players at six goals or higher are permitted on a high-goal team."

She grinned. "Does that make you one of the chosen few?" she asked teasingly.

"Something like that." He stopped what he was doing and peered at her more closely. "Are you sure you feel like going tonight?"

"I wouldn't miss it for the world. Why?"

His eyes narrowed suspiciously. "You don't look too good."

"Thanks. That's just what I wanted to hear."

"I'm serious," he insisted. "You're so pale—you look like walking death."

She shook her head. "Jet lag, that's all," she said with a dismissive wave of her hand. "Anyway, I enjoy the nonstop teas and parties."

"I'm glad somebody does." He hated any function, social or otherwise, that required the wearing of a tie.

She twisted around to look up at him. "Stop yanking at your collar," she scolded. "You look wonderful in formal attire. Sophisticated."

"I feel like a victim of the Spanish Inquisition," he grumbled. "Where's Travis?"

"Pouting. He wants to go along."

"Why can't he?"

"He'd never last through the evening," Sloane maintained.
"He'd be bored to death. I think he'll be better off here with
Emma tonight. He's like you—he hates formal or even semi-
formal affairs." She put down the hairbrush she'd been pulling
through her long hair. "The two of you are so much alike. If
I didn't know better, I'd think you were his real father—" She
stopped short, realizing what she'd said.

He looked at her. "What was he like?" he asked, settling
down on the foot of the bed.

Sloane frowned. "It's been so long . . . he's just a blur in
my memory now," she answered finally. "When we met, I
was young and naïve, I had a lot to learn about a lot of things.
I actually believed—for a while—that I was in love with him."

"And now?" Jordan asked.

She shrugged. "I wonder what I ever saw in him," she said
simply. "He lacked any real drive or ambition. He also lacked
nerve." She sighed heavily. "Looking back on it now, I have
to admit that Travis was the only good thing to come out of
that fiasco."

"He's not like the man at all?" Jordan asked, unable to refer
to anyone else as her son's father when he already considered
himself Travis's father.

"Not at all," Sloane said with a shake of her head. "He
doesn't even look like Mitch. There have been times I've wondered if Mitch really was his father."

Jordan's eyes met hers. "He isn't. Not anymore."

"You gotta be kidding!"

The bar was on the Boston waterfront and the clientele was
questionable at best. Mostly dockworkers, big and burly and
loud. Definitely loud. It was a Friday night, payday for most
of them, and the majority of the customers that night were
spending a large chunk of their hard-earned dollars on beer and
whiskey. Two men, clearly not part of the regular crowd, went
unnoticed as they sat alone at a table near the door, speaking
in hushed but urgent tones.

"What's so difficult about—"

"It's a fuckin' *island*, man! They're right on the goddamned
shore!"

"That should make things easy for you. You can simply do it, then depart by boat."

"Evidently you ain't familiar with the security around that place. It's like fuckin' Fort Knox, man! If I managed to get *in*, which I doubt, the odds against me gettin' out again are nil."

"So get a job there. Then there won't be a problem."

"You must be nuts, man. You know how I work. I don't let nobody see my face."

There was a pause. "Look—I don't care how you do it. As long as it gets done."

The low hum of the voices engaged in conversation throughout the ballroom at Whitehall, the estate of polo patrons Harry and Sarah Harwood, almost drowned out the music provided by a small string orchestra, and the entrance foyer was congested by a steady flow of late arrivals attended by servants who took their expensive evening wraps. Light from the magnificent chandeliers overhead reflected off the elaborate jewels adorning the female guests, turning the room into a glittering sea of constant movement. White-coated waiters moved throughout the crowd with trays of chilled champagne.

Sloane stood at Jordan's side while he talked polo with Gavin Hillyer, who had once again turned up at a social function minus his elegant wife. She scanned the faces in the crowd with interest, recognizing many of them even though she had never met them personally. The more she traveled with Jordan, the more apparent it seemed to her that wherever they were, whether it was London or Palm Beach or Sydney or Deauville, they were surrounded by the same people. She recognized Owen Rinehart, who was chatting animatedly with ten-goaler Memo Gracida; Julian Hipwood and his attractive wife Pamela; Cornelia Guest; Geoffrey and Jorie Kent; and Alan Kent, who had just arrived with his long-time fiancée, Fiona Eckersley.

"Looking for someone?" Dusty Welles asked as she approached, champagne glass in hand.

Sloane took one from a tray as one of the waiters passed by. She shook her head. "Just thinking about how surprising it is that no matter where in the world we are, we seem to cross paths with the same people."

Dusty smiled. "That's what happens when everyone's pursuing the same thing," she said lightly. "I see Gavin's latched on to Jordy already. Does this mean you've become a polo widow before the wedding?"

Sloane gave a little laugh. "I hope not!"

"Is Gavin alone again tonight?" Dusty sipped her champagne.

"As far as I know. He was already here when we came."

"Nadine's had so many headaches in the past few months, I'm surprised Gavin isn't insisting on a brain scan—or hiring a private detective, at the very least," Dusty commented with a knowing smile.

Sloane looked at her. "Then there is some fact behind the rumors? About Nadine Hillyer and her lovers, I mean?"

Dusty shrugged. "Nobody's ever been caught hiding under her bed as far as I know, but it does seem pretty obvious—don't you think?"

"Jordan thinks she's got her eye on Lance," Sloane said then.

Dusty almost choked on her drink. "Lance? No way," she disagreed, shaking her head. "He's still upset about his soon-to-be-ex-wife. If he'd loved polo as much as he loved her, he'd have been a ten in nothing flat. There's never been anybody but Paula, no matter what kind of front he puts up."

Sloane didn't hear her last few words. All of her attention had suddenly been focused on the elegant couple who had just arrived. Max and Jilly Kenyon. Jilly's red hair stood out like a beacon in a sea of blondes and brunettes of varying shades. *Like a red flag waving in front of a bull,* Sloane thought, hating herself for letting the woman get to her this way, yet feeling powerless to fight it. Every time she thought of Jordan with that woman, every time she imagined the two of them together, every time she thought of how Jilly still schemed to get him back. . . . She turned to Dusty. "I'll be right back," she said, excusing herself.

She went to the nearest bathroom and was violently ill.

Lance lay on the bed, stark naked, his arms folded behind his head. Nadine, also naked, straddled him, riding him, moving her hips so that he could feel himself sliding in and out of the dampness within her. Her large breasts bounced with every movement, her nipples still hard and bruised from the assault of his lips and teeth only minutes before. She arched her back and gave little moans of pleasure as she rocked back and forth, constricting her inner muscles around him, urging him to come and come quickly. Lance, however, was in no hurry.

He liked things just the way they were. Their relationship suited him perfectly. Nadine took care of his sexual needs but made no demands on him emotionally. She didn't want from him what he couldn't give. What he didn't want to give. After Paula, he wasn't capable of loving any woman. After Paula, no one else could make him happy. Sex was all that mattered now, pure physical release. She gave him expensive gifts—usually jewelry—which he always sold to finance his increasingly expensive cocaine habit. It took more and more to do the trick these days. Pills had stopped being enough months ago. But Lance knew he had to be careful. If Hillyer ever found out he was bedding his wife—and that she was supporting his drug habit—there would be hell to pay.

"Don't play games with me, Jilly," Max Kenyon snarled, advancing on his wife menacingly. "The entire time we were at the Harwoods' party, you never stopped watching him! I'd have had to have been blind not to be aware of it—in fact, I'm sure everyone present was aware of it!"

"Is that what bothers you, Max?" Jilly asked, removing her large emerald earrings. "What everyone else was thinking?"

"What bothers me, my dear Jillian, is knowing that my wife is still carrying one huge torch for her ex-lover!" he snapped, tearing off his white dinner jacket. He threw it down on the bed. "I wonder, Jilly—when we make love, is it me you're making love with up here"—he thrust a finger to his own temple—"or is it Jordan?"

She glared at him. "What do you think, Maxwell?" she demanded hotly.

"Bloody hell! I think you've been unfaithful to me since the day we were married!"

"Think what you want," she responded indifferently, turning away from him. "I *am* married to you."

"A fact you seem to remember only when it's convenient

for you to do so,'' Max pointed out. He pulled off his watch
in a fierce jerking motion and dropped it on the nightstand.

"You don't make it easy, you know," she stated calmly.
"Your jealousy is positively suffocating. If I even speak to
another man, you fly into a rage!"

He turned to her, furious. "We both know damned well that
talking to Jordan Phillips isn't at all what you have in mind,"
he said, his face dark with rage. He took her face in both hands.
"Let me warn you now, my darling wife—if I ever catch you
with him, I'll kill both of you! Understand?"

"Perfectly," she said in a small voice, her entire body trembling.

He released her abruptly. As he pushed past her and stormed
into the bathroom, slamming the door as a pointed reminder
of his displeasure, Jilly stared after him, knowing with a sickening certainty that Max was perfectly capable of doing exactly
what he'd threatened to do.

"But, Sloane—what's the fun in coming to England for the
first time if I don't get to see anything?"

Sloane looked at her son disapprovingly. "What happened
to 'Mom'?"

"I've outgrown that," he informed her as he half dragged
her down the street. "Anyway, it's not classy."

She looked at Jordan, who was trying not to smile, then at
Travis again. "Since when are you concerned with being
classy?" she asked suspiciously.

He regarded her with impatience. "You're avoiding the real
issue here," he accused. "Why *can't* we go sightseeing today?
Jordy isn't playing—"

Jordan came to Sloane's defense. "I think your mother's a
little under the weather," he told the boy. "She's really not
up to doing a lot of walking." He turned to Sloane again. "Are
you?"

"I'm just tired, that's all."

Travis persisted. "Could we at least go to Buckingham Palace?" he pressured his mother. "It's close by."

Jordan looked at Sloane questioningly. "You up to it?"

She nodded. "I told you—I'm just tired," she repeated.

He wasn't convinced. "You've been like this for weeks

now," he said, concerned. "I think you should see a doctor."

"There's nothing wrong with me!" she snapped irritably. She turned back to her son. "Buckingham Palace it is."

"Great!" Travis led the way across a busy London street, headed for Constitution Hill. "Will we be there for the Trooping of the Color?"

"No. That's next week," Jordan replied, remembering he'd been younger than Travis the first time his mother had brought him to England. He recalled the pageantry of the annual event, which honors the Queen's official birthday on June thirteenth. Each year, a different Guards regiment presents itself for inspection, and the colors are those of its regimental flag. The Queen, on horseback, rides to the Horse Guards' Parade off Whitehall, where she receives the salute amid marching bands. As a child, Jordan had been fascinated by it—as Travis was now. Maybe if Sloane was up to it, they'd stick around another week.

Sloane. He couldn't figure her out sometimes. Why did she so stubbornly refuse to admit that something was wrong? He had only to look at her to know she wasn't well. She hadn't been herself in weeks. Why did she feel she had to be superwoman? Did she still have hang-ups about the age difference between them? Didn't she realize yet that it didn't matter?

"Why are you suddenly so quiet?" Sloane asked.

"Just thinking." He took her arm as they crossed Piccadilly and headed up Constitution Hill toward the palace.

"About what—or shouldn't I ask?"

He gave a low chuckle. "About you, woman—about how stubborn you can be sometimes."

She smiled. "I guess that makes us two of a kind," she said promptly.

Travis enjoyed Buckingham Palace even when it was made clear to him that he would not be permitted to climb the high iron gates as he would have liked. He spent the better part of twenty minutes taunting and harassing one of the guards stationed at the gates, trying in vain to elicit a response of any kind from the motionless, stone-faced guard. He stuck out his tongue, made incredibly ugly faces, and tried everything he could think of, but to no avail.

"I think you'd better give up," Sloane advised.

Travis shook his head emphatically. "Not a chance!" he insisted. "No way am I going home with a blot on my otherwise perfect record!"

"My son could test the patience of a saint," Sloane told Jordan, who looked uncertain as to what, exactly, they were talking about. "He's sent more Manhattan teachers into early retirement than anyone in the history of the school system."

Jordan laughed. "Look—it's eleven-fifteen now. Why don't we stick around for the changing of the guard?" he suggested.

"Great!" Travis exclaimed excitedly.

Jordan turned to Sloane. "Well?"

She nodded. "Whatever you want," she agreed without much enthusiasm. All she really wanted was to find a place to sit down.

She felt as though she were about to faint.

"I'd have been better off with a newspaper," Sloane said wearily, putting down the paperback novel she'd been reading for the last hour. She pulled off her reading glasses. To her right, Travis looked out the window of the 747, enjoying the view as he always did at thirty-five thousand feet. Jordan sat in the aisle seat to her left, leafing through a magazine.

He looked up with a half smile. "That bad?"

"Worse." She frowned, laying her glasses on top of the book. "It reads like a long synopsis—a very long synopsis."

Jordan covered her hand with his. "Do I detect just a bit of arrogance there?"

"A bad book is a bad book," Sloane maintained. "Even now, Adrienne would kick my ass if I turned in something this bad."

Jordan studied her for a moment, aware that she was critical of everyone and everything when she wasn't quite up to par physically—or emotionally, for that matter. He knew she hadn't been feeling well, though she'd done her damnedest to hide it. "Maybe you should forget reading for a while and try to sleep," he suggested. "It's going to be a long flight."

She forced a tired smile. "Maybe you're right."

He hesitated momentarily. "This has gone on long enough," he said finally, his tone firm. "I want you to promise me you'll see a doctor as soon as we get back to the States."

"I'm sure it's nothing serious—"

"I think we should be sure."

"Jordan—"

"I want your word," he insisted.

She hesitated for a moment, then nodded. "All right, if it'll make you happy."

She didn't tell him she fully intended to see a doctor, that she'd made that decision shortly after they'd arrived in London. She didn't want him to know how worried she really was.

↻ New York City, July 1987

"You're pregnant."

Sloane stared at the doctor in disbelief. "You can't be serious!"

He smiled. "On the contrary. I'm very serious," he assured her, making some notes in her file. "You're approximately three months pregnant."

"Three months," she repeated, numb with shock.

"You really had no idea?"

She shook her head. "None," she admitted, somewhat embarrassed. "My cycle's been irregular before when I've been under stress, so I never gave it a thought."

He raised an eyebrow. "Have you been under a great deal of stress lately?"

Sloane shrugged it off. "There's been a lot going on."

"Obviously." The doctor smiled. "There are some things you should be aware of," he went on, tapping his pen on the desk absently as he spoke. "You'll be thirty-six next month, and it has been eleven years since your last pregnancy—"

She smiled wryly. "I'm painfully aware of both of those facts," she assured him.

"Let me finish," he said firmly. "Your blood pressure's a little on the high side. Pregnancy won't be as easy for you as it would be for a woman in her twenties. There are elements of risk involved."

"Meaning what, exactly?" she asked carefully.

"You're going to have to slow down," he told her. "Later on, I'm going to want to do an ultrasound and amniocentesis."

"Define 'slow down.' "

"Less traveling. A lot less. Shorter hours—for working and socializing. More rest," he said. "In other words, pamper yourself."

She gave a little laugh. "I thought I'd been doing that all along."

"There's a big difference in pampering and indulging when it comes to pregnancy," he said as he took a blank prescription pad from the drawer. "I'm going to prescribe some special prenatal vitamins. I want to see you once a month for the next two months, twice a month during the sixth and seventh months, and every week after that until you deliver." He wrote out the prescription and gave it to her.

"When will you do the amniocentesis?" she asked, tucking the prescription into her bag.

"Not until the fourth month."

She was silent for a moment. "I've heard there's a risk involved," she said finally, looking down at her hands in her lap.

"A necessary risk, I think."

Sloane nodded, frowning. "I suppose so," she said quietly.

She was still trying to digest the reality of being pregnant. Dealing with the potential risk was more than she could handle at the moment.

December. The baby was due in December.

She couldn't believe it. The worst part of it was that she wasn't even sure she wanted a baby. She wasn't sure she could cope with two A.M. feedings, teething, dirty diapers, and all the other unpleasant tasks that went with a new baby. It hadn't been easy with Travis. It was bound to be ten times worse now.

But Jordan wanted a baby.

She thought about it as she walked alone up Park Avenue. After nine years, she was accustomed to her fast-paced lifestyle. She had always loved traveling, and she loved traveling with Jordan even more. She wasn't sure she could slow down even if she wanted to.

But Jordan wanted a baby.

And Sloane wanted Jordan. She wanted him to be happy, happy with her. If she went through with this pregnancy, she would be proving to him—and to herself—that there was nothing he could have with a younger woman that he couldn't have with her.

Besides, she thought smugly, she could always hire a nanny to do the dirty work.

"Are you sure?" Jordan, seated on the couch looking up at her, looked as though he were afraid to get excited, as though he thought there might be some mistake.

Sloane, standing in the middle of the living room facing him, nodded. "Very sure," she replied in an uncharacteristically timid voice.

"Are you okay? I mean, is everything all right?" he asked, suddenly concerned. "There won't be any problems?"

"Dr. Halsey says I'll have to take it easy toward the end," she started carefully. "He says I'll have to slow down until after the baby's born, but other than that, I'll be fine." She saw no reason to tell him of the concerns the doctor had expressed, at least not yet.

He got to his feet. "When's the baby due?"

"December. Just before Christmas." She was silent for a moment. "You *are* happy about it, aren't you?"

He broke into a big grin. "Of course I'm happy!" he declared, sweeping her up in his arms in a big hug.

Sloane laughed with relief. "Careful, you big lug!" she shrieked. "You'll squash the baby!"

"Are you sure this is what you want?"

Cate was leaning against the edge of her desk, supporting her weight on her hands as she eyed her client warily.

Sloane's smile was tired. "Of course it's what I want," she insisted. "You've known me long enough to know I wouldn't go through with it if it weren't what I really want."

"I think you're doing it more for Jordan than for yourself," Cate stated bluntly.

"No," Sloane said with a shake of her head. "At first, maybe, but not now. This is Jordan's child. I love him—and I can't think of a better way to express that love." She paused. "Besides, I think it'll be nice to have a little one running around the house again after all these years."

Cate raised an eyebrow. "Nice? That's it?" she asked. "You think it would be nice?"

"I don't know a better way to put it," Sloane responded frankly. "As much as I love Travis, I didn't love his father. I've always wondered what it would be like to have a baby with a man I love."

"These are not exactly practical reasons to have a baby," Cate pointed out.

Sloane smiled. "Are there really any practical reasons for having a baby? Perpetuating the species, maybe?" she asked. "Is there ever any real logic behind any woman's decision to get pregnant?"

"Decision?" Cate asked. "As I recall, you weren't exactly trying to get pregnant."

Sloane shook her head. "No, actually, I wasn't. Not consciously," she admitted.

"I hope you've thought this through," Cate said, unconvinced. "I hope it's what you really want."

"It is," Sloane assured her. "Just be happy for us, Cate—and keep your fingers crossed."

Cate laughed for the first time. "My dear," she said, "my fingers have been crossed as long as I've known you."

૨ Martha's Vineyard, July 1987

"How did I ever get talked into this?" Sloane despaired as she looked over the proposed list of wedding guests. Frustrated, she tossed it down on the coffee table in front of her and took off her reading glasses. "There's just no way on earth we can have a small, intimate gathering for five hundred guests!"

"My mother's fault," Jordan chuckled, attempting to pass the buck. "I think she knows everybody in the Social Register. She just had to invite this old and dear friend—and once she had that name on the list, there was no way she could not invite good old so-and-so." He waved his hand dismissively. "You know how it is."

Sloane laughed, rolling her eyes upward. "How well I do know," she said with an exaggerated groan. "But as fond as I am of your mother, darling, this is not going to work. Some of these names—no, most of them—will have to be crossed off the list, or we'll have to move the wedding back to New York. To St. Patrick's Cathedral!"

"I'll let *you* tell my mother," Jordan said as he got to his feet. He reached out and patted her thigh. "I think I'd better go look in on Lady Spade."

"Thanks a lot!" She grabbed his wrist. "Dump all the dirty work off on me."

"You're the one who wants a small, intimate wedding. We can get married in the middle of Fenway Park at the bottom of the ninth for all I care," he told her. "Just as long as it's legal."

"She's *your* mother!"

"But this is *your* production." He laughed. "And I really

do have to check on Lady Spade.''

Sloane frowned. ''You're worried about her, aren't you?''

''Yeah,'' he admitted, taking a deep breath. ''She's going to foal any day now—and after two failed attempts, I'm not taking any chances.''

Sloane understood how he felt. Lady Spade had been a thorn in Jordan's side for as long as Sloane had known him. Sired by Secretariat, with two Derby winners in her lineage on the dam's side, her bloodlines were what could only be described as equine royalty. Her own racing career had been short but impressive, and now that her racing days were over, Jordan had high hopes for her as a brood mare. The first time he'd bred her, she'd lost the foal early on. The second time, the foal was stillborn. Determined to get at least one promising foal from her, he'd bred her again, vowing to train her for polo if it didn't work out this time around, but knowing even as he made that vow to himself that he didn't intend to honor it. No—Lady Spade came from the best racing lines, and he was certain she would produce equally good foals.

Sloane shook her head, smiling to herself as she turned her attention back to the wedding invitation list. Her money was on Jordan, no matter what the odds.

''How's she doing, Cappy?''

The stable manager turned as Jordan entered the large box stall in the brood mare barn. ''She's been a little restless today,'' he commented without too much concern. ''She knows her time's near.''

Jordan patted the black mare's neck. ''Has Doc been out yet?''

Cappy shook his head. ''Not so far today,'' he answered, pulling his cap low on his forehead. ''I called. He's runnin' a little late. Had to deliver a foal this morning over at Longworth.''

Jordan frowned. ''Let me know when he does come. I want to talk to him.'' He looked the mare over thoughtfully from head to tail. ''I think we just might make it this time, Lady Spade.''

''Sure looks good,'' Cappy said with a grin. ''Could be three's the charm.''

"It had better be," Jordan said, finally optimistic. "If it doesn't happen this time, we're giving up—aren't we, girl?" The mare nudged his shoulder affectionately.

Cappy looked skeptical. "I'll bet you are," he snorted.

"No point in throwing good money after bad," Jordan said with a shrug.

"That's what I've been telling you all along," Cappy pointed out, "but I don't recall you ever listening."

Jordan laughed. "Lady Spade is worth a certain amount of risk—aren't you, girl?" He hooked an arm under the mare's neck and stroked her muzzle with his free hand. She nickered softly.

"It's been a damned expensive risk so far," Cappy stated. "I hope this foal is worth it."

Jordan grinned. "It will be," he said confidently. "This year, Cappy, I've taken the biggest risks of my life—and so far, they've all paid off."

Sloane stood sideways in front of the antique full-length oval mirror in the bedroom, studying her reflection thoughtfully. It had been a long time, but she hadn't forgotten the last time. A mother never forgot such things. She remembered her last pregnancy as clearly as if Travis had been born last week. She remembered checking her reflection then, standing on the bed in her small apartment in Chicago because she didn't have a full-length mirror, just the small one over her dresser. She remembered waiting for the bulge that eventually came, and it had come with a vengeance, she recalled now, remembering the thirty-eight pounds she'd gained, ten of which had stuck around long after the birth. She'd have to be more careful about that this time. After this baby was born, she wanted to get back in shape right away. She wanted to be in good shape for Jordan. He insisted he thought pregnant women were especially beautiful, but she was sure he didn't want her to look pregnant all the time.

She remembered the first time she felt Travis move within her womb, that first faint fluttering sensation she'd felt lying on the bed in the darkness during a violent thunderstorm. She recalled the blimp jokes she'd endured from friends when she was near full term and uncomfortably large. Then there was the birth itself, punctuated by a lot of agony and too much yelling and swearing on her part until her obstetrician finally surrendered to the demands of the delivery room nurses and gave her an anesthetic. She smiled to herself. Her son's birth hadn't been the dramatic, profound experience of books and movies, but it had been no less a miracle. And the birth of this child was going to be even more of a miracle.

This child had been conceived in love. This child was the result of all that was good and right in her life, the living proof of what existed between herself and Jordan. And that, when all was said and done, made this pregnancy worth any risk.

She drew her loose red cotton shirt as tightly around herself as she could and checked the mirror again. Was she beginning to show—or was the slight roundness of her belly the result of her first pregnancy? She took a small pillow off a nearby chair and stuck it under her shirt, then looked again. She made a face at her reflection. For once, she was actually looking forward to getting fat. For once she wasn't going to mind having a big belly and not being able to hide it. She didn't want to hide it. Not now. She wanted to show the world . . . but, for now, she was glad she wouldn't have to have the waistband let out on her wedding dress.

As much as Sloane wanted that happy ending Jordan had talked about that afternoon in the restaurant in Honfleur, she was too much of a realist—and a cynic—to believe that it was going to come easy. The problems that existed in their relationship weren't going to vanish with the speaking of the marriage vows. The wedding ceremony wasn't an occult ritual that would banish all their troubles. Some of the problems would never go away. Still, she had the feeling that being married would make a difference. Marriage was important to Jordan. Commitment was important to him. By marrying him, she was giving him proof of her commitment to him, to their relationship. It was the first step. *Every journey begins with a single step,* she thought.

But they still had a long way to go.

"It's a good thing it's a big house," Sloane told Jordan when the wedding guests began to arrive. "I'd have hated to have had to put everyone in sleeping bags in the library."

Jordan laughed as he sat down on the edge of the bed and pulled off his boots. "It could have been worse," he reminded her. "Can you imagine having to put up five hundred guests?"

"No, I can't—and we couldn't," she said with a shake of her head. She unbuttoned her mauve cotton shirt and shrugged it off her shoulders. "We would definitely have had to send them to a hotel—all of them."

"I think I might have preferred that anyway," Jordan chuckled, pulling his green polo shirt up over his head. He tossed it aside and unbuckled his belt. "Not that I'm antisocial or anything, but—"

"I know," Sloane assured him as she looked through the closet in search of something suitable for an informal dinner with those guests who had already arrived. Moonstone was Jordan's Shangri-la, the one place in the world where he could be assured of absolute privacy. Sloane understood his passion for privacy because, in a sense, she shared it. It was wonderful being in the spotlight—as long as it was possible to walk away from it from time to time and remember who and what you really were.

"Why aren't any members of your family here for the wedding, Sloane?" Jordan asked then.

Sloane flinched inwardly but tried not to let it show. She still hadn't told him everything. He still knew nothing of Sammy Douglas, of what Sammy's life in Chicago had really been like. "My father hasn't been well," she said, pulling a dress from its hanger. "He can't travel in his condition, and my mother didn't feel she could leave him, even for a day or two." She paused in front of the mirror, holding the dress in front of her, then she turned to Jordan. "What do you think?"

"I've always liked that dress. You know that." He was silent for a moment. "What about your brother?"

She shrugged. "We were never all that close, Jordy. His not being here doesn't surprise me at all." She put the dress on the bed and slipped on a robe. "I think I'll go take a shower." She bent down and gave him a quick peck on the cheek.

He grinned. "Want some company?"

She laughed. "Not this time," she said, pulling away as he made a grab for her. "What would our guests think if we didn't show for dinner?"

"They won't mind." He grabbed at her again, but she dodged him and ducked into the bathroom. "Maybe next time," she told him, closing the door.

"Definitely next time," he corrected.

"It's a date."

Once inside the bathroom, with the door closed so he couldn't see her, her smile evaporated. He'd finally come right out with it and asked her about her family. She knew it would happen eventually. There was no way to avoid it. Cate had been right. She should have told him. She should have told him everything. If she didn't tell him herself, he'd find out anyway, sooner or later. That would be worse. It should come from her.

The truth was, her parents would have loved to have been there for her wedding—and nothing could have kept them away had they known about it. It was possible they did know she was getting married—it certainly hadn't been a well-kept secret—but they couldn't know where and when it would take place. They didn't know because she hadn't told them. In fact, she hadn't seen or spoken to them in years. She hadn't even written to them. It wasn't that she didn't care. She did. And she knew they cared about her, in their own way. But it was better this way. The fewer ties she maintained with her past, the less likely it was that anyone was ever going to learn the truth. Cate knew, but she was the only one Sloane had ever confided in. No . . . too much had happened. Too many unpleasant memories. It was all a part of a past she'd left behind when she arrived in New York nine years ago.

A past she wanted desperately to forget.

The wedding took place on a hot Saturday afternoon in the garden behind the main house. Jordan and Sloane took their vows in the gazebo that was at least a hundred years old but had been given a fresh coat of white paint in honor of the occasion, with only Jordan's parents and a handful of their closest friends in attendance, Carlo and Gaby serving as their attendants and Travis as ring bearer. The strong scent of the honeysuckle that grew up around the gazebo filled the air.

Having vetoed any possibility of wearing a tux, even for his own wedding, Jordan's only concession to formality was the blue suit he wore. An informal afternoon wedding suited him perfectly. He would have been married in his polo jersey and boots had Sloane been willing to allow it.

Sloane herself looked like a southern belle in a simple, off-the-shoulder white silk dress with a full skirt and wide-brimmed white picture hat. Around her neck she wore a single strand of freshwater pearls, a wedding gift from Jordan. He'd teased her about the snug fit of the waistband of the dress, telling her they'd have to get married quickly or she'd never be able to get into the dress, and now, standing in the gazebo taking her vows, she realized he hadn't been too far off base. The waistband was already tight.

They spoke the vows they'd written themselves, drawing from contemporary poets and composers whose words best expressed their own feelings about each other and about the commitment of marriage. The music they chose for their wedding was unconventional, from contemporary artists, like John Denver's "Follow Me" and Neil Diamond's "Story of My Life." Even their wedding invitations had been unconventional in design and color. Instead of the traditional white, they'd chosen a pale gray paper on which an announcement they'd written themselves was printed, along with a line from Kahlil Gibran: "It is when you give of yourself that you truly give."

After the ceremony, a buffet reception was set up in the garden, where the guests were serenaded with lively music while they feasted on smoked salmon, chilled shrimp, lobster tails, and oysters. Later, Jordan and Sloane cut the wedding cake, a magnificent four-tiered cake topped with a specially made spun sugar bride and groom on a white horse. Jordan refused to have an all-white cake no matter what the tradition happened to be, so one tier of the cake was devil's food beneath the snow-white icing.

"Well, you've done it," Cate told Sloane as they watched Jordan dancing with Gaby, who wore a beautiful apricot silk dress, on the soft grassy carpet beyond the gazebo that served as their dance floor.

"Done what?" Sloane asked, not sure she understood.

"You've gotten married, my dear." Cate smiled. "You always said you never would."

"And you never believed me."

"It only takes the right man to change a woman's mind—

and vice versa.'' Cate smoothed the side of her iridescent green two-piece dress.

Sloane smiled but said nothing. Watching Jordan now, she was more aware than ever that she had married not only a man but a way of life, one that was entirely possible for Sloane Driscoll, the best-selling novelist, but out of the reach of Sammy Douglas, her alter ego. It made her wonder.

Would a man like Jordan have looked twice at a girl like Sammy?

''Somehow, I thought it was going to be different.''

Jordan looked down at Sloane in the darkness as he hovered over her, supporting his weight on his elbows. He grinned at her, and even in the darkness she could see the devilish gleam in his eyes. ''Different?'' he asked, amused. ''Different how?''

''I don't know.'' She lifted her head off the pillow to kiss him fleetingly. ''I just figured married sex would be different.''

''The difference, my love, is in the emotions,'' he told her. ''There's a big difference in having sex and making love.''

''Mmmm . . . so I've discovered.''

His lips brushed her forehead. ''Did you want it to be different?'' he asked lazily as he kissed her lips again and again.

She wrapped her arms around his neck. ''No,'' she said softly. ''It can't really get any better, can it?''

''Not as far as I'm concerned.''

She nuzzled his lips gently. ''You know, this is going to get harder and harder to do in the next few months,'' she told him.

''How so?''

''I think we'll have to switch places eventually.''

''That's not so bad.''

She giggled, fingering his chest hair. ''I never thought of you as the passive type.''

''Being on the bottom doesn't necessarily mean I'm going to be passive.'' He bit her neck playfully.

Sloane shrieked. ''Cannibal!''

''I vant to bite your neck,'' he said in his best Bela Lugosi imitation as he drew the sheet up to cover both of them completely. She squirmed frantically, laughing, as he bit her neck again and again.

''Fire! Fire!''

The shouts were coming from outside. Jordan and Sloane stopped what they were doing abruptly. He kicked the sheet off and scrambled to his feet. He ran naked to the window in time to see four of the stable hands running toward a bright orange glow coming from beyond a thick patch of trees.

"There's a fire in the brood mare barn!" someone shouted.

"Jesus Christ!" Hearing that, Jordan grabbed his pants and pulled them on quickly, then searched frantically for his boots.

Sloane sat up, groping in the darkness for her robe. "What's wrong?" she asked, finding the robe in a heap on the floor next to the bed.

"The brood mare barn's on fire!" He struggled into his polo shirt as he headed for the door.

She pulled on her robe and slippers. "I'm going with you."

"The hell you are," he snapped without looking back. "You're going to stay here where it's safe—or have you forgotten that you happen to be pregnant?"

"I haven't forgotten anything!" She followed him down the stairs. They reached the front door at the same time. "I just want to help."

"Fine—you can make coffee for the men. They're going to need it." He pushed past her and flew out the door.

She followed him. "If you think I'm going to hole up in that kitchen doing nothing but making coffee and wondering if you're out there risking your life, you're nuts!" she yelled at him as she struggled to keep up.

He didn't argue. There wasn't time. He broke into a run and headed for the stables, with Sloane following as closely behind as she could manage. She let out a painful yelp as she lost one slipper in the rush and stepped down on a sharp twig with her bare foot. It broke her stride momentarily. Hopping on one foot as she tugged the slipper on again, she followed him down the shell-rock drive past the stables to the brood mare barn.

By the time they reached their destination, the huge structure was engulfed in flames. The stable hands had evacuated most of the horses and were leading them to safety, some of them with foals. Jordan turned to Cappy, who was struggling to unroll a heavy rubber hose. "You call the fire department?" he wanted to know.

"Yeah," Cappy shouted over the din of the men's raised

voices, the horses' screams of terror, and the roar of the blazing fire itself. "They're on their way!"

"All the horses out?" Jordan yelled.

"Dunno," Cappy responded, pausing to wipe the perspiration from his brow. "Six of the boys went in—ain't been time for a head count!"

"Where's Lady Spade?" Jordan's eyes scanned the cluster of nervously prancing horses moving past him.

"We can't get to her!" one of the grooms yelled, fighting to control the two horses he was leading as they strained against the ropes. "The fuckin' flames are everywhere—it's an inferno in there!"

Before either Sloane or Cappy could stop him, Jordan took off in a dead run, heading straight for the burning barn. "Jordan!" Sloane screamed. She started to go after him, but Cappy grabbed her.

"You can't go in there, and you can't stop him!" Cappy shouted above the noise around them. "He won't do anything stupid!"

"What do you call this?" Sloane tried to break away, but he was holding her tightly.

"That mare means a lot to him—he's gonna get her if there's any way. But he won't kill himself to do it," Cappy assured her. When she stopped fighting him, he released her. "If he sees there's no way, he'll be back."

Jordan stopped just long enough to grab one of the hoses and thoroughly soak himself and a heavy horse blanket with the ice-cold water before running into the burning building against the protests of the other men. One arm raised to shield his face from the intense heat, Jordan made his way through the flames toward the back of the barn. Along one wall, stacks of baled straw ignited and became one huge fireball. Flames licked up the walls, bringing down beams. Almost drowned out by the roar of the fire, he could hear Lady Spade's panicked screams, her hooves drumming wildly against the floor of the stall. He dodged burning debris falling in his path but moved on with a fierce determination. Flames mushroomed with a crackling roar, the heat within the barn unbearable. Sweat poured from Jordan's face and body as he struggled for breath, half suffocated by the oxygen-stealing flames. By the time he reached her, the walls of the stall were ablaze. The half door wouldn't open. He tugged at the latch, but it was stuck. Maybe he could force it down. He kicked it as hard as he could, but it wouldn't budge. Finally, desperate, he threw all of his weight against it and the latch broke. He threw it open and ran to his mare just as a beam came crashing down on top of her. She let out a scream of agony. Knocking the beam out of the way, he took the horse blanket and threw it over her. Moving quickly, he grabbed her halter and tried to lead her out. She fought him, terrified. He yanked his large handkerchief from his back pocket and covered her eyes with it, stuffing the corners into the halter since it wasn't big enough to be tied around her head. Physically and mentally drained, he led her, balking all the way, toward the exit. More than once in that normally short journey that now seemed to take forever, Jordan doubted that either of them was going to make it out alive. Halfway to the exit, their path was blocked by a falling beam still ablaze. He pulled the old blanket from Lady Spade's back and beat at the flames furiously, while at the same time fighting to maintain control of the frightened mare. In the back of his mind he wondered if he'd be around for the birth of his child. . . .

Outside, Sloane watched helplessly as the barn was completely consumed by fire. She was only dimly aware of the wail of the approaching sirens as she silently prayed that Jordan was all right. Her heart was racing, the sound of her own blood pounding in her ears like war drums. She couldn't remember ever being so frightened in her life—not even in those awful days in Chicago. . . .

Please let him be all right, she prayed silently. *Let him be all right.*

Three fire trucks, lights flashing and sirens blaring, came barreling up the drive, screeching to a halt as they moved into position near the burning barn. The firemen leaped off the trucks before they came to a full stop, unrolling their hoses rapidly.

''There he is!'' Cappy shouted, the sound of his voice cutting through Sloane's thoughts. She looked up as Jordan emerged from the barn leading Lady Spade. Her entire body sagged with relief as she broke into a run, dodging the firemen and their equipment as she raced to meet him, with Cappy close behind.

She threw her arms around him while Cappy tended to the mare. "I was so worried you'd never make it out of there," she gasped, wiping soot and perspiration from his face with her hand. "I don't think I've ever been so scared in my life!"

"That makes two of us," Jordan admitted wearily. "I wasn't sure I was going to be able to get out once I was in there."

"Jordan," Cappy called to him. "I think you'd better come here."

They both turned. Lady Spade was down. Cappy was on his knees, hunched over her. Jordan dropped to his knees next to the other man. "What is it?"

Cappy frowned. "She's not gonna make it, Jordy," Cappy said gravely. "She's been pretty badly burned."

"A beam fell on her."

Cappy nodded. "Her leg's probably broken. I don't know how you ever got her out of there in this condition."

"You're saying we have to put her down?"

Cappy nodded.

Jordan shook his head emphatically. "I can't do that, Cappy," he insisted. "I can't."

"You're gonna have to!" Cappy snapped irritably. "This mare is suffering! Put her out of her misery, goddamnit!"

"If there's a chance—"

"There isn't. The vet's on his way. I called him to check the horses over. Let him take care of it," Cappy urged.

"What about the foal?"

Cappy shook his head. "If the vet gets here in time—"

"No," Jordan said firmly. "I can't take that chance. If I can't save Lady Spade, I might be able to save the foal." He scrambled to his feet.

Cappy looked up at him. "What've you got in mind?"

Jordan sucked in his breath. "I'll deliver it myself." He turned to one of the grooms. "Go down to the tack building and bring back the medical supplies—and a shotgun."

Sloane looked at him, horrified. "A shotgun!"

He nodded, wiping his face with the back of his hand. "I've got to do it," he said quietly. "I've got to shoot her."

"But Jordy—"

"You heard Cappy. She's not going to make it," Jordan

said grimly as he stared down at the mare. "I have to do what I can to save her foal."

The young groom returned minutes later with everything he'd asked for. Sloane stood next to Cappy unable to watch, as Jordan loaded the shotgun and took aim. Sloane's eyes were closed when she heard a single shot fired, and her body jerked involuntarily. She opened her eyes slowly as Jordan handed the shotgun back to the groom and went to his knees again, opening the box of medical supplies. "I need a knife. A big one," he instructed the groom. "And sterilize it."

The groom did as he was told. Sloane moved up behind Jordan, looking over his shoulder as he worked quickly to save the foal he'd had such high hopes for. His hair was damp and his face dirty and glistening with perspiration in the orange glow of the dying fire. His hands were steady in spite of the tension she could feel surging from him like a physical presence. She thought she might vomit when he sliced the mare's belly open, but she forced herself to watch, to stay by Jordan's side no matter what. Even though there was nothing she could do, she felt he needed her there. She felt she needed to be there. She looked down at him. Was that sweat rolling down his cheeks—or was it tears? She had never seen him cry before, but she knew if anything was capable of bringing tears to his eyes, this was it. This mare, this foal, meant everything to him. They were, in his own words, the future of Moonstone's racing bloodlines. They were a big part of his future. He hadn't been able to save Lady Spade, even though he'd risked his own life to do it. If he lost the foal, too. . . .

Jordan pulled the foal from the mare's open womb and cleaned the membranes off its face. At first it was still and didn't appear to be breathing. He continued to work with it frantically. "Live," he muttered as he moved furiously, doing everything he knew how to do to make the foal come alive. "Live, damn you!"

Finally, it began to move. First, its sides heaved in a deep intake of air, then one tiny hoof fluttered involuntarily. "He's breathing," Jordan gasped, wiping his face again with the back of his dirty hand. "He's alive!"

Jordan had been sure the fire was caused by the carelessness of a groom smoking in the barn. At first.

The next day, he and Cappy questioned everyone on the Moonstone payroll at length. No one admitted to smoking on the job, of course. Quite the contrary. They all denied it fiercely. Not that this surprised Jordan. They all knew the rules.

"What did you expect, Cappy?" he asked when they were alone in the trainer's office. "Nobody's going to be stupid enough to confess and put his job on the line."

"Yeah," Cappy agreed with a reluctant sigh, "I guess you're right."

"Mr. Phillips?"

Both men looked up. One of the young grooms, Danny Tyler, stood in the doorway, looking more than a little hesitant to come forward.

"Well, don't just stand there, boy—come on in here," Cappy said impatiently, waving him in.

"What is it, Danny?" Jordan asked.

"Well, sir, uh—I saw this guy coming out of the barn that night—" He stepped forward timidly. "I don't know that he was smoking for sure, but—"

"Who was it?" Jordan asked, looking from the boy to Cappy and back again. The Irishman looked as if he might explode at any moment.

"I don't know his name," Danny went on, "but it was the new guy."

"What new guy?" Jordan asked carefully.

"The one who just started the other day."

"Can't be," Cappy interjected, shaking his head.

Jordan looked at him. "What makes you so sure?"

"I haven't hired anybody new in over a year."

♻ Boston, September 1987

Hamilton, Massachusetts, a small town of approximately seven thousand residents, is located some twenty-five miles north of Boston, overlooking the Atlantic Ocean. It is characterized by rolling green hills, white pine forests, and a number of large estates. There are a few working farms but only traces of modern industry. A large portion of Hamilton's population commutes daily by train or car to work in Boston. In the Hamilton town park stands a statue of General George S. Patton, the local hero, whose family still calls Hamilton home.

Hamilton, Massachusetts, is also home to the Myopia Polo Club, founded in 1888 by a group of nearsighted sportsmen from Boston who had formed a hunt club in nearby Winchester six years earlier. Finding the rural ambience in Hamilton more to their liking—as well as having more space for fox hunting—they relocated. They added polo to their activities and, in the fall of 1888, played their first real match against a team from the Dedham Country Club on what would become known as Gibney Field. It has been said that the first match, which literally started with a bang—an accident—ended with a whitewash when the two team captains, Myopia's George Meyer and Dedham's Percival Lowell, collided in a mad dash for the ball. Lowell was sidelined for the duration of the game, and his team suffered a humiliating 13–0 defeat.

As Sloane crossed the now quiet Gibney Field to join Jordan at the far end of the field, she tried to imagine what Myopia had been like at the turn of the century, the club's so-called "tuxedo days." She tried to picture well-heeled Bostonians arriving in their elegant horse-drawn carriages, sipping tea un-

206

der their parasols along the sidelines on a sunny Sunday afternoon. Fashion had changed drastically since then, and modes of transportation had also undergone a number of marked changes, but Myopia's old-world elegance had endured, more as a feeling than as a physical presence.

She waved to Jordan, who was mounting up. He smiled as she approached. "Didn't expect to see you out here so early," he called out to her. "Was the interview canceled?"

Sloane nodded. "For the third time," she said wearily, whipping off her wide-brimmed white hat. "There was a plane crash at Logan Airport—no way can I compete with hard news."

He grinned. "As I recall, you weren't put off for hard news last time." He put on his helmet and fastened the chin strap.

She shook her head. "The reporter had to go interview a baseball player who was only in town that day." She preferred not to be reminded of that; she *did* like to say it made her realize why she'd never been overly fond of baseball.

Jordan laughed. "Hardly what I'd call 'hard news.'"

"Hardly," Sloane agreed with a shake of her head. "I need a shoulder to cry on."

He smiled knowingly. "Wish I could oblige you, love, but you came at a bad time," he told her. "After practice, I promise."

She looked up at him with mock hurt in her eyes. "Taking a back seat to polo, am I?" she wanted to know. "Does this mean the honeymoon's over?"

"Not a chance," he answered her, taking the mallet handed up to him by a groom. "It's just on hold—till after the match."

Sloane shook her head as she watched him ride onto the field with the other players. Even in the joking tone of their exchange, she would never have pointed out to him that today's match was only a practice game. Whether it was a practice match or the U.S. Open, every match was important to Jordan. They all mattered deeply to him. It wouldn't do to minimize their importance, even in fun.

Most of the players on the field today were from Myopia polo families—the Littles, Fawcetts, Daniels, Carpenters, McGowans, and Snows. It seemed to Sloane that this was the case wherever they went. Players almost always came from families of players; the fathers taught their sons and so on.

Jordan had often said he'd like to have his own family team one day. Watching Jordan make an offside backhand shot that sent the ball flying, she found herself wondering if he would teach Travis to play. She wondered if he would teach his own child to play. Her hand moved down to her belly, already beginning to swell. She smiled to herself. A year ago, if anyone had told her she'd be going through another pregnancy, she would have laughed. But then, if anyone had told her a year ago that she'd even want to get married—let alone do it—she would have laughed. She'd always been too much of a skeptic to believe it could work.

But now . . . now she believed anything was possible.

"I don't care what time it is on the West Coast!" Gavin Hillyer barked into the telephone receiver. "You just get that bastard on the phone and get it done! I don't give a damn if you have to drag that S.O.B. out of bed to do it! What? You'd damn well *better* call me back!"

He slammed the phone down and turned to his wife, who was calmly finishing her breakfast. "Problem, darling?" she asked, dabbing at the corners of her mouth with a napkin.

"Incompetence is always a problem," he growled, taking a seat at the table across from her. "There are times I think I have to do every goddamned thing myself in order to make sure it gets done," Hillyer complained, lifting the cover from his plate. He hoped the food here at the Copley-Plaza was better than at the last hotel. It had been deplorable, especially considering what it had cost him.

"I thought you already were," Nadine said, mildly amused. She tasted her orange juice, then turned her attention back to her crepes.

He ignored her comment, his mind clearly still on business as he ate in silence. Nadine watched him, aware there was unrest in the Hillyer empire but ignorant of any details since her husband rarely, if ever, confided in her.

Still . . . this time he seemed worried, really worried. He'd dealt with setbacks and reverses in the past without even batting an eye. Troubles just rolled off him like water off a duck's feathers. Nadine had always believed he could deal with anything. But now . . . now he didn't hide his concern. That worried Nadine. If the business was in serious financial trouble, it could mean that they were in serious financial trouble personally.

Nadine could not imagine herself broke. She could not imagine herself living the life of an ordinary woman, an ordinary housewife. A life without servants, without furs and jewels and travel and four-star restaurants and luxury hotels was unthinkable. A life any less opulent than the one she now led was unthinkable. No . . . she couldn't deal with that, she realized now.

She couldn't deal with that at all.

The first thing they saw when they drove through the gates at Myopia were the police cars—two of them, parked in the circular drive in front of the clubhouse. Jordan braked the rental car, a 1985 white Mustang, to a stop behind the second squad car. "What the hell's going on?" he wondered aloud, craning his neck as he scanned the group of people gathered at the clubhouse entrance for familiar faces.

"Think there's been some kind of trouble?" Sloane asked.

"The police wouldn't be here for any other reason." Spotting Lance and Eric Langogne in the crowd, he got out of the car and went around to open the door for Sloane.

She trailed behind as he joined the group of people talking with the police, wondering what could have happened. In the year she and Jordan had been together, she'd seen a lot of accidents on the polo fields. There had been more injuries than she could count. She was accustomed to the ambulances that were always parked at fieldside. Police cars were another thing. Polo, for all of its excitement and danger—more people died playing polo than any other sport—was still a gentleman's sport.

"Some maniac got into the stables at Silver Leaf Farms last night," she heard Lance saying as she joined the group. "Two of Hillyer's horses were pretty badly injured. They had to be put down."

"How did it happen?" Jordan asked.

Lance frowned. "Somebody rammed something up Diamond Gem's rectum—the vet said it might have been a broom handle—and cut through the intestine. They did the same thing to Crown Jewel, but didn't completely puncture the rectum. Still, it was bad enough for the horse to have to be put down.''

"How the hell could any one person have done it?'' Jordan asked skeptically. "There's no way one man could hold a horse still for something like that. He would have gotten his brains kicked out!''

Lance shrugged. "Obviously, he found a way,'' he said grimly.

"Or it wasn't just one person,'' Jordan speculated.

"How would a group of people get into the stables—even at night—without being seen?'' Sloane asked then.

Jordan was thoughtful for a moment. "A lot more easily than one man could make one very large horse stand still for torture,'' he muttered angrily.

Sloane shuddered. She thought she was going to be ill.

"They don't have any idea who did it?'' Jordan asked.

Lance shook his head. "That's why they're here,'' he said, gesturing toward the two policemen. "They're talking to everyone connected with polo.''

Jordan frowned. "Where's Hillyer?'' he asked. "Surely he's been notified—''

"Not yet,'' Lance said gravely. "They tried to call him, but he'd already left the hotel. I talked to Nad—Mrs. Hillyer—about fifteen minutes ago. She said he was on his way out here.''

Sloane looked at Lance, then at Jordan. The look on her husband's face told her he'd picked up on Lance's slip of the tongue and didn't have the slightest doubt as to why he'd really called Nadine Hillyer.

Jordan nodded but didn't comment on Lance's conversation with Hillyer's wife. "He should be here soon, then,'' he said, looking around. "Not that he gives a damn about the horses. He'll only be concerned about collecting from the insurance company.''

This came as a surprise to Sloane. "The horses are insured?'' she asked.

"Of course,'' Jordan answered, frowning. "Hillyer's ponies are valuable animals. Some of them were bred and trained on the pampas of Argentina. He's paid as much as fifty thousand dollars apiece for them. You can bet that when Gavin Hillyer puts out that kind of money, every one of those horses is going to be heavily insured.''

Lance nodded in agreement. "He's not about to come out the loser.'' It was clear that Lance shared Jordan's low opinion of the man they both worked for.

Jordan was the first to spot Hillyer's car coming up the drive. "Speak of the devil,'' he murmured.

It was times like this that made Sloane wonder why Jordan had ever agreed to play for White Timbers. He never bothered to hide his dislike of Gavin Hillyer. He didn't like the way Hillyer treated his players *or* his horses. And he didn't need the money—so why had he ever accepted Hillyer's offer, even if it was for a quarter of a million dollars a year? Oh, he'd given his reasons, but she wasn't sure she would have compromised herself to that degree.

Oh, come on, she told herself. *You're a fine one to talk— you sold your soul in the fine print in your contracts!*

The police approached Hillyer as he got out of his car. Sloane could see them talking but couldn't hear what they were saying. She could see that Hillyer was upset. Maybe Jordan and Lance had been wrong about him on that count. Maybe he did care about his horses after all.

"Here he comes," Lance said in a low voice as Hillyer turned away from the two uniformed policemen and started toward them.

"He looks pissed off.''

Jordan frowned. "What did you expect?'' he asked. "Hillyer hates like hell to lose.''

"How the hell did this happen?'' Hillyer demanded angrily as he approached them. "Don't they have any goddamned security at that stable?''

"They don't hire Wells Fargo to provide twenty-four-hour security, Gavin,'' Jordan said darkly. "They've never had to. This sort of thing doesn't exactly happen every day, you know.''

"They were responsible for the care and safety of *my* horses,'' Hillyer said crossly, glancing around as if he were looking for someone.

"What did the police say?'' Jordan wanted to know.

Hillyer shook his head, irritated. "No leads. No possible

suspects,'' he said. ''Do you realize what this means? The insurance company won't pay off right away. There will have to be an investigation. It could take months, dammit!'' Spotting the owner of Silver Leaf Farms, where the horses had been at the time of the attack, he abruptly headed off for a confrontation.

''He really doesn't care,'' Sloane observed, amazed, as she watched him stalk away. ''All he cares about is the money.''

Jordan looked disgusted. ''Sentimental fool.''

They'd been there before, that same dingy tavern on the Boston waterfront. Normally they never met at the same place twice. That was one of the rules of the game. Never take unnecessary chances. Never be seen anywhere either party might be recognized.

But there was no chance of that here. Not here. Even though it was clear that neither of the men belonged, they were completely ignored, just as they had been the first time. They sat alone, heads lowered toward each other as they spoke, keeping their voices low.

''Here's your money.'' One of the men produced a thick brown envelope.

The other reached across the table and took it. Opening it just enough to look inside, he did a quick check of the currency inside. Mixed denominations, nothing larger than a fifty, unmarked bills.

''It's all there.''

He nodded, then tucked it inside his jacket.

''I'll be in touch.''

The other man was silent for a moment. ''When's this all gonna end, man?''

''When I say it ends, that's when.''

The bizarre events of the night before certainly hadn't lowered the team's morale, Sloane decided as she watched the action from the sidelines. If anything, they were more determined than ever to win. She wasn't sure how the other players felt, of course, but she knew Jordan was working off a lot of aggression. He felt a great deal of anger, both at the person or persons who had so savagely attacked the White Timbers horses and at Gavin Hillyer for his lack of compassion. Jordan's aggressiveness on the polo field was his way of dealing with that anger.

Now Jordan was involved in a showdown with the opposing back, at times evoking wild cheering from the spectators. The other player was giving him a run for his money, but Jordan wasn't about to let him make the goal. Sloane held her breath as a collision was narrowly averted. When, she wondered, would she ever get used to the dangers that were so much a part of professional polo?

The answer was simple: never.

She would never get used to the fact that the man she loved, the man she'd married, knowingly put his life on the line every time he rode out onto the polo field. She would never get over feeling sick every time Jordan took a spill. She would never get over the fear that one day polo, which took away a part of him that could never be hers, might take all of him from her.

Permanently.

Several yards away from where Sloane was sitting, Max and Jilly Kenyon were watching the match with British shipbuilder William Spencer-Whyte, the sponsor of Max's team, and his wife, Lady Margaret. Lady Margaret's understated elegance—simple dove-gray suit, single strand of pearls, and upswept pale blond hair—provided a sharp contrast to Jilly's wild, wind-blown hair, large jewelry, low-cut polka-dotted dress, and wide-brimmed black straw hat. The two women had nothing in common beyond their husbands' involvement in polo and spoke no more than a few words to each other though they found themselves sitting side by side while their husbands talked polo.

Why did Max do this to her? Jilly wondered resentfully. He knew how much she hated playing hostess to the dreary wives of his stuffy friends. She was young. She wanted to surround herself with young people who enjoyed life in the fast lane as much as she did. She wanted to have a good time. She wanted to have *fun*.

Max was barely into his thirties himself. Why couldn't he understand that? Was he so determined to make sure she didn't look at another man—and no other man looked at her—that he would go to such extremes to guarantee it?

Doesn't he realize it won't do any good? she wondered as she watched Jordan ride off his opponent to wild applause from the spectators. She'd been such a fool to let him get away. Jordan Phillips was the best lover she'd ever had. The best lover? Yes—that and more. Much more. He was the best thing that had ever happened to her, and she'd been such a damned fool to let him get away. She'd not only *let* him get away, she'd all but shoved him out the door that morning at Chukka Cove.

It was a mistake for which she'd never stopped paying.

"What're *they* doing here?" Jordan asked irritably, catching sight of Jilly and Max near the pony lines as he handed his mallet to a groom and dismounted.

"Who?" Sloane asked, pretending not to have noticed the presence of the Kenyons at Gibney Field, when, in fact, she'd been aware of them from the moment they arrived.

"Jilly and Mad Max." He gestured toward them. "When did they get here?"

Sloane shrugged. "I have no idea. Like I said, I didn't even know they were here," she lied. "Anyway, why should it surprise you? We run into them all the time." *Unfortunately*, she thought.

Jordan pulled off his helmet. "His team isn't scheduled to play," he said tightly.

"So?"

"Kenyon's not the type to fly halfway around the world just to *watch* a match," he said, taking the damp towel she offered him. Wiping his face and neck thoroughly, he ran it over his already damp, tousled hair, then draped it over his shoulders. "Not without a damned good reason."

"Reason?" Sloane asked, pouring him a glass of iced tea. She handed it to him. "Like what?"

"I wish I knew." Jordan took a long swallow. The truth was he did have his suspicions, but he wasn't about to say anything to anyone, not even Sloane, until he was sure.

Until he was absolutely certain of Max Kenyon's whereabouts the night the White Timbers horses were attacked.

↻ Sydney, September 1987

"Honestly, Daddy, the longer I'm with Maxwell, the more convinced I am that our marriage is nothing but a bad joke," Jilly lamented, twisting the large diamond ring on her left hand nervously as she spoke.

She and her father, John Fleming, were having lunch at the Abbey, an Italian restaurant in Glebe, a few miles west of the city. The Abbey is a restored stone church said to be over a hundred years old. It is ornately furnished and surrounded by a garden, and a cocktail bar now stands where once there was an altar.

Fleming, still a fit and attractive man in his late fifties, settled back in his chair and studied his daughter. Jilly had grown into a beautiful woman, there was no question about that. She was the mirror image of her mother—which, Fleming supposed now, was the reason he'd found it so hard to spend much time with her once she'd grown up. For all his womanizing in his youth, he'd loved Sarah deeply. From the moment he'd met her, he'd known his bachelor days were numbered. While she was alive, he never looked at another woman. After she died, there had been women, of course, but only to satisfy his sexual needs. None of them was ever a part of his life for very long, and that was the way he wanted it. But now, looking at his daughter . . . it made him think of his Sarah, and the memory was painful.

He reached for his drink, and took a long swallow. "Maxwell loves you, Jillian," he said quietly.

"Loves me?" Jilly's laugh was hollow. "It's not love, Daddy—it's more like a very strange obsession. You don't see him every day—you don't know what he's really like.''

"He's a jealous man," Fleming maintained. "Nothing wrong with that.''

"Were you jealous when it came to Mother?" she asked hesitantly.

His smile was sad. "I would have killed any man who even looked at her the wrong way," he answered truthfully. "As a matter of fact, I was in a number of brawls for just that reason. Spent more than one night in jail, cooling off.''

"I'm afraid of Max's temper," Jilly admitted. "There are times . . . God, he's so violent at times.''

"You've done more than your share to cross him these days, Jillian," Fleming pointed out.

That remark angered Jilly, so much so that she was unable to keep quiet. "How can you take his part like this?" she demanded. "I'm your *daughter*!"

"You're also Maxwell's wife," he reminded her, lighting one of the long, slim cigars he always smoked. "The way I hear it, you haven't been acting much like a wife lately.''

"Meaning what, exactly?" Jilly asked carefully, biting off each word.

"Meaning I've heard about your recent behavior from some of my friends stateside," Fleming told her. "You're a married woman, Jillian. Jordan Phillips is married now as well. Whatever possessed you to throw yourself at him the way I hear you've been doing?''

"I was in love with Jordan a long time before either of us was married. I'm still in love with him.''

"You're married to Max now.''

"I'm thinking about getting a divorce," she said, frowning. "I'm thinking very seriously about it.''

"Don't do anything foolish, Jillian." His tone held a warning note.

Her expression was grim. "The only foolish thing I've done, Daddy," she began evenly, "was marrying Max Kenyon to start with.''

That, she thought, *and throwing away the only chance I've ever had to really be happy. But I'm not giving up . . . not without a fight.*

Jilly wished she could talk to her father. She wished he would listen, that he would care. But he'd never believe her if she told him what Max was really like, and what her husband was entirely capable of doing. . . .

Max Kenyon's frustration was evident in the way he stalked across the practice field to his parked car. He didn't look back as two grooms went on about the business of tending his horses. He pulled off his helmet and gloves in sharp, angry gestures and tossed them, along with his whip, into the back seat of his convertible. Raking his fingers through his hair, he sucked in his breath.

Damn Jilly, anyway!

His wife was driving him to distraction. Didn't she realize what it did to him when she flirted openly with other men? Didn't she care how he felt when he noticed the look in her eyes as she watched Jordan on the polo field—or at the sidelines with his new wife? Didn't she care how it made him look?

He got in the car and slipped the key into the ignition. He sat there for a long time, half listening to the low hum of the car's perfectly tuned motor as he considered the matter of his wife's roving eye. He simply could not tolerate such unacceptable behavior any longer. She was his wife and it was time she started to act accordingly. Her blatant flirting had to stop and stop right now. She had to get Jordan Phillips out of her system.

Jilly, he decided with finality, had to be taught a lesson. They both did.

₪ San Antonio, September 1987

Nothing seemed to work.

Gavin Hillyer was worried but trying damned hard not to let it show. Sitting in the back of a limousine leaving the San Antonio airport, he pulled his brown leather attaché case up onto his lap and unlocked it. He opened the case slowly as if it contained some dangerous radioactive substance. *It's just as bad,* he thought as he sifted through the papers and files inside. *Maybe worse.*

The company was in trouble. He needed to get his hands on some capital—and a lot of it—fast. But where? That was the problem. It seemed to him now that every major bank in the country had been approached, and they had all turned him down. Southwest Steel was teetering on a shaky foundation, and that was the sort of thing that made bankers nervous. Regardless of the company's past performance, and it had certainly withstood the test of time, they saw it now as a bad risk. The pompous bastards! Didn't they realize that the Hillyer empire had been in trouble before? In those times, however, bankers had more guts. They weren't afraid to take risks, not with a proven performer like Southwest Steel. Not even in its darkest hours. But now . . . .

While Hillyer pondered his rather bleak situation, his wife, seated next to him in the limo, was ruminating over her own problems. Staring through the tinted glass window into the traffic around them, she was aware only of her own reflection. In spite of all of her efforts, in spite of the skill of the plastic surgeon, in spite of the striking face she saw looking back at her from the tinted glass, Nadine still felt like an old woman.

An old woman whose young lover was losing interest.

It was true. Lance *was* losing interest in her. His interest in her had never gone beyond recreational sex, but these days even his interest in that seemed to be waning. Half the time he wasn't available when she wanted to be with him, though she suspected that he often made excuses simply because he didn't want to see her. And when they did go to bed, it was always over much sooner than Nadine would have liked. He didn't bother much with foreplay. He just got on top of her, satisfied himself, and sent her on her way.

Nadine frowned. In that respect, he was no different from Gavin.

Jilly hadn't wanted to come.

She'd made her feelings on the subject quite clear, but Max had insisted. He could be so bloody unreasonable. He wouldn't hear of her staying behind in Sydney because, quite simply, he didn't trust her any further than he could see her. Max wasn't an easy person to take under any circumstances—he was arrogant and demanding and generally humorless—but his jealousy, constantly growing in intensity, made him unbearable.

When she looked at him, when she thought of the things he'd done and the things she suspected he'd done but had never been able to prove, it made her blood run cold.

She watched as Max spoke with the porter collecting their luggage from the baggage carousel, wishing they'd hurry. She hated crowds and crowded airports in particular. They made her nervous.

Max made her nervous.

Lance leaned on the fence, watching the horses that frisked about in the paddock. *Must be nice,* he thought dismally. *Damned nice. Human beings are the so-called superior species, but animals really have it made. They eat, they play, they mate with whoever happens to be handy, but they don't fall in love. It's the only way to be.*

It had been more than a year since Paula had left him, and he still hadn't gotten her out of his system. He was still in love with a woman who'd dumped him, but he couldn't manage to shake a woman he didn't want. He ran one hand through his hair as his frustration surfaced once again. Why did he ever get involved with Nadine Hillyer, of all people!

I must have a death wish, he thought.

Sloane was beginning to wish she hadn't come.

She'd had a blinding headache on the plane, and now, alone in their suite at the Hyatt Regency, as she attempted to unpack, a wave of nausea swept over her. She stopped what she was doing and sat down on the edge of the bed, drawing in a deep breath. Maybe she should have listened to Jordan. Maybe she should have stayed home. After all, he was going to be here only three days. And she did need to spend more time with Travis. Not that she really believed he missed her all that much . . . her son had begun to live a life of his own, with his own circle of friends, pursuing his own interests. *My baby's growing up,* she thought with a mixture of pride and regret. *He doesn't need me anymore.*

And now here she was, starting all over again. A new husband. A new baby on the way. *Am I crazy?* she asked herself, though not for the first time. Probably. As much as she'd always loved Travis, from the moment he was born—no, she'd loved him *before* he was born—she had never been a traditional mother. *Nobody's ever going to compare me to June Cleaver,* she thought, recalling a time when Travis was only five years old. She'd been so absorbed in the manuscript she was working on, she'd forgotten that her son was in the bathtub. Only when he began to complain loudly, hours later, did she remember. She'd barely gotten through the early months of late-night feedings, diaper changings, and teething. Later on, it had been touch and go when she'd had to help him with his homework; she was hopeless at all but the simplest forms of math, and history and science had completely eluded her. Only when it came to English was she able to be of any help to him.

And now she was going to go through it all again.

The sound of the key turning in the lock cut through her thoughts. She could hear the door opening and closing in the next room, and a moment later Jordan appeared in the doorway of the bedroom.

"I thought you were going to spend the afternoon practicing," Sloane said as he crossed the room and bent to kiss her forehead.

"Couldn't. It rained last night. The fields at Retama might as well be a swamp." He paused. "You feeling okay?"

She made a face. "I'm just a little nauseous, that's all," she said. "Goes with the territory, remember?"

"You're six months along," he reminded her. "Isn't that all supposed to subside after a few weeks?"

"Sometimes, but not always. My mother had morning sickness the entire nine months." She resumed her unpacking.

Jordan looked at her for a moment. "Now that *is* a surprise," he commented.

"What?"

"What you just said. Do you realize that this is the first time you've ever told me anything of significance about your family?" He took off his watch and put it on the dresser.

She shrugged it off. "So my mother had morning sickness the entire nine months she carried me. What's the big deal?"

He dropped into a chair in one corner of the room, drawing one leg up across the other, his arms folded behind his head. "It *is* a big deal to me," he said, "since I know practically nothing about your background. You never talk about your childhood. You don't tell me funny little stories about growing up in Chicago—"

She concentrated on the suitcase she was emptying. "There are no funny little stories to tell," she said quietly.

"Okay, so your childhood wasn't so great," he conceded, "but was it so bad that you can't bring yourself to talk about it at all?"

Unable to take it anymore, Sloane dropped the sweater she'd just picked up and turned to face him. "Which is more important to you, Jordan?" she wanted to know. "Who I was then—or who I am now? Which one did you marry?"

His eyes met hers. "Is there a difference?"

"I like to think there is, yes." She turned her attention back to her unpacking.

Jordan watched her, puzzled. What in her past could be so terrible that she was trying so desperately to forget?

• • •

Nadine got out of the rented BMW and walked to the front of the car where her husband stood, surveying the rain-soaked polo field. "Is the match going to be canceled?" she asked, attempting to make conversation.

He shrugged. "Who knows?"

Nadine gave a little sigh, resigned to the fact that Gavin was once again shutting her out. She didn't know why that sort of thing still came as a surprise to her. She and Gavin had never really shared things the way most husbands and wives did. If they'd ever shared that kind of closeness, even without a great sex life, she wouldn't have found it necessary to turn to other men. Gavin didn't need her. He needed the company to make him powerful, to fulfill his destiny, so to speak. He needed polo to fill his head for a constant challenge. He needed the trappings of success—the numerous homes, the cars, the yacht, the private jet, the racehorses and polo ponies—to prove to the rest of the world that he'd made it.

But he didn't need her. He didn't need her at all.

"What are they doing?" Sloane asked.

She and Dusty were sitting on the lowest level of the Retama Polo Club's unique double-sided grandstand, watching as two helicopters, flying dangerously low, moved back and forth across the polo field. At one end of the field, players gathered under a tent while grooms tended ponies. A group of spectators en route to the cantina—an authentic army barracks brought to Retama plank by plank from Fort Sam Houston—crossed at the edge of the sand-dressed Bermuda grass field.

"They're blow-drying the field—or trying to, anyway," Dusty explained. "It's an expensive procedure. I've only heard of it being done once before, at Oak Brook, some years ago. It was a big event, and supposedly the date couldn't be changed for a lot of good reasons."

"They look like they're about to crash," Sloane worried aloud.

Dusty shook her head. "Those guys know what they're doing."

"It seems like it would be smarter to cancel the match."

The other woman studied her for a moment, realizing it wasn't the helicopters—or how they were flying—that bothered her. "Don't worry about Jordy, Sloane," she said then. "He's been at this for a lot of years. He's played under more adverse conditions than you could imagine."

"I could imagine a lot of things," Sloane said quietly. "I could imagine—I *have* imagined—him taking a fall on a field just like this. I've imagined him not being able to roll clear of the horse and—"

"Don't," Dusty said as she reached out to touch Sloane's arm reassuringly. "Don't let the 'what ifs' make you crazy. I know what that can do to you. My mother used to travel with my father, but it made her a nervous wreck. Dad's taken a lot of spills in the years he's been playing—I think he's broken just about every bone in his body—but it took a bigger toll on Mom. She'd get hysterical every time Dad took a fall or was involved in a collision. After her heart attack the doctors advised her not to travel with us anymore. They knew what it did to her."

Sloane turned to look at her. "She doesn't attend the matches at all?"

Dusty shook her head. "It's for her own good," she said. "Not that she really misses it, because I don't think she does."

"She doesn't like polo?"

"She doesn't like the risk involved."

"I know the feeling," Sloane said quietly.

It's becoming riskier and riskier every day, Sloane thought grimly. There had been too many "accidents" lately for them to be seriously considered accidents any longer. *They really are the Four Horsemen of the Apocalypse. Death and disaster seem to follow them everywhere.*

Where would it all end?

The play was fast and furious in spite of the less than perfect conditions on the field. Jordan's team won by only a slim margin, 11–12, but he declined to join in the postgame festivities, preferring to spend a quiet evening alone with Sloane. They had dinner at a Creole restaurant, La Louisiane, after which they took a long walk in the moonlight. San Antonio is a city rich in Spanish-American history, clearly in evidence wherever one turns, from the Alamo to the Paseo del Rio to the pedal boats in which sightseers can pedal themselves up and down the river, admiring the sights at leisure, to La Villita, an eighteenth-century Spanish city within a city.

"You've been awfully quiet all evening," Jordan observed as they walked. "Feeling all right?"

Sloane looked at him. "Why do you keep asking me that?"

"You've been looking a little pale. You haven't been yourself. So naturally"—he gave a little shrug—"I worry."

"Well, don't." She gave him an affectionate peck on the cheek. "I'm fine. I swear I am."

He took her in his arms and kissed her forehead gently. "Sorry, love—you're not doing a very good selling job."

She looked up at him, smiling. "Then maybe we should go back to the hotel," she said softly, "so I can prove it."

At midnight, Gavin Hillyer was on the phone with his people in New York and Los Angeles, ranting and raving at them—but to no avail—while his wife slept soundly in the next room. Normally, he would have been amazed that she was able to sleep—even with the aid of those strong sleeping pills she almost always took at bedtime—but tonight he was too involved with his business affairs to care whether or not he might be disturbing Nadine.

"I don't want to hear any more of your goddamned excuses, Mathison!" Hillyer barked into the receiver. "I'm paying you for results—and I damn well expect to see some and fast! . . . No, that won't do. Not good enough . . . No. You know what I expect you to do! You just go *do* it—or submit your resignation!" Slamming the phone down, he ran a hand over his thinning hair. He felt as though it were all closing in on him. Everything seemed to be moving too fast.

Time, unfortunately, was running out.

"Now do you think I'm ready for the convalescent home?" Sloane asked, stroking Jordan's chest lightly with her fingertips.

He smiled down at her in the darkness, drawing the sheets up to cover both of them. "Is that all there was to it?" he asked in a mildly teasing voice. "You trying to prove something?"

"You know better than that." She traced his lips with the

tip of her index finger, then raised her head to kiss his chin.

"Uh-hmm." He threaded his fingers through her hair, kissing her forehead. "There are times, love, when I wonder how well I really *do* know you."

"About as well as anyone could," she said simply.

"There are times I seriously doubt that."

She raised her head and looked at him oddly. "What makes you say that?"

"Well," he began thoughtfully, "there *are* times . . . times I feel as if you're keeping a part of yourself locked away, not allowing anyone access to that part, no matter what."

"You mean because I don't talk about my childhood," she concluded.

"No. That's part of it, sure, but—"

"My childhood was nothing to write home about, Jordy," she said quietly. "I wasn't happy, and there was little about it I care to remember. In fact, I've spent a lot of years actively *trying* to forget."

"Even an unhappy childhood must have *some* happy memories."

"Offhand, I can't think of any." She snuggled against him. "You know, Phillips, this is depressing as hell. Could we please talk about something else?"

"Like what?"

"Oh, I don't know." Her hand moved down over his chest, stroking, caressing, moving downward slowly, leaving no doubt as to her destination. "How about this . . . "

Ian Welles was alone in the trailer in which the White Timbers tack was kept. It wouldn't have mattered if there had been anyone with him. He wouldn't have noticed or, for that matter, cared. What he'd stumbled onto during a casual inspection of the tack puzzled and concerned him . . . though he wasn't quite sure why. This sort of thing happened all the time; he'd lost track of how many times in the years he himself had played the game. It wasn't all that unusual. Still . . .

"Dad?"

His head jerked up, startled by the sound of his daughter's voice as she entered the trailer. "I thought you'd be out practicing," he said quietly, absently fingering the bridle in his hand.

"Where?" she asked, pulling the door shut. "It rained again early this morning. Sixteen fields here and all of them looking more like the Florida Everglades than southern Texas." She moved a pile of martingales aside and seated herself on an old trunk near the door.

Ian was examining the bridle thoughtfully.

Dusty studied him for a moment. "You okay, Dad?"

"I'm not sure," he started slowly. He looked up then. "Have you noticed any problems with your tack lately?"

"What kind of problems?"

"Anything. Frayed girths, broken bridles—"

Dusty laughed. "All the time. I think it falls under the heading of 'occupational hazard.' " She paused, puzzled by the look on his face. "Why do you ask?"

"I'm not sure," he admitted as he passed the bridle to her. "Take a look."

Dusty did as he asked. "It looks almost as if it's been deliberately cut," she commented, holding the damaged rein up to the light.

"Maybe it was."

She looked at him. "What are you suggesting?"

"That lately there have been too many coincidences."

"I don't—"

"Think about it, Kirsten." He called her by her real name only when he was upset about something. "How many near misses has the team had in the past year? How many falls? And how many of those were the result of damaged tack?"

Dusty shook her head. "Don't you think you're overreacting?" she asked, handing the bridle back to him. "Jeez, Dad—you've been playing long enough to know that this sort of thing happens just about every day."

"They break. They're not deliberately cut."

"You can't be sure it was."

"You saw it. What do you think?"

She shook her head. "I'm not sure *what* to think."

Ian did. He was thinking of the horses that had to be put down at Myopia.

And wondering if there could be a connection.

BOOK FOUR
SPADES

New York City, October 1987

The pain was unbearable.

Sloane was only vaguely aware of being taken off the plane at La Guardia Airport by paramedics who transported her by ambulance to the hospital in Manhattan. She remembered Jordan being at her side in the ambulance, holding her hand, trying to comfort her. She remembered not being able to hear what he was saying to her above the loud wail of the siren.

And she remembered the pain. The terrible, intense pain that ripped through her body. Pain that felt as if her insides were being torn apart. Relentless pain that didn't let up for even a moment.

And now she was being wheeled through a busy, brightly lit hospital emergency room. Jordan was still gripping her hand, half running alongside the gurney as two attendants maneuvered it through a crowded corridor and into an examining room. A nurse yanked the heavy green curtain shut as the attendants retreated. "The doctor'll be in right away," she told Jordan as she checked Sloane's pulse. "How far along is she?"

Jordan frowned. "Six months. The baby's due at the end of December."

The nurse strapped a wide cuff around Sloane's upper arm and checked her blood pressure. Shaking her head, she removed the cuff quickly. "Severe pain," she noted. "Any bleeding?"

"Some."

"Nausea?"

Jordan nodded.

The doctor came in then, a tall, thin man who looked to be in his late forties, dressed in green surgical scrubs. He and the nurse spoke briefly in hushed tones, then he turned to Jordan. "You'll have to wait outside in the—"

"No!" This was Sloane.

"Only until I've examined her," the doctor said.

Jordan nodded. He looked down at his wife. "It won't be for long," he promised. "Just long enough for them to check you over."

"No!" She gripped his hand tightly.

"I'll be right outside." He pried himself free. "I'll come back in just as soon as they say it's okay." He bent down to kiss her forehead, then left the room quietly.

The doctor looked down at Sloane. "When did the pain start?"

"On the plane . . . we were flying in from Texas . . . I don't know," Sloane answered with uncertainty in her voice. The pain was making it hard to think clearly. "An hour, maybe longer."

"That's all? You're sure?"

"No—I'm *not* sure." Why did he have to ask so many questions? Couldn't he see how much pain she was in? "I just know it started on the plane."

"What about before that?" He pulled back the sheet covering her. The crotch of her white slacks was soaked in blood. "Any nausea, cramps?"

She was silent for a moment. "This morning . . . I couldn't eat. I felt like I was going to throw up," she recalled. "Even though my stomach was empty, I felt like I was going to throw up."

"Cramps?"

"Some. Not severe," she gasped. "Not like now."

He turned to the nurse. "Let's check her blood pressure again."

"Her blood pressure is dangerously high," the doctor told Jordan. "Right now, the possibility of a stroke is a very real danger."

Jordan looked up at him. "What do we do?"

"We feel it will be necessary to terminate the pregnancy as quickly as possible."

"There's no other way?"

The doctor shook his head. "I'm sorry."

"Have you told her?"

"We've tried," the doctor said with a heavy sigh. "She's made it clear that she will not consent to a termination of the pregnancy even though she's about to abort anyway."

Jordan looked at him questioningly.

"There's nothing we can do," the doctor said quietly as if reading his mind. "Losing the baby is inevitable now, but if we can speed it along, we might be able to save your wife."

"Might?" Jordan wanted to hit him. Rationally, he knew the doctor was only doing his job, presenting the situation as it existed, but did he have to be so goddamned cold and clinical about it?

"As I said, her blood pressure is extremely high," the doctor said gravely.

"I want to see her. Now."

"No. It's out of the question."

Jordan paced the small room, frustrated. For someone in her condition, she still had a lot of fight left in her. "Haven't you heard anything I've said?" he asked irritably. "The doctor says you're on the verge of a stroke! This could *kill* you, dammit!"

"They're not taking my baby," she said stubbornly.

"You're going to lose the baby anyway!" he blurted out, regretting the words the moment they'd left his lips. He turned to face her. "I'm sorry," he said softly as he took her hand. "I'm just worried about you, that's all."

"You wanted a child," she said. "Your own child—"

"Not if it means risking your life," he said with a shake of his head. He was fighting back tears. "Nothing is worth that. Not to me."

"It's my choice—" She stopped short, suddenly gripped by another sharp pain.

Alarmed, Jordan called out to the doctor. He turned back to Sloane. "If you don't sign the consent, I will," he told her.

"You can't do that!"

"The hell I can't! I *am* your husband!"

"If you do, I'll never forgive you."

He looked at her, his expression grim. "If I don't," he said quietly, "I'll never forgive myself."

• • •

The past few hours had seemed like days. Jordan sat in a small lounge on the hospital's maternity floor, waiting to be allowed to see his wife. It seemed cruel that they had put her on a floor where she would not only be surrounded by women who had just given birth but would be within earshot of the nursery, where she could hear the newborn babies crying. How was she going to take it? he wondered. She'd been heavily sedated since they brought her up here, but she'd be coming around soon. Any time now, the doctor had said. He was anxious to talk to her, to know she was all right. He dreaded having to tell her she'd lost the baby. She'd blame him because of what he'd said to her in the emergency room. She might not even give him a chance to tell her that he hadn't signed any consent. There hadn't been time. The pregnancy had terminated on its own.

Jordan looked at Travis, who sat next to him on the red leather couch. The boy had been sitting there in a daze since the housekeeper had brought him to the hospital shortly after Sloane was brought up to her room. He reached out and touched the boy's shoulder in a gesture of reassurance.

"She's going to be all right."

Travis nodded.

"She is. You've got my word on it."

The boy looked at him, his face serious. "Who are you trying to sell, Jordy? Me—or yourself?"

Jordan hesitated for a moment, surprised by Travis's directness. *He is his mother's son,* he thought. "Both of us," he said aloud. "Both of us."

"Does she know? About the baby, I mean."

Jordan shook his head. "Not yet."

"You going to tell her?"

"I think I should be the one to tell her, yes."

"She really wanted the baby, you know."

Jordan nodded. "I know."

"She didn't, not at first."

I know that, too. "Yeah. She told me."

"It surprised me—that she was going to have another baby, I mean," Travis said then.

"Oh?"

"Well—Mom's not very domestic, you know."

Jordan forced a smile. "So I've discovered."

"She was always there for me," the boy told him. "She always made sure I knew she loved me. But she was never good at mother things."

Jordan smiled. "Mother things?" he asked.

"You know—cooking, playing room mother at school, helping me with my homework, stuff like that." He gave a little half smile. "It's a good thing I'm smart, 'cause Mom can't do homework."

"She *is* going to be all right, you know," Jordan said then.

Travis looked down at the floor. "I hope so," he said, unconvinced.

She looks so pale, Jordan thought as he looked down at Sloane, still sleeping. She was normally fair—so fair she had to use a sunblock outdoors—but now her face was deathly white, as white as the pillow on which she lay. She was also restless, tossing her head and mumbling to herself, things that made no sense at all. The sedative was probably wearing off. That meant she'd be coming around soon.

He took a chair beside the bed and waited. He had no idea how he was going to tell her about the baby. She was going to be devastated, and coming on the heels of that scene in the emergency room, she would probably blame him. Hell, why not? Hadn't he been blaming himself since all of this started on the plane?

He never should have allowed her to go on the road with him. The doctor had made it clear that she had to take it easy. He should have put his foot down. But he hadn't. Instead, he'd been a selfish idiot, dragging her all over the world because it was what *he* wanted. *He* had wanted her with him. Oh, he'd worried about her, all right, but not enough to insist she stay home. *And now it's too late,* he thought dismally.

She was stirring again. She was trying to talk, but he couldn't hear most of what she was saying—and what he could hear didn't make any sense.

"Got to get out of here," she whispered. "Go now . . . before they come . . ."

He leaned closer, wiping her face with a damp cloth. "It's

all right,'' he said softly, soothingly. ''You're safe now.''
What's she talking about? he wondered. *Who—or what—is
she running from?*

''I'm going to have a baby . . .'' Sloane was mumbling again.
''If they catch us . . . they can't catch us . . . God, they'll take
my baby . . .''

Of course, he thought, *she means the doctors. She thinks
the doctors are trying to take the baby. She doesn't know. . . .*

''The police can't catch us, Roddy . . . we'll go to jail . . .
they'll take my baby . . . Roddy, I can't let my baby be born
in jail, Roddy . . .''

Jail? That didn't make any sense at all to Jordan. *And who
the hell is Roddy?*

Sloane was dreaming. In her drugged state, she'd gone back
in time, back to another troubled period in her life. . . .

Chicago, November 1975.
*Sloane was only six months pregnant, but she looked as if
she'd reached full term. Dressed in a taupe suit—with specially
made maternity slacks—and a forest-green turtleneck sweater
that covered her bulging tummy snugly, she sat across from
Roddy Daniels, who had been many things to her in the years
they'd known each other—including, on an off-and-on basis,
her lover. They were sitting in a red vinyl booth in a small
greasy spoon on the city's south side.*

''Sammy, I think you're worryin' for nothin','' he told her
as he took a bite of his sausage. ''The cops aren't onto us.
That old gal was off her trolley, if you know what I mean.''

''Roddy!''

''It's the truth and you know it,'' he maintained. ''She was
an easy mark. A real easy mark.''

''I feel like a louse, Roddy.''

He laughed—at her. ''Come on, Sammy!'' he chided her.
''You've been doin' this a long time. This is a hell of a time
to get cold feet!''

''It's not cold feet—not exactly,'' she said carefully. ''It's
just that, well, things are different now. The baby—''

''That baby's going to be expensive.'' He took a long swallow of his coffee. ''How do you think you're going to cover

all those expenses? Get a job? How're you gonna get a job now, in your condition? Even with that college degree of yours, the best you can hope for right now is a job as a waitress in a dive like this. Or maybe you could be a Kelly Girl. Don't pay too well, you know.''

She frowned. ''Don't remind me.''

''You want that kid to have everything, don't you?''

''You know I do.'' She picked at her food. ''And I want 'everything' to include a mother. Preferably one who isn't doing ten to twenty.''

''You worry too much.''

''I want out, Roddy . . .''

''I want out, Roddy . . . I don't want my baby born in jail . . .''

Jordan looked down at her, puzzled. Who was this Roddy? he wondered.

And why was she afraid her baby would be born in jail?

''When can I see her?'' Travis wanted to know.

''Not for a while yet,'' Jordan told him. ''She's still not completely awake. They've had to keep her medicated because she's in so much pain.''

''But she *is* going to be all right, isn't she?''

''Yeah, she is,'' Jordan promised. ''But she'll have to stay in the hospital for a while. She needs a lot of rest.''

Travis looked grim. ''When can I see her, then?''

''Maybe tomorrow,'' Jordan said, patting the boy's shoulder. ''We'll see, okay?''

He gave a reluctant nod. ''Okay.''

''Right now, I think you should go home with Emma.''

Travis opened his mouth to protest, but Jordan cut him off.

''There's nothing you can do here right now except wait,'' Jordan pointed out, ''and I think you'll be a lot more comfortable doing that at home, don't you?''

Travis looked down at his Reeboks. ''I guess so.''

''I'll call you if there's any change at all,'' Jordan assured him. ''You've got my word on it.''

Travis nodded. ''Okay.''

''Make sure he gets to bed early tonight, Emma,'' Jordan told the housekeeper.

She nodded. "If you don't mind my saying so, Mr. Phillips, I think you could do with some rest yourself," she observed.

"Yeah," he said in a tired voice. "I'll rest—just as soon as I know my wife's all right."

Emma forced a smile. "I'm sure she will be."

But as he watched them disappear into the elevator, he was thinking of something else: *I wonder if Travis was the baby she was afraid would be born in jail*.

Sloane opened her eyes. At first they refused to focus properly. She could distinguish light from dark, but the images were blurred. Her mouth felt as though it were full of cotton. She tried to talk, but the words wouldn't come out. Not at first, anyway.

"Water . . ."

Someone was bending over her. She couldn't tell who it was. She could only distinguish a shadow blocking the brilliant white light that felt warm against her face. A familiar scent—cologne, perhaps?—reached her nostrils.

"Jordan—" she breathed.

"I'm here, love." His voice was soft, reassuring.

Her eyes were finally starting to focus. "Where am I?" she asked, her voice still weak.

"You're in the hospital," he told her.

The hospital. I'm still in the hospital. Something was terribly wrong. "The baby—"

"Ssh. The doctor says you need to rest."

He's keeping something from me. I can see it in his eyes. "Jordan . . . what about the baby . . ."

"The doctor says you're going to be fine." He touched her face gently, stroking her hair.

What about my baby? her thoughts were screaming. *Tell me about my baby!* "The baby . . ."

Silence.

"What aren't you . . . telling me?" she wanted to know. But a part of her already knew. She just didn't want to believe it.

There was a long pause. When he finally spoke, he avoided her eyes. "You—you lost the baby," he said quietly.

It took a moment to sink in. She knew it, deep within herself, but she didn't want to believe it. "I didn't lose it," she said hoarsely. "They took it. You let them take it."

"No." He shook his head emphatically. "I didn't let them do anything—"

"You told me!" She started to cry. "You said you'd give them permission to take my baby!"

He turned to face her. "I said I'd do whatever was necessary to save your life!"

"Damn you." Her voice was cold, flat.

"You would have *died*!"

"Damn you." She wouldn't look at him.

"They didn't take the baby," he said finally.

She took a deep breath. "You're just saying that."

"No, I'm not." He was silent for a moment. "I was willing to sign. I admit it. They told me I couldn't. Some legal reason or other." He turned to the window, his discomfort obvious. "It didn't matter anyway. You lost the baby before anyone could do anything."

Sloane turned her head so he couldn't see the tears welling up in her eyes. That baby had been her last chance. She'd been trying to prove that there was nothing he could have with a younger woman that he couldn't have with her. She'd done it all for him, and she'd failed miserably.

I should never have married him in the first place.

Jordan brought Travis to the hospital as soon as Dr. Halsey allowed Sloane to have visitors. Cate came in, as did Adrienne, Dani, and Caroline. Jordan thought having visitors would lift her spirits, but it seemed to have the reverse effect: she was becoming more depressed, more withdrawn.

Physically, she was recovering nicely. Dr. Halsey was pleased with her progress and had said he'd have released her from the hospital days ago had it not been for her questionable mental state. Sloane was deeply depressed, and Dr. Halsey admitted he thought it might be necessary to call in a psychiatrist for consultation.

Jordan wasn't sure he liked the idea at all. "Of course she's depressed!" he responded defensively. "She's just lost a baby—that hardly makes her a schizophrenic!"

"I'm not implying that she's a schizophrenic, as you put it," the obstetrician maintained. "Even though there *is* an external cause for your wife's depression—the loss of the baby—she's showing no signs whatsoever of coming to grips with it. She hasn't accepted what's happened."

This made Jordan angry. "What do you expect?" he asked irritably, shoving his hands down into his pants pockets. "It's only been a week—I can't say I've really 'come to grips with it' myself."

"It's very different for your wife, Mr. Phillips." The doctor tried to explain. "It's normal, entirely normal, to be depressed after losing a baby. To grieve that loss. But there is normally an adjustment, a process of coping with that grief. In your wife's case—" He shook his head.

"She just needs time," Jordan insisted stubbornly. "No way am I going to push her into therapy when I'm not convinced she really needs it."

The doctor's face was serious. "I can't insist, Mr. Phillips. I can only make a recommendation," he said. "I urge you to at least *think* about it."

"Dr. Halsey says you'll be able to go home soon." Jordan pulled up a chair, sitting on it backward near Sloane's bed, his arms folded across the back.

Sloane frowned. *What is there to go home to?*

"I thought we'd go up to Moonstone for a while," Jordan went on, resting his chin on his forearm. "We both need to get away from it all—for a while, anyway."

"Don't you have a match coming up right away?" There was no emotion in Sloane's voice.

"I'm not playing," he said. "I've already talked to Hillyer."

"I'll bet he loved that."

Jordan didn't smile. "Doesn't matter whether he did or not. It's necessary—for both of us."

She avoided his eyes. "You don't have to look after me, Jordan."

He forced a smile. "I know I don't *have* to. I *want* to."

"I don't want to be looked after," she said sullenly.

Jordan was silent for a long moment. Finally, he drew in a deep breath. "I lost a baby too, Sloane," he said quietly. "I'm hurting too."

"Don't you think I know that?" Her tone was cross.

"Sometimes I wonder."

She looked at him for the first time. "It's not the same," she said tonelessly.

"How do you figure?"

"It's not. It can't be," she said. "I carried that baby inside of me. I felt it move, felt it grow."

"That makes you capable of caring more than I possibly could, is that it?" he asked with a twinge of resentment in his voice.

"It's different."

"How?"

"It just is."

"I wanted that baby just as much as you did," he said angrily. "When the doctor told me you were going to lose it, I felt so goddamned helpless—I just wanted to punch something, anything. I think I did, I don't really remember." He paused, choking up at the memory. "You know, I went out to Meadowbrook a few days ago. I borrowed a horse and spent the afternoon beating the hell out of the ball to blow off a little steam."

"Did it help?" she asked, though her tone—or lack of it—indicated minimal interest.

"Not really," he admitted. "Oh, it did for a little while. But not for long."

"Why are you telling me this?" she asked then.

He just looked at her for a moment. "I wanted you to know how I feel," he said finally. "I wanted you to realize you're not the only one who's lost a child."

"I see." Sloane turned away. "If you don't mind, I'd like to be alone for a while."

Was it a dream, or did she really hear a baby crying?

It sounded as though it were coming from the next room. Or somewhere very, very close. Crying. Continually crying. Where was it coming from? She couldn't tell because it was so dark. Pitch dark. *I can't see my own hand in front of my face.*

The darkness lifted, just a little. Enough to see light. Dim light. A figure moving in the shadows. A doctor—it had to be a doctor, he was wearing green surgical scrubs. He was holding

a newborn baby. Her baby? She reached out to take the squall-
ing infant, but the doctor withdrew. She tried again and again,
but he kept moving away from her. *Let me have my baby! I
want my baby!*

The baby continued to cry. The man was running away,
farther and farther away. She called out to him, pleading with
him, begging him to come back, but to no avail. The baby was
still crying. . . .

Sloane woke with a start. She sat up in bed, at first not sure
where she was. Then she remembered. She remembered everything. She was still in the hospital. On the maternity floor. The
nursery was just down the hall.

And the babies were still crying.

➷ Martha's Vineyard, December 1987

Christmas was just around the corner, but the atmosphere at Moonstone was anything but festive.

Jordan was beginning to wonder if he'd made a mistake. Maybe he should have listened to Dr. Halsey. Maybe Sloane *did* need professional counseling. It had been six weeks since he'd brought her home, and in that time he'd seen no significant change in her emotional state. She was prone to exaggerated mood swings—remote and withdrawn one day, unnaturally cheerful and talkative the next. She could sleep—only with the aid of pills—but she was always restless. He suspected she was troubled by nightmares. She didn't want anyone around, not even those closest to her. Most of the time he had the feeling she didn't even want him around. Once, she'd come right out and said it. That had been a day he wasn't likely ever to forget. She'd been home from the hospital for three weeks. Gavin Hillyer had called, wanting him to play at Eldorado. He'd refused. Sloane, having overheard his end of the conversation, surprised him with her response.

"Why didn't you go? You've always liked playing at Eldorado."

He'd been unable to hide his surprise. *"I want to be here for you."*

"There's nothing you can do for me, Jordan," she said indifferently. *"There's nothing anyone can do."*

"Maybe if you'd give me a chance—"

She shook her head. *"There's nothing you can do,"* she insisted. *"Besides—I like being alone."*

She'd all but sent him packing, he recalled now as he stood

at the window in the library, watching her walking in the garden. She'd been serious. She wanted to be alone.

Jordan was frustrated by this feeling of powerlessness. He wanted to help her, but he didn't know how. Hell, he didn't even know how to *reach* her! Their loss, he reasoned, should have brought them closer. They should have been able to turn to each other for consolation. They hadn't.

And now it was driving them apart.

"Where is she?" Cate asked.

Jordan, seated in a black leather armchair in the library, shrugged. "She left an hour ago. She said she was going for a walk," he answered. "She never confides in me anymore."

Cate put her leather briefcase on the desk. "She's still depressed?"

"Most of the time," Jordan said sullenly. "Her moods change so drastically from day to day, it's hard to tell. I never know what to expect."

"Then she hasn't been writing?"

Jordan's laugh was hollow. "Surely you're joking. These days she doesn't even *read* a book, much less attempt to write one." He got to his feet. "She doesn't really *do* much of anything these days."

Cate raised an eyebrow questioningly.

Jordan frowned. "She sleeps late most of the time," he said. "When she finally does get up, she either stays in her room or goes for walks—long walks. On the beach, in the woods—"

She raised a hand to stop him. "Back up. She stays in *her* room?"

He nodded. "I've been sleeping in one of the guest rooms."

"For how long?"

"Since I brought her home from the hospital."

Cate shook her head. "Your idea?"

"Hardly," he snorted. "She said she thought it would be for the best, that she wasn't sleeping well—which she wasn't. But—" He paused. "But the truth was she didn't want me in her bed, and she still doesn't because she's afraid I'll want something from her she isn't prepared to give."

"Jordan, have you considered seeking professional help?" Cate asked then.

"You mean a psychiatrist."

She nodded.

"I've thought about it. As a matter of fact, Dr. Halsey spoke to me about it while Sloane was still in the hospital," he admitted, turning to the window. "I thought he was way off base."

Cate said nothing, but looked at him expectantly, waiting for him to go on.

"I brought her home against his recommendation," Jordan recalled, staring through the window into the garden without really seeing it. "I thought all she needed was to be away from that damned hospital. They had her on the maternity floor—right down the hall from the nursery. Seeing the other women with their babies, hearing them cry—how could she *not* be depressed?" He looked at Cate. "Was I wrong to take her away from that?"

Cate shook her head. "You were doing what you thought was best for her."

"But I was wrong," he concluded.

"It's not too late. If you were to get her into therapy now—" Cate began.

"I'm not sure she'd even agree to talk to someone, let alone go into therapy," Jordan said quietly. "She's convinced there's nothing anyone can do."

"Then you have to convince her," Cate said promptly. "*We* have to convince her."

The sun was warm on Sloane's face, but she didn't feel it. The scent of pine trees and saltwater was in the air, but she didn't smell it. She was barely aware of her surroundings as she walked alone in a wooded area near the beach. It wouldn't have mattered where she was because she was aware only of what was going on within herself.

She was aware only of her own pain.

The physical pain had diminished with the passing weeks. Her abdomen had shrunk back to its normal size, and the bleeding had stopped. The emotional wounds, however, were still open. Still painful. Still very much with her. Still a reminder of her failure as a wife, as a woman.

She didn't want to turn away from Jordan, didn't want to shut him out, but how could she face him knowing she'd failed him? Jordan wanted children—children of his own—more than anything. He'd made no secret of that, even before they were married.

She'd worried about it then. She'd been hesitant to marry him for that reason. Hadn't she told him he needed a younger woman, someone who could give him the large family he'd always wanted? He'd insisted that none of that mattered, that she was the only woman he wanted.

But it *did* matter. It mattered to her.

And it mattered to him. She was sure it did—no matter what he said. He'd wanted that baby, even more than she did, right from the beginning. She still remembered how uncertain she'd been about having another child. She remembered the ambivalence she'd felt when she discovered she was pregnant.

And it made her feel even guiltier.

Had she lost the baby because there was still a part of her that didn't really want it? She'd never been superstitious, but now . . . that thought nagged at her constantly. She'd had doubts, and she'd lost her baby. Didn't a lot of people believe in the mind's power over the body? Wasn't it *possible*?

If it *was,* then it meant this really was her fault.

"She's lost fifteen pounds. She barely eats these days."

Cate looked at him, concerned.

"No appetite," Jordan said grimly. "That's what she says."

"A loss of appetite is often a symptom of depression," Cate said, nodding. "You said she *was* sleeping well?"

He shrugged. "She sleeps, but she's usually pretty restless. I think she has nightmares. I've looked in on her during the night and found her tossing and turning. Sometimes she talks in her sleep." He paused for a long moment. "Do you know if Sloane ever knew someone named Roddy?"

Something registered on Cate's face; Jordan wasn't sure if it was recognition or alarm, and it was gone before he could identify it. He opened his mouth to ask, but before he could get the words out, Sloane appeared in the doorway. "I'm going up to my room—" She stopped short when she saw Cate. "What brings you up here, so far from Manhattan?" she asked, without any real interest in her voice.

Cate hesitated. "I wanted to see how the book is coming along."

Sloane looked at her blankly. "It isn't," she said. And she turned, without another word, and headed up the stairs.

Sloane climbed the stairs as if it took every ounce of energy she could summon. She went directly to the master bedroom and closed herself up there. As she collapsed onto the bed, she idly wondered what had brought Cate all the way up to Martha's Vineyard. It wasn't the book, as she'd said; Sloane was sure of that. If she'd only wanted to know how the new book was "coming along"—the longest aborning of her projects to date, it was hardly a "new" book anymore—she would have called. No, she was here for another reason.

Jordan had probably called her.

A knock at the bedroom door cut through her thoughts. She raised herself up on her elbows. "Jordan, I really don't want—"

"It's not Jordan," Cate said, opening the door. "All right if I come in?"

Sloane hesitated for a moment, then nodded. "Sure."

As Cate entered the room, Sloane pulled herself upright, sitting cross-legged in the middle of the bed. Cate crossed the room and sat on the edge of the bed, smoothing the skirt of her jade-green suit over her knees with one hand. "How have you been feeling?" she asked softly.

So that's why she's here. "About as well as can be expected under the circumstances," Sloane said aloud. She avoided eye contact with Cate, methodically picking at the tiny fabric pills on her oversize blue sweater.

"Jordan tells me you're not eating."

"I eat."

"Barely enough to keep yourself alive."

"Maybe that's not such a good idea either."

Cate was silent for a moment. "You don't mean that," she said finally.

"I don't know if I do or not," Sloane responded truthfully. "There are times . . . but my body seems to want to survive even if my soul doesn't."

"You'll get through this, Sloane. You're strong. You've weathered a good many storms over the years—"

"This is different." Sloane continued to pick at her sweater.

"Different, yes," Cate acknowledged. "But you *will* get through it. I have every confidence in you."

"I guess I should be glad someone does," Sloane said darkly.

"Jordan wants to help you if you'll let him."

"Is that why you're here?" Sloane wanted to know. "Did Jordan send for you?"

Cate hesitated for a moment. "He called me, yes," she admitted.

"He wasted your time."

"He's worried about you. You're shutting him out."

Sloane looked up for the first time. "He told you that?"

"No—yes—yes, he did," Cate said with a slight nod. "He thought I might be able to get through to you—since he doesn't seem to be having any luck himself."

"There's nothing to 'get through to,' as you put it." Her voice was cold. "I need some time alone. I need to think."

"About what?"

"Things."

"Jordan?"

There was a pause. "In a way, yes."

"About whether or not you can get back to being his wife again?" Cate asked.

"Why would you ask a question like that?"

"I think that should be pretty obvious, even to you," Cate said quietly. "*Especially* to you. You're so wrapped up in your own grief that you've shut him out. He's hurting, too, Sloane. He grieves for that baby just as much as you do. He wants to comfort you—and wants you to comfort him—but you won't allow it."

Sloane drew in a deep breath. "He told you we're not sleeping together," she concluded.

"He told me he'd moved into one of the guest rooms. He said you were restless, that you've been having trouble sleeping."

"He didn't tell you the truth, then."

"That depends," Cate started carefully. "What *is* the truth?"

Sloane looked away. "That I don't want to sleep with him because I'm afraid he'll want to make love and I can't."

"He understands that, Sloane."

"No, you don't know what I mean," Sloane said, shaking her head emphatically.

"Then why don't you tell me?" Cate suggested gently.

"I'm not talking about—medical reasons."

"What, then?"

"I'm afraid to."

"Why?"

"I don't want to get pregnant again. I *can't* get pregnant again." There was anxiety in her voice.

"There's no hurry—"

"I can't get pregnant again." Sloane scrambled to her feet, pacing the room nervously. "Not now, not ever."

"Don't you think it's a little too soon to be making a decision like that?"

Sloane turned to face her, their eyes meeting for the first time. "I can't go through that again," she said softly, her fear apparent in her voice and in her face. "I *can't.*"

Alone in one of the guest rooms that night, Cate was having trouble sleeping herself. She was worried about Sloane. She'd had her ups and downs over the years—and some of the down times had been pretty extreme—but Cate had never seen her like this before. It was as if she'd given up on everything: her marriage, her career, the life she'd created for herself. As Cate stood at the window, staring into the night without really seeing anything, she found herself wishing Sean had come with her. If Sloane needed anything now, she needed professional counseling.

Cate wasn't sure what bothered her more—Sloane's present state of mind or the near miss she'd had herself, this afternoon in the library.

If Jordan asked her about Roddy again, how was she going to handle it?

I do love him. I don't want to lose him. But I'm afraid.

Sloane looked at the clock on the nightstand. Three-twenty. And she hadn't been asleep at all. Yet. She lay on the bed, wearing only a short lavender silk nightgown, thinking about the things Cate had said earlier. She'd thought of little else all evening.

She hadn't stopped loving Jordan even if she wasn't able to *show* him she loved him. She knew she was hurting him, and she felt powerless to do anything about it. She'd lost her baby, and now she was losing Jordan. Both were her fault, and that knowledge made her sick inside.

She got up off the bed and went to her dressing table. Opening the top drawer, she took out a small amber-colored vial bearing a prescription label from a Manhattan pharmacy. Barbiturates. Prescribed for her by her internist over a year ago. She'd been having trouble sleeping while she was on the promotional tour. The bottle was almost full, because she'd tried not to take them. *Only if I absolutely had to.*

She picked up a second vial. Amphetamines. Diet pills. It was half full. She'd been on them a couple of times, but they hadn't really done her any good, so she'd stopped taking them.

The third vial was Darvocets. Dr. Halsey had prescribed them for pain, and they certainly did their job. They dulled the pain, all of it. But she had the feeling he wouldn't refill it. *When these are gone, I'm on my own.*

She went into the bathroom for a glass of water, then came back and took one of the Darvocets. She wanted to take two. She'd taken two before. *Better make them last,* she thought. Then she reached for the barbiturates. Thank God she'd kept them.

She hadn't needed them before, but she did need them now.

Jordan slept fitfully. Tossing and turning in the darkness, he changed positions at least a dozen times before finally accepting the fact that he was not going to get more than brief snatches of sleep. Not tonight.

Bunching up the pillow under his head, he lay back again, staring up at the ceiling. He wondered if Sloane was sleeping. Was she also restless? Did she realize what she was doing to him—to them—by keeping him at a distance this way? He loved her, but even he had his limits.

He wasn't sure how much more of this he could take.

The door opened then, slowly. He looked up and saw her

standing there in the doorway, wearing just her sheer night-gown—and there wasn't much to it. He sucked in his breath. No point in jumping to conclusions until he knew why she'd come.

"Jordan?" Her voice was low and unusually soft.

"Yeah," he responded. "I'm awake."

"May I come in?"

They'd been reduced to an uncomfortable politeness. *Is this all we have left now?* he wondered. Aloud he said, "Sure."

She came into the bedroom and closed the door. He could barely see her in the darkness as she moved toward him. Without a word, she pulled back the covers and got into the bed beside him.

"I love you," she said as she nestled in his arms. "I *do* love you, Jordan."

"I love you, too—and I've missed you." He started to kiss her, but she drew her head back.

"I want to be a real wife to you again," she said in a tremulous voice, "but it's going to take me a little while—"

"Ssh! It's all right," he said, holding her close. It *was* all right. It was a beginning.

And, knowing that, he could wait.

₪ Palm Beach, February 1988

As his mount galloped across the otherwise vacant polo field toward the ball, a small white speck on the uniformly green turf, Jordan raised his mallet high in anticipation of the shot he was going to make. He brought it down forcefully in a wide arc but hit the ball at such an awkward angle that he sent the ball bouncing off to one side. It came to rest several yards away. Jordan reined in his mount and surveyed the situation for a moment.

"Damn," he muttered under his breath as he removed his helmet. It had to be the worst shot he'd made all morning—and that was pretty bad.

He wasn't surprised. Lately, his mind hadn't been totally on his game, a fact that was all too obvious in the way he played. No . . . these past few months he'd been too preoccupied with Sloane and what she'd gone through to be able to give one hundred percent to his polo.

He thought about her as he rode across the field. Sloane hadn't been the same since she lost the baby. After that initial period of withdrawal, he'd been convinced the worst was over, that she was definitely making progress.

Now, he wasn't so sure.

There were times . . . times she seemed like a total stranger to him. Her extreme mood swings were unnerving. One moment she was remote and withdrawn, not wanting to see or speak to anyone, sometimes not even able to get out of bed. The next, she was bright and bubbly, in good spirits and even better humor, ready to dance all night and a tigress in bed. A more exaggerated version of the old Sloane, the woman he'd fallen in love with. I must be crazy, he thought.

He didn't know which side of the coin bothered him more.

"You know what to do."

The other man nodded. "Right. Make it look like an accident."

"No one must be the least bit suspicious."

"Yeah, right." He'd heard it all before.

"I'll call you when it's done, let you know where and when to pick up the money."

"You do that."

"I have to go now. I can't risk being seen with you."

The other man frowned. "I ain't exactly crazy about bein' seen with you, either."

"No unnecessary risks—your rule, remember?"

"Yeah, right." Then he asked, "How long you gonna keep going with this? Mind tellin' me why you're doin' all of this?"

"Yes, I *do* mind. As long as I'm paying you, my reasons for doing what I'm doing are none of your business."

And he turned and walked away.

"If I didn't know better, I'd think you were avoiding me."

Lance stepped back to let Nadine enter his room. "Why would I avoid you?" he asked, trying to make his voice light as he closed the door.

"I don't know." She started unbuttoning his shirt. "Suppose you tell me."

"Your husband *has* been keeping me busy—"

"Not *that* busy." She parted the fabric of his blue cotton shirt and started nuzzling his chest. "As a matter of fact, I happen to know he's been thinking of dropping you from the team."

Lance froze inside. "He told you that?"

She gave a throaty laugh. "Of course he told me," she said as she unbuckled his belt. "I *am* his wife." Reaching inside his pants, she took his limp organ in one hand and stroked it gently. "Don't worry, Lance," she breathed, feeling him harden under her manipulations. "I've talked him out of it— and I can do so again if necessary." Though she didn't actually say the words, she made her message quite clear: *Your place on the team is safe as long as we continue to be lovers.*

"I suppose I should thank you," he said.

Her eyes met his. "Actions speak louder than words," she said in a suggestive voice.

He kissed her hard as he fumbled with the zipper down the back of her cobalt Valentino dress. "Get out of this thing," he growled, "and we'll play a little show and tell."

Nadine stepped back, shedding her dress with a shrug of her slim body. She felt exhilarated. She'd finally discovered the key to holding her young lover.

Now things would be different.

Sloane took the small vial from her overnight case and gave it a little shake. Empty. *Damn—I should have had it refilled before I left New York,* she thought. *Now what am I going to do?*

She thought about it for a moment. There *had* to be a doctor somewhere in Palm Beach who would prescribe amphetamines without asking a lot of questions. After all, this *was* Palm Beach—a town full of rich, beautiful, *thin* women. Doctors willing to dash off prescriptions for "diet pills" probably did a booming business here. The problem for her was going to be in finding one of those doctors.

She couldn't just walk up to someone on the street and say, "Hey, can you tell me where I can find a good pill pusher posing as an M.D.?" She had to be careful. She couldn't let anyone find out. God, if Cate or Adrienne ever found out. . . .

No . . . it had to remain a secret. *Her* secret. She couldn't even let Jordan find out. Especially not Jordan. He wouldn't understand. Nobody would understand. How could they? How could they possibly understand that the pills were all that kept her going? The barbiturates warded off the demons of the night. They made it possible for her to sleep. They dulled the pain. And the amphetamines took away the mental fog induced by the barbiturates. They enabled her to get out of bed in the morning. They made her able to be more like her old self. As much her old self as she was capable of being, anyway. They made it possible for her to function. She *needed* them.

The sound of the door slamming in the next room interrupted her thoughts. Jordan. She dashed across the room and hurriedly stashed the bottle in the bottom of her overnight case, snapping it shut just as he came into the bedroom.

"How was the practice?" she asked, trying to sound casual.

"Uneventful." He kissed her lightly on the lips. "I didn't expect to find you here."

She gave him a quizzical look. "Why not?"

"I guess because you told me this morning you planned to do some shopping." He pulled off his jersey and went to the closet for a clean shirt. "Since it's two o'clock in the afternoon and you're still in your nightgown, I'm assuming you didn't go anywhere."

"No, as a matter of fact, I didn't." She paused. "The muse came to visit."

He looked at her over his shoulder. "You've been writing?"

She nodded. "Twenty-five pages in one morning," she said. "Of course, there are another ten in the round file." She pointed to the wastebasket.

He let out a low whistle. "Cate's going to be pleased."

"She will be when she gets it," Sloane agreed. "I'm expressing it home to be typed tomorrow—thought I'd see if I could knock off another twenty-five pages tomorrow morning."

"You *are* a ball of fire today, aren't you." His tone was mildly teasing. "I hope this sudden burst of creative energy doesn't mean you're not going with me to the awards banquet tomorrow night."

"Not at all." She embraced him from behind. "We're not going to be at the Hillyers' table, are we?"

"Sorry, love. He *is* my team sponsor, after all," Jordan reminded her. He knew Sloane didn't much like Nadine Hillyer and had an even lower opinion of her husband.

"Look, Ian and Dusty'll be there and Erin and Sam and Dan—"

"And Lance?"

Jordan's mood changed abruptly. "Who knows with Lance these days?" he said more than asked in an irritated tone. "You only know he's coming when you see him. Most of the time he's so spaced out he doesn't even know what planet he's on."

Sloane hesitated momentarily. "What do you think he's on?"

"God only knows. Pills, maybe coke—it's hard to tell." He paused. "I'd be willing to bet Nadine Hillyer's supporting his habit, whatever it is."

Sloane drew back. "How so?"

"Rumor has it she pays extremely well for stud service," Jordan said, pulling a shirt off its hanger. "Watches, cuff links—payments disguised as gifts. Tokens of her affection. Lance isn't interested in that sort of thing, so my guess is that he pawns them to pay for drugs."

"He doesn't appear to be having any trouble getting the stuff," Sloane said thoughtfully.

"Lance can be very resourceful when he wants to be," Jordan said, his tone grim.

Sloane didn't hear him. She was thinking about how she was going to approach Lance. She'd have to be careful about how she did it. He might not trust her. He probably wouldn't. After all, she *was* Jordan's wife, and he knew how Jordan felt about drugs. Yes . . . she'd have to be very careful.

For her present need, Lance was the only game in town.

"We have to do this more often," Nadine cooed.

Lance was lying on the bed, naked. Nadine, also naked, was on her knees, straddling him, riding him while he played with her breasts. There were no more remarks from him about her age or her plastic surgery, no more sexual indifference. They'd made love all afternoon, and Lance had been an enthusiastic participant. Nadine was pleased. She no longer had to worry about losing him. She'd found the perfect way to keep him in line.

His hands moved down, gripping her buttocks as his hips started to jerk beneath her. She arched her back and grasped his forearms to keep her balance as he reached an explosive climax. She stayed on top of him, holding him inside her, as they both struggled to catch their breath. Finally, she bent forward, supporting her weight on her hands, until her breasts were directly above his face. He reached up and cupped them in his hands, nuzzling them lazily for a long time.

"Suck them, Lance," she whispered. "I love it when you suck them."

He flicked his tongue over one; it hardened at his touch. He took it in his mouth and sucked at it lazily. "Harder," she breathed. "Harder!"

He began to suck fiercely. Nadine shivered with pleasure as she moved forward, allowing his now limp organ to slip out of her dampness. Not yet having reached an orgasm herself, she rubbed herself against the hard muscles of his abdomen, relishing the sensations the movement created, the sensations his mouth created.

She kept him at her breasts until she, too, had been satisfied. From now on, she *would* be satisfied. Lance would see to that. She was sure of it. She pulled back, rearing over him, and took a deep breath. "That was wonderful," she praised. "Take a breather, darling, and we'll try it again."

She got off him, off the bed, walked naked across the room to the dresser, and picked up her handbag. As she was rummaging through it, Lance came up behind her, wrapping his arms around her, over her breasts. When he pressed himself against her, she could tell he was aroused again. He nuzzled her right earlobe, kissing his way down her neck to her shoulder.

"Get down on your knees," he growled.

She gave a little moan as she sank down to the carpet on her hands and knees. Lance, on his knees at her bottom, entered her from behind, moving rhythmically as he reached around to stroke her clitoris with his fingers. With his other hand, he lightly pinched her left nipple. Nadine moaned with pleasure as he moved within her, surprised by his initiative.

The moment was interrupted by furious pounding on the door. Before Lance could make a move to respond, the door was forced open and Gavin Hillyer burst into the room, his face purple with rage. "You lousy son of a bitch!" he hissed as Lance scrambled to his feet and went for his pants. "I ought to tear you apart with my bare hands. I gave you a chance when everybody said you were washed up in professional polo. I put up with you no matter how poorly you performed, and how do you respond? By screwing my wife, you bastard!"

Lance said nothing. There was nothing he *could* say.

Hillyer turned to Nadine, who made no move to cover her nakedness. He snatched up her dress, lying in a heap on

the floor, and threw it at her. "Get dressed," he snapped.
"The car's waiting downstairs."

And he turned and walked out.

"I should divorce you," Hillyer told Nadine when they were
alone in their suite at the Breakers. "I should throw you out
on your surgically perfected little ass without a cent." He turned
to face her. "I could, you know."

"You could," Nadine said evenly, "but you won't." She
was terrified he would and trying desperately not to show it.

"You're sure of that, are you?" He went to the bar and
poured himself a drink, a double.

"Yes—I am." There was a slight tremor in her voice. She
hoped he didn't notice. "Whatever else you are, Gavin, you're
a proud man."

"Meaning . . . ?"

"Meaning you wouldn't want anyone to know your wife
had been with another man," Nadine replied.

"Other *men*," he corrected, taking a long swallow of his
drink. Seeing the surprise that registered on her face, he gave
her a wintry smile. "I know about *all* of them, my dear. I've
known all along."

"Then why now—" she started.

"Now, my darling wife, I have too much on my mind to
be distracted by your little indiscretions. I decided it was time
to put a stop to it."

"You've had me followed," she concluded.

"You bet I have," he said crossly. "You *are* my wife."

"You seem to remember that only when it's convenient for
you to do so."

"If I were *you*, Nadine, I would not press my luck." His
voice held a warning note. "Push me too far, and you just
might end up out on the street with nothing but the clothes on
your pretty backside."

Now she *was* frightened. "What are you going to do?" she
asked cautiously.

"Nothing," he said flatly. "That is, as long as you agree
to my terms."

She hesitated momentarily. "What terms?"

"That this doesn't happen again—with Whitney or anyone

else," he said, refilling his glass. "That you start acting like a wife—a woman your age—instead of trying to look and act like a twenty-year-old nymphomaniac."

She nodded. "What about Lance?"

"What about him?"

"What are you going to do about him?"

"Nothing—for the moment." His smile was cold. "As you said yourself, I have my pride. Wouldn't want this to get out now, would we?"

Putting down his glass, he turned abruptly and left the room.

"Why aren't you practicing?" Sloane asked casually as she approached Lance, who leaned against the hood of his rental car, watching the early-morning practice game.

"What's the point?" His tone was dismal.

She looked at him, puzzled. "Come again?"

"After today I'll probably be dropped from the team." He kept his eyes on the polo field.

"Why?" She climbed up on the hood of the car next to him. He shook his head. "It's a long story."

"I've been told I'm a good listener."

"I'd rather not talk about it, okay?" His tone was abrupt.

She gave a little shrug. "If that's the way you want it." There was a long pause. "If you won't let me help you, then maybe you can help me."

"How?" He never took his eyes off the field.

"After I lost the baby," she began carefully, "I had a lot of problems. I sort of went off the deep end. My doctor prescribed barbiturates." She looked at him out of the corner of her eye. There was no visible reaction on his face. She went on: "They did their job, but I was pretty dopey most of the time, so I started taking amphetamines, some diet pills I'd had for a while but had never taken before. Now"—she drew in a deep breath—"I'm out of pills and my doctor won't refill them."

Lance looked at her for the first time. "I'm sorry about the baby, Sloane," he said quietly. "But I don't know how I can help you."

"I—that is, Jordan told me you went through a pretty bad time when your wife left you," she said, her eyes meeting his.

"He said he thought you had—used something for a while."

Lance's blue eyes narrowed suspiciously. "What else did he tell you?" he asked, his deep voice suddenly cold.

She shook her head slightly. "That's all," she insisted. "I'm sorry if I've said something wrong. I just thought you might be able to help me get—"

He cut her off. "Well, I can't. I'm sorry." He straightened up. "No point in me sticking around here," he decided. "Sorry I can't help you, Sloane. I really am."

She slid off the hood and stepped back as he got into the car and started the engine. Frowning, she watched him drive away.

Now what was she going to do?

On Saturday, February 27, at the Polo House of the Palm Beach Polo and Country Club, five of the world's six ten-goal players were in the audience the night *Polo* magazine's third annual Polo Excellence Awards were presented. Called the "Tommys"—for polo legend Tommy Hitchcock, in whose image the bronze statuette was created by sculptor Tom Holland—they are polo's equivalent of the Oscars.

One of the five ten-goalers in the audience that night was Gonzalo Pieres, of Peter Brant's powerhouse White Birch team. Considered by many to be the best player in the world, he was named Player of the Year. Accepting his award, Pieres thanked his wife, Cecelia, Brant, and his ponies. "Without them, I couldn't have won this," the Argentine said of the statuette in his hand.

A Special Mention Award was presented to Piaget's Chukkers for Charity team, not only for their success in raising two million dollars in three years for various nationwide charities, but for their active promotion of polo itself. The award was accepted by four members of the team, actors Alex Cord, William Devane, Jameson Parker, and Doug Sheehan. Sheehan, referring to an exhibition match the celebrity team was to play the next day as a warm-up of sorts, preceding the Camacho Cup match, joked, "We call ours the No Macho Cup."

The highlight of the awards presentation, however, came when another polo legend, Australian-born Bob Skene, was named to the Polo Honor Roll. Skene, overcome by emotion, received a standing ovation as he stepped up to the podium to make a brief acceptance speech in which he thanked his wife of fifty years, Elizabeth, who also received a round of applause.

At the White Timbers table, Jordan talked with Ian Welles while Dusty attempted conversation with Sloane, who was visibly nervous and distracted. Nadine Hillyer, elegantly turned out as always, sat at her husband's side, but the coldness between them cast a chill felt by everyone at the table.

Lance Whitney was conspicuously absent.

The effects of the amphetamines were beginning to wear off, and Sloane felt as if she were about to crash, physically *and* mentally. Only the barbiturates kept her from running, screaming, into the streets now. Her hands were trembling, her head was pounding, and every noise, every voice sounded ten times louder than it really was. At times, visual images seemed grossly distorted.

She could only hope that Jordan would not want to make a night of it, that they would be leaving soon. She didn't think she could handle a late night. Not tonight of all nights.

"Are you all right, Sloane?" Dusty asked.

There seemed to be an echo in the room. Sloane shook her head emphatically. "I'm fine," she insisted. "I just—I just need to go to the ladies' room, that's all."

"Want me to go with you?"

"No!" she said quickly, almost too quickly. "I'll be fine."

"You don't look well."

Sloane hesitated. "I *am* a little under the weather," she admitted. "Probably just a virus."

She got to her feet, the movement so awkward it caught Jordan's attention. He looked up. "What's wrong?" he asked, taking her hand.

"What makes you think anything is wrong?" she asked. And to herself: *Is it that obvious?*

"*Is* there anything wrong?" he pursued.

"No." She forced a smile. "You worry too much."

"Maybe I love you too much."

She lowered her voice to a whisper. "I hope so."

Her head was throbbing as she made her way through the crowd toward the rest rooms. She was having trouble breathing. Once inside the ladies' room, she leaned against the wall, struggling to catch her breath. Her heart was racing as she bent over the sink and splashed cold water on her face, not caring what it was probably doing to her makeup.

She needed something to calm her nerves, and she needed it now. Checking to make sure no one else was in the room, she dug into her evening bag with a shaking hand and took out a small pillbox that resembled a miniature compact. Her fingers trembled so badly, that when she finally managed to open it, she dropped both of the red barbiturate capsules into the sink.

"Damn!" she swore under her breath as the two capsules eluded her grasp and disappeared down the drain.

Taking a few deep breaths, she straightened up and stared blankly at her own reflection in the mirror. She couldn't face going back in there. Not yet. Not without something to calm her nerves. No . . . what she needed was some fresh air.

She left the bathroom and headed straight for the exit, hoping Jordan didn't see her. Once outside, she found a quiet spot and took a few deep breaths of the cool night air. It didn't really do much good, but inside she'd felt as though she were suffocating.

"Sloane?"

She jerked, startled, as Lance stepped out of the shadows. He obviously hadn't planned to attend the awards presentation; he wasn't wearing a tux. He was dressed in denim jeans and jacket and a red polo shirt. "I figured you'd come out sooner or later," he said as he came forward, out of the shadows. "It's part of the pattern."

"What pattern?" She wiped her sweaty palms down the sides of her low-cut beaded gown.

"The pattern of the user. I'll bet you were nervous as hell in there."

"Well—yes."

"You felt like you couldn't breathe in there, didn't you?" She nodded.

"I thought so." He took a small brown envelope from his jacket pocket and offered it to her. "I think this'll help."

"What is it?" she asked.

"Bennies. I don't know what you've been taking, but they should do the trick." As she reached out to take it, he pulled it back. "There's a condition."

She looked up at him. "What?"

"Nobody knows where you got them."

She nodded. "Nobody's even going to know I have them."

"Not even Mr. Straight-Arrow Phillips?"

"Especially not Jordan."

He seemed satisfied. Pressing the envelope into her palm, he turned to go.

"Lance?" she called after him.

He turned. "Yeah?"

"Did Hillyer drop you from the team?"

He shook his head. "Not yet. I got off with a warning—this time."

As he disappeared into the darkness, Sloane emptied the contents of the envelope into the palm of her hand. Six capsules. *Thank God,* she thought, flooded with relief.

Now, maybe, she could get through the night.

⇄ Sydney, February 1988

"You can't be serious."

Jilly stared at the doctor in disbelief as he wrote out a prescription. "I'm quite serious," he said, tearing the top sheet off the pad. He gave it to her. "You're two months pregnant."

"I can't be!" she protested. "I'm on the pill."

"Well, Mrs. Kenyon," he began thoughtfully, "no birth control method is one hundred percent effective. And there is always the possibility of human error."

"Human error?"

"Have you been taking your birth control pills religiously?" he asked. "Without missing even a day?"

"Yes—that is, I think so," she said, suddenly uncertain. So much had gone wrong in her life in the past year—who was she kidding? Most of her life had gone wrong! But in the past year, in particular, there had been so much turmoil . . . yes, she had to admit that it *was* possible. She *could* have forgotten. . . .

"What's this?" she asked, looking down at the written prescription in her hand.

"Prenatal vitamins," he told her. "I want you to have that filled and start taking them right away."

"I see," she said without much enthusiasm.

The doctor suddenly looked concerned. "You *do* want this baby, don't you?"

"I'm not sure," she answered truthfully.

He was silent for a moment. "Are you considering abortion?" he asked finally.

"I may be," she said quietly. "I have to think about it."

262

"Until you do, I want you to take care of yourself as if you were going to have that child," he said then. "Prenatal care can never begin too soon. You have to start looking after yourself."

Jilly only nodded. *I certainly do,* she was thinking.

In more ways than one.

She didn't *want* to be pregnant.

That much she knew for sure, Jilly thought as she drove along the coast headed for her father's place. She didn't want to be pregnant with Max's child—she never had, really, and certainly not now—the state of her marriage being what it was. No . . . being pregnant was one more complication she didn't need. Especially now.

Jilly didn't consciously realize where she was going until she arrived. She wasn't even sure why she had come to her father. She'd tried to talk to him before, but he'd never understood, never showed her any sympathy. He was the last person she should be talking to about this. And yet . . .

She spotted him out on the practice field, practicing an off-side backhand shot. She braked her car to a stop and got out, watching him intently as she made her way to the white rail fence and climbed up to the top rail. From her perch she waved to him, but he didn't acknowledge her. She wasn't sure he even knew she was there. When he played polo—even if he was only practicing—nothing else mattered. Nothing else got through to him. Not even his only daughter. It had always been that way.

As he rode toward her, finally aware of her presence, he pulled off his helmet and waved to her. She forced a smile and waved again. *Why am I here?* she asked herself again. *I already know what he's going to tell me. What's the use?*

"What brings you here?" Fleming asked as he rode up to the fence and dismounted.

Jilly tried to keep her voice light. "Does a girl always need a reason to pay her father a visit?"

"No, but I've never known you to come without one," he pointed out, "so why don't you tell why you're here now?"

She sucked in her breath. "I just saw the doctor," she started.

He looked mildly concerned. "Are you ill?"

"No," she said with a shake of her head, "I'm pregnant."

Fleming studied her for a moment. "You don't seem very happy about it, Jilly girl."

"I'm not," she admitted.

"You don't want children?" He ran a towel over his hair and draped it over his shoulders. "Hand me that thermos bottle over there." He gestured toward the green and tan polo bag and other items on her side of the fence.

"I'm not sure *what* I want right now," she said glumly, hopping down from the fence. She retrieved the thermos and handed it over the fence to him.

He opened it, taking a long swallow of its contents. "You should have taken precautions if you didn't want to get pregnant."

"I did. I was taking birth control pills," she said quietly.

"So what are you going to do?" Her father sounded genuinely interested.

"I don't know." Jilly hugged herself as if trying to shut out the cold when there was none. "I might have an abortion. I don't know yet."

"Have you discussed this with Max?"

Jilly frowned. "Max doesn't even know I'm pregnant."

"You *are* going to tell him, of course."

"I don't know," she said again.

"You *have* to tell him. It *is* his child—isn't it?" Fleming suddenly looked uncertain.

"Yes, Daddy—it is," Jilly said with a sigh. "If it weren't, I'd want to keep it."

"Jillian!"

"It's the truth, Daddy," she said sullenly. "I might as well speak the words as think them. I don't want Max's child. It might be like him."

"Maxwell's a fine man," Fleming maintained.

"He's sick," she argued. "He's insane. When I married him, I knew he was jealous. I knew he had a terrible temper. I could have lived with that. But it's worse, much worse, than I thought. He's obsessed, Daddy. He's lost control of himself. He frightens me. I think he's capable of anything."

"Are you sure you're not blowing things out of proportion

because of the problems in your marriage?'' Fleming mounted up again.

"Max's problems are the cause of our troubles," Jilly maintained.

"Along with your inability to get Jordan Phillips out of your system." Fleming put on his helmet and fastened the chin strap.

Jilly stared at him for a moment. "Why must you always put the blame on me?" she asked finally. "Why is it always my fault?"

"You haven't been trying, Jillian," he said. "Even now— this baby may be just what the two of you need to get back on track, and all you're thinking of is having an abortion."

Jilly shook her head. "Daddy, I know you loved Mother," she said carefully. "Grandmother told me everything some years ago—how you met, fell in love—"

"Get to the point, Jillian." Even under the helmet, the tension in his face was apparent. She'd obviously struck a nerve.

"You loved her very much. Why do you expect me to settle for less?" she wanted to know.

"Love doesn't last, Jilly girl," he said tightly. "The sooner you realize that, the better off you'll be." He turned his mount and rode away without so much as a good-bye.

Jilly thought about it as she drove home. Losing his wife, her mother, had left her father bitter and unwilling to let himself care about anyone or anything. It wasn't that he didn't *believe* in love—he was afraid of it.

Just as she was afraid now.

"This is a switch," Max greeted his wife sarcastically as he entered the apartment. "My dear wife—at home, waiting for me."

"Don't flatter yourself." Jilly's voice was cold. "It's coincidence. That's all."

"Really?" He tried to kiss her, but she jerked away. She could smell liquor on his breath.

"You've been drinking."

"Fancy that." He turned and headed for the bar. "I suppose there's really no point in stopping now, then, is there?"

"One more—or a dozen more—certainly couldn't make any

difference as far as you're concerned," she agreed indifferently.

"Such a loving wife." He poured himself a double, downing it quickly, then poured another. "I'm such a lucky man."

"Drop it, Max." Her tone held a warning note. "I'm not in the mood." She felt the beginning of a monumental headache coming on.

"You're never in the mood these days, are you, Jilly sweet." He gulped down his drink. "At least not for me."

"I wonder why."

"Funny—when we were married, I was under the impression that a wife had certain—responsibilities," he said then.

"I believe both parties had those responsibilities," she corrected icily.

"We're a fine pair, aren't we? A real loving couple." He filled his glass again.

"The perfect couple," Jilly said, turning to face him. "We're going to make wonderful parents, aren't we?"

His laugh was hollow. "Come again?"

"I'm pregnant."

"That's a lousy joke, Jilly sweet," he said with a smirk.

"Our *marriage* is a bad joke," she responded. "Unfortunately, however, *this* is not."

His eyes narrowed suspiciously as he came forward. "Just what are you saying?" he asked carefully.

"That should have been clear enough, even for you, Maxwell." She didn't like the way he was looking at her. "I'm pregnant. I saw the doctor this morning. I'm just as surprised as you are—"

His hand lashed out across her face. "Bitch!" he hissed. "Whose is it?"

"It's mine—ours—"

"You lying cunt!" He backhanded her across the face again. She fell back onto the couch, her hands raised to shield her face. "Whose is it?"

"It's your baby!" she screamed, afraid he might actually kill her.

"The truth!" He grabbed the front of her red silk blouse and hauled her to her feet. "Whose bastard are you carrying?"

"It's yours—"

"Think you can make a fool of me, do you?" There was pure, uncontrollable rage in his eyes. "Well, you're not going to get away with it!" He drew back his fist and punched her in the stomach—hard.

Jilly cried out in pain, but Max wouldn't let go of her. "You're not passing off someone else's bastard as mine!" he shouted. And he hit her again.

"Max, listen to me—please—" she begged.

"It's Jordan's, isn't it?" he demanded. "I should have finished him off when I had the chance!"

"I haven't been with anyone else—"

"Bitch! What kind of fool do you think I am?" He slapped her again and again.

"Max, listen to me—" She was sobbing uncontrollably.

"I'm through listening to your lies—and Phillips's!" He punched her again, and the last thing Jilly remembered as she slumped to the floor and lost consciousness was the terrible pain—and the sudden feeling of dampness between her legs.

At first, Jilly didn't know where she was.

When she opened her eyes, her vision was blurred for a few moments. When she was finally able to focus, her surroundings were unfamiliar. She wasn't at home—thank God! Max wasn't there. She gave an inward sigh of relief. Someone had heard her screams. Someone had gotten her out of there before Max killed her.

Even the intense pain she'd experienced had subsided, replaced now by a dull ache in her abdomen. There was a faint throbbing sensation in the back of her head, and she felt drugged. When she tried to speak, her voice was weak.

"Where . . . am I?"

"It's all right, Jillian." It was her father's voice, comforting her. "You're in the hospital."

"The hospital—" She turned her head to look at him. He was seated in a chair beside the bed, looking more concerned than she could ever remember him being. "How did I get here?"

"The police. Someone in your building called them. When they arrived, you were unconscious and Max—Max is in jail now." He paused. "What happened?"

"I took your advice," she said coldly, staring up at the ceiling. "I told him I was pregnant. He was drunk. He didn't believe the baby was his. I didn't have a chance to tell him I wanted to have an abortion—he decided to take care of it himself." She fell silent for a long moment. "I lost the baby, didn't I."

Fleming nodded. "I'm sorry."

"It's a little late for sorry, isn't it, Daddy?" Her voice was cool. "It's a little late for a lot of things."

"They tell me you can press charges against Max," Fleming said then.

"I don't know," Jilly responded. "The only thing I'm certain of now is that I want to end this farce of a marriage—as soon as possible."

Maybe now, she thought, *if I tell him what Max is really capable of . . . maybe now he'd believe me.*

But she was still afraid.

⇄ Singapore, May 1988

"We're going to have to fly back to the States," Hillyer told his wife. "Today."

"What's the great hurry?" Nadine asked without much interest as she scanned the closet of their room in the Hotel Shangri-la in search of something to wear. They had only arrived yesterday, and the White Timbers team wasn't playing until tomorrow.

"Business," he said tersely, not looking up from the newspaper he was reading. His breakfast had been barely touched, and what remained was most likely cold by now.

"Now, why doesn't that surprise me?" Nadine asked coolly as she selected a sapphire-blue Valentino and lay it on the bed, still on its hanger. "It usually *is* business, isn't it? Especially these days."

"The business, as you call it, is having serious problems. I'm needed at home." His voice was ice cold.

"Really? Where *is* home, Gavin?" she asked, a sarcastic edge to her voice. "In all the years we've been married, we've owned a total of eighteen homes and I have yet to feel that any of them was a real home. Did I miss something?"

"I can do without this, Nadine," he responded curtly, folding his newspaper carefully as if the gesture enabled him to maintain his self-control.

"That's wonderful to hear," she shot back at him. "It's wonderful to know you can do without something. I've had to do without a great deal in the course of our marriage. I've had to do without love, without sex, for the most part, without a real husband—"

He looked up at her, his face void of emotion. "The lack of regular sex has an adverse effect on your temperament, I see," he commented.

"I *am* a normal woman," she said stiffly. "I do have needs—"

"Obviously."

She was silent but only for a moment. "If you knew about me," she began carefully, "if you knew about other men— why now? Why make such an issue of it now? Why not do it sooner?"

He took a deep breath and put the newspaper aside. "In the past, I looked the other way because I knew you had needs I couldn't satisfy, and you were discreet about it. I figured it made you happy and made my life considerably easier, so I could live with it." He paused. "With Whitney, you weren't discreet. There were rumors. It was quickly becoming a joke. I had enough on my mind already. I simply couldn't deal with it. I had to put a stop to it."

"And that's why you didn't drop Lance from the team," Nadine concluded.

"Exactly. Had I dropped him, I would have been as much as admitting the rumors were true," he said grimly. "I would have been a laughingstock."

Nadine gave him an icy smile. "And that's all that matters to you, isn't it," she said incredulously. "*Your* pride, *your* image?"

He stood up. "If you're so unhappy, Nadine, I *will* give you a divorce," he told her. "If that's what you want."

She looked at him for a moment. She didn't hate him, but she didn't love him, either. But he was all she had left—or, more precisely, her position as Mrs. Gavin Hillyer was all she had left. She wasn't about to lose that, too.

"No, thank you," she told him.

"I can't believe you had me come all the way to Singapore." The man unzipped his black leather jacket and took out a pack of cigarettes. "This ought to be good."

"Let's just say it will definitely be worth your while," the other man told him.

"What do I have to do, kill your wife?" he chuckled.

The other man wasn't smiling. "Don't tempt me."

Jilly was sure Max was in Singapore.

He'd left Sydney as soon as he was released from jail. He'd left the country. She wouldn't have been able to press charges against him if she'd wanted to. And by the time she left the hospital, she'd wanted to.

The doctors told her she'd never be able to have children now. Max had beaten her so badly that day . . . there had been internal bleeding, other injuries. The morning they told her—the day after Max was released from jail, the day after he left Australia—she wanted to kill him. She wished him dead. She had never hated anyone so much in her life.

But now she had to find him.

As much as she hated him, she also feared him. She'd discovered firsthand how violent he could be. What he was capable of doing. He had almost killed her. He'd tried to kill her. Good God, he'd actually *wanted* to kill her! He'd claimed he loved her, yet he'd tried to kill her. He was insane. She'd suspected it before, but she was sure of it now.

She would never forget the look on his face as he stood over her, having beaten her within an inch of her life. She couldn't forget the rage, the unquestionable madness blazing from his eyes. Nor could she forget his last words to her before she lost consciousness, the clear threat he'd made.

Not against her, but against Jordan.

Lance was in limbo.

Ever since Hillyer caught him having sex with Nadine that day in Palm Beach, he'd been waiting for the ax to fall. He *expected* Hillyer to drop him from the team. He'd expected it to happen long before now. The fact that he hadn't left Lance perplexed—and more than a little uneasy. Why *didn't* Hillyer get rid of him? The man had made it clear he wasn't satisfied with his performance as a polo player, and after catching him with Nadine—what could he possibly have in mind?

Lance wasn't at all sure he wanted to wait around to find out.

• • •

"I'm worried about you, Dad," Dusty admitted over dinner at the Great Shanghai, a crowded, noisy Singapore restaurant.

Ian looked up from his dinner and smiled. "May I ask what brought on this sudden concern?" he asked in a mildly amused tone.

"You haven't been yourself lately," she said thoughtfully. "Your mind's not on your game."

"My mind is *always* on my game," he disagreed.

"Not like it used to be," Dusty said, shaking her head.

"I'm not as young as I used to be," he pointed out.

She sipped her drink. "That's not what I mean, and you know it," she scolded.

"I know what you mean, honey," he admitted, taking another bite. "I'm all right. I've just got a lot on my mind, that's all."

"But you don't want to talk about it," she concluded.

He shook his head. "It's not that I don't want to," he told her. "I can't. Not yet."

"It must be catching," Dusty remarked, keeping her voice light. "First Lance, then Jordy, and now you. Is there something in the water, or what?"

Ian forced a smile. "It only seems that way, honey," he assured her.

It was better not to tell her the truth, he decided. She'd only end up being more worried than she was already.

"Coincidence?" Ian sighed deeply. "I don't think so."

"So you think these accidents are deliberate?" Jordan asked.

"I'd put money on it."

"Any idea who's behind it?"

Ian shook his head.

"How about motive?"

"Revenge looks like a safe bet from where I sit."

Jordan frowned. "That would put at least half a dozen people I know under suspicion."

And Max Kenyon is at the top of the list.

Sloane dug to the bottom of her overnight case hastily, retrieving the small bottle of barbiturate capsules bearing a legitimate pharmacy label. From the other side of the closed bathroom door, she could hear water running in the shower.

And Jordan singing "Rhinestone Cowboy." *Some things never change*, she thought. *And some things change too much.*

Far too much.

She took two capsules from the bottle and washed them down with water from a glass on the nightstand. She was tempted to take one more. Lately, they didn't seem to be doing their job. She took another capsule from the bottle, thought about it for a moment, then put it back. If she found she needed another one, she'd take it later after Jordan was asleep.

In the bathroom the singing had stopped, and the water had been turned off. He'd be coming out soon. She returned the pills to their hiding place at the bottom of her overnighter, locked it, and put it in the closet. Then she got into bed and switched out the lamp.

When Jordan emerged from the bathroom, she pretended to be asleep. She lay very still in the darkness, her eyes tightly closed, hoping he'd think she really was asleep. She was lying on her side, facing away from him, when he slid into bed beside her.

"You asleep?" he asked in a low voice.

She didn't respond.

He pressed against her from behind, putting one arm around her, across her breasts. She flinched at the caress of his arm through her sheer nightgown. "So—you *are* awake," he murmured, hugging her close.

"Hmm?" She tried to sound as if she were at least half asleep.

"For a minute there, I thought you were asleep." He nuzzled her ear.

"I was—almost."

He kissed her neck. She pulled away. "Please, Jordan," she sighed heavily, "not tonight."

He withdrew abruptly, surprised by her response—or, rather, the lack of it. "Have I done something wrong?" he asked, trying to make his voice light. "If you'll tell me what I'm guilty of, love, I'll know how to plead."

"You haven't done anything wrong," she said quietly. "I'm just not feeling well, that's all."

"Oh?" His voice was suddenly cold. "Headache, right?"

"No. I just don't feel well."

"Sorry. I'll try not to disturb you." As a pointed reminder

of his displeasure, he drew back and turned away from her, silent, though she knew he wasn't asleep.

She lay awake in the darkness for a long time, tears streaming down her face. Even though Jordan was still in bed beside her, she had never felt more alone in her life.

Jordan woke in the middle of the night. Beside him, Sloane was tossing and turning, mumbling in her sleep as she often did these days. And not making sense. Which she never did. He lay there in the darkness, listening to her for a long time.

"I can't do this, Roddy . . . my baby . . . can't let them take my baby . . . what if I go to jail . . . what will happen . . . they'll take my baby, Roddy . . ."

Jordan frowned. Who was this Roddy? What had he been to Sloane? What had they been to each other? Why did the memories so obviously trouble her?

What did it all mean?

He decided to ask her about it.

He was up early the next morning, but he didn't go to practice as he normally would have. Instead, he called room service and had breakfast sent up while Sloane was in the shower. It had arrived and was set up in the bedroom when she emerged from the bath.

"I thought we'd eat in here," Jordan told her. "Hungry?"

"Not really." She wasn't. The amphetamines killed her appetite, and most of the time she did little more than pick at her food. She'd lost a great deal of weight—almost forty pounds—but instead of looking svelte, she only looked gaunt and haggard.

"Try to eat anyway," he insisted. "It'll do you good."

She sat down across from him and lifted the cover from her plate. Even the smell of food made her nauseous, but she forced herself to take a bite.

"We need to talk, Sloane," Jordan said then.

She looked up at him. "About what?"

"About someone named Roddy."

Sloane froze, her eyes wide with fear. "Roddy?" she asked weakly. Her mind was racing. How did he know? How did he find out? "I—I don't know what you're talking about," she stammered nervously.

"Roddy," Jordan repeated. "Do you or do you not know somebody named Roddy?"

She hesitated. "I did," she said finally. "A long time ago."

"Well, at least we've established that there *was* a Roddy," he said, his eyes fixed on her. "What was he to you? Friend? Lover?"

Sloane took a deep breath. "I thought he was my friend, but he wasn't," she said. Now that the truth was out, she had no choice but to tell him all of it. "He was my lover off and on. But mostly, he was my partner."

Jordan looked confused. "Partner?"

She nodded. "Before I was Sloane Driscoll, before I was a best-selling novelist, I was Sammy Douglas from Chicago. Sammy Douglas was a con artist."

He stared at her incredulously. "A *what*?"

"A con artist," she repeated. "Roddy was my partner. He taught me everything I knew."

"Everything being exactly what?" Jordan suddenly looked pale.

"Con games. We had a fortune-telling racket going for a long time," she told him. "We took a lot of people for a lot of money—a lot of people who needed something to believe in." She looked down at her plate, clearly not proud of what she'd done. "When the bunko squad got wise to us, we'd switch tactics, come up with a new scam. Roddy was a master. He knew every trick in the book and invented almost as many of his own." She paused again. "Roddy taught me to cheat at poker. He worked with me, day after day, until I was as good as he was. Then he got me into as many high-stakes games as possible. He said nobody would ever suspect me. I didn't look the part. They all thought I was green."

Jordan was silent for a long time. "Why, Sloane?" he asked finally. "Why did you do it at all?"

She frowned. "For reasons I'm sure wouldn't seem important to anyone but me," she answered.

"Try me."

Sloane thought about it for a moment. "I grew up in midwestern suburbia, Jordan," she began slowly. "My father was a blue-collar worker, my mother a very traditional housewife. Sometimes I think June Cleaver could have taken lessons from *her*. My folks were perfect for each other. Dad was stubborn, opinionated, very domineering. He wanted to tell all of us what to do, when to do it, and how to do it. Mom was just the opposite. She was quiet, easygoing—maybe *too* easygoing, I don't know. She was always the peacemaker in the family, always the one making concessions.''

"You sound as if you disapprove," Jordan observed.

She nodded. "I did—I do," she admitted. "I thought it really stunk that she was always the one giving in."

"So what did all of this have to do with you becoming a— a con artist?"

"I'm getting to that," she assured him. "My life, up until the time I finished college, was incredibly dull. I used to think if I were any more bored, I'd sink into a coma. I wanted something more from life. I wanted excitement." She paused. "Roddy came into my life almost on cue. He was the embodiment of everything I was looking for—good-looking, smart, daring, fun. He provided the excitement that was missing from my life."

"So the two of you became lovers," Jordan concluded.

"Something like that," she said quietly. "He introduced me to his world—not that he had any problem there—and trained me as his partner. I was a quick study. It was no time before I was out running scams myself."

"You sound as if you enjoyed it," Jordan commented.

"I did," she admitted. "I was looking for thrills, and with Roddy I found them in spades. For a long time, I loved it."

"When did that change?"

"When I got pregnant with Travis."

Jordan looked at her. "This Roddy—he was Travis's father?"

She shook her head. "I met him during one of my off periods with Roddy." She made a wry face. "Roddy was never capable of being monogamous."

"So what happened when you decided you wanted out?"

"Roddy didn't like it at all," she recalled. "He claimed he was on the verge of something really big and needed me to pull it off—but I was scared. We'd had a couple of close calls. Too close. I was afraid we'd get caught and I'd end up having my baby in prison. If that happened, he would have been taken from me, put in a foster home. I couldn't bear that.''

"What did you do then?" Jordan asked.

"I lived on my share of the money Roddy and I had made in the time we worked together. I started writing about that time—and right after Travis was born, I finished *Revelations*." She paused. "I never saw Roddy again after that. I always figured he'd turn up one day and try to blackmail me, but he never did.''

"He still could, you know."

She made a face. "How well I know."

"Is that why you changed your name?"

"One of the reasons."

"What will you do if he does turn up one of these days?" Jordan wanted to know.

She gave a little shrug. "I honestly don't know." Her eyes met his. "What are *you* going to do, Jordan—now that you know the truth?"

He looked puzzled. "What do you mean—what am I going to do?"

"You now know what I am," she said. "I'm a criminal, Jordan—and, worse than that, I'm a phony. I'm not even who I claim to be."

"You are now." Jordan got up and came around the table, pulling her to her feet. "And now that I know who and what you *were*, it doesn't make a damned bit of difference. I married the woman you are now."

She stared at him in disbelief. "You're not angry?"

"Angry? No, I'm not angry," he said, taking her in his arms. "I *am* a little hurt that you didn't trust me enough to tell me before now."

She took a deep breath. "I was afraid. I didn't want to lose you," she said.

His lips brushed over her hair. "Lose me?" He gave a low chuckle. "It would take a lot more than that, love."

But he was thinking: *What else is she hiding?*

☡ London, June 1988

Had Jordan *really* accepted her past?

Sloane still wasn't sure. Ever since she'd told him about her past, about Sammy Douglas and her questionable life-style, she'd had doubts. Oh, he went through all the motions and said all the right words, but somehow it just *felt* different. *She* felt different. *It's true,* she thought, *you can never go back. Once it's done, it's done.*

Leaning against the hood of their rental car, she watched Jordan mount up, and she thought about that morning in Singapore. He knew everything now. Well, almost everything. And he was still with her. So why didn't she feel more secure?

Though she would never have admitted it, to Jordan or to anyone else, she'd never felt so *insecure* in her life.

He was riding out onto the polo field with the other players. He was so handsome. So young and strong. An athlete. Any woman would be attracted to him. And here she was, an older woman whose life was falling apart. She was a wreck, both emotionally and physically.

How long could she expect to hold him?

"You look like you could use a friend."

She looked up at the sound of a familiar voice. Lance was coming toward her. He was not wearing polo attire. "You want to be my friend?" she asked lightly as he leaned against the car beside her.

He forced a smile. "I had a different kind of friend in mind," he said, withdrawing a small brown envelope from his shirt pocket. He pressed it into her hand as discreetly as he could.

She looked at him, unsmiling. "Thank you."

He nodded. "They help, but only for a while," he said. "You have to keep taking larger and larger doses to get the same effect."

"So I've discovered." Sloane fixed her gaze on the polo field.

"How long?" he asked.

"What?"

"How long have you been on the stuff?" he wanted to know.

"Long enough."

"Meaning you don't want to tell me."

"No, I don't." She continued to watch the action on the polo field. "Does it matter?"

"Not really."

Out on the field, Jordan's path to goal was blocked, forcing him to make a difficult pass to Eric Langogne. It was in the nature of a miracle that Jordan was able to perfectly place his thirty-yard backshot.

"Why aren't you playing?" Sloane asked.

"Hillyer wants to win this one," Lance said with a shrug.

Sloane turned her attention to the polo field once again. The opposing team had launched an all-out attack. Jordan and the opponent's number one were racing for the ball. Then, suddenly, so quickly no one could have predicted it, the two horses collided, and both of them went down.

Sloane straightened up quickly, her heart racing. When she saw Jordan scramble to his feet, she breathed an inward sigh of relief.

Then she heard the sirens.

An ambulance raced onto the field; lights flashing, sirens blaring. A crowd was gathering. Sloane started across the field, with Lance trailing behind. Jordan caught her at midfield.

"What happened?" she asked anxiously.

"He came down hard. A head injury, I think." Jordan put an arm around her. "He's unconscious."

"My God." It came out a whisper.

It could so easily have been Jordan, she was thinking.

The injured player, a British six-goaler named William Markey, remained in a coma at a hospital some thirty miles from the polo grounds at Windsor Great Park. The other players, some of them accompanied by their wives, kept a vigil at the hospital, trying to offer comfort to Markey's wife, Frances, as they awaited word from his doctors.

Jordan and Sloane were among them. They had come directly from the polo grounds, and Jordan was still in his soiled polo jersey and white trousers. They sat in a busy hallway on metal chairs that offered little in the way of comfort. Ian, Dusty, Eric, and Lance were with them, no one doing much talking but all of them watching the double doors leading to the intensive care unit, waiting for Frances Markey to emerge.

"Do they think he's going to make it?"

". . . something about brain damage . . ."

". . . if he doesn't live . . ."

"How is Frances holding up . . ."

"If he doesn't pull through . . ."

"Someone said he was wearing a defective helmet . . ."

". . . still in a coma . . ."

"If he doesn't make it . . ."

Sloane felt as if she were suffocating. She tugged at the collar of her blue linen dress, taking several deep breaths. She couldn't stop thinking about how close it had been.

It could have been Jordan.

"Are you all right?" Jordan asked in a low voice.

She nodded. "I can't stop thinking . . . it could have been you. It could so easily have been you."

"But it *wasn't* me."

"It could have been."

He reached out and took her hand. "Sloane, it's a waste of energy to worry about what might have been. I'm here. I'm all right."

She nodded again, rising slowly on unsteady legs. "I'll be right back," she told him.

"Where are you going?" he asked.

"I need a drink of water."

He gave her hand a little squeeze before releasing it. "It'll be okay," he said reassuringly.

She forced a smile. "Sure."

She found a water fountain at the other end of the long corridor, around a corner. Looking around to make sure no one was watching her, she dug into her bag for her pillbox and took one of the capsules. As she bent over the fountain to wash it down, she caught sight of Max Kenyon stepping out of the elevator. She watched him for a moment. He didn't join the group outside the ICU. Instead, he went off in the opposite direction.

What was he up to? she wondered.

Hillyer and his wife stopped by the hospital late in the evening. As they stood outside the double doors looking into the ICU, Nadine felt a twinge of envy at the obvious devotion Frances Markey shared with her husband. The woman sat by his bedside, holding his hand, talking to him as if he could hear every word she said.

Or was she praying?

What must it be like to love someone that much? she wondered. *To have someone love you that much?* At that moment, Nadine realized she had never really been in love. She'd made a good marriage, a financially sound marriage—though even that was in question now—and she'd had a number of affairs with younger men. But love? No . . . she wasn't even sure what love was.

"She's a lucky woman," Nadine said aloud.

Hillyer looked at her, surprised. "How can you say that?" he asked. "Her husband is dying—"

"But she loves him. They love each other." Nadine turned to look at him. "If he doesn't make it, at least she has that. What do *we* have, Gavin? For all our material possessions, that's the one thing we've never had and never will have."

Hillyer said nothing. After all, what could he say?

He certainly couldn't deny it.

"What do the doctors say?"

Sloane was alone in the waiting area when Frances Markey emerged from the ICU. The older woman walked slowly, her shoulders slumped in defeat. She walked over and sat down next to Sloane. There was blood on the front of her simple pale pink suit. *Her husband's blood,* Sloane remembered. She'd ridden with him in the ambulance. Her honey-blond hair looked disheveled, and even under her heavy makeup she looked deathly pale.

"They say he'll never come out of it," she said, looking down at her hands in her lap. "They say he's brain dead."

Sloane looked at her, stunned. "Brain dead?"

Frances Markey nodded. "There are no doubts," she said gravely. "They've done all the tests. He'll never be normal again. He'll just be like this until he dies."

"What are you going to do?" Sloane asked.

"What *can* I do? I know Bill would not want to go on like this," she said, frowning. "He couldn't cope with being a vegetable, kept alive by artificial means. Never having any hope of a normal life again."

"You're not thinking of—" Sloane began.

Frances shook her head. "I don't really have any choice," she said. "This is the only thing I can do for him now."

Neither of them spoke for a long time, not knowing what to say to each other. Finally, Sloane broke the silence. "How did you do it?" she wanted to know.

Frances looked up. "I beg your pardon?"

"Your husband played for a long time, didn't he?"

"Almost thirty years."

"How did you do it?" Sloane asked again. "How did you handle it, knowing every time he played this could happen?"

The older woman was thoughtful for a long moment. "I dealt with it because I had to," she said simply.

Sloane looked at her, not sure she understood.

"I knew Bill was a polo player when I married him," Frances said. "I knew he'd never give it up. Polo was as much a part of him as his name or the color of his eyes." She paused. "Oh, he knew the risks—and so did I. God knows he's had his share of falls. I think he's broken every bone in his body at one time or another while playing polo."

"Didn't it scare you?" Sloane asked.

"It terrified me," Frances admitted. "It terrified me every time he played. I kept it to myself because I loved him."

Sloane said nothing. *How well I know that,* she was thinking.

William Markey died three days later. At the funeral his wife held up incredibly well, her emotions held in check throughout the lengthy graveside service.

It was Sloane who fell apart.

She sobbed uncontrollably during the service. Afterward, Jordan had to hold her up as they walked to their car. He took her back to their suite at the Dorchester and put her to bed. It didn't make any sense, he thought, puzzled. Why was she taking it so hard? She didn't even really *know* William Markey.

He drew the drapes in the bedroom, hoping she'd get some sleep, then went into the next room to call the front desk. He was worried about her. He hoped the hotel doctor might be able to help.

"*Jordan!*"

Startled by her scream, he dropped the phone halfway through dialing and ran back into the bedroom. She was sitting up in bed, terror reflected in her eyes. He sat down on the bed and held her close, stroking her hair. "It's all right," he cooed reassuringly. "I'm right here."

She buried her face in his shoulder and cried. "It could have been you," she sobbed. "Oh, God—it could have been you!"

"But it *wasn't* me."

"The next time, it *could* be."

"It could," he admitted. "There are no guarantees."

"Don't let it happen," she begged. "Get out of polo— before it's too late."

"I can't do that, Sloane." He had to make her understand. "I am a professional polo player. It's what I do for a living. There are risks, sure. Lots of professionals take risks every day—airline pilots, stuntmen, even politicians these days."

"It's not the same—" she whimpered.

"It *is*," he disagreed. "We all take risks every day—traveling by air, by car, even walking across the street. Like I said—there are no guarantees. And I'm not sure I'd want any."

She looked up at him, bewildered.

"Dying is a terrible thing," he said, stroking her cheek with the back of his hand, "but there is something worse."

"What could be worse?"

His smile was sad. "Dying without ever having lived," he said quietly. "That's what it's like, you know, always playing it safe. It's like not really being alive."

There was fear in her eyes. "And watching you deliberately risking your life day after day is like being in hell," she said. "A living hell."

But like Frances Markey, she would have to accept it.

♜ Margaux, October 1988

Sloane stood at the edge of the polo field watching Jordan practice, and she was filled with apprehension. No matter how he tried to reassure her, no matter how many times he told her how the risks "went with the territory," there was nothing Jordan or anyone else could say or do to erase her fears. Too much had happened. There had been too many "accidents."

And she was afraid Jordan would be next.

Jilly was beginning to wonder if coming here had been a mistake.

As she got into a taxi outside the Merignac International Airport at Bordeaux, she felt a knot of fear forming in the pit of her stomach. She knew Max was in Margaux. She knew he would be playing in the Tournoi International de Giscours Challenge Louis XIII de Rémy Martin. That was why she was here. Because of Max—and Jordan. Because Max had threatened to kill Jordan, and Jilly was sure it hadn't been an idle threat. But now that she was here, she wasn't sure her presence would do any good.

It might actually make matters worse.

"Paula, I just want to see you." Lance clutched the telephone receiver, his voice desperate. "That's all, I swear. Is that too much to ask?"

"What good would it do?" the all too familiar feminine voice on the other end of the line asked. "What's the point in reopening all of the old wounds?"

"I love you, Paula," he told her. "I've always loved you.

284

There's never been anyone else as far as I'm concerned.'' He paced the floor of his hotel room, phone in one hand, the receiver cradled on his shoulder, his free hand repeatedly raking through his hair in a nervous gesture as he spoke.

There was a pause on the other end. ''Yes, Lance—there is,'' she said finally.

''You don't know what you're talking about!''

''I'm not talking about another woman, Lance,'' she told him. ''I know there was never another woman.''

''Then what—''

''I'm talking about your father, Lance,'' she said gravely. ''Your father ran your life—and our lives, after we were married—even from beyond the grave. He controlled your fate. I couldn't live with it. I still can't.''

''Paula, you still haven't told me,'' he began hesitantly. ''Do you feel anything at all for me now?''

''I love you, Lance. I always have,'' she confessed. ''But I can't live with you.''

At the Grand Hotel de Bordeaux, where the Hillyers were staying, Gavin Hillyer reviewed the latest reports from his comptroller. Things were getting worse by the minute, if that were possible. He didn't know how much longer he could keep the wolves at bay.

· Not now that they'd smelled his blood.

Max Kenyon ate dinner alone at a small bistro outside Libourne. He'd had a large meal but had devoured it without really tasting a bite of it. It could have been raw horsemeat for all he cared. His mind was on something far more important. Tomorrow, he and Jordan would face off once again on the polo field.

For Jordan, it would be the last time.

Jordan was worried.

Not about the tournament, about winning, but about Sloane. About the change in her since she lost the baby. In the beginning he'd tried to tell himself it was all quite normal. She'd lost a baby. She'd get over it. In time.

But she hadn't—and now *he* was afraid he was losing *her*.

• • •

Nadine Hillyer watched the stick-and-ball session with an indifferent eye. She could still recall a time when she enjoyed watching Lance practice, enjoyed looking at him, thinking about what he was like in bed.

Now she felt only sadness.

Before, her relationship with Gavin had been fairly good, even if it did lack passion. Now she didn't even have that. Their marriage was like a state of cold war, strained and unfriendly.

And she wasn't at all sure she wanted it to continue.

Two of Hillyer's most valuable polo ponies were killed when the truck pulling their trailer overturned on a busy Texas interstate. He didn't seem concerned—beyond the time it took to notify his insurance company. Nor did he care that the driver of the truck had been killed as well.

Or that the truck's brake line had apparently been cut.

Hillyer played his first string—both players and ponies—in the first round of semifinals. They played a French team, a team they'd never been up against, and were leading 8–4 at the end of the first half. That impressive lead left them somewhat overconfident, and they were outscored by the end of the fourth chukker.

Eric Langogne missed two penalty shots, but the team still managed to tie the game and send it into overtime. Jordan played aggressively, even more so than usual, and it made Sloane nervous.

"What's he trying to prove?" she asked, unaware she'd spoken the words until Dusty, sitting beside her, responded.

"He's proving he won't take any shit off Julien."

Sloane looked at her. "Who?"

"Julien Richaud—the French number three," Dusty offered in explanation. "I've heard he can be a real prick when he wants to be."

Sloane gave a weak laugh. "Sounds like a real charmer."

Out on the field, Richaud had pushed Jordan too far. Having taken all he could take, he swung his mallet across his pony's neck and in the direction of Richaud's face in a most unsportsmanlike gesture. Angered by the altercation, Richaud leaned his pony into Jordan's. A miscalculation on Richaud's part brought both ponies down. Standing with Dusty at the sidelines, Sloane screamed. It was the last thing she remembered before she fainted.

Both players were taken to a hospital in Margaux. While they were being examined in the emergency room, Sloane paced the floor in the small waiting room, worried and frustrated and angry. Worried because she had no idea how seriously Jordan had been injured. Frustrated because there was nothing she could do. And angry because he knew the dangers and he played anyway. Angry at herself because she hadn't been able to talk him out of it. Mostly angry because she loved him so much but couldn't accept him for who and what he was, which she had when she'd first married him.

Ian brought her a cup of coffee. She didn't really want it, but she accepted it graciously. She walked over to the only window in the small room and stood there for a long time, staring off somewhere in the middle distance, until she was sure no one in the room was watching her. Then she took a pill. She had a feeling she was going to need it.

"Madame Phillips?"

She jerked around, spilling the coffee. The emergency room doctor stood in the doorway. He was looking right at her.

"Y-Yes," she blurted nervously, "I'm Mrs. Phillips. Is my husband all right?"

The doctor smiled. "He will recover, if that is what you ask," he answered slowly in English. "You may see him now if you will come with me."

She nodded, wiping the spilled coffee from her left sleeve with her right hand. Dropping the paper cup in a trash can on her way to the door, she followed the doctor down a long, busy corridor to a bank of elevators.

"We have taken your husband up to a room. He will have to stay for a few days," the doctor explained. "After that, I have strongly advised him it would not be wise of him to play polo for a while."

"Thank God," Sloane breathed.

He looked at her. "I beg your pardon?"

"Nothing," she said quickly. "How bad—how badly was he injured?"

"Three of his ribs are broken. He also suffered a mild concussion," the doctor said. "The best medicine I can prescribe for him is rest. Time and rest. But these polo players, they are so stubborn. He will be back on the fields within a week no doubt."

Sloane shook her head. "Not if I can help it."

"How do you feel?"

Sloane forced a smile as she bent to kiss Jordan's cheek. She pulled up a chair and sat by his bed, holding his right hand in hers, trying not to let her nervousness show.

He gave her a tired smile. "Like I'm on display," he admitted. "They've done so many damned tests—chest X-rays, skull X-rays, CAT scans, you name it. I think that in the past few hours the inside of my head's been viewed more often than the reruns of *I Love Lucy*."

"They only want to make sure you're all right," she pointed out.

He grimaced. "Yeah."

"They tell me you should take some time off from polo," she said then.

Jordan shook his head. "I can't."

"You have to."

Their conversation was interrupted at that moment by Jilly, who barged into the room unannounced and uninvited. At the sight of her, Sloane was on her feet, ready for a fight.

"What do you want?" she demanded angrily.

Jilly's voice was cold. "I came to talk to Jordan—alone, if you don't mind."

"Oh, but I *do* mind," Sloane assured her. "I think you'd better just turn around and leave, Jilly. You're not wanted here."

"I'm not going anywhere until I've spoken with Jordan," Jilly responded stubbornly.

"Then suppose you tell us what's on your mind, Jilly." This was Jordan.

She stared at him for a moment. Her eyes moved from Jordan to Sloane and back again. Then she nodded. "Max is here," she said.

Jordan gave her a puzzled look. "I know that," he said.

"No—you don't understand." Jilly shook her head emphatically. "Some months ago I discovered I was pregnant. It wasn't planned. It was a mistake. When Max found out, he went crazy. He was sure it wasn't his. He beat me so badly I lost the baby and ended up in the hospital. Max was put in jail—but he got out before I was released from the hospital."

"I don't understand," Jordan started slowly. "What does all of that have to do with me?"

"He's convinced the baby was yours."

"*What?*"

"He wants to kill you."

♻ Martha's Vineyard, December 1988

"Does it still hurt?" Sloane asked.

Jordan smiled wearily as he pulled himself upright in bed. "Only when I do mundane little things like breathe," he said as she placed the breakfast tray across his lap. He looked at it for a moment. "Eggs, ham, potatoes, fruit—there's enough here for three people!"

"Emma thought you might be hungry." Sloane sat down on the side of the bed, brushing a strand of hair away from her face. "You've lost a little weight since we've been home."

He cut into the thick slice of ham and took a bite. "Pain does have a strange way of killing the old appetite," he muttered as he chewed.

"If that's the case, then you must be feeling pretty good this morning," she said lightly.

"It comes and goes."

She was silent for a long moment. "I've been thinking, Jordy . . . With everything that's been happening, don't you think it would be a good idea to maybe get out of the line of fire for a while . . ."

He looked up. "The line of fire?"

"You know. Maybe you shouldn't play for a while," she said.

His laugh was mirthless. "This isn't a hobby, Sloane. It's the way I make my living. I can't just take six months off because I feel like it," he pointed out.

"Can't you take six months off to save your own life?" she asked sharply.

He shook his head. "Don't you think you're overreacting

just a little?'' he asked. He didn't tell her about Ian's suspicions. Telling Sloane could only make matters worse, given her present state of mind.

"No, I don't.'' Her face was serious. "There have been too many accidents, Jordy. Too many so-called coincidences. Every time you ride out on the polo field, I'm scared to death something's going to happen to you. I have nightmares about it.''

"I've taken those risks every time I've played, Sloane, and I've been playing almost sixteen years now,'' he told her. "This is nothing new.''

"This *is* different, and you know it.''

"I know you worry too much.''

She wasn't about to let go. "I don't want to lose you, Jordy,'' she said softly. "I love you. Sometimes I think I love you too much.''

He looked at her for a moment, wishing there was something he could say or do to put her mind at ease. There wasn't, so he did the only thing he could do. Lifting the tray off his lap, he set it aside and took her in his arms, holding her close. He did love her. He'd never stopped loving her. But was love enough? Was it strong enough to get them through this?

"What's happening to us?'' he asked aloud as he stroked her hair.

She looked up at him. "I don't know,'' she admitted, "and it scares the hell out of me.''

He kissed her tenderly. "I love you,'' he said. "Do you believe that?''

"It's one of the few things I still do believe.''

When Jordan thought about it later, it bothered him. Their lovemaking that morning had been wonderful—slow, gentle— better, in fact, than it had been in a very long time. For that time it was like having the old Sloane back, but when it was over, he was faced with the realization that something was terribly wrong. He knew that by sundown her mood could change completely.

She wasn't the old Sloane, the woman he'd fallen in love with, the woman he'd married, and what scared him most was that she might never be again.

Never in his life had he felt so totally helpless. It was like watching this woman he loved drown and not being able to swim well enough to save her. Still . . . when people were drowning, weren't there other ways to save them, ways other than jumping into the water after them? Yes . . . there had to be a way.

If he just knew where to begin. . . .

"I thought I'd find you here."

Jordan didn't turn around. He lifted the lightweight English saddle onto Solitaire's back. "You know me pretty well," he said lightly as he secured the girth.

"You have a *very* predictable routine," Sloane said, opening the gate just wide enough for her to pass through.

"Too bad I can't say the same for you." Satisfied the girth was tight enough without being too tight, he pulled the flap down and adjusted the stirrups.

She stroked the mare's neck affectionately. "Solitaire . . . such a lovely name," she murmured softly. "It does suit her. She's a gem. One of a kind."

"Sometimes I think it would suit you better than it suits her," Jordan said.

She looked surprised. "Me? How?"

He shrugged. "I don't know. A lot of ways, actually. You're a solitary kind of person. A loner. No matter how important we've been to each other, how close we are—or were—I've always had the feeling you've held something back, that you've always kept a part of yourself isolated. Even from me."

She looked at him oddly, as if not knowing what to say.

"There are times I feel as if I don't really know you at all," he went on. "One minute you're passionate and giving—like you were this morning. The woman I fell so hard for in Deauville. You're laughing and ready to take the bull by the horns— like you were when we first got married. But it's like flipping a light switch. Ten minutes later you're moody and withdrawn, not wanting to talk to anyone or do anything but hide out up there in the bedroom."

Sloane looked down at the ground. "So much has happened—"

"We're not the only couple who's ever lost a baby, Sloane,"

he reminded her. "It happens to lots of people, but they get through it."

"This is different," Sloane responded sullenly.

"It's only different because of that frustrating habit of yours of keeping everything bottled up inside yourself," he disagreed. "How much *have* you kept to yourself since we've been married, anyway?"

"So that's what this is all about," she said carefully, biting off each word as if she were taking a bitter-tasting medicine. "I knew it would be a mistake to tell you about Chicago. I *knew* you'd never be able to forget it—or let me forget it!"

"It's not what you did or didn't do back in Chicago," he insisted. "That's history—water under the bridge and all that. What matters is that you kept it to yourself for so long, that you didn't trust me enough to tell me the truth. And now— for over a year we've been drifting further and further apart because you've thrown up this invisible wall around yourself, and even I can't seem to penetrate it."

Not knowing how to respond, Sloane said nothing; she turned to walk away. Jordan, not finished with her yet, grabbed her arm and spun her around to face him again.

"Solitaire is a game for one person, Sloane," he told her. "Life isn't—and marriage sure as hell isn't."

"Are you and Sloane having problems?" Travis wanted to know.

He was helping Jordan muck out one of the stalls. Jordan often worked off tension through physical labor, and in spite of the discomfort caused by his mending ribs, it was something he needed right now. "What makes you ask a question like that?"

"I dunno," Travis said with a shrug. "She just seems different lately."

So Travis had noticed it too. Jordan looked at the boy. "Different how?"

"Weird. Like there's two of her," Travis said thoughtfully. "Like maybe she was snatched by aliens, and they left a clone in her place."

Jordan suppressed a chuckle. In spite of his own concerns about his wife, his stepson's observation *was* amusing, if a little farfetched.

"Don't you think she's been acting different lately?" Travis asked.

"She's had a lot of problems lately," Jordan said quietly.

"It's been more than a year since she lost the baby," Travis said, digging into the manure.

"Some things aren't easy to get over." Jordan found himself trying to explain something even he didn't fully understand. "Losing the baby hurt your mother very badly. It's going to take her a long time to heal."

"Can't she have another baby?" Travis wanted to know.

"Sure she can—that is, I think she can," Jordan answered.

"So why doesn't she?"

Jordan stopped what he was doing and dug his pitchfork into the ground. He turned to face the boy. "I'm afraid it's just not that easy, sport," he said. "You see, when parents have children—whether they have two or twelve—they love all of them equally. Not always in the same way, but equally. Trouble is, kids can't be replaced the way you'd replace a pair of shoes. When you lose a child, you can't have another one to take its place."

Travis was thoughtful for a moment. "Then if you and Sloane have a baby, it won't take my place?" he asked.

Jordan laughed. "Of course not!" he said, putting an arm around the boy's shoulder. "No one could ever take your place with your mother."

"She's pretty special to me, too," Travis admitted.

"There is one thing you could do that would really make her happy," Jordan said then.

Travis looked up at him. "What?"

"Try calling her 'Mom' again."

Alone in the master bedroom, Sloane retrieved her overnight case from the back of her closet. She put it on the bed and unlocked it with trembling fingers. Yanking it open, she hastily rummaged through it until she found the vials of pills hidden at the bottom. She opened one and took out one of the amphetamine capsules, then went into the bathroom for a glass of water. She stuck the pill in her mouth, chasing it down with the water, and silently prayed it would begin to work quickly.

Where, she asked herself, *is this all going to end?*

• • •

"I'm making up for lost time," Sloane told Cate over the phone. "I wrote seventy-five pages in three days."

"I suppose it would be too much to hope for that you'll be able to maintain the momentum long enough to finish the book." Cate's tone was mildly reproachful.

"Depends on how long the muse decides to stick around," Sloane said lightly. *Actually, it depends on how long the pills hold out,* she was thinking.

"I'll keep my fingers crossed," Cate said, laughing.

"Whatever makes you happy."

She ended the call and replaced the receiver slowly. Since she'd seen Dr. Leonard in New York, she felt a hundred and fifty percent better. The stuff she'd been taking wasn't doing the job anymore. He'd given her something different. Something stronger. They made her feel positively *wonderful*.

If only her heart would stop racing.

The first step was obvious. He had to find the stuff.

Jordan entered the bedroom and closed the door. He had to find the pills, find them and get rid of them. They had to be here somewhere. Though he knew she probably kept them well hidden, he started with the obvious places: the medicine chest in the bathroom, her dresser drawers, the drawers in her nightstand. Nothing. He searched her shoulder bag. All he found was a small bottle of aspirin and some antacid tablets. He checked her hatboxes. Zip. He went for her luggage, going through each suitcase carefully.

The last piece was the overnighter. Frustrated, he dumped its contents onto the bed and rummaged through it hastily until he found what he was looking for: two large vials, one filled with barbiturates, the other with amphetamines.

"What are you doing?"

He jerked around. Sloane was standing in the doorway, looking at him accusingly. *"What are you doing?"*

"With any luck, I'm saving your life—and our marriage!" He held up the two vials. "Tell me, Sloane, how long have you been on this crap?"

"None of your goddamned business!" She made a grab for the vials, but he pulled away quickly.

"No way!" he snapped. "No way in hell are you getting your hands on these again!"

"You don't have any right—"

"Like hell I don't!" Jordan's anger rose. "You're my wife and you're killing yourself with this shit! I have *every* right!"

She lunged at him, grabbing for the pills again, but he threw up an arm to deflect her attack. The movement unbalanced her, and she fell backward onto the bed. Pulling herself upright, she focused her energy. She realized now that a direct frontal attack was not going to work. Trying another approach, she looked up at him, her facial expression softened. "You don't understand, Jordan," she said softly.

His gaze was cold, angry. "You're right. I don't," he said. "Suppose you make me understand."

"I *need* the pills."

"Obviously."

"I can't get by without them." She was pleading with him. "They're all that keeps me going."

"I see," he said irritably. "Says a lot for Travis and me, doesn't it?"

"That's not what I mean."

"Then maybe you'd better tell me what you *do* mean." He stood facing her in an unquestionably angry stance, feet spread apart, arms akimbo.

Eyes cast downward, she spoke slowly, hesitantly. "You know how bad things were after I lost the baby."

He nodded.

"I thought I was going to lose you, too."

He looked surprised. "Where did you get an idea like that?"

She shook her head. "I knew how much you wanted children, and since I can't give you any—"

"Nobody said you can't have another child," he pointed out.

"I can't go through that again, Jordan," she said gravely. "I can't go through losing another baby."

"It's not preordained that you'll lose every baby you conceive," Jordan maintained. "You carried Travis to term."

Sloane laughed mirthlessly. "That was twelve years ago, Jordan," she pointed out. "I'm thirty-seven years old now, I have high blood pressure—"

"And a drug problem," Jordan finished.

"And a drug problem," she echoed with a slight nod. "I needed the pills after I lost the baby. I needed them to sleep, to drive away the nightmares. I started taking the amphetamines because the sleeping pills made me feel dopey all the time—"

"And now?" he asked.

"I can't stop," she admitted.

"Yes, you can."

She shook her head emphatically. "No. I can't," she said in a firm, quiet voice. "I really can't."

He saw the look on her face and knew she meant it. She really believed what she was saying. Jordan knew what he had to do. He drew in a deep breath and faced her squarely. "You're going to have to," he said quietly, "because I'm not giving them back."

Sloane didn't waste any time. As soon as she was sure Jordan had left the house, she retrieved her secret stash from its hiding place in the long, deep compartment at the back of her portable tape recorder where, had she been using the machine, the batteries would have been placed.

Thank God he hadn't found them. She'd figured all along that sooner or later he'd get suspicious and start looking. She hadn't been able to put all of the pills in the tape recorder—there were too many—but at least she'd been able to hide some of them.

He doesn't understand, she thought as she took one of the barbiturate capsules from the small plastic bag in which she'd wrapped them. *He can't understand.*

She looked at the yellow capsule in the palm of her hand. Given her present state of agitation, one probably wouldn't do it. Not this time. She'd probably need two. She took another capsule from the bag before closing the back of the tape recorder and returning it to the top drawer of the nightstand.

Just a little something to calm me down, she thought as she put both capsules in her mouth and washed them down with the contents of one of the small, airline-size liquor bottles she found at the back of the drawer.

Just a little something to calm me down.

• • •

When Jordan returned, Sloane was sprawled facedown on the bed, sleeping soundly. Too soundly. From the doorway he couldn't even tell if she was breathing. As he started toward the bed, something lying on the carpet caught his eye, and he bent to pick it up. One of the yellow capsules.

Damn, he thought. He must have dropped it when they were arguing earlier.

As he straightened up, he caught sight of the empty liquor bottle on the nightstand. He snatched it up, turning it upside down to see if there was anything left in it. Not a drop. *Terrific,* he thought. *She probably took pills, too. She said it herself. She took pills to sleep and pills to wake up.*

But how many had she taken? And what kind? He couldn't be sure. He'd taken the pills from her, sure, but he had no idea how many she might have already taken before he got to them.

First things first, he thought, his mind racing. *Got to wake her up.* He grabbed her by the shoulders and shook her roughly. "Come on, Sloane," he urged. "Wake up. Come on—wake up!"

She gave a little moan but didn't open her eyes.

"No," he said gruffly. "I'm not going to let you sleep. Not until I know you're all right." He dragged her to her feet. "Come on—we're taking a little walk."

She was like a rag doll in his arms. He staggered around for a few moments before finally regaining his balance, then proceeded to walk her around the room, half walking, half dragging her limp form, slapping her face lightly in an attempt to rouse her. She shook her head from side to side, murmuring her protests, but to no avail. He kept at it, determined to bring her around.

"Come *on,* Sloane!" he growled. "You've got to wake up!"

"No . . . just let me sleep," she muttered. "Just a little . . . while . . ."

"Not a chance," he said crossly. "How many did you take?"

"Don't know . . ." She leaned against him, her legs weak.

He patted her face vigorously. "How many, Sloane?" he pressed.

"Two," she muttered in a drugged voice. "Just two . . ."

"Are you sure?"

"Two . . . think so . . ."

"Two and some liquor. How much liquor, Sloane?" he demanded.

"Just a little . . . just two."

Two? Did she mean two miniatures of scotch—or was she still talking about the pills? He couldn't be sure, therefore he couldn't take any chances. He dragged her into the bathroom. Opening the shower stall, he supported her with one arm while he turned on the cold water. He took her into the stall and closed the door, standing with her under the spray of cold water.

She shrieked loudly when it hit her, her speech garbled when she begged him to turn it off. "I'm awake—I am!" she wailed.

"Sorry, love, but I've got to make sure you *stay* that way," he shouted over the roar of the water. Both of them were soaked; hair plastered to their faces and necks, clothes clinging to their bodies like a snake's skin.

Sloane shivered violently in Jordan's arms. "Please—turn it off," she cried. "I'm all right—I only took two!"

"What about the booze?"

"Only one—one of those little airline bottles! I swear it!"

His whole body sagged with relief as he reached down and turned off the water. *Thank God,* he thought. It was a false alarm—this time.

It was also the last straw as far as he was concerned.

"We've got to talk."

Sloane, sitting up in bed, looked up as Jordan came into the bedroom. "I thought you'd already said it all," she said quietly.

"Not quite." He closed the door and crossed the room to the bed.

"What's left?" she asked with a shrug.

"Us. *We're* left, Sloane," he said quietly. "Don't you think we're worth saving?"

She looked at him blankly. "I don't know what you mean."

"The hell you don't," he said irritably. "Things haven't been the same between us since you got on this crap—"

"Since I lost the baby," she corrected.

"We could have survived that," he maintained. "Jesus, it should have brought us even closer. But this . . ."

"*This* was the only way I was able to get through it," she replied without much emotion.

"Only because you didn't feel you could turn to me," he reminded her.

"How could I? I let you down—I couldn't give you the one thing you really wanted."

He stared at her for a moment. "All I wanted—all I still want—is you," he told her. "Sure, it would be great to have a whole houseful of kids. I don't deny that. But if we can't have them, I can live with that. We have Travis—and we have each other."

"That's not enough," she said flatly.

"It is for me."

"For how long?"

"I want you to enter a drug treatment program, Sloane," he said then.

She looked genuinely surprised. "I don't need a treatment program!" she snapped angrily.

"You told me you *needed* pills, that you couldn't get through a day or a night without them," he said, recalling their earlier conversation. "Are you trying to tell me those aren't the words of a woman who needs—desperately needs—a rehab program?"

"I can't stop," Sloane sobbed. "I'm *afraid* to!"

"You *can!*"

"Please, Jordan—"

"You *have* to, Sloane," he said firmly. "You have to beat this thing if we're going to save our marriage."

Sloane looked at him, not sure she understood.

"I love you, Sloane. I love you more than I've ever loved anyone in my life," he said, his eyes meeting hers. "But I *won't* stay here and watch you destroy yourself."

"Jordan, I can't . . ."

"Then you leave me no choice," he said with finality. "I'll be leaving for California in the morning—alone. If you change your mind before then, I'll be across the hall—packing."

Speechless, Sloane watched him leave the room.

Her worst fears had been realized.

⇄ New York City, December 1988

It was early evening when the train pulled into Grand Central Station. Sloane remained on board until the last passenger had disembarked from the car, then she collected her bags and left the train slowly, numb with shock. Her mind still couldn't accept the reality that Jordan had walked out on her, yet his parting words to her echoed through her thoughts now like a knife stabbing at her heart: *You've got a serious problem. . . . I'm not going to stick around and watch you kill yourself. . . . I love you, but I just can't take it. . . . You know where to find me when you're ready to let me help you. . . .*

She made her way to the busy main concourse, with its high, vaulted ceilings painted pale blue and decorated with the constellations of the winter sky that were painted backward—"as God would see it," according to the artist, Whitney Warren. The day was as gray and gloomy as Sloane's mood as she wandered through the mob of harried commuters, oblivious of the jostling crowd and the grandeur of her surroundings. She finally pushed her way to the nearest exit, emerging on East Forty-second Street.

Several taxis were lined up at the curb, a number of them taking on passengers. It was snowing, and the brisk wind was bitterly cold, but Sloane felt nothing. She tossed her bags into the back seat of the first empty cab she came to and slid in beside them, jerking the door shut. She leaned back in the seat and opened the front of her fur coat.

"Where to, lady?" the driver asked, switching on the meter.

She looked somewhat confused. "What?"

' ' "Where to?"

She shrugged indifferently. "What difference does it make?"

"A lot. The meter's runnin', in case you ain't noticed," he pointed out. "'Course it's your nickel—you can go all the way to East Jesus if you got the fare."

Sloane stared at him for a moment, frowning. "Take me to Sixty East Eighty-eighth Street," she said finally.

"You sure?" He was looking at her as though he thought she might be on something, looking at her the way Jordan had before he left.

"I am," she said quietly.

I have nowhere else to go, she thought dismally.

The apartment was in darkness when she entered the gallery. Sloane could feel the emptiness like a physical presence, reaching out, grabbing at her. Funny . . . it had never bothered her before. How many times in the past had she come back to this apartment, when both Jordan and Travis were at Moonstone and Emma was out for one reason or another, and never been bothered by the emptiness? Sure, she'd missed them and hated being away from them, but she'd never been *afraid* to be alone. But now . . . she wished she hadn't dismissed the doorman who'd offered to bring her bags up for her. She wished someone—anyone—were here with her now.

She put one suitcase down long enough to turn on the lights, then carried both bags to the master bedroom, the bedroom she and Jordan had shared. She ran one hand over the silk comforter, remembering the first time they had made love in that bed. They'd returned from an exhausting two weeks on the road, physically drained but mentally high. They'd taken to that bed with a bottle of Bollinger Brut and ended up drinking too much. She'd made a few clumsy attempts at seduction, and Jordan had finally taken over, taking her slowly because he'd been incapable of any quick or sudden movement. Afterward, they'd fallen asleep locked in an embrace, and Sloane had been so happy she was almost afraid to go to sleep, afraid she'd wake up and discover it had been only a dream, a beautiful dream. . . .

Sloane blinked back a tear. Even then, she'd lived in dread

of the day she would lose him. She'd been afraid that sooner or later he would begin to feel he'd made a mistake, that he'd leave her for a younger, more beautiful woman. She'd worried that he might go back to Jilly. Never once had she imagined that she would *drive* him away.

She sank down onto the bed and took a deep breath. She took off the wide-brimmed black hat that had served as her shield on the train, making it possible for her to avoid eye contact with the other passengers and therefore discourage any attempts at conversation. Putting the hat aside, she kicked off her shoes and lay back on the bed. She knew what she had to do, and yet she dreaded doing it. She had to get herself into a drug treatment program, and she had to do it fast. She had to beat this thing. She had to prove to Jordan that she could do it. First thing in the morning she would check into the treatment program.

And hope it wasn't too late for her and Jordan.

The mantel clock read two-fifteen. Sloane wanted to go to bed, but she knew she wouldn't sleep. She was so charged up now, she could probably stay awake for a week. She hadn't had a pill of any kind in twenty-four hours, and she was beginning to feel the stress, mentally and physically. She knew relief was only as far as the bedroom, and the bottles of yellow, red, and orange capsules buried in the bottom of her shoulder bag. Two of those reds would guarantee her at least ten hours of uninterrupted sleep. It would be so easy.

But she wasn't going to do it. She was determined *not* to do it.

There was too much at stake. Even amphetamines and barbiturates would never be able to ease the pain of losing Jordan for good. She knew that only too well. Withdrawal, no matter how difficult, would be easier to endure.

Death, she thought grimly, *would be easier*.

Sloane woke with a start. Her heart was pounding. She lay back, staring up at the ceiling in the darkness, trying to determine if it was one of the first physical signs of withdrawal or if it was a reaction to the dream she'd been having.

She couldn't remember all of it, and what she *did* remember

didn't make a hell of a lot of sense. She was on a polo field—
God only knew where—during a match. She'd lost her wedding
ring. She was down on her hands and knees, searching for it
in the grass, only the grass wasn't as green and well tended as
it was on most of the polo fields she'd seen. It was dry and
brittle and brown. Dead grass. The sky was full of dark, threat-
ening clouds, and yet the sun was getting through somehow.
It was unbearably hot. The action around her was fierce. The
players were all around her, swinging their mallets over her
furiously as she searched for her missing ring. They were laughing—hollow, malicious laughter. They were laughing at her!
She searched the faces around her for Jordan's, but he wasn't
there. Jordan wasn't there. . . .

What did it all mean? she wondered as she struggled to catch
her breath. Her heart was still racing. She was sure there had
to be some deep, underlying meaning behind that troubling
dream. She'd lost her wedding ring—lost Jordan. Was it actually Jordan she was looking for in the dream? Were the other
players laughing at her because they knew he'd never come
back, that she'd lost him for good? She closed her eyes tightly,
trying to block out the images that raced through her mind,
distorted, frightening images of men and women on polo
ponies, their laughter echoing inside her head. Her tears came
freely. There was no escaping their taunting ridicule. No escaping the reality of her loss. . . .

She rolled over on her side and threw one arm across the
pillow on the other side of the bed. Jordan's pillow. She froze.
Was it her imagination, or was there an indentation in the pillow
where Jordan's head would have been? She moved closer,
pressing her cheek to the cool softness of the pillow. Only a
faint trace of his cologne lingered on the surface. A tear escaped
from the corner of her eye and rolled down her cheek as she
inhaled the woodsy scent. Everywhere she turned, there were
reminders of Jordan.

She sat up in the darkness and turned to look at the digital
clock radio on the nightstand. Four-thirty. She couldn't have
been asleep for more than half an hour. She'd finally given up
and gone to bed at three o'clock, after a long, hot bath and
enough cocoa to float a yacht, but even then sleep had not
come easily. She couldn't recall how long she'd been lying

awake, unable to stop thinking, unable to stop feeling, until overwhelming exhaustion finally claimed her.

She pressed one hand to her chest. Her heart was still thudding wildly, and breathing took a monumental effort. She looked at the three plastic bottles on the nightstand next to the clock radio. She'd put them there when she went to bed . . . just in case. Just in case she needed them. Like now. . . .

She knew if she took a couple of the reds, she'd sleep. They'd give her relief. She also knew if she took them, the vicious cycle would begin all over again. She'd be lost. Jordan would be lost. All because of the pills. . . .

"Damn you!" She lashed out violently, knocking the vials off the nightstand with such force that the caps popped off and their contents spilled onto the carpet. Sloane made no move to pick them up. She fell back against the pillows, sobbing uncontrollably.

For what she had lost, and for what she had become.

She was still awake when the first rays of sunlight invaded the darkness in the bedroom. Her eyes were swollen and painfully dry. She'd cried so much she was convinced there were no tears left in her to be shed. There was nothing left in her, just a vast, empty wasteland incapable of sustaining life of any kind.

"My God!"

Startled, Sloane's head jerked toward the door, where Emma stood looking down at the capsules scattered on the carpet. She pulled herself upright, pulling the sheet up around herself. "What are you doing here?" she demanded irritably.

"I-I came back early, Mrs. Phillips," the housekeeper stammered, obviously unnerved by what she'd seen. "I'll clean this up immediately—"

"Leave it!" Sloane snapped.

The older woman looked stunned. "Are you all right?"

"I'm all right, dammit!" Having gone too long without the pills on which she'd become dependent was taking its toll on Sloane. "I just want to be alone—is there anything wrong with that?"

"No, of course not, Mrs. Phillips, but I don't think—"

Sloane was fighting for self-control. "I *need* to be alone

now, Emma,'' she stated firmly, insistently. "Travis is at Moonstone. His father—that is, Mr. Phillips—is out of the country. I would feel better if you were there with my son.''

"If you wish,'' Emma responded with uncertainty.

"I wish,'' Sloane said tightly. "I'd like you to leave right away. Right now.''

"Yes, of course.'' Emma knew better than to argue with her in her present state of mind, but she also knew something was very wrong. She'd do as Sloane had instructed. She'd leave.

But before she did, she'd call someone to look in on Sloane.

Sloane wasn't sure why or when she'd decided to do this on her own. Maybe it was her fear of the resulting publicity that had changed her mind about entering a treatment facility. It had been her secret for so long, she couldn't bring herself to suddenly share it with the world. Not now. Especially not now.

She knew what she was doing was risky. She knew it was going to be rough. She knew she needed medical supervision. But just as she knew all of those things, she knew she *had* to go it alone. There was no other way. Not for her. Not now.

Up until now, the effects of withdrawal had been primarily psychological, but now the physical discomfort had begun. By nightfall, she was experiencing abdominal cramps. Even the simplest task, like holding a glass, became difficult because her hands trembled so severely. She couldn't even look at food without being overcome with nausea.

She'd begun to doubt the soundness of her own decision. Twice, she had reconsidered. She'd almost called the treatment center. She'd almost asked for help, but in the end her fear had held her back. Fear of discovery. Fear of publicity. Fear of reopening all the old wounds. No . . . she'd have to deal with it alone. There was no other way. She'd get through it okay. She had to.

She took a hot bath and went to bed early. She was exhausted, both physically and mentally, but sleep did not come easily. She tossed and turned for the better part of three hours before she finally drifted off.

The sleep that finally came was fitful and haunted by troubling, all too vivid dreams. She was standing in the middle of

Grand Central Station. She could see Jordan in the middle of the crowd on the other side of the main concourse. He was calling her name . . . there was an echo, though she wasn't quite sure why. She was running toward him, pushing her way through the crowd, trying to get to him. She was reaching out to him, calling to him . . . but when she reached the spot where she'd seen him, he was gone. Then she saw him in another part of the concourse—still waving, still calling to her. And it started all over again. She was running to him, fighting her way through the mob—but when she reached her destination, once again he was gone.

She woke in a cold sweat. She sat up in bed, fumbled in the darkness for the switch on the lamp, and turned it on. Her hands were shaking and her heart beat wildly as she struggled to catch her breath. Suddenly, a wave of severe nausea swept over her. She scrambled out of bed and stumbled into the bathroom, making it just in time. On her knees, she hugged the cold porcelain bowl as she vomited continually until she was certain there was nothing left inside her to come out. Her throat was raw, and her insides felt as if they'd been ripped apart; tears streamed down her cheeks as she sobbed uncontrollably. Could she do it? Could she beat this thing?

Did she have the strength to survive what lay ahead?

The red light was flashing on the answering machine. Sloane didn't check to see who had called. She didn't care who had called. She was sure Jordan *hadn't*, and he was the only one she wanted to talk to now.

She curled up on the couch, still in her robe. She didn't get dressed because there was no reason to get dressed. Her hair was dirty and tangled, badly in need of a shampoo and brushing. She'd lost weight; she'd had no desire for food, so she hadn't eaten. She had no idea how many days she'd been holed up here. She'd lost all track of time: she wasn't even aware of day or night most of the time. The drapes were all drawn, and every light in the apartment remained on around the clock. Sloane was terrified of the dark, of the loneliness it brought, of the memories it stirred.

There had been a time—had it been so long ago?—when she had loved the night. Welcomed it. She'd looked forward to the long, passionate nights with Jordan, looked forward to that time alone with him. Now, the night only made her more acutely aware of her loss. She went to bed alone. Either she didn't sleep at all, or when she did, she slept fitfully, haunted by dreams of loss, of being alone. She was never quite sure which was worse.

So this is what hell is like, she thought.

The nausea and vomiting finally passed. The lethargy that had immobilized her began to dissipate, and she felt her energy beginning to return—slowly, so slowly that she was barely aware of it at first, but returning nonetheless. It was a beginning, she told herself repeatedly. But a beginning of what?

She woke one morning wanting nothing more than a hot bath. Filling the bathtub with hot water and perfumed oil, she bathed slowly, thoroughly enjoying it as she never had before. It seemed to her, soaking in the hot fragrant water, that her tightly knotted muscles were finally beginning to relax. Still, she fought the urge to stay there, to go to sleep there.

Afterward, she washed her hair. It felt wonderful. She'd never gone so long without washing her hair before. She didn't blow-dry it as she normally would have. She combed it out, letting it dry naturally. Wet, it felt wonderful.

By the next day she was ready to eat, even though her insides still ached from so much vomiting. She decided to start with something light, so she soft-boiled two eggs and lightly buttered a single slice of toast. She ate slowly, not sure she was going to be able to keep it down. Eggs had never tasted so good! She was still hungry when she swallowed the last bite but decided against eating too much at once. *Quit* while you're ahead, she thought.

On the third day, she ventured out onto the terrace. Even the cold winter air smelled different than it had before— cleaner, somehow fresher than she remembered. She didn't even mind the cold; on the contrary, she welcomed it. She could feel it, and being able to feel was a wonderful thing. It meant she was still alive. It meant there was hope. . . .

That afternoon, she played back all the messages left on her answering machine. Cate had called three times, concerned because she didn't know how to reach Sloane. Adrienne called.

But there was nothing from Jordan. Nothing.

Sloane didn't know why she felt so disappointed. She hadn't really expected him to call. He'd told her he wouldn't. And yet a part of her still clung to the hope that he would.

Hope, in the end, was all that kept her going.

♻ Cairo, December 1988

Jordan wondered if he'd made a mistake.

Had he been too hard on Sloane? He'd asked himself that question again and again since the day he walked out on her at Moonstone. Would his leaving force her to face the truth about her problem and do something about it—or would it push her over the edge? Had he made a mistake?

He wished he could talk to her, but he didn't even know where she was now. He did know she'd left Moonstone not long after he left. When he called—he had tried to call her—Emma had told him Sloane was already gone. She had *not* taken Travis with her. Why? What did it mean?

His first thought was that she'd gone to New York. He'd called the apartment several times, but he always got the answering machine. He never left a message since she obviously wasn't there, either.

The question remained: Where was she?

He called Cate Winslow. She had neither seen nor heard from Sloane since Thanksgiving, and she was more than a little concerned. It wasn't like Sloane not to stay in touch.

But she was also aware that Sloane hadn't been herself for some time now.

"How long do you think you can keep this up?" Ian wanted to know.

Jordan shook his head. "I don't know," he answered truthfully. "I really don't know."

They were having coffee in a small café near their hotel since most establishments in Arab countries do not serve alcoholic beverages of any kind.

310

"I don't know what happened between you and Sloane," Ian began, "but I can see what it's doing to you. Is it worth this, Jordy? Is it so bad that you can't work it out?"

"It's pretty bad, Ian, but it's not what you think," Jordan said quietly, swirling the small amount of coffee that remained in the bottom of his cup. "Sloane's on drugs."

If Ian was surprised, he gave no indication of it. "How did it happen?" he asked.

"After she lost the baby." He waved to their waiter to bring more coffee. "She took it pretty hard."

Ian nodded. "I remember."

"Dr. Halsey didn't want her to leave the hospital as soon as she did," Jordan started. "He was worried about her mental state. He thought she needed a psychiatrist."

"And you didn't," Ian concluded.

"I was worried about her, sure, but I figured there wasn't anything wrong with her that getting her out of that damned hospital wouldn't cure. They had her on the maternity floor, for chrissake, right near the nursery. She had to lie there all day and all night, hearing the babies crying . . ." His voice trailed off.

"So you took her home too soon."

Jordan nodded, not speaking until the waiter had refilled their cups and moved out of earshot. "She was having trouble sleeping, so the doctor prescribed sleeping pills. Barbiturates. She already had the amphetamines—a prescription for diet pills she'd had filled some time ago. She'd take the barbiturates to make her sleep and the amphetamines to wake her up. When she ran out, she found some doctor in New York who'd prescribe anything to anybody, and when she couldn't get to him, she got them from Lance."

Now Ian was surprised. "Lance?"

Jordan frowned. "Yeah, my former best friend was supplying my wife with drugs. How's that for friendship?"

"This is what split you two up?" Ian asked, somewhat confused.

"I couldn't take it anymore," Jordan admitted. "Too much was wrong between us. Sloane was like a stranger to me. She went through these wild mood swings. She was shutting me out. Finally, I felt I had to do something."

"Such as?"

"I confronted her. I told her I wasn't going to stick around and watch her destroy herself," Jordan said sullenly. "I told her I was leaving, that I wasn't coming back until she cleaned up her act."

Ian paused thoughtfully. "Do you think that was wise?" he asked.

Jordan gave him a puzzled look.

"Anyone going through what Sloane's going through now needs all the support she can get," Ian reasoned. "In other words, she needs you now more than ever to help her get through this. Instead of walking out, you should have pushed her into a rehab program—and stuck around to help her through it. That is, if you still love her."

Jordan's head jerked up. "Of course I do!"

"Then go home, Jordy," Ian told him. "Tell Hillyer to get a replacement for you. Tell him you have to go home."

"And if he won't go for it?"

"Tell him to go to hell."

Jordan forced a smile. That was something he'd wanted to do for a long time anyway.

He lay awake that night, thinking about it. Ian was right. Walking out on Sloane the way he did was probably the worst thing he could have done. If only he'd taken the time to think things through, he would have realized that. But he hadn't thought it through. He'd acted out of desperation.

And now he didn't even know where she was.

He telephoned Gavin Hillyer the next morning. He refused to tell Hillyer what he wanted to discuss over the phone, so Hillyer told him to stop by his hotel later in the day. Jordan knew Hillyer thought he was going to say he was leaving the team. *That's probably not a bad idea,* Jordan thought now. He'd never really been happy working for Hillyer—and like it or not, that *was* what he was doing—and getting out had been in the back of his mind long before Sloane's problems came to a head. After this was all over. . . .

It was just past one in the afternoon when Jordan arrived at Hillyer's hotel. Nadine let him into the suite, and he was amazed by the change in her. She seemed to have aged ten years in a matter of months. Physically, she was pale and drawn. She seemed more subdued in her speech and mannerisms; the old cattiness was gone.

"I'm on my way out," she told him as she put on her earrings. "Gavin is on the phone in the bedroom—business as usual—but you're welcome to wait if you like."

He nodded. "Thanks, I will."

She gave him a tired smile. "I'd offer you a drink, but they don't seem to believe in well-stocked bars here, I'm afraid."

"That's okay." He paused. "Are you all right?"

She thought about it for a moment. "I will be, yes," she said finally. "Very soon now I will be."

Jordan wasn't sure exactly what she meant by that, but he was too preoccupied with his own problems to give it much thought. After she'd gone, he walked around the room, looking without really seeing. Without really caring. Until he caught Hillyer's end of the conversation coming from the bedroom.

"... I don't care *how* you do it, dammit! Just make sure it gets done! Look, I don't like this any more than you do, but I don't have any choice—and for the record, neither do you! No—you just do as I say, do you hear? I don't want excuses; I want results. I need that money, and I need it *now*!"

Jordan frowned. What did it all mean?

↹ Berlin, August 1989

The plane circled Tegel Airport, waiting for clearance. Sloane closed her eyes and took several deep breaths. Very soon now she would be face-to-face with Jordan again, and she wasn't at all sure how he was going to react. She wasn't even sure how *she* was going to react. It had been more than seven months. Seven months that seemed like a lifetime.

In a way it is, she thought. *It's a new beginning. Another lifetime. But is it too late for Jordan and me?*

What was she going to say to him? What would he say to her? How would he feel about seeing her now? She would never forget what he said to her the day he walked out....

"I love you, but I just can't take it.... I'm not going to stick around and watch you kill yourself.... You've got a serious problem.... You know where to find me when you're ready to let me help you...."

Sloane blinked back a tear. *I'm ready now, Jordan,* she thought. *I'm ready to be your wife again—if you still want me.*

Jordan dismounted and handed his pony over to a groom. Carrying his helmet by its chin strap, he walked past the line of parked horse trailers at Maifeld Park and flopped down in one of the canvas director's chairs. Draping a damp towel around his neck, he reached into a cooler and took out a bottle filled with ice water. He unscrewed the cap and took a long swallow.

It was no good, he decided, as he stared thoughtfully at the players practicing out on the polo field. He'd given it his best shot, but it was no good. He couldn't give one hundred percent to his game right now because his mind was on Sloane. It had always been on Sloane, ever since he'd walked out on her.

He'd made a mistake. He knew that now.

He'd searched for her, off and on, since the beginning of the year. He'd flown back to the States. He'd gone to Moonstone. No one there knew where she was. If Emma, who was looking after Travis, knew, she wasn't telling. He'd gone to New York. She wasn't at the apartment. She wasn't there, though he suspected she had been at some point. He'd found evidence of her presence there. He'd talked to Cate and Adrienne. Neither of them had seen or heard from her. It wasn't like her to go off and not tell anyone where she'd gone.

He couldn't stop thinking about it, couldn't stop worrying.

Alone in the back of a taxi, Sloane struggled to control her anxiety. It had been a long time since she'd had to do it without pills. She wondered if she could do it now.

I have to, she thought. *I can't go back.*

That was the one thing—the most important thing—she'd learned in the past seven months, first during that trying two weeks at the apartment, then at the drug treatment center in California where she'd spent the better part of three months cleaning up her act.

I can never go back.

Not much longer now.

Max Kenyon was looking forward to this match more than he had any other at any time in his career, not only because it was the International Polo Federation world championship, the World Series of polo, but because he would be facing off with Jordan.

For the last time.

Lance's hand was shaking so hard he almost dropped the glass.

He was losing control. In the beginning the stuff helped. It got him through the bad times, made those bad times bearable. It made him *feel* good, even when things weren't so good. But now . . . now it was as if *it* controlled *him,* as if there were a terrible war going on inside him—and his side was losing.

He still wasn't sure why Hillyer, a man so bent on winning, had insisted he play in a tournament as important as the IPF World Cup. Especially the way he'd been playing. Hell, he still hadn't figured out why Hillyer kept him on the team at all after catching him with Nadine. It didn't make sense. *Oh, well—never look a gift horse in the mouth and all that,* he thought, pouring himself a drink from the bar in his hotel suite. The IPF World Cup—jeez, the old man would have been proud, he thought, as he raised his glass in a solo toast.

"Here's to you, Dad—I'm sure you're having the last laugh, wherever you are."

Sloane drove out to Maifeld that afternoon. She parked at the edge of the polo field and sat in the car for a long time, watching the practice match in progress. She wondered if Jordan had changed much since she'd last seen him.

She knew that she had changed a great deal—hopefully for the better.

He was riding toward her now. She'd know her husband anywhere, even at a distance, even with his helmet and face guard on. She got out of the car and walked to the front of it, leaning against the hood. He rode up, bringing his mount to a stop several yards from where she stood, and dismounted. He didn't speak at first, just removed his helmet and started toward her.

"I wasn't sure you'd want to see me," she said weakly.

He took her in his arms. "See you? I've been looking for you all year!" he told her. "Where in God's name have you been?"

"California—in a drug treatment center. Then I was . . . by myself for a while." She drew back and looked at him. "You were looking for me?"

He nodded. "Nobody knew where you went—not Cate, not Adrienne, not Emma, not even Travis," he said.

"I wanted it that way." She told him what she'd gone through while she was alone in New York. "I had to be sure I was really over it."

"And are you?"

She nodded. "It's scary sometimes," she admitted. "When were you looking for me?"

"Almost the entire time we were apart," he told her. "I even hired a private detective to look for you. I was sure something had happened to you—and that it was my fault for leaving."

She kissed him. "I was so afraid I'd lost you," she said softly.

"Not a chance!" He brushed a strand of her hair off her face with his fingers. "I wouldn't have left at all, except I couldn't take standing around watching you kill yourself."

"I love you, Jordan. You're the only man I've every really loved," she said then. "I *would* have died if I'd lost you."

"Like I said—not a chance." Jordan grinned. "It's been a long time, love. What do you say we go back to the hotel and make up for lost time?"

Ian was puzzled.

None of this made any sense. He'd known Gavin Hillyer long enough—longer than he would have liked, actually—to know that winning was everything to the man. Having his polo team win the IPF World Cup would be like having one of his racehorses win the Triple Crown. So why had he insisted Lance play in the finals, knowing Lance's game was at an all-time low?

And why had Max Kenyon been brought in as a last-minute replacement on the British team, against whom the U.S. team would be competing in the finals? What was Kenyon up to? Ian didn't trust the man one bit.

He'd heard too many stories. . . .

"It's good to have you back, love," Jordan told Sloane as they lay together, their bodies entwined, basking in the afterglow of their lovemaking. "I mean *really* have you back, the way you were before all the troubles."

"It's good to *be* back," she said, snuggling against him. "I didn't think it would ever be like this again."

"I never wanted to leave you, you know."

She looked up at him. "That was pretty hard to believe at the time," she said. "More than once while I was at the clinic, I wondered if you'd left me to be with Jilly."

He looked genuinely surprised. "Jilly?"

"Sure. Now that she's left Max—"

"It doesn't matter whether Jilly's left Max or not," Jordan told her. "Jilly and I are history and have been for a long time now."

"She's still in love with you."

"That's her problem."

Sloane looked skeptical. "Are you telling me you don't feel *anything* for her now?"

He thought about it. "I feel sorry for her," he said finally. "I think I always have, in a way. She's a strange lady."

"But you're not still in love with her?"

Jordan frowned. "Looking back on it, I don't think I ever was," he said, tightening his embrace. "It was lust, not love."

"But you *love* me."

"Of course."

She smiled wickedly. "So it's always one or the other?" she asked. "Never both?"

He knew immediately what she was getting at. "Not at all," he insisted, placing one hand under her chin and lifting her face to his. He kissed her tenderly. "It only works, love, when you have both."

"Oh?" Her tone was playful. "And do we have both?"

Jordan grinned. "In spades." He rolled her over on her back and hovered over her, kissing her deeply. "God, I've missed you," he muttered, burying his face in her neck.

"You need a shave," she giggled, squirming under him as he nibbled at her neck.

"Later," he growled. "I'm very busy right now."

"Mmmm . . . I can tell," she murmured, his arousal unmistakable as he pressed himself into her. She buried her hands in his hair as he left a trail of kisses across her collarbone and down over her breasts. His lips brushed over her nipples, first kissing and nuzzling, then licking, then sucking. Sloane arched her back, desire shooting through her like an electrical current. She grasped his shoulders as his lips left her breasts and moved further downward, over her belly, across the tops and then along the insides of her thighs, nuzzling between her legs. He kissed her there, his tongue wet and hot as he sought out just the right spot and began licking her intently. She moaned, thrusting her hips forward, urging him on. He kept at it until

he felt her shudder violently at his touch, letting out a muffled
cry that told him she'd reached an orgasm. He reared over her,
thrusting himself into her with an urgency that left her breathless. She gripped his upper arms as he moved within her, taking
her swiftly. It had been such a long time since she'd felt like
this, since she'd been able to feel anything at all. It felt so
wonderful to be here with him, to be making love with him—
to be alive. God, she loved him! She raised up off the pillow
and kissed him as he reached his orgasm.

"Welcome back," he whispered, returning her kiss.

This was going to be Jordan's big day. Sloane was sure of
it.

She would have liked to sit at the picket line as she normally
did, where she could be with him between chukkers, but Gaby
and Carlo had flown in from Rome—she hadn't seen them in
ages—and she'd agreed to sit with them in the stands. There
would be time to celebrate later, she told herself. She and
Jordan would have all the time in the world.

The stands were full. *Standing room only,* she thought. *Jordan's got to be thrilled.*

"I've never seen Jordan play better," Gaby commented as
they watched the action on the field. "If he keeps playing like
this, he's going to make the ten this year for sure."

"What are you talking about?" Sloane said with a laugh.
"He should have *already* made the ten, and you know it!"

Gaby laughed too. "You wouldn't be biased, now, would
you?" she chided.

"Not at all!"

Then it happened, without warning. The three horses collided
and went down. Two of the men got to their feet, apparently
unhurt. One was still down, not moving. People were on their
feet in the stands, running onto the field. There was an ambulance on the field, lights flashing.

"My God!" Sloane screamed.

She was on her feet, straining to see what was happening
on the field over the heads of the spectators standing in front
of her. Over the loudspeakers, the announcer was speaking
excitedly in German. Sloane couldn't understand what he was
saying. She didn't know what was happening. She knew only

that she had to get down there. Somehow. She had to find Jordan.

This can't be happening. Not now....

Ignoring Gaby's protests, she fought her way through the crowd, down to the bottom of the stands, onto the polo field. *Please, God—not now,* she prayed as she pressed onward. *Not now....*

"I should have killed you a long time ago, you son of a bitch!" Jordan exploded. He had pinned Lance to the ground in the stable and was straddling him. His hands clutched Lance's throat, throttling him. "I should have killed you when I found out you were giving Sloane drugs!"

"She asked me to get the stuff for her," Lance gasped, struggling to free himself. "She was desperate—"

"You almost killed her, you bastard!"

"Jordan—no!"

He looked up, maintaining his grip on Lance's throat. Sloane was coming toward him, her form silhouetted by the bright light streaming through the entrance.

"Jordan!" she called out to him again. "Let go of him!"

"Stay out of it, Sloane!" he shouted angrily. "This is something I should have done a long time ago!"

"You're killing him!"

"Damned right I am!" Jordan snapped. "Should have done it long before now—"

Lance had stopped fighting. His face was turning blue. He was strangling. Sloane attempted to pull Jordan off him, but Jordan pushed her away. She lost her balance and fell backward to the ground. She scrambled to her feet and made another attempt to restrain Jordan, but to no avail. He was too strong—and too angry.

"Let him go, Jordan!"

Sloane looked up. Ian Welles was coming into the stable. Moving quickly, he pulled Jordan off Lance and physically restrained him. "Calm down!" he ordered harshly.

"Stay out of this, Ian!" Jordan's angry voice held a warning note.

"I said calm down!" Ian snapped.

"That son of a bitch almost got me killed!" Jordan argued.

"It wasn't his fault!"

Jordan showed no sign of calming down as he looked past Ian to Lance, who, with the help of one of the grooms, was getting to his feet. "The hell it wasn't!" he raged, struggling to break free of Ian's grip. His face was flushed and glistening with perspiration, his hair mussed from the physical struggle. "He could have gotten us killed out there—"

"It wasn't Lance!" Ian repeated. "He was a pawn—just like the rest of us!"

Jordan stopped fighting and stared at him, confused. "What—?" he began.

"Jordan—it was Hillyer!"

An hour later, they were all back at the polo fields, surrounded by reporters as Gavin Hillyer, in police custody, was taken away by German law enforcement officers. "We are sure to make the newspapers this time," Eric Langogne commented, raking a hand through his dark hair.

"For all the wrong reasons," Dusty said, nodding in agreement.

"I still don't understand," Sloane told Jordan. "Why did he do it?"

Jordan frowned. "Hillyer's steel company was in trouble. Deep financial trouble. Stood to lose everything," he said. "He tried to keep it all quiet so the stockholders wouldn't panic, but he'd racked up a lot of debts and had no way to cover them."

"But why would he want to kill you—" Sloane began.

"He didn't," Jordan said. "It was Lance who was supposed to be killed."

Sloane looked at him, still puzzled.

"He knew Lance was having an affair with his wife—knew it all along, apparently."

"Why didn't he just drop Lance from the team?"

Jordan shook his head. "He couldn't—or at least he felt he couldn't. Hillyer's a man who really cares about his public image. There had been too many rumors about Lance and Nadine. To drop Lance from the team would have been like admitting the rumors were true—and Hillyer figured he'd end up looking like a fool."

"Still, how would killing Lance—or anybody else—solve Hillyer's financial problems?"

"In a word, insurance—if he'd taken a large enough policy, which he had," Jordan told her. "Hillyer was running out of options. He'd sold some of his racehorses, one or two of his homes, part of his art collection, but it wasn't enough. So he started off by cashing in on the insurance on the ponies."

"The horses that were put down at Myopia—" Sloane looked horrified.

Jordan nodded. "He didn't do it himself, of course. He hired a pro, a contract man. He paid the guy a lot of money in the hopes of making a hell of a lot more on the insurance. Interpol's got a file on him as thick as the Manhattan phone book. Trouble is, he seems to have dropped off the face of the earth."

Sloane shuddered at the thought. He could be anywhere right now. Maybe somewhere close.

"When he realized cashing in on the horses wasn't going to do it, he decided he was going to have to cash in on the players," Jordan went on. "He had large policies on all of us. He decided to start with Lance for a lot of reasons. It was a good way to do away with his wife's latest lover, for one. Lance's drug problem was another. Ian discovered somebody had slipped some pretty deadly stuff into Lance's malletier. Pure. Since there's no mandatory drug testing in professional polo, he—Hillyer, that is—could get away with telling the insurance company he knew nothing about Lance's problem."

"Even if it had been directly responsible for his death," Sloane concluded.

"Exactly."

But it wouldn't have been enough, Sloane was thinking. *Sooner or later, it would have been Jordan.*

"Your husband is certainly full of surprises," Jilly commented, sidling up to Nadine Hillyer after the furor had died down.

Nadine frowned. "I've known for a long time what a cold-blooded bastard Gavin could be," she said quietly, "but I never believed he could be capable of murder."

Jilly looked genuinely surprised. "You never suspected him? Not at all?"

"Not for a moment."

"Well, *I'm* surprised," Jilly admitted. "I was convinced Max was behind it."

Nadine didn't respond.

"What will you do now?"

"I have no idea," Nadine answered truthfully.

Jilly flashed a smile. "Would you like the name of an excellent divorce attorney?"

♻ Martha's Vineyard, May 1990

Sloane sat in the window seat in the master bedroom, proof-reading the yellow pages stacked neatly at her side. When she'd dotted the last *i*, she breathed a sigh of relief. *Winner Take All* was finally finished, almost a year behind schedule but some of the best writing she'd ever done. Given the events of the past two years, that was amazing. That she'd been able to write at all was incredible. Still, when she stopped to think about it, really *think* about it, it had been a catharsis for her. She felt differently about finishing this book than she had about any of the others. There was always a degree of sadness, yes, always the feeling she was saying good-bye to old friends, but this time it was different. Finishing this book made her feel as if she were ending a chapter of her own life.

And beginning another.

In a sense, it was true. Since she got off the pills, she'd felt as though she were truly starting over. Correction. *They* were starting over. She and Jordan. They'd weathered the storm, and as a team they were stronger than ever. She smiled to herself. Lately, they'd been discussing a possible addition to their family. Maybe more than one. She was thirty-eight now and in the twilight of her childbearing years, but for some reason she knew she could cope with all that now. The five-year age difference between Jordan and herself no longer bothered her. It was just as he'd said—mind over matter. *If you don't mind, it doesn't matter.*

Rising from the window seat, she collected the stack of pages and put them into a cardboard box. Tomorrow, she'd express it to her secretary in New York to be typed, and with luck, she'd be able to deliver the finished product within a few weeks.

Then, she promised herself, she'd take a year off. She'd stop being Sloane Driscoll, the best-selling novelist. She'd stop trying to bury the part of her that was and always would be Sammy Douglas. She'd just be Jordan's wife. That, in the end, would be enough to make her happy.

More than enough.

"I've decided to put together my own team," Jordan announced as he came into the bedroom. Taking a deep breath, he flopped down on the foot of the bed and started pulling off his boots.

Sloane, curled up in a large chair in one corner of the room, looked up from the newspaper she was reading and smiled. "Your father will be happy to hear that," she responded.

He shook his head. "I'm not going to ask my father to sponsor the team."

She looked mildly confused. "But how do you plan to—"

"I'm taking on a partner." He put the boots aside and pulled his shirt off over his head. "Antonio Alvarez."

Sloane literally dropped the newspaper. "Alvarez? But the two of you can't stand each other . . ."

Jordan grinned. "We've always competed against each other," he pointed out. "But on the same team we could be a force to be reckoned with, even if I do say so myself."

Sloane looked at him dubiously. "But could you stand to work with him so closely on a regular basis?"

He paused for a moment as if considering it. "We'll soon find out, won't we?"

"Then you're really serious about this?"

"I wouldn't have asked Tonio to come here if I weren't."

"He's coming here? To Moonstone?"

Jordan nodded. "He'll be here in the morning."

"This *is* going to be a year of major undertakings," she said promptly, "for both of us."

He raised an eyebrow questioningly. "Why do I get the feeling you're not just talking about the polo team?"

She smiled. "I'm not," she said simply. "I finished *Winner Take All* today."

"Great!" He grinned broadly. "Still planning to take that year off from writing?"

"You bet," Sloane assured him. "Which brings me to my surprise."

"Surprise?" He looked at her suspiciously.

She nodded. "Over there—on the dresser."

He looked in the direction in which she was pointing. On the dresser was a home pregnancy test—the box still unopened—and a bottle of Dom Perignon. It was also unopened. He looked at Sloane again. "Are you trying to tell me—"

"Not yet," she said quickly. "What that means, my love, is that I want to start working on it. The day we get a positive test, we'll open the bubbly and celebrate."

"Now *there*'s an incentive if I ever heard one," he said with a wicked gleam in his eye. He held out his arms, beckoning her to join him on the bed. "There's no time like the present to start working on it."

She smiled too. "You're absolutely right." As she went to him, the newspaper she'd been reading fell to the floor.

She never made it as far as the brief article on the society page detailing the Hillyers' divorce—and Gavin Hillyer's conviction.

⮰ London, May 1990

Max Kenyon was smiling when he entered the small, carpeted, russet-toned lobby of the Connaught Hotel. He nodded to the doorman but did not speak. Passing the wide, sweeping flight of polished mahogany stairs, he made a sharp right turn into the corridor leading to the restaurant. Oblivious of the flowers and small mirrored bar in the hallway, he entered the restaurant, where he was immediately escorted to a table across the large dining room.

Though he was still smiling when the maître d' departed with his order—the wild duck with peaches he always ordered at the Connaught—Max Kenyon was far from happy. Around him, other diners enjoyed the superior cuisine and clubby atmosphere created by the walls of highly waxed, honey-colored wood, crystal sconces with peach-colored shades, burgundy-striped velvet upholstery, and engraved glass, but all Max could think about was the legal document upstairs in his suite. Divorce papers. Jilly had had him served the morning he left Sydney.

Jilly was divorcing him. He didn't know why he was surprised. She'd been talking divorce for some time now. Still, he'd never really believed she'd do it. Jilly had always been restless, always had a roving eye. He'd suspected she had been unfaithful to him on more than one occasion, and he'd felt it was necessary to come down hard on her in order to keep her in line. But he had never considered divorce an option because he'd had no intention of giving her up. Jilly was his wife, and she would remain his wife.

Till death do us part, he thought grimly. *It's the only way, Jilly love. The only way.*

"Is everything all right, Mr. Kenyon?"

The maître d's words cut through his thoughts. His head jerked up sharply. "I'm sorry," he said absently. "I didn't—what did you say?"

"I asked if everything is all right." The maître d' looked mildly concerned.

Max nodded. "Quite all right. Thank you."

Quite all right, he thought ruefully. *As all right as a man about to lose the only woman he's ever loved can be.*

He *did* love Jilly. She called it an obsession, but she just didn't understand. If she understood, if she really understood, she wouldn't be leaving him now. She'd know he behaved the way he did because he loved her. She'd know what it did to him when she looked at other men. She'd know what it did to him when he made love to her knowing it was Jordan she really wanted.

Jordan. Jordan Phillips, who had once been his friend. Jordan, who had been Jilly's lover first. Jordan, who had a wife of his own now and was no longer interested in Jilly. Jilly had never accepted that, but Max had. Trouble was, it was too late. There could be no going back, not now.

Not ever.

He ate slowly, mechanically, finishing everything on his plate yet never really tasting a bite of it. He paid the check by credit card and left a generous tip. He smiled at everyone he encountered as he left the restaurant, but his smile never quite reached his eyes. If people noticed, they made no comment. Not that he would have cared if they had. No . . . he'd stopped caring what anyone thought of him a long time ago. He'd stopped caring about anything the day Jilly walked out on him.

He went upstairs to the room where he'd spent the past four days, most of that time drunk on his ass because it was the only way he'd been able to deal with what Jilly had done. He locked the door because he didn't want to be disturbed.

The divorce papers were lying on the nightstand next to an empty whiskey bottle. He sat down on the edge of the bed and picked up the papers, staring at them for a long time. When he finally put them down, he reached for the bottle. Checking it to make sure it was completely empty, he dropped it into the wastebasket, then got to his feet and went to the small bar across the room for another.

All the while, he moved automatically, like a robot, without thought, without emotion. He opened the bottle and took a long swallow, not bothering to use a glass. Then he took another. Straight bourbon burned his throat going down, but he didn't care. It dulled another pain deep within him, a worse pain. It galvanized him, gave him strength. He needed that strength now.

He drank all of it. When he had finished, he put the bottle aside, then went to the window and opened it. As he stared down at the heavy traffic passing through Mayfair, he thought of Jilly and what she'd done to him.

Then he jumped.

↻ Los Angeles, May 1990

It's true, Lance thought as a white-uniformed nurse escorted him down a long, antiseptic-looking corridor to the room he would occupy during his stay at the Valleyview Drug and Alcohol Rehabilitation Center. *You really do have to hit rock bottom before you can dig your way back out.* He knew because he had hit bottom in Berlin. His problems, his weaknesses, had nearly killed him and two other men. And it was only then that Lance had realized that cocaine was destroying him. *That's not quite true,* he admitted, but only to himself. *I destroyed myself. Cocaine was just the instrument.*

Just being able to realize that meant he'd come a long way, and that knowledge gave Lance reason to hope. When he arrived in L.A. two days ago, he hadn't believed there was a hell of a lot to feel hopeful about. His personal life was in shambles. His career was ruined. There was nothing, no one left in his life that mattered. There was only cocaine, and that was no longer enough.

The nurse led him into his room, showed him where everything was, then left him alone—leaving the door open, of course—to get settled in. Lance paused for a moment, looking around. It was a large room. And, fortunately, a private room. He hadn't wanted a roommate. No . . . he wanted to be alone.

He sat down on the edge of the bed, frowning. He was thinking about the long road that brought him here, starting with Paula. No . . . his problems went back much further than that, now that he thought about it. His ill-fated marriage had been a casualty of his troubled life, not a cause.

It had actually started long before he met Paula. It had started with his stern, unyielding father who had pushed him into professional polo, though Lance himself had never been quite sure he wanted to pursue polo as a career. It had been his father, who in death had managed to control Lance even more than he had in life, who had ruined Lance's life.

Because I let him, Lance thought. After a moment he took a pen and paper from the top drawer of the bedside table. Sitting on the edge of the bed, he started to write.

My darling Paula. . . .

London, May 1990

As the Qantas flight from Sydney began its final approach to Heathrow Airport, Jilly stared through the small window to her right at the familiar view of the city below. It was funny, she reflected, how you could fly into a city so many times and never really take notice of the view. It was only at a time like this, when a person was incapable of doing anything else, that such things were noticed at all.

The call from the police in London had come as a shock, waking her from a sound sleep. Legally, she was still Max's wife—the divorce wasn't final yet, after all—and so they had telephoned her. Still shaken by the news of her soon-to-be-ex-husband's suicide, she'd taken the first available flight out. She wasn't sure why she had to come, what they'd wanted her for. She hadn't really asked. She hadn't been thinking clearly. She supposed she would have come anyway, though at the moment she wasn't quite sure why.

It was still so hard to believe. Max . . . taking his own life. She'd known him to be many things in the years they were together—some of them quite ignoble—but she had never thought of him as suicidal. She'd believed he could be capable of taking someone else's life, but not his own. There had been times she thought he might be contemplating Jordan's murder. There had been moments when he was so angry he was out of control, and she thought he might actually kill her. But if anyone had told her Maxwell Kenyon might actually kill himself, she wouldn't have believed it.

Until now.

Max had been sick, much sicker than Jilly had realized. She

couldn't help wondering how much of her husband's sickness had been her fault. She should never have married him to start with.

For the first time in months, Jilly allowed herself to think of Jordan. His marriage was solid. For a time there had been rumors of trouble between them, but that was all in the past now. If Jilly had ever held out any hopes of getting Jordan back, they had vanished. She'd lost him, and it had been entirely her own fault. If only things could have been different. If only her mother had lived. If only her father could have cared more about her than he did about polo. If only she could have grown up as part of a real, loving family.

So many ifs, she thought. *So many things that couldn't be changed.*

She noticed that the man seated across the aisle was looking at her. When their eyes met, she smiled. He smiled too. He was quite attractive, Jilly decided. A strong, angular face. Blue eyes. Dark hair just starting to go gray. Well built, from what she could see. Well dressed. She glanced at his left hand on the armrest. He wasn't wearing a wedding ring.

Maybe she'd stay on in London a while longer than she'd planned. . . .

↻ New York City, July 1990

"Well? What do you think?" Sloane wanted to know.

Adrienne leaned back in her chair and looked at the thick manuscript on the desk in front of her thoughtfully. "It packs an emotional wallop," she said finally.

Sloane leaned one shoulder against the bookcase, her arms folded across her chest. She smiled wryly. "You sound surprised," she observed.

"Frankly, I am," the editor admitted.

Cate, who sat placidly in a chair in front of the desk, spoke up. "You mean because of the problems Sloane's experienced in the past," the agent concluded.

"Well, yes."

Sloane drew in a deep breath. "For a while there, I wondered myself if I'd ever finish it at all—let alone to my satisfaction. Or anyone else's," she confessed.

"Nonsense!" Cate scoffed. "I, for one, always had complete faith in you. And for the record, *Winner Take All* is some of the best work you've ever done." She turned to Adrienne. "Don't you agree?"

"Absolutely." There was still a note of surprise in the editor's voice, but with it the conviction that she really believed what she'd just said.

Cate looked up at Sloane, who knew immediately what the agent was thinking: that the events of the past two years had freed her emotionally somehow, had loosened the tight controls she'd always had on herself. Made her capable of expressing her deepest feelings. *She's right,* Sloane thought. *She's absolutely right.* The funny part was, she was no longer afraid to let those feelings show. The ghosts of the past—Sammy's past—no longer frightened her. It was hell, she recalled now, but it was worth it. It was all out in the open now. The ghosts had all been exorcised. There could be no looking back now; she could only look ahead. To the future.

"So when do we roll up our sleeves and get to the dirty work?" Sloane asked aloud.

Adrienne smiled, knowing that, in spite of her derogatory remark, Sloane genuinely enjoyed the editorial process. "It's going to be at least a month before I can even begin the line editing," she answered. "While you're waiting, why don't you start playing with ideas for a new book?"

Sloane shook her head. "Wouldn't be a good idea," she said.

"Why not?" This came as a surprise to both Adrienne and Cate. Normally, Sloane was working on ideas for new books while still working on the previous book.

"I've decided to take a year off," Sloane told them.

"Are you serious?" Adrienne asked.

"Very."

Adrienne looked at Cate, who shrugged. "This is the first I've heard of it."

Adrienne looked up at Sloane again. "Think you'll be able to stand doing nothing for a whole year?"

Sloane smiled slyly. "Oh, I think I'll have plenty to keep me busy," she stated with certainty. She was thoroughly enjoying the looks of confusion the other two women were exchanging. "Didn't I tell you?"

"Tell us what?" Cate wanted to know.

"I just came from the doctor's office," she said with a triumphant gleam in her eyes. "The rabbit died this morning."

Author's Note

Solitaire is a work of fiction—and yet, like most works of fiction, there are threads of fact woven through the tapestry of this novel, threads taken from the world of international polo and book publishing in order to provide a colorful and believable backdrop for the story.

The characters are fictional. They are products of my own imagination, as are their stories. All of the polo players I've had the pleasure of knowing are dedicated, hardworking and totally committed to their sport, and it is my hope that they will not be offended by some of the conflicts and weaknesses of my fictional players, necessary to enhance the storyline. Occasionally I had to exercise literary license for the good of the story, and I take full responsibility for any factual errors.

Real people are mentioned throughout the novel. The Pieres and Gracida families, as well as Owen Rinehart, Julian Hipwood and his wife Pamela, Cornelia Guest, Geoffrey and Jorie Kent, Peter Brant, William Devane, Doug Sheehan, Alex Cord, Jameson Parker, and Robert Skene are all well-known names in the polo community. I have taken care not to mention any of them in a way they might find offensive.

Real tournaments are also featured—the Coupe D'Or, the Argentine Open, the International Polo Federation's World Cup, and others are actual matches played annually. The celebrities mentioned actually do play for the Piaget Chukkers for Charity team, a fine organization raising money for worthwhile charities all over the country. And the Polo Excellence Awards, sponsored by *Polo* magazine, are awarded each year in Palm Beach.

In closing, I would be remiss not to thank the many people who contributed to this novel through research, publishing expertise, and good old-fashioned moral support, for they are all deeply appreciated: Linda Besade, Director of Operations for the Museum of Polo and Hall of Fame; Mary Hurlock of the Greenwich Polo

Club (Connecticut); Bob, Ann, and Susan Human of St. Louis Benefit Polo, Inc.; as always, my agent, Maria Carvainis; my editor, Leslie Gelbman; the great team at Berkley who make it all happen: Sabra Elliott, Donna Gould, Liselle Gottlieb, Joni Friedman, and Gail Fortune; my picky copy editor, Sybil Pincus; and all the people whose shoulders I cried on during the writing, revising, and publication of this novel—Anna Eberhardt, Donna Julian, Mary Martin, Sally Schoeneweiss, Karyn Witmer-Gow, Eileen Dreyer, Sue Easterby, Suzanne Boyle, Carla Neggers, and Carrie Feron. Special thanks are due those no longer a part of the Berkley team but who continue to be an influence on my work: Damaris Rowland, Amy Barron, and Kirsten Kreimeier; and the two very special friends and fellow authors who took the time from their busy schedules to read and endorse *Solitaire*—Sandra Brown and Susan Elizabeth Phillips.

I love you all!

Norma L. Beishir
St. Louis, Missouri
April 1990

<u>New York Times</u> bestselling author
CYNTHIA FREEMAN

Cynthia Freeman is one of today's best-loved authors of bittersweet human drama and captivating love stories.

___ILLUSIONS OF LOVE   0-425-08529-5/$4.50
___SEASONS OF THE HEART   0-425-09557-6/$4.95
___THE LAST PRINCESS   0-425-11601-8/$4.95